Whispers in the Mist

By G. J. Woosley

ISBN 9780983840008

Published by GJWNovels.com

A Note from the Author

I've always been fascinated by the rugged beauty that still exists in the Pacific Northwest. There are so many places that have been unspoiled by man. The pristine areas are rapidly fading because of development and *progress*. I've always tried to imagine what the area looked like before freeways, railways, and the arrival of logging crews.

The story that follows is a fictional account of people with vision and tenacity. Although they may not have existed in real life, portions of their visions did and are still alive today. The history of this area is both remarkable and sad. With progress and development comes great loss. I'm proud to have been a resident of this area for 18 years and saw many changes during my time there. The influx of people may have been great for the economy but not for the landscape. I have only glimpsed what the native tribes must have seen more than a century ago with the passing of their customs, traditions, and way of life.

The women in this story are more a part of history of this area than most people know. They were strong, determined women who couldn't play by the pre-determined rules in a man's world. It's of women who had to learn to cope with a white man's world, with the help of some visionary white men. I hope you enjoy the story that follows.

G. J. Woosley
Wooster, Ohio
July, 2011

Dedication

This book is dedicated to the women who helped build the Pacific Northwest. You will never see their names in the history books. It is also dedicated to all the strong women in my life from my grandmother to aunts. Lastly, but most of all, it is dedicated to my rock, my strength, my life partner, Bonnie. I could never have gotten these pages to you without her love and support. I thank you and love you all from the bottom of my heart.

G. J. Woosley

Chapter 1

The light misty rain fell as she stared at the grave marker. March is always rainy but the temperature was colder than usual. It had taken her ten years to finally get to this spot. Ten years of searching, researching, and getting to the point of emotional bankruptcy before everything fell together. The story ended here in this back corner of a Renton, Washington cemetery.

She brushed away some leaves that covered both of the markers. She knelt between them and read the first marker. "Sara 'Two Trees' Monroe. Born Dec. 17, 1858 and Died June 14, 1928." She looked over at the other marker that was almost identical, and read, "Anne Elizabeth Monroe. Born July 9, 1889 and Died Dec 12, 1961." She stood up and looked back at the first marker. "These people are my relatives," she whispered. She wished she could have known them.

"It's pretty small, isn't it?" a voice behind her said. She was startled and turned around. She had no idea how long he had been standing there. She had no idea how long she had been there herself.

"Yes, it is," she said. "It took me a while to find it. I had a map that I got from the office, but it's hard to get your bearings in here." She looked into the steel gray eyes of the caretaker. He was old and frail but had strangely familiar twinkle in his eyes.

"You were looking for these two specific markers?" he asked.

"Yes," she answered.

"I come to this back corner, often," he admitted. "Anne and I knew each other, but I'd never met her mother. Do these people mean something to you?"

"My grandmother and great-grandmother," she admitted. "I've been searching for ten years to find them. You said you knew my grandmother?"

"Yes, I met her right after her mother died," he began. "She was the most beautiful woman I had ever seen. No one could hold a candle to Anne."

"I'm sorry," she said, "I've not introduced myself. I'm Beth Monroe."

"Nice to meet you," he smiled. "I'm Zack McGill. I've been the caretaker here, off and on, since 1928. That's how I met your grandmother. I saw her at her mother's funeral. I was just a kid then. I was eighteen, and she was thirty-nine."

"Don't tell me that you remember every funeral over the years,"

Beth remarked.

"No," Zack answered. "That one was special. There were only 3 people there and I thought that unusual for a woman of Sara Monroe's stature in this community."

"Mr. McGill," she started, "can we sit down and talk? There are some questions I'd like to ask you about my grandmother."

"It's 5pm now and I'm finished," he said. "I have a little place just around the corner. If you have time, let's go now. I haven't been in the presence of a young lady in some time."

They left the cemetery and walked to the house that Zack owned. This was a man that knew her grandmother. He could fill in a few of the holes she had about her family history. She needed these holes filled, especially about her grandmother. She had been able to piece together some things, but the picture in her head wasn't as clear as she needed it to be.

Zack chatted about the weather and the state of the economy as they walked. She was cold and hungry and wished she could get something to eat before talking with Zack. They reached the small, but well-kept, house just outside of the cemetery. She had admired that house when she went into find the grave markers.

As Zack opened the door one of the first things to strike her were the pictures around the room. This is what made a house a home. There was warmth in this house that didn't come from the furnace.

"Take your coat off and hang it by the fireplace," Zack said as he turned on a switch. The fireplace began to burn, and he smiled. "I love not having to carry wood for this thing. Its gas and I love the convenience. I have a pot of stew I made last night. Would you join me for dinner?"

"I'd love to," Beth said. "I'm starving and all I have at my apartment are instant things."

"No one cooks anymore," Zack yelled from the kitchen. "I don't understand that."

Beth looked at the pictures and found one that drew her in. This was of a beautiful woman holding a baby. Her dark hair and light eyes were such a contrast. She was beautiful and you could see the glow coming from her. Zack caught Beth looking at the picture.

"That's your grandmother," Zack said as he came over and carefully picked up the frame. "I told you she was beautiful," he said as he handed the picture to Beth. "That's your father that she's holding. She was so proud it was a boy. She wanted someone to carry on the family name."

"I never knew my father," Beth said. "He died before I was born in Viet Nam. My mother told me about him, but never could tell me about anyone else from my father's side of the family." Something finally struck her. "Her name was Monroe. What about my grandfather? My father's birth certificate says "Unknown" for the father's name. I can't seem to find out anything about him or who he was."

"Let's take things one step at a time," Zack said. He went to the kitchen and brought the hot stew, fresh bread, and a pot of tea. "Let's eat and I can tell you what I know."

They sat down at the table and started to eat. The stew was hot and tasty. Beth didn't realize how hungry she was and how much she had missed a good home cooked meal. She stared across the table at Zack. There was something familiar about his face and something comforting about this demeanor. Beth felt like she knew this man, but didn't know from where. Maybe she had seen him in the grocery store or some other public place.

"You look like her," he said.

"Like who?" Beth responded.

"Like your grandmother," he said.

"What did you know about my great-grandmother?" Beth asked. "I'd like to start at the beginning. From what I could find out, she was an amazing woman. She was a woman of vision and was tenacious."

"She was a woman of vision," he said as he rubbed his beard and smiled. "She was the first woman to run a logging camp in the Pacific Northwest. She was respected and feared by many of the local businessmen because of her connection to the local Indian tribes. She was a pioneer in environmental concerns. She respected the land and was devoted to her family. She also was able to balance her Native American heritage and her responsibility therein, with her life in the white man's world."

"I should have talked to you ten years ago," Beth said. They had finished dinner and Zack suggested they sit by the fireplace. He handed Beth a mug of tea and sat down in the rocker next to her.

"I'll tell you the story," Zack said. "This is what you won't find in the history books. This is the true story as told to me by your grandmother."

***

It was the summer of 1864 and Sara Two Trees was 5 years old. There were 3 white men in her Nez Perce camp. Sara was a name given to her by the white priest that had settled near their camp and had built his church in the Wallowa valley. Sara was the niece of

Chief Joseph and her mother was well respected and had earned her choice of places in the multi-family long house.

Sara's gifts were recognized at a young age. She was quick to learn the ways of the animals that inhabited her world. She recognized the vegetation, herbs, and mosses her mother used for healing others in the tribe. The people had many more illnesses since the white man had entered their world. This did not keep the tribe from trading with them. This was the first time she had seen Edmundson Monroe.

He had not visited her tribe before. He was tall and spoke very softly. The other white men would bring something they called whiskey and would be loud after drinking this. Sara noticed that he did not drink this. She also noticed that he didn't let his face hair grow. This was different from any other white man she had ever seen.

Her people would trade with these men, and they brought many new things to her people. They had brought the fire stick that they called a gun. Sara had picked up on the English language very quickly. She understood their language and would listen to their conversations. She heard them talk about the fighting beyond the big mountains. She heard them talk about the Rebel army and someone they called The President. Her mother said this was the 'Great White Father' who lived in a place called Washington.

These words meant nothing to Sara but she listened anyway. She loved the sound of the new language. Monroe spoke the words differently than the men who had visited the people before. The other two men had been coming to the village long before Sara was born. Frenchy and Pierre had taught Sara the words but she liked the way that Monroe said them. The words were soft and flowing.

Sara saw Monroe looking at her. She was nervous and aware of his eyes. He came over and sat beside Sara.

"Hello," he said. "My name is Edmundson Monroe. What's your name?"

"Sara Two Trees," she said.

"You speak our language very well, Sara Two Trees," he smiled. "Who taught you this?"

"The white men have been coming here since before I was born. I just listen to them. I like the sound of the words," she said.

She smiled at him and he smiled back. She liked his clean face and his white teeth. The other white men had brown teeth from the brown weed that they would chew. They would put it in their mouth and chew it and spit brown juice out. This was very ugly. Why would they do this? What was in the brown weed that they wanted? She found some of the weed and tried it once. She did not spit out the brown juice and was ill for 3 days.

Sara's mother knew what she had done and let her suffer with the consequences. Sara would not die from this, but a lesson would be learned from the experience. Sara did learn and would not try anything again without knowing what it was.

Sara spent many more days talking with Monroe. She liked him and felt a bond unlike she had known with even her own people. Her mother saw this too and was concerned. She also knew if her people were to survive they would have to learn the white man's way. They were passing through their valley every day. They were like the sickness that they brought in. Most of them were on their way to Oregon or California.

After 7 days, the white men were ready to move on. Sara was sad to see Monroe leave, but he said he would come back. The people were getting ready to move low down the valley to prepare for winter. The snow would come in 2 months and the food stocks were being stored. Monroe found Sara before he left gave her a beaded necklace with gold and silver. It was the most beautiful thing she had ever seen.

"This is my promise that I'll be back," Monroe said as he put the necklace around Sara's neck. "Every time you look at this, think about your friend, Monroe."

With that he was gone.

The next few years passed and each summer brought Monroe. He would return with Frenchy and Pierre and trade with the people. Sara was now 16 and she had become a beautiful young woman. Monroe saw this but so did Frenchy and Pierre. They would sometimes spend nights with other young woman, but only with the permission of the family. They were well aware of the customs of the Nez Perce and would not dishonor these people.

Monroe would not do this. He had spoken to Sara's mother about taking Sara for his wife. He had even spoken with Chief Joseph about the marriage. There was a price for Sara and she must agree to this and he must be able to pay the price. Sara already was a woman of property by the people's standards. She had 5 Appaloosa ponies and her own lodge. She had learned the healing ways of her mother and was respected. Many young braves had asked for her but she turned them down.

Sara preferred to spend time with her ponies and another young woman in the tribe. The Shaman said she had the gift of seeing both worlds. Sara could live in the woman's world but also live and experience the man's world. She was looked upon as special and holy. No man had ever stirred anything in her except Monroe. When he was in the village, she preferred to talk the white language with him. Between his visits, she would spend her time with Mary Laughs with Her Eyes.

Mary's parents had both died of the white man's lung sickness during the winter of the heavy snows. Mary had lived with Sara and her mother for 4 years. It was at this time that Sara had found the pleasure of another woman's touch. The people accepted this practice. Sara and Mary would work with the ponies together. Mary seemed to know what Sara wanted or needed without being told. Sara taught Mary the white man's language.

Mary had a gift for the language and even Monroe was amazed. He knew of the relationship between Mary and Sara. When he returned this summer, he had the payment for Sara's mother and had brought many extras. He brought these extras for a reason. He knew the army was going to round up the last of Chief Joseph's tribe to place on a reservation. These were the needed items so they could remain free as long as the Chief saw necessary. He had planned to use these things to bargain with.

He wanted to marry Sara and this was the summer for it to happen. He wanted to make sure that Sara was safe with all the military activity beginning in this area. Mary knew this time was coming and grew sad. Her beloved Sara would be leaving. Monroe had crossed the great mountains to the west and wanted to take Sara there.

Monroe talked to the priest that lived in the valley about the marriage. He said that Sara had not fully accepted the Christian faith so he could not perform the ceremony. Monroe was not unhappy about this and was disappointed at the narrow attitude displayed by a man of God. He told Sara about his meeting with the priest.

"I will never accept the white man's God," she said. "He is a God of hate and division. The Great Spirit sees all of us as equal. He has given us this land to live on. It is not ours to own but to care for. The white man's God says it's okay to take the land and ruin it."

Monroe was overcome by Sara's wisdom and agreed to have the Shaman say the marriage words. The day before the ceremony, Sara and Mary spent time with the ponies and rode to the far ridge. This was their favorite place. You could see the entire valley and the great mountains to the west. From this place they could also see the white man's settlements.

"I will miss you, Two Trees," Mary said with a quiver in her voice.

"I will ask Monroe to take you with us," Sara said, "if you want to go over the great mountains. We are sisters of the heart. Do you want to go with us?"

"Yes, Two Trees," she said. "There is nothing here without you."

"I will talk to Monroe," Sara said.

They returned to camp and Sara found Monroe. She was not afraid of his answer. She somehow knew that he would do as she asked. His eyes met hers and he smiled.

"I will speak with your mother and the chief," he said. "Mary will be coming with us if that's what she wants. I have enough to pay for her and will do so."

"This is what she wants," Sara said. "This is what I want. Thank you Monroe."

"Let's tell her together, Sara," he said.

They found Mary in Sara's lodge. She was very happy and hugged Sara. Mary kissed Monroe's hand and knelt before him. He quickly helped her to her feet.

"Never do that, Mary," he said. "Never bow your head to anyone. You're not a servant or a slave. You are part of this family and will be part of my family. You are my Sara's sister and you will have all the respect that goes with that."

The marriage ceremony was beautiful. Monroe and Sara said their words of promise to each other. The Shaman explained the duties of a husband and the duties of a wife. Each agreed to these duties and when the Shaman was finished, Monroe kissed Sara gently on the lips. She had never before touched her lips to anyone but Mary or her mother, and the feeling was strange but not unpleasant.

The first night with Monroe was different than any experience she had. She had never been with a man and didn't know what to expect. She had sexual experience with Mary but that was all. Monroe was gentle and tender. Sara had never experienced this and Monroe knew this was one of the most important times of a new marriage. He was aware of her sexual history so he carefully and artfully took the extra time to allow Sara's desires to build.

After their first consummation was complete, Monroe held Sara and she found that his arms were comforting. He told her of an accident he had several years ago. He didn't know if he was able to have children or not. He showed Sara the large scar in the glow of the campfire inside of their lodge. Sara fell asleep in Monroe's arms. They were not Mary's arms, but they held her and she found she enjoyed their strength and gentleness. She did miss Mary when she awoke the following morning.

During the next two days Monroe packed up his horses and supplies he had gathered for the trip west. Sara spent most of her time with her mother. She had not been well this year. She had contracted a sickness during the winter and had not recovered, as Sara would like to have seen. She was weak and tired easily.

"Monroe will be a good husband," her mother said.

"Yes, Mother," she agreed. "He is a good husband. He wants to take care of me and of Mary."

"You're going far away, Sara," her mother said. "You will not be back to see the people for many years, if ever and I will be gone." Sara knew this to be true and was sad about that.

"You will be with the Great Spirit soon, Mother," she said.

"Yes, my daughter," her mother responded. "I will wait to meet you there when your time comes. I have loved you always. I will watch out for you after I'm gone. Do not cry for me, but live for me. See all the things that you can. Take care of the land, take care of Mary, and learn the white man's ways. Our ways are ending and will never return."

Sara and her mother spent their last night together in mother's lodge. She knew that her mother would not see the next snow. She had given Sara a medicine bag with the herbs and mosses needed for any occurrence on her trip west. She, Monroe, and Mary would start out early the next morning on their 400-mile trip west.

Morning did come and the weather was warm. Sara and Mary had gathered their ponies and loaded their possessions on the others. Sara's mother, the Shaman and the Chief saw them safely on their way. Moving on horseback would be quicker than moving with a wagon train. Monroe had done this on his first trip west. He grew tired of the whining from the people in the wagon train. They moved at a slow pace and didn't understand how to take care of themselves.

He had some experience in making maps. This was an art passed down to him by his father. He made mental notes during his first trip and drew a crude map. Each trip after this added more to his map. There were places noted with good hunting, fishing, and places to avoid. He had even laid out land belonging to specific tribes. He would, occasionally, pull out his map and make notes.

"What is that?" Mary asked him one night.

"This is called a map," he said. He went over and sat by Mary, "This tells us where we are, and where we're going." He continued to explain the use of the map and saw Sara smiling at him. She was pleased that he was taking so much time with Mary. There was no jealousy that Mary may want Monroe. If Monroe wanted her, this would be all right with Sara.

During this trip Mary would sleep in one side of Sara and Monroe on the other. This seemed right to all and there was no reason to change this. At the times when Monroe and Sara were intimate, Mary would go to sleep. Mary and Sara continued their physical relationship. Monroe had full knowledge of this and never interfered. This made Sara happy and Monroe only wanted that for her.

Monroe continued to talk to Mary about the map. Sara listened intently. She was pleased with how quickly Mary had picked up the white man's language. This was important to Sara. She knew that their way of life was ending. It was going to be even more important to learn to write this language.

"Where are we going, Monroe? What is the name of the place across the big mountains?" Sara asked.

"The area is outside of the great city of Seattle," Monroe said. "It's on the Snoqualmie River above the great waterfall. I have been there each winter since we first met. I have a lodge built for us. It's beautiful and peaceful. The trees are unlike any you have ever seen."

Sara watched Monroe talk of this place and watch the delight in his face as he described the area. Mary was as excited as Monroe and found she couldn't contain her enthusiasm. The next day, as they rode along the Columbia River, Mary continued to ask Monroe about this green land.

"Will we follow this river through the mountains?" she asked.

"No, Mary," he answered. "We will leave this river and head north. This river will take us too far south. We will continue down through the cliffs and then we have to cross this river. Once we cross, we will rest for a few days."

"Why must we rest, Monroe?" Mary asked.

"I will need to replenish our food stores, and give the horses some time to graze before we start through the mountains," he explained. "We should be across the mountains and to our new home within 30 days."

They did just as Monroe said. They reached the crossing place.

Monroe made sure that there was very little food left before they crossed. This made it easy for the horses to swim across this cold and refreshing river. The temperature was well over 100 degrees that day in this land of scrub and sand. There were rich grazing places along the banks. They got to the other side and Monroe found a protected place to build camp. Mary staked out the ponies to graze and Sara fashioned a fishing pole as her people had done for many generations before she was born.

It was mid-afternoon and it felt good to rest. Mary made a fire pit and started a fire. Monroe had set off with his gun to hunt for meat. Sara headed to the riverbank to catch fish for their dinner. She had been unsuccessful the other times she had done this. She could see the large silver fish but could not find anything they would bite on. She remembered seeing the men in her village catch for these fish. They would not leave the line in the water. They would move it back and forth above the water to draw the fish up.

Sara did this and then when she saw the fish at the surface, she let the line drop and he grabbed on. She was fighting with this big fish when Mary appeared behind her. She handed Mary the pole and Sara pulled in the line. By the time she got the fish to the bank, Sara was tired.

"This fish has a fighting soul," she said as she panted.

"I can see why," Mary said as she lifted Sara's prize. It was more than 2 feet long and weighed 10 pounds. "This will feed all of us, with some left over. I'll clean it and lay it over the fire."

They walked back to the camp to find Monroe had returned with a deer. He remarked about Sara's prize and smiled.

"That's beautiful and it smells wonderful, Sara," he smiled. "You finally figured out how to get one of those. I was never any good at it."

"We can have that tonight," Sara said as she pointed to the fish. "I'll help you with your deer."

Monroe watched with awe as Sara skinned the animal by only making one cut in the hide. Her hands worked, expertly, as she removed the insides. Monroe helped her cut the pieces for smoking and jerky. By the time they finished, Mary had their evening meal prepared.

The salmon was warm and tasty and a nice switch from the food they had been eating. Monroe looked at these two women in amazement. They knew what the other would do before it happened. They had a rhythm about them that he had not seen in white women. Neither was lazy or afraid of getting dirty. They were not like the women that his mother had lined up for him while he was still in London.

He thought about one in particular. She was refined and cultured. She came from a well to do family in London. He spent the better part of two years in a well-defined courtship with her. His mother was pleased with the match but something delayed his asking for her hand. He had no true feelings for her. She was like the crystal clock his mother had on the fireplace mantle. It was a work of art and beautiful, but, it was only useful to look at. There was no depth to the crystal clock, or to Daphne. The amount of warmth that came from each of them was the same. He could not see Daphne having, let alone, raising children. He wanted more from a mate. He wanted more for his children. He wanted more from his life.

His mother was angered about him not wanting to have Daphne's hand. She said he would not see a dime of the inheritance that his father had left him. This money meant nothing to him. He didn't want it. He had saved money over the years and wanted only to come to America. He spent endless nights reading books on the frontier and how to survive. His father had taught him maps and how to read the stars for direction.

He had made up his mind and had purchased a ticket to sail the following spring. His mother was devastated, but understood his need to leave. Edmundson was always adventuresome and she knew he would leave someday. She also saw she could save face in society about him not marrying Daphne. Her anger had subsided and she allowed him to have his inheritance.

He was adamant about not wanting the money. His mother convinced him to leave it in an account where he could access it when he wanted. The summer he met Sara was his first trip. He knew as soon as he met her, why he had come to this new land. He also knew the first time he saw the Snoqualmie River area that this is where he wanted his life to be.

He thought about Sara and the tenderness she showed to him, her mother, and to Mary. He knew that this would be the same for his children. She was a woman of depth. He knew this the first time he saw her as a child. His opinion had not changed of her. As she took care of him, he would take care of her, and they would both take care of their children.

As Sara handed him some coffee, he was brought back to reality. Their trip had gone as Monroe had planned. He was a stickler for timetables and schedules. He was not so inflexible, though, to not allow for things unplanned. The next few days stop was not a planned delay. He saw the need in the horses for a rest, and he could use one himself.

He found himself very tense on this trip. He found himself staying very alert to any danger that may be ahead. He had precious cargo with Sara and Mary and didn't want to see any harm come to them. They had been traveling through some harsh country and water had been a concern for him. This was a needless worry as was crossing the Columbia River.

The next few days rest would be needed as they headed north into more rugged territory. Only half of their journey was completed. He thought the women may slow him down, but he was ahead of his schedule. He looked back at these women and smiled to himself. There had not been a single complaint. He wondered how Daphne would have handled this trip. He then chuckled almost aloud and looked in his coffee cup.

He went to sleep looking up at a blanket of stars. He looked at the constellations his father had taught him. They would head north-northwest in two days. Tomorrow would be spent smoking the rest of the venison and cleaning the hide for clothing. He could hear Sara's soft words to Mary. They had not spent time together since he and Sara had been married. He was drifting off listening to the sighs of the women. He would dream about the great falls and his home. The whispers in the mist made by the great waterfall seemed to call to him.

Chapter 2

They broke camp and started heading away from the Columbia. It didn't take long to see the forests and great wall of mountains with the snow-capped peaks that lay ahead. Sara and Mary were in awe for they had heard stories of these mountains and had seen the peaks from their valley. They never imagined the size or the beauty of them.

"Monroe," Sara sighed, "I never imagined such beauty. The Great Spirit must live here."

"They are beautiful, aren't they?" he said. "They can be difficult to travel through. I found a low pass a few years ago. Pierre gave me the direction, but he died before he could show me, but I found the pass later that summer and made sure it was on my map. I've not shared this pass location with any other white man. I'm sure the Indians are aware of it, but no one else. It's good for horses, but not for wagons. That's why no one uses it."

"The large hairy men live in these mountains," Mary said quietly.

"What large hairy men?" Monroe said. "What are you talking about Mary?"

"She's talking about the Sasquatch of the mountains," Sara said. Sara saw the look on Monroe's face and she knew that he knew nothing of these mystical beings. "Let me tell you of these things, Monroe," she started.

She began to tell him the legends that came to the people. She told him of the legend's beginning and the stories passed down through the generations. Monroe listened intently as Sara spoke. He had heard of this legend on the other side of the mountains. He'd heard this from loggers, Indians, and fur trappers. He'd heard stories of camps and equipment being destroyed by a large creature, yet he didn't believe this legend, until he heard Sara speak of this thing. She began a story of how she became lost as a child. She and her mother were picking berries the fall before she met Monroe. She was following a rabbit and lost her mother. When she realized that her mother was nowhere around she began to yell to her. Sara remembers hearing rustling in the leaves behind her and turned to find the large hairy one looking at her. Sara told Monroe that she should have been afraid, but somehow knew this creature would not harm her. He came and walked past her and turned again to look at her.

"It was as though he wanted me to follow," Sara said. "We

walked for some time and then he stopped. I then heard my mother calling my name. When I turned to look at the creature, he was gone."

"That's when the Shaman said that Sara was special and had the gifts of understanding with all the creatures," Mary smiled proudly.

"Our people and other tribes have lived in peace with these creatures," Sara said. "They are everywhere and can be seen if they want to be seen. They are very illusive and powerful."

"I had heard this legend, but never knew of anyone who had seen these creatures," Monroe said. "I didn't believe that these creatures were real until now."

"They are real, Monroe," Sara said. "I have seen them many times since that day when I was a child."

They rode on a few more miles when Monroe found a quiet spot to make camp. He still was thinking about the stories that Sara had shared with him. He felt he needed to write these stories down. He had always kept a journal when he made his maps and he had been making notes during their trip, but decided to write down this history. He had no idea if anyone would ever read this, but would keep it just the same.

***

"What ever happened to these journals?" Beth asked.

"I have them here," Zack answered. "I have been offered a great deal of money from the Historical Society for them, but your grandmother was very rigid about the selling of family history."

"I would like to see them, if that's alright," Beth said.

"I think you should see them, after all, they belong to you," Zack smiled. "This is your family, and your history. I need to get them from the attic, but I'll do that tomorrow."

Beth noticed the time. It was past 11pm and she didn't know where the hours went. Zack sat and looked at the fire. He had a far away look on his face and Beth wondered what he was thinking.

"I need to get home," she said. "I'd like to come back tomorrow, if it's alright."

"Tomorrow is Saturday, so I'm not working," Zack replied. "I'll expect you around 11am."

Zack saw Beth to the door. She looked so much like her grandmother that Zack felt that same feeling he had when he had first seen her. Her blue eyes were such a contrast to her dark hair and as he watched her walk to her car, he could see Annie. His eyes began to tear as Beth turned to wave goodbye. His mind flashed back the first time he saw her in 1928.

***

Zack remembered that June morning in 1928. He had come to this country when he was 7 with his mother. His father was killed during a drunken brawl in Chicago less than 6 months after they arrived. His mother took in laundry and worked for a bakery near their flat. Zack remembered his father and all he did remember was that he was always drunk and usually violent during his worst binges. He remembered the many beatings he and his brother Kevin endured from this man, but he would never lay a hand on his mother. Michael Wesley McGill may have been a drunk, but he dearly loved his wife.

After their father's death Zack and Kevin found part-time work to help with the living expenses. Kevin found he liked to write and investigate. He secured a job with the newspaper as a reporter. He was only 17 but the editor liked Kevin and gave him a chance. Kevin, in turn, got Zack a job delivering newspapers. Life without their father proved to be much easier than before he died. Zack's mother didn't have to hide money to pay the bills, buy clothes or food. Zack and Kevin's help made life so much easier for her, and she was happier.

Zack remembered thinking that he never wanted to leave Chicago. He and his brother were close and cared deeply for his mother. She was the reason why he wanted to go to college. He wanted to make sure that he could care for her in her old age. He wanted to make sure that she didn't have to worry about a home, food, or any of the things associated with day-to-day life. As Zack excelled in school, Kevin worked his way up in the newspaper. Over the next few years he had become chief reporter and was getting known around the city.

Zack was proud of his brother. He had gained a reputation for honesty. Kevin was also very outspoken about Prohibition. He believed in following the letter of the law. He also remembered his father and the grief that alcohol brought to his family. His special mission, so he stated, was to put the bootleggers out of business. He wrote articles and exposed some of the people working with organized crime. He had received threats from those same people although he could never prove it. They were threats none the less.

"When you receive threats, you've hit a nerve," Kevin used to say with a smile, but he never took these threats seriously. Zack was concerned about them and the safety of his brother. Zack was now 17 and had graduated from high school and had planned to go to the University of Chicago. He was interested in medicine and wanted to be a doctor.

"Some of my classmates are going for coffee," Zack told Kevin and his mother. "I'll be home by 8pm."

"Don't get into any trouble, Zack," Kevin said. "I'm very proud of you."

"I'll see you at home," his Mother said. "I love you, Zack." She gave him a hug that seemed to last forever.

Kevin and Mother never came home that night. When Zack got home, Kevin's boss was waiting at the house with a policeman. Kevin's car ran off the road and both in the car were killed. The policeman explained that the conditions surrounding the accident were "suspicious" and it would be investigated.

That single act changed Zack's life forever. His dreams of never leaving Chicago were shattered. His dreams of his future were shattered. He wanted nothing more than to get away. Kevin had a tidy nest egg built up, and Zack had saved a good amount for his education. He wasn't going to go on to school, now, so he would use the money to settle somewhere else.

He arranged the funeral, with Kevin's bosses' help and tied up the loose ends. He packed what things he wanted, and saved the things with sentimental value, said good-bye to the people in his neighborhood, and a few classmates. With that he boarded a train to leave Chicago behind. This city held no attraction for him. The train stopped in Seattle. Zack collected his things and headed for the sleepy little town of Renton, but why he didn't know.

Zack had rented a small house next to a cemetery. He had wanted to pursue a career in medicine, but the dream had passed with his mother and brother's death. The mortuary connected to the cemetery was looking for help. Zack applied and they offered him a job. Included in this job was training in being an undertaker. Zack had never considered this. He wanted to save lives at one time, but found that restoring dignity in death pleased him. He had been there for 4 weeks when the body of an Indian woman arrived.

Even in death, he could see that she was a beautiful woman. Her dark hair had some gray, but was still shiny and thick. Her high cheekbones and her straight nose gave her an aristocratic air. When this combined with her flawless beige skin, the look was striking.

"Beautiful, isn't she?" Bill said.

"Yes, she is," Zack said. "Who is she?"

"This is Sara Monroe," he said with surprise.

"This is Sara Monroe?" Zack asked. "I didn't know that she was an Indian. I've heard such wonderful things about her from you, and some of the other businessmen in town. She looks to be around 45, and way too healthy to be here."

"Sara was 70 years old," he said. "Her daughter wouldn't allow an autopsy, but we have been allowed to embalm. The doctor said she probably died of a heart attack. One of her estate hands found her dead this morning."

"I'll get right to this," Zack said. He turned around and saw her for the first time. She looked like her mother, but with paler skin. She had deep blue eyes that looked right through you.

"I'm Anne Monroe," she said in a soft melodious voice.

***

Beth watched the door close as she drove away. Her mind was swimming with all of the information she had been given. This was just the beginning and she was thirsty for more. She knew there were things that Zack hadn't told her. She wondered why he had all of the journals and the pictures. Why didn't her father have them, and why didn't he ever tell her mother any family history.

She had so many questions now. She had spent years searching for her family history and thought she had completed her quest when she found the graves. Meeting Zack was a stroke of luck, or was it? It was as though he was watching and guarding those graves. She looked in the rear-view mirror and agreed that she had her grandmother's eyes. Who was Zack? He was more than a kind old gentleman, who knew her grandmother. Why did he know so much?

She opened the door to her apartment. It was cold and dark. This place never did feel like home. Zack's house felt like home. She got ready for bed and couldn't shut off her brain. As she crawled into bed, she could see Sara, Mary, and Monroe riding through the mountains. She could see the trees, the sky, and the snow covering the peaks. She could see those same peaks that she loved to drive through when she needed to think. She drifted off to sleep to the sound of Zack's voice telling the story that was unfinished.

Beth was at Zack's door at 11am sharp. She was always punctual. Zack was waiting for her and greeted her with a smile.

"How about some coffee?" he asked. "I also found the box with the journals for you." He handed her a mug and pointed to the neatly packed box on his table.

"Thanks for the coffee," she said as she took the mug. "I have so many questions I need to ask you."

"I'm sure that you do," he smiled. "Let me get on with the story and I think all of your questions will be answered. Let's see, where were we?"

"Monroe had just begun to write down the stories," Beth said with enthusiasm.

***

Traveling in this country was hard. They would only make 10 to 15 miles a day. Monroe didn't want to stress the horses, and he loved this country. The pristine beauty of these mountains impressed him every time he came through this area. He would write in his journal at night. He found it good to recall the events of the day and could lose himself in his thoughts.

"Why do you make marks in that book?" Sara asked.

"I'm writing down the story of our trip," he said.

"Can you teach me to make the marks of the white language?" Sara asked.

"Yes, I can teach you," Monroe said. He felt guilty about not offering to do this for Sara many years ago. Sara was going to live in this world. Writing would be an important thing to learn. He would make sure that Mary knew how to do this also. Monroe figured they could help each other. "We can start now if you like? I'll teach you and Mary to write the language."

With that the teaching began. Monroe started with the alphabet and worked from there. He was amazed at the quickness of their minds. Mary was grasping this concept quickly. Monroe found her helping Sara. He was afraid that Sara would not accept her help, but was pleased with her willingness to accept the help from Mary. By the time they reached the mountain pass, Mary could recite and write the alphabet. Sara had quickly picked up the sounds of the letters and could associate them with words like sky, tree, and mountain.

Monroe would give them simple words and ask them to read them and then spell them. They camped for two days on the west slope of the pass. Sara had noted the difference in the trees and foliage. Traveling would be more difficult now because of the undergrowth. Monroe wanted to do some hunting to add to their food supply. They were 5 days from the cabin that sat above the great waterfall. He was hoping that Sara would like her new home.

He returned from his hunting trip to find Sara and Mary practicing their letters. He pulled the elk from his horse and they started to skin it. Monroe was always in awe at the speed that they worked. Their hands made this difficult task look effortless. Within 20 minutes the elk was cleaned, dressed, and ready to be smoked. He had a temporary smokehouse built and the fire was going.

Sara saved some of the elk to cook for supper. Mary worked with the hide so it could be tanned in a few days. After their meal, Monroe wrote in his journal and the women practiced their writing. Monroe knew that some of the people he knew would not be thrilled at his choice for a wife. They would be less thrilled that they could read and write. They would be the narrow-minded and the cruel, but he would try to protect them as much as he could.

He had purchased clothing for them, mainly Sara, to wear once they arrived at the cabin. Mary was about the same size as Sara, so these would suit her too. He had not told them about getting rid of their buckskin clothing. This would be safer for all concerned. The clothing arrived before he left for Sara's camp. The furniture he had ordered was with this shipment. The inheritance that his mother allowed him take came in handy. He had built and furnished his cabin and still had much more in the bank.

If he never did another day's work in his life, he and Sara would be comfortable. He was not one to remain idle. The area outside of Seattle was beginning to grow and it would be many years before the remote area he chose would be settled. This was how he liked it. He didn't like the urban life he had in England. The people were phony and didn't understand what it meant to work for something. He did like the convenience of an urban life, because it was a two-day trip to go into to Seattle, so he made the most of each trip.

"Monroe? Is this right?" Sara said as she brought him back to reality. She handed him a paper with the words 'Sara Monroe' written on it.

"This is your name," Monroe smiled. "That's right, Sara," as he handed the paper back to her.

They were on their way down the mountain while Mary talked about the difference in the land. She was surprised at the large trees, the coolness of the air, and there was a heavy dampness everywhere. Some of the leaves were starting to change. It was September and fall was in the air. Sara found a large patch of berries and encouraged Monroe to stop so they could pick some. He couldn't say 'no' to her, for, she rarely asked for anything.

The berries proved to be a nice addition at supper. Monroe was anxious to get home. He was ready to settle in for the winter. He would need to make a run into town for some staples for the winter. He also needed to go into Seattle before winter. He had some business he was conducting with a timber mill for lumber. They were building like crazy in Seattle and the mill would take any logs he could provide and pay him well.

He had seen what some of the logging camps were doing. They would clear every tree from an area. They left the area in a shameful mess and never replanted a single tree. His plan was to purchase a large tract of land and only log a portion of it each year. As the land was logged, it would be replanted so it could be logged again. For the last 3 years he had planted seedlings to be replanted from the land he would log.

He began to talk to Sara about his plans for this. She was very interested and suggested that he not cut all the trees. He could leave trees for the birds and animals and those that were too small to be of any use yet. This would not drive away all the wildlife or cause problems when the rains came.

"The Great Spirit wants us to take care of the land, not ruin it," Sara said. "If we must cut the trees, let's do what's good for the land."

"I didn't think about erosion, Sara," Monroe admitted. "I did consider the animals."

They rode on and Mary made some suggestions for Monroe's logging operation. They both had a wealth of knowledge about the land, and could grow anything. Monroe would consider them partners in his operation and his life. Sara had a good head for numbers, seasons, and could see the future. Mary understood plants, and trees and asked of she could maintain the seedling nursery.

For the next two days they discussed how they would help Monroe. When they camped that last night, Monroe knew they would be home the next day. He held Sara close that night with the sky clear and aglow with stars. Their 400-mile journey was without incident. It would be good to sleep in a bed again. That was the only comfort he really missed and he hoped Sara would learn to like a bed also. She had spent her life sleeping on the ground. This was one of the many things that would change for her.

He hoped she would accept this change in her life. I don't think she realized how much she would lose. Her culture would be gone. The way of life she grew up was ending and if he hadn't married her, she would have ended up on a reservation or dead. A reservation would have been a prison for her. Maybe this new life would be a prison, also. Monroe would try to not let that happen. He wanted to keep her safe, warm, and loved.

By noon the next day, the cabin was in sight. Monroe pointed it out to Sara and Mary. They reined in their horses and looked at each other. He saw them both smile. They rode up the long lane through the trees and Monroe stopped his horse in front of the barn. They were met by two men and both beamed with smiles.

"It's good to have you back, Mr. Monroe," Charlie said.

"Charlie, this is my wife, Sara, and her sister Mary," Monroe said. "Sara this is Charlie, and that's his son Samuel."

"How, do Ma am, and Miss," Charlie said as he removed his hat. "Let me help you get your animals unpacked." Samuel tipped his hat and his eyes met Mary's. They seemed to look at each other forever. Monroe could swear that he saw Samuel blush and he knew what Samuel was feeling and knew that look.

Sara turned to look at the place that Monroe called his cabin. This was unlike any cabin that Sara had ever seen. It was tall and massive. There were three buildings near the cabin. There was a large barn with enough room for all of Sara's ponies. There was room for grain, hay, and Monroe had saddles and harnesses. There was a small cabin that belonged to Charlie and Samuel and the other building housed wood for the fireplaces, and tools for construction.

Monroe escorted Sara and Mary into the large two- story house. It was warm and sturdy and Sara saw strange and new things inside. There was a large metal machine in the corner of what Monroe called the kitchen.

"It's called a cook stove," Monroe smiled. "It's like an indoor campfire. I'll show you how it works."

There was an indoor well and storage area like Sara had never seen. The upstairs boasted 4 large bedrooms with fireplaces in each room. The room that Monroe called his also had a desk and many books. Mary looked, with longing, at these. She wanted to know what was in these books. That story did they tell, and why were these words written down?

Mary's room was down a short hall from Monroe's. There were large windows that faced the morning sun. There were also shelves with books in this room. She gently ran her hand over the books. She wanted to open each of them and read the words. She wanted to know the story. She looked at the large bed and looked back at Monroe.

"It's a bed," Monroe explained. "Come, sit down on it," he encouraged as he sat down on the bed. Mary sat next to him and was surprised at the softness. She ran her hand over the multi-colored quilt that covered this bed. She looked at Monroe and smiled. "You'll like sleeping on this. It's softer than the ground."

"This is mine?" Mary asked. Monroe nodded his head and got up and left the room. Sara was watching from the doorway and smiled at Mary. She was so grateful to Monroe and saw Mary's eyes filled with tears. Mary had never expected such treatment from a white man. Many of the women in her village had chosen to become involved with them but Mary never felt the desire. She was so in love with Sara and didn't want to explore any other types of intimacies.

She didn't understand why Sara chose to marry this man at first. She didn't understand how Sara could have feelings and want to be with this white man. During their trip from their village, Mary had seen the side of Monroe that Sara had seen years before. His kindness and gentleness was like nothing she had ever seen, even with her people.

Monroe left Mary to get settled. He was pleased that Mary was happy with her new home. When Mary was happy, Sara was happy and this was Monroe's hope. He didn't think, or get jealous about the time that Sara and Mary spent together. In certain social circles this was expected and accepted behavior. He knew of many women who would spend time with other women prior to marriage. Men seemed to think this made them better wives.

He had an aunt that never did marry. She lived for 30 years with the same woman and was happy. He knew they were lovers, but it was never discussed. Monroe was always pleased with the thought that she was happy. When she died he felt bad for her 'friend'. To everyone else's surprise, she died two days later. He always smiled at the thought of them being together where ever we go after we die.

He went back to his and Sara's bedroom to find Sara looking at the closet, and the clothes hanging there. She turned to him with a puzzled look in his face.

"Those are for you," he said.

"Why?" she said flatly.

"I thought it might make things easier," he said tentatively. He didn't want her to think that clothes weren't good enough. In all honesty, he preferred the buckskin clothing she wore. He also knew that for she and Mary, to better be accepted in the white man's world, they would have to look less like Indians. He hated this but it was a fact of life. He saw Sara take the dress from the closet and inspect it closely. Monroe's heart was in his chest. He didn't want Sara to think that he wanted to change her.

"I like these clothes. Can I wear them now?" she asked.

"You can wear them anytime you want, Sara," he smiled. "I have some for Mary, too. I got each of you these large trunks for your buckskins. I don't want you to throw them away. They're far too beautiful. I didn't have time to show Mary the things in her closet. Would you like to help me with that?" Sara nodded and smiled and they left to find Mary.

Monroe went down the stairs and found Charlie and Samuel had unpacked the horses and had brought the things into the house. Monroe looked at this father and son and marveled. Charlie was half dead when he found him and that was 11 years ago. Samuel was only 5 but was doing his best to take care of his father after being mauled by a bear.

Monroe was amazed that he didn't die. He had come across them 2 days after the encounter on his way back from his first visit to Sara's village. He had just started to build the house and was going to hire some help. He happened upon these two and knew that Samuel wouldn't make it without his father. He knew Charlie wouldn't make it without his help, which Charlie was reluctant to accept. Charlie had been a slave and was freed by the civil war, but wanted to come somewhere and start over after Samuel's mother died.

Monroe helped Charlie and Samuel until Charlie was strong enough to travel. He saw the tenderness in Charlie after watching him with his son. Charlie was a carpenter on the plantation where he was enslaved as a small child after his own mother had died. Charlie liked Monroe and felt he could trust him. After some long discussions by the campfire, Monroe decided to ask Charlie to work for him. Charlie was reluctant at first. Monroe explained that it was different from what he had been used to. This was a job. This was by his choice and he could stay or leave at his own free will. They agreed on a wage and shook hands on the deal.

"You need a job and I need the help," Monroe said. "Will you work for me, as a free man? If you don't like the work, you and Samuel are free to leave anytime you like."

"That's very kind, sir," Charlie said.

"There is no need to call me sir," Monroe said. "You're a free man, and so am I. My name is Edmundson Monroe, but most people call me Monroe."

With that Charlie and Samuel had a home, work, and a good life. Monroe trusted these men with his life and now the lives of Sara and Mary. Samuel was now 16 and was handsome and strong. His father had taught him the art of carpentry and Monroe had taught him to read and write. Samuel was like his father in many ways. He was quiet, smart, and had a dignity that was rare in any man. His respect for his father and Monroe was sincere.

Charlie and Samuel had a bond that was rare. They had a love that they demonstrated and they talked constantly. Samuel kept up on the news especially politics. Charlie seemed to be in tune with the building and expansion of the Puget Sound area. They both had their interests and Monroe continued to provide information to keep their interests alive.

Samuel had some interests of this own, which worried Monroe. He saw the look in Samuel's eyes when he saw Mary. Monroe felt very protective of Mary and hoped if Samuel was interested in a relationship with her that he would be patient. Mary had gone through many changes in the last few months. Sara had also, and they needed to get settled into their new surroundings. As Monroe continued to watch Charlie and Samuel he could, again, hear the whispers in the mist. They called to him from 400 miles away. He was so happy to be back with his wife, who would now make this large empty house a home. He asked for only one thing more in this life and that was for the chance to raise a child. All the doctors he ever spoke with told him this was not possible, but something told him otherwise. Something had called him to this place and who knows what the future would hold.

He looked back to see Sara standing on the front porch in one of her new dresses and she was a vision. He walked toward his bride, toward his life, and toward a future filled with promise.

Chapter 3

The next few months saw some wonderful things for Sara. Monroe had taught her to use the stove, indoor pump, and the other modern conveniences in the kitchen. She, in turn, had taught Mary these things. Their lives had changed drastically since leaving their village 4 months earlier. There was no daily concern about food or cutting wood for the fire, there was little concern about snow, rain, or cold, for the house was well built and warm.

Mary had begun to read the books in her room. She would stay up late at night and get engrossed in the stories being told. She would find words she could not say or understand the meaning. She would ask Monroe about these, but lately she had been turning to Samuel. Monroe was glad to see this, in a way. Both she and Samuel had curious minds and a desire to learn. Over the last month Monroe had seen Mary's vocabulary and grammar improve.

There had been one change in the large house that Monroe was ashamed to admit he hadn't thought about. Sara had noted that Charlie and Samuel usually had meals in their cabin.

"Why don't Charlie and Samuel share meals with us?" Sara asked Monroe.

"I don't know," Monroe stated.

"I think that they should share the meals with us," Sara stated.

"Why do you think this, Sara?" Monroe asked. He was interested in why this was on her mind.

"Charlie and Samuel are part of this family and families should be together," she said directly.

"Yes, they should. Do you mind cooking extra for them?" he asked. She shook her head agreeing that there would be no problem.

"This will start tonight," she smiled.

From that night on, Charlie and Samuel ate in the main house. Sara had a small motive for her question. Mary liked Samuel and enjoyed talking with him. This was a way for them to spend time together and no one would be the wiser. This seemed important to Mary. She didn't want Monroe to think that she wasn't grateful for all he had done for her, but Samuel could explain things in a way that was easy to understand.

Over the last month Samuel had stayed and worked with Mary after dinner. He would have her read and had taught her how to use the Dictionary to learn the meaning of the words in the books. There were times when Sara had joined them and listen to the story as Mary read aloud. They would laugh and cry with the characters in the story. Mary displayed emotion openly, but Sara had always been reserved in this respect.

Sara kept her feelings guarded and only showed emotion when she was comfortable with those around her. She could easily smile and laugh with Monroe and Mary, but even they never really knew what she was thinking. She was still reserved around Charlie and Samuel. It was getting easier with Samuel, but Charlie was different. She didn't know him well, but she saw how Monroe relied on him. She knew he was a fine man and she trusted him, but she tended to avoid him whenever possible.

Charlie had been gone for the last few days. Monroe sent him to Seattle for one last stock of supplies that would carry them through the winter. It had rained consistently for the last 2 weeks and Sara understood why everything stayed green. Nothing had a chance to dry out.

Monroe and Samuel were finishing the last of the work inside the barn. They added 5 more stalls for Sara's ponies. Monroe didn't like for animals to be in the weather unless it was unavoidable. Charlie had just finished the addition on the barn when Sara first arrived, but didn't have time to finish the inside work before leaving for Seattle. This was the first time that Samuel didn't accompany him. He seemed content to stay behind this time. He was enjoying his time with Mary more and more and didn't want to be away from her.

Samuel was whistling a tune as he and Monroe worked on the stalls. Monroe was pleased at his good mood. Samuel was never sullen or showed anger. His temper was always very even.

"You seem exceptionally happy today," Monroe teased.

"Life is a wonderful thing, Edmundson," Samuel said. Samuel was the only one who used Monroe's first name. He did this as a child and it continued. Monroe never minded this.

"Life is wonderful," Monroe agreed. "Why do you think this?"

"I'm in love with Mary," he said directly. He had stopped working and looked at Monroe.

"How does she feel?" Monroe asked. "Have you told her of your feelings for her?"

"She said she wants to be with me always," Samuel said. "I want to marry her Edmundson. I asked her to be my wife." Monroe had stopped working and looked at Samuel. He had just turned 17 and Monroe would like to see him wait before taking a wife. Marriage was hard enough when you're prepared for it. To want to take on that responsibility at his age was remarkable.

"What was her answer?" Monroe asked.

"She said, yes," he smiled. "I'm asking your permission to marry her."

"You don't need my permission, Samuel. You have Mary's answer and what she says matters," he said. He walked over and shook his hand. "Well, have to spoken to your father about this?"

"Spoken to me about what?" Charlie said as he walked into the barn. Samuel looked at Monroe and smiled.

"Mary and I want to get married," he said. "I asked her and she said, yes."

"I guess there's nothing to talk about," Charlie said as he smiled. He looked at Monroe and winked. "Samuel, can you start unloading the wagon?"

Charlie walked over to Monroe and shook his head as he smiled. "He's just like his father. I had many women to choose from, even in those days of slavery. I knew the minute that Samuel's mother's eyes met mine that she was the one. He never seemed the least bit interested in the girls we saw while we were in Seattle, and let me tell you, there are some brown beauties there."

"I'm concerned about how young he is. If I were to choose anyone for Mary, it would be Samuel. His gentleness of spirit and common sense are his greatest qualities," Monroe said. "What am I doing? It's not my decision, it's theirs' and it's been made, so it looks like we are going build another house, Charlie. Does Samuel want to stay here?"

"I believe that he does, but let's ask him," Charlie said.

Samuel did want to stay and this was good news to Monroe because of the things he wanted to start in the spring. He would need Samuel's help, hands, and ease with numbers for his new business venture. Sara was already aware of Mary's feelings for Samuel and they had not been intimate in weeks. Sara missed her soft touch on many nights, but she didn't force the issue. She was happy for Mary and for Samuel.

Charlie agreed to move into the main house and let Mary and Samuel have the cabin until their house could be built. Monroe thought they should have their privacy and Charlie would move into the downstairs bedroom. Mary asked Monroe if she could take her bed and books.

"You can take anything you want, Mary," he said. "They belong to you."

The wedding was small and simple. Sara pulled out her buckskins she wore for her wedding. They were special to her. Her mother had made these for her and Mary was pleased that Sara had offered them for her wedding. The hand made beading and design was in the traditional Nez Perce fashion. Charlie and Monroe bought a suit for Samuel.

Monroe had found a preacher to perform the ceremony. He was a quiet and unassuming man. Patrick Reilly was nothing like the priest that refused to marry him and Sara. This preacher was what Monroe thought a man of God should be. He had spent enough time with the Indians to understand their customs and not want to change them.

Samuel and Mary stood before this man and promised to love and take care of one another. As they held hands, Monroe remembered his marriage to Sara just 8 months earlier. He reached over to hold Sara's hand and saw her crying. He placed his arm around her and held her close. These were tears of joy for Mary. Sara was happy that Mary had found someone that she could love and build a life with. She was happy it was Samuel. He was a kind and gentle man who was mature for his age, and would take care of Mary.

They spent the next few days getting the newlyweds settled in the cabin. As soon as the weather cleared, they would start on their house. Samuel had picked out a spot that was quiet about 200 yards from the main house. Monroe and Charlie started removing the trees to clear a spot for the house. This was cold and wet work with the rain. Monroe had contacted a friend of his who ran a logging crew.

"We can clear these trees in a week," Ivan told Monroe. "We'll pull the stumps for you, too."

"Thanks, Ivan," Monroe said. "What are you looking at for payment?"

"I'll take half the trees, if that's okay," he said. Monroe looked at him strangely. "We get a good price from the lumber mill and I can pay my people."

"That's great," Monroe smiled. He thought about this later. He had purchased 3000 acres of land in this area. His house and buildings were on the west edge. He was wondering, recently, why he had purchased so much land. He had no set plans for it, and the land was cheap 10 years ago. His mind was racing now with thoughts of being able to secure his and Sara's future. This would also secure the future of his children that he wanted so desperately.

***

Beth was looking through the journals that Monroe kept on his trip. She saw the maps he had made and the detail in them. Zack was on the phone about schedules for next week at the cemetery. As Beth read the journal she could picture their trip that took 5 hours by car today. How she wished she could have seen this area before all the bankers and lawyers got their hands on it.

She could see the Columbia River and where they crossed it. This is where Ellensburg now sits. She could see how they turned north from there and where they crossed the mountains just north of where I-90 now exists. How pristine this area must have been. To see this area unscathed by towns, roads, and clear-cuts would have been an amazing sight. She would never travel this route again without thinking of Monroe, Sara, and Mary.

"What are you thinking about?" Zack asked.

"How this land looked before," Beth said. "What I wouldn't give to be able to see through Sara's eyes right now."

"I remember what this looked like in 1928," Zack said. "It was a long trip by train back then. I remember the long tunnel threw the mountain by what is now Steven's Pass. I remember thinking about how long that tunnel was. It was pitch black as you passed through it and it seemed to go on forever."

"They still use that tunnel, don't they?" Beth remarked.

"Amtrak still runs trains through there," Zack said. "I was only through it once and that was when I came out here."

"Where were you from Zack?" Beth asked.

"Chicago," Zack said as his smile faded. "I grew up there."

"What made you leave?" Beth asked, but was sorry she did. She saw how the look on his face was one of remorse.

"My father died when I was young," he said. "I never wanted to leave Chicago, but my mother and brother died in an accident. I wanted to start over somewhere else, so I hopped a train and ended up here."

Zack had that faraway look in his eyes again and Beth wondered what he was thinking about. She decided the look wasn't remorse as she had first thought, but one of longing. It was a longing for something he couldn't have, or maybe he had once had and lost. She thought about his mother and brother and assumed it was those lost he longed for. She missed the mark on this one.

***

"Hello, Miss Monroe," Zack said. "I'm Zachary McGill. I'll be taking care of your mother."

"I've brought the clothes for her to be dressed in," she said. She held up the buckskins that Sara wore across the mountains on her first trip with Monroe. "She wanted to wear this to the spirit world."

"Yes, Ma'am," Zack said. He couldn't take his eyes off of her. She was the most beautiful woman he'd ever seen. Her dark hair, but not completely black was shiny and thick. There was a hint of auburn in it that caught the light. Her eyes were the color of a mountain lake. They were so blue you could swim in them. She had her mother's high cheekbones and narrow aristocratic nose. She seemed to glide across the room when she walked. Her tall lean stature gave her the appearance of a graceful panther.

"There's no need to call me ma'am. My name is Anne. It's nice to meet you Zachary," she said as she extended her hand. "I know almost everyone in town, but your name, McGill, is not familiar to me. Have you been her long?"

"No, ma'am, I mean Anne. I've only been here for a couple of months," Zack said and paused not wanting to end the conversation. "It does rain a lot, though."

"You'll get used to it," Anne said. "There's no more beautiful place on Earth." She picked up her mother's cold hand. "This is the only place she ever wanted to live, although she grew up in Eastern Washington." She kissed her mother's hand and put it back at her side. "Do what you need to do, Zachary. The funeral will be in 2 days. There will be a private funeral. The public viewing will be tomorrow and tomorrow, only. I don't want this to turn into a circus."

"I'll make sure that Mrs. Monroe is ready," Zack said. He watched as she left the room. His heart was in his throat, his hands were sweating, and his heart was pounding. Zack couldn't take his eyes from the door and he hoped, against hope that she would come back in. He had never seen a more exotic, beautiful, cultured woman in his life.

"You look like you've been struck by lightening," Bill chuckled.

"What an amazing woman," Zack said.

"Well, don't fall in love. She can be hell on wheels, but she doesn't hold a candle to her mother when it comes to determination," Bill said. "She is quite beautiful, though."

"That she is," was all the Zack could manage to say. Bill looked at him and started to laugh and left the room.

Sara Monroe was ready for viewing the following day. Zack took extra care with her and made sure the buckskins were just right. Anne arrived prior to the viewing to check on her mother. She was pleased with Zack's work.

"You did a good job Zachary," she smiled as she touched her mother's hand. "I'd forgotten how good these buckskins look. They're well over 60 years old. She almost threw them out, several times, and I stopped her. I'm glad I did."

"Bill told me that this is not the casket she will be buried in," Zack said.

"That's right," Anne responded. "There will be one brought in tomorrow. She'll be placed in that and buried. It's hand made by an old friend of hers."

"It's time to open the doors, Anne," Zack said quietly.

"Okay, Mother," she said. "Don't try to piss anybody off." She looked at Zack and he started to smile. She smiled back and her face lit up the whole room.

Anne was the model of decorum throughout the afternoon. Zack counted well over 500 people who walked past Sara Monroe's coffin. There were flowers everywhere and no more room for them, but they kept coming. They all stopped and expressed their condolences to Anne. Bill even pointed out a man that he said was the Governor of Washington. There was one couple in particular that Zack remembered seeing. It was as though Anne had waited all day to see these people. The small attractive woman had to be 75 years old, and her husband the same. Anne's face lit up when she held the small body. They didn't leave her side for the rest of the afternoon.

By 5pm Zack closed the doors. Within 10 minutes the room had cleared and Anne said good-bye to the old couple and was again alone with her mother. She sat down and suddenly looked tired. Zack watched her as he closed up the outer doors. Anne had her head down and he saw tears. He wanted to comfort her, but knew nothing he could say, would help.

"Well, Mother," she said softly. "Not a bad showing for someone who broke all the rules, defied the government, and was an Indian on top of it. I think some of them just wanted to make sure that you were dead." She stood again at the casket and saw Zack out of the corner of her eye. "I'll be out of here in a couple of minutes."

"Stay as long as you like," Zack said. "I've nowhere to go."

"Zachary?" she started to ask. "Would you care to have dinner with me?"

"Yes, Anne," he said as he felt his face flush. "I'd like that very much."

As they left the mortuary Zack was aware of his desire to be with this woman. He liked walking next to her with her stride that was long and flowing. Although Zack was almost six foot tall, he had to work to keep up with her. There was a small restaurant down the street that Zack always wanted to try but hadn't gotten around to yet. He liked fixing his own meals, and was good at it.

Their meal was quiet and peaceful. Many heads turned as he and Anne entered the room. Anne nodded 'hello' to several people. They were seated in a small private booth in the back of the dining room. The food was Italian and Zack had forgotten how much he had missed this kind of food. He and his brother would frequent someplace similar when he was in Chicago.

Zack and Anne spoke of many things during the next 2 hours. Zack told about his life in Chicago and the death that surrounded his family. He found her easy to talk to. She told him of her father's death and how her mother seemed to take everything in stride.

"She seemed to handle the situation with such dignity," Anne said. "Or so I was told. I was very young when he died. Very few people really knew how alone she felt. The old couple that sat next to me today, they were the rare ones."

"It was a blessing when my father died," Zack said. "I did love him, but he drank too much and would be abusive. He never hit my mother, though. I will give him that much." Zack paused for a moment, "I wish I could have known your mother and father."

"My mother would have liked you," she smiled.

"Why do you say that?" Zack asked.

"Because I like you," she said as she looked into his eyes. "You have that rare gift about you. You are kind, gentle, and intelligent. How old are you Zachary?"

"I'll be nineteen next month," he said quietly. He was feeling very young. He had guessed her age at mid-twenties.

"You seem much older Zachary McGill," she smiled.

"Age really doesn't matter between friends, does it?" he smiled back.

"No it doesn't," she said.

They continued to talk as they walked back to the mortuary. The rain had stopped and the skies had cleared. Anne said her good-bye and left and Zack watched her as she walked away. He wondered why she asked him to dinner. He was glad she did. He wanted to see more of her. He would get that opportunity tomorrow at her mother's service.

The morning that Sara "Two Trees" Monroe was laid to rest was clear and sunny. The clear skies remained and the temperature was warm for June. There was to be no service except for the few words said at the grave sight. Zack was working when a man appeared behind him.

"I'm Samuel Washington," he said. He was a tall handsome black man. He estimated his age at 65 or 70 years, but was still physically fit.

"Hello," Zack responded. "What can I do for you?"

"I have a casket for Sara Monroe. Where can I put it?" he said.

"I'll help you bring it in," Zack said.

Samuel nodded in agreement and Zack followed him to the wagon that held the casket. Zack had never seen such craftsmanship. There wasn't a nail to be found in any part of it. It was unlike anything that Zack had ever seen. As he ran his hand over the lid, he felt that it was as smooth as glass.

"This is the best work I've ever seen," he said. "Who was the craftsman?"

"I am," Samuel said. "I learned from my father."

"You have a gift, sir," Zack said.

"I wanted it to be perfect for Mrs. Monroe," he said as he turned and picked up the one end of the casket. They carried the casket into the room where Sara lay and they carefully placed it on the stand. Samuel turned to look at Sara and tears came to his eyes as he gently touched her hand. Zack didn't want to disturb him during his time of reflection. "I'll miss you Sara. I'll never forget you and I'll continue to take care of Mary as long as I can."

Zack turned to a rustling behind him and was surprised to see a women standing there. She slowly walked over to Samuel and touched his arm. She looked at Sara and back to Samuel.

"She's gone to the spirit world, my husband," Mary said. "She is with her mother, her husband, and her son. She will always be watching us. She will always be guarding us." She turned and bent over and kissed the body in the casket. "We will join you soon, my sister. We will join you soon." She turned and looked at Zack.

"Hello, ma'am, I'm Zack McGill," he said as he extended his hand.

"I'm Mary Washington. You've met my husband," she said as she looked at Samuel. "You've done a fine job with Sara. I want to thank you." She removed her coat and she was wearing a set of buckskins similar to those that Sara had. "My husband and I will place Sara in her burial box."

"I can do that ma'am," Zack responded.

"Miss Anne will be here shortly. She wanted us to take care of it," Mary said.

"Hello, Zachary," said another voice from the doorway. "Mary is right. We would like to prepare Mother, if you don't mind."

"That would be fine," Zack said. "I'll be next door if you need me. We can start the service when you're ready." Zack left with Samuel behind him. He turned and said, "Would you care for a cup of coffee?"

"That sounds good," he said. They sat and drank their coffee and talked. Samuel told Zack some of the history of the area. The next hour passed quickly. Zack was entranced with Samuel's stories of his travels and how he met Sara and then his wife, Mary.

"I believe we're ready, Zachary," Anne said from behind him. He was so engrossed in what Samuel was saying that he didn't hear Anne come into the room and the sound of her voice made him jump. Zack stood up quickly and Anne smiled. "I'm sorry if I startled you, Zachary. It looks as though Samuel has been spinning his tails again."

They left and there was a team of beautiful appaloosas hitched to a wagon. Samuel, Zack, and Bill loaded the casket in the wagon and Anne lead the wagon to a far corner of the cemetery. There was a large hole awaiting the casket. Zack always hated this part. He hated the look of the large square hole. He knew this beautiful work of art would rot away in this hole after a few years. It didn't seem a fitting end for anyone, but especially for Anne's mother.

Waiting at the grave was a man with snow-white hair. Samuel, Mary, and Anne all smiled at the same time. The casket was removed from the wagon and this man started to talk about Sara. He spoke in a strange tongue for part of the service.

"It's the Nez Perce language," Bill whispered to Zack.

After 30 minutes he finished. Although Zack couldn't understand all of what the minister said, he found the words refreshing. It was so much better than the priest at the funeral for his mother and brother. Zack watched as he hugged Anne and talked with Samuel and Mary. It sounded as though this minister had known these people for many years. He did hear him say that Mary looked as pretty as the day he married she and Samuel. Samuel took a few minutes and secured the coffin lid and turned to join his wife.

Mary took the lead rope for the appaloosa team and headed back to the mortuary with Samuel by her side. Anne stayed at the grave sight for a few minutes. Zack didn't want to leave her alone and the minister saw him standing there.

"I'm Patrick Reilly," he said as he shook his hand.

"Zachary McGill," Zack said.

"You wouldn't be from Chicago, by any chance would you?" Patrick said.

"Yes," Zack said in a surprised voice. "Why do you ask?"

"I used to read articles in a Chicago newspaper written by Kevin McGill," he said. "I used to enjoy them and admire Mr. McGill's passion. I'm sure that this is a common name in Chicago."

"That was my brother," Zack said. "He died a few months ago in a car accident."

"I heard that. It's a small world isn't it? I miss your brother's articles and I'm sorry for your loss, Zachary," he said as he put a hand on Zack's shoulder. He turned and headed back to the mortuary. Zack looked up to see Anne walking toward him. She had a smile, but tears were in her eyes.

"Thank you for waiting, Zachary," Anne said. "Will you walk with me?"

They started the long walk back to the mortuary. The sun was high in the sky and Zack wanted to put his arm around Anne and comfort her, but he felt that this was inappropriate. He wanted to gather her in his arms and kiss her tears away. He had not felt this way about anyone before and he couldn't stand it anymore. He took a risk and took her hand in his. She stopped walking and looked at her hand in his, then looked into his eyes. Zack felt himself blush.

"I'm sorry, Anne," he said but didn't let go of her hand.

"Don't apologize, Zachary," she said as she turned to him and stepped in close. She laid her head on his shoulder and he hugged her as she gently cried. The feel of her body close to his was heavenly. It was as though he had held her before at some other time, or in some other life. He felt like he had come home and no words written could describe this feeling.

***

Beth sat and watched Zack as he made tea. She wondered how much he knew and how well he knew her Grandmother. She never knew her father, let alone her mother. All she knew was a set of foster parents and then the people who had adopted her. She didn't want to think about that now. She wanted to concentrate on her true family history and not on what she had been told.

It wasn't her foster parents' fault for not telling her much, either. They didn't really know anything, except a few bits and pieces. They did let her keep her real name. She did give them credit for that and for the many other things they did for her. They were good people and they did help her as much as they could find out about her real family.

    "Here you go, my dear," Zack said. "Let's get back to the story."

Chapter 4

Ivan and his crew were true to their word and the area was cleared in 4 days. Samuel was on site for the entire time. He was very specific about which trees he wanted removed. He wanted his house and out buildings to be nestled amidst the trees and had a rough plan drawn out. He talked with Ivan and marked each tree to be removed. On the last day, Monroe went to Samuel's site and was amazed at the transformation.

"What do you think?" Samuel asked as he walked up behind him.

"Why did you choose to leave some?" Monroe asked.

"These trees are the Redwoods. I didn't want to remove these. The fir, hemlock, and alder are everywhere. The Redwoods are not as common here," he said. "I understand that there are stands of these in California that are a thousand years old."

"I've heard that, too," Monroe smiled.

"I want to see those trees, someday," Samuel said. "Let me show you what I have planned." Samuel walked over to his wagon and pulled out some drawings of what he wanted his house to be. "I've asked Mary what she wanted and I had my father help me with the design."

"This is interesting," Monroe said. "This house is on one level. I don't see any stairs."

"It is on one level," he said. "Mary is not fond of stairs, and neither am I. I wanted it to look like a large cabin with minimal interior walls. Dad helped with the design and the support structure."

"Have you calculated the lumber amount?" Monroe asked.

"Somewhat," Samuel answered. "I spoke with Ivan and he was going to have the trees that I kept taken to the mill. He wants to see if they will trade him those trees for milled lumber. If they won't then I'll pay to have the logs milled."

Monroe continued to talk to Samuel for a few more minutes and when Charlie arrived Monroe left. Samuel was a smart kid. He handled himself well and knew what he wanted. Monroe liked the fact that he had talked to Mary and asked her what she wanted. Samuel would be a good husband.

Sara had been sullen since Mary had married. They still worked together daily with their daily chores, but Mary's absence from the house was noticeable. Sara had started reading more and she asked

Monroe to teach her math. This was never his strong area but Charlie was a whiz with this. Monroe asked Charlie to help Sara with this. Sara was hesitant at first, but when she started to get excited about numbers, the tension she had felt around Charlie disappeared.

After the first month, Monroe was a student, too. Charlie's ability to calculate board feet from raw logs was precise. As these classes progressed on a nightly basis, Monroe's thoughts were about the future. He thought about the thousands of acres of land he had purchased many years earlier. Small towns were starting to spring up everywhere as the area west of the Cascades was settled. These people would need lumber to build their homes and he had thousands of acres of trees, ready to harvest. He would need loggers, a mill, and some knowledgeable partners. He looked at Sara and Charlie, and thought about Samuel. The partners he needed were right in front of him.

Spring had come early this year. By March the weather had warmed and the rain had subsided. Samuel and Charlie were busy with the house. The deal that Samuel had made with the mill had paid off. The milled lumber was delivered for the frame and roof. They had even milled shakes for the roofing material. Monroe was now the hired hand as Charlie and Samuel accepted his help and put him to work. Monroe was learning more about carpentry than he ever knew was possible.

Samuel was using the timber frame knowledge he had learned from his father. The 6" X 12" beams were hard to work with, but by the time they were ready to go into to place the measurements, angles, and peg holes were never wrong. Charlie was working on the trusses. The time had come to place the ridgepole beam and this took more that just Charlie, Samuel, and Monroe. Ivan and four of his loggers arrived and helped to set the beam.

They stayed and worked the day and help set the rafters and start the roofing. They were happy for the large meals fixed by Sara and Mary. The weather had cooperated with them and, over the course of the next 3 days, they finished the roof. During this time, Monroe had talked with Ivan about going into to business together. He talked about his plan of logging his holdings, but not in the way that Ivan was used to. He talked about only logging a portion and then replanting that area.

"That's an interesting concept," Ivan said. "You could then log it again in the years to come."

"There would be no need to keep finding new areas to log," Monroe said. "It would renew itself. Sara also gave me the idea about not cutting all of the trees."

"Why?" Ivan asked.

"If we left a few and were selective, then the wildlife would stay in the area," Monroe said. "We need to leave trees of varying ages and sizes. These would be marked and left standing." Monroe paused for a minute and let Ivan think. "What do you think?"

"I trust you Edmundson," Ivan smiled. "I think we will do well. I'll try anything new. Who knows, maybe we will be the pioneers in this new logging process. Where did you get this idea about selective logging?"

"My wife was reading a book on it," Monroe said. "Her Nez Perce background helps, too."

They shook hands and sealed their deal. Ivan told Monroe that he would talk to the mill owner and make sure that he could take the logs there. Ivan liked to have a written contract, especially when it came to payment for logs. If the mill owner agreed then he and Monroe would get the contracts in order to start as soon as possible.

That evening, Monroe asked Samuel and Mary to join them for dinner at the main house. During this meal, Monroe talked about the business venture he had planned. He talked about the selective logging process that Sara had suggested and the idea of replanting. Charlie would be used to estimate the board feet and interact with the mill owner. Samuel would be in charge of marking the trees, or even stands of trees, to remain. Mary said that she would plant and maintain the seedlings for replanting.

The only person left out was Sara. She was feeling sad that Monroe didn't have a job for her. He looked at her and reached over and held her hand.

"Sara will be my right-hand person," he said. "She will be in charge of everything, when I'm not available. Charlie I want you to teach her about estimating board feet, and the finances with the mill. Sara and I will work together on this and I promise you, we will not fail."

"I need to get my house finished, Monroe," Samuel said softly.

"I know this Samuel, and this should be your first order of business," Monroe said. "I've talked to Ivan, and the four men that helped with the ridge beam will stay to help you as much as they can, if that's all right with you."

"That's fine. They're good men," Samuel smiled.

"Mary," Monroe said. "When can you start new seedlings?"

"I've already started them," she said. "I wanted to see how well they did over the winter and see how quickly they grow."

By the time they finished their meal Monroe's plans were in place. There was an excitement that Sara hadn't felt since leaving the valley she grew up in. Monroe had listened to her about not ruining the land and would enact this when the business took off. Monroe said that Ivan would set up his logging camp about 3 miles from the main house just outside of the town of Snoqualmie. All of his equipment would be moved as soon as the contracts were in place.

As Monroe and Sara lay in bed that night, Monroe reached over and held her hand.

"I love you, Sara," he whispered.

"I love you, Monroe," she said as she placed his hand on her abdomen. "I carry your son in me."

Monroe was thinking that Sara was sullen because of Mary leaving the house. Sara was sullen because she was fighting with morning sickness. She didn't want to tell Monroe until she had skipped her second bleeding cycle and then she was sure. Sara was very happy about this and Monroe was beyond happy. She told Mary and Samuel later that week. Although Samuel spent long days working on his house, he found time to work with Charlie and built a cradle for the new arrival.

For the first time since arriving, Monroe wanted Sara to go down to the small settlement in the valley. This town sprang up about a year ago and it was booming. They could get most of the things that Monroe used to go to Seattle for. Sara had never been to a General Store but she would have to get used to going alone. He wanted to make sure the people knew who she was, so there was no question when she used his account for supplies.

Sara normally let her hair flow freely, but today she put it up on her head. When she met Monroe on the front porch, she was dressed in her gray dress and was wearing a bonnet that matched. She looked beautiful and Monroe was pleased. He helped her into the buggy and they were on their way.

As they entered the town of Snoqualmie Sara saw the logging camp that belonged to Ivan. Monroe saw Ivan and stopped.

"Good morning, Mrs. Monroe," he said as he tipped his hat to Sara. She nodded a smile to him.

"Hello, Ivan," Monroe said. "Have you heard anything from the mill?"

"Better than we could hope for," he said. "There's a new mill right here and this owner is fighting for the business from the established mills. He'd like to see us. As long as you're in town, can we head down there?"

"I'd love to, but I wanted to show Sara around a bit first," Monroe said.

"Why don't you stop back here and I'll have the Misses fix us some lunch. Is noon okay with you?" Ivan asked.

"That would be fine," Monroe said as he looked at his pocket watch. They drove down the main street, which was busy with wagons, horses, and people walking the streets. It was noisy and Sara wasn't crazy about that. They stopped in front of the General Store and Monroe got out of the buggy and came around to help Sara out. Monroe had tried to explain why men did this and she never understood the custom. She had been reading about American customs and was ready to try out these. She didn't tell Monroe about this book she had read but thought any information in it would be useful.

They walked into the store and a man with an apron came out from around the counter.

"Edmundson," he said as he shook his hand. "It's good to see you."

"Jacob Walker I'd like you to meet my wife," Monroe said. "This is Sara."

"It's a pleasure to meet you ma'am," he said as he shook her hand.

"It's nice to meet you, Mr. Walker," Sara said.

"You can call me Jacob. What can I do for you folks?" Jacob asked.

"I wanted to introduce Sara to some people in town," Monroe said. "This town gets bigger every time I come here."

"Families are moving in like crazy," Jacob said. "They just built a school and we have a doctor now. I can't keep up and Suzy is fit to be tied." About that time a woman appeared from the back room. Sara knew that she was Indian, but she wasn't from her tribe.

"Sara, this is my wife, Suzy," Jacob said.

"Hello, Sara," Suzy said with a smile. "What tribe are you?"

"Nez Perce," Sara said. "And you?"

"Snoqualmie," she smiled. "If you need anything, you come see me. I know everyone in town." She turned to Monroe and said, "We have a doctor now. Did Jacob tell you?"

"Yes, he did," Monroe said. "I think we'll pay him a visit this morning to introduce ourselves. Sara is going to have a baby."

With that announcement Jacob and Suzy engulfed Sara in hugs. She liked these people. She liked Suzy and felt she was a kindred spirit. Monroe gave Jacob the list of supplies he needed and they went to visit the new doctor. They walked out the door and Sara spotted the sign before Monroe. She pointed to the building across the street and started to walk over.

"Dr. E. McLaughlin," Sara read. "Why are we going here? I'm not sick."

"I know this, Sara," Monroe said. "I know nothing about women having babies, and I'd like to know that everything is as it should be. This doctor will have to deliver it, because I don't know how." Sara was thinking about having some strange man helping her deliver her baby. This was not a pleasant thought. If she were back in her lodge with her tribe, many women would be available for this. If this was the white man's way, she didn't like it but would have to get used to this custom.

"May I help you?" a woman's voice came from the back room.

"Yes, ma'am," Monroe said. "We'd like to see Dr. McLaughlin if that's possible."

"It is possible, and you just have," she said. "I'm Dr. Emily McLaughlin. What can I do for you? You both look pretty healthy."

"I, well, I," Monroe stammered.

"My husband seems to think that having a baby is an illness," Sara said. "I'm Sara Monroe, and this is my husband, Edmundson."

Monroe was even more tongue-tied. Never had Sara called him by his first name. She took charge of the situation and Monroe was proud of her. He had not expected a woman doctor, or one so attractive. Monroe had heard that more women were going into medicine. He had also heard that they were coming west because it was hard for them to work in the east. The combination of her accomplishments and her beauty left him speechless. Sara accompanied the doctor to an exam room and she removed her bonnet. Dr. McLaughlin explained what she was doing and Sara followed every instruction to the letter. They talked briefly and returned to the waiting room.

"Your wife is extremely healthy, and should have no problems with this baby," Emily said. "I calculated that you should have a child around October or the end of September."

"Thank you Dr. McLaughlin," Monroe said. "What do I owe you?"

"My name is Emily, and you owe me nothing, she's not sick," she said. "I wanted to thank you for coming in. I just got into town last week, and folks aren't breaking the door down to see a woman doctor. I'd like to see you next month, Sara."

"I thought you said she wasn't sick?" Monroe piped up.

"She's not, but I like to follow my patients that are pregnant so there are no surprises. I think Sara will do just fine," Emily said.

"Thank you, Emily," Sara said. "Would you like to join us for supper some time? Monroe can show you where we live."

"I'd like that very much, Sara," Emily smiled. "Thank you."

They left the office and Monroe was puzzled by Sara's invitation. He thought he would ask her about it later. He had a meeting with Ivan and they needed to pick up their supplies from Jacob's store yet. They walked across the street and were greeted by Suzy's beaming smile.

"What do you think of our doctor?" Suzy teased.

"I think she's wonderful," Sara piped up. "I think Monroe was surprised."

"I knew he would be," Suzy giggled. "That's why I didn't tell him."

The supplies were ready and loaded in the wagon. Monroe asked Sara to sign for them. She took the pencil and signed her name in a smooth, fluid cursive style. Monroe remembered the first time he taught her to sign her name. She had been practicing and he was so proud of her. They talked with Jacob and Suzy for a few minutes longer and headed for Ivan's camp.

"Why did you invite the doctor to supper?" he asked. "I don't mind that you did, but you surprised me."

"I think that she is trying to fit in this world, as I am," she said. "Samuel and Mary will have children, too. Mary will need to know this person, and feel comfortable with her." She paused for a few minutes and continued. "She is from the east and can help me with the customs of being a 'lady'. You can only teach me so much about this."

They reached Ivan's and lunch was ready for them. Ivan's wife was a large woman from Europe. She said Germany, but this meant nothing to Sara. Her food was hot and filling. Helga didn't cook with many spices, but it was still very tasty. After the meal, Monroe and Ivan left to talk with the mill owner. Sara and Helga talked about many things during that hour. Helga was fascinated with her Indian background. She wanted to hear stories about how Sara grew up and the way she lived.

Sara found out that Helga's father was killed during a Sioux raid some 20 years ago. She held no grudge against them, though. Sara asked her why.

"They were protecting their land," she said. "We were trespassers. I would kill to protect my house, land, and family if I had one. I would certainly protect my husband at any cost." She paused, "they were protecting their way of life, their culture. I understand that they're losing that now, and it's a shame. I've never seen a prouder people."

"Pride doesn't go very far," Sara responded and she thought about Chief Joseph.

They continued to talk and soon they heard the men outside. Sara stood and extended her hand to Helga.

"I'm very happy to know you, Helga," Sara said.

"Stop in anytime you come to town," she said with a smile. "We will probably see much more of each other if our husband's go into business."

"That's exactly what we've done," Ivan said from the doorway. "We got a good contract for the next two years."

"Why is the contract only for two years?" Sara asked.

"I have a feeling that we may want to re-negotiate by then," Monroe said. "I think that there will be more of a demand than there is now. That's what I'm banking on, anyway. I've followed the lumber prices for the last 10 years and it's never gone down. We're taking a chance on the mill owner, and he's counting on us to deliver as we have promised."

"I think we can meet the contract with the men I have," Ivan said. "We may want to add on more help next year. I'll see how it goes. I will not work my men 7 days a week. They need that 2-day break to rest, or spend with their families. I'll tell them that we have a two year contract, and many will move their families here."

"When do we start work?" Helga asked.

"We make our first delivery on May 1st," Monroe said. "This gives us a couple of months to get organized. The mill will be ready for the added volume by then."

Sara and Monroe said their good-bye, but not before Helga hugged Sara. Ivan looked strangely at his wife and then smiled. The trip back to the house was quiet and peaceful. Monroe took a different road and showed Sara the great falls. She could hear the sound long before they could see it. It was unlike anything Sara had ever seen. There was a mystical feel about the place. Monroe told Sara that this was a holy place to the Snoqualmie tribe. Suzy could tell her more about it than anyone else he knew.

"I will ask her about this place," she said. "I believe the Great Spirit must live here. You must not cut trees here, Monroe. Promise me this."

"I promise, Sara. I will cut no trees here," he said.

He had no desire to desecrate this place. He wanted it kept like this forever. He had bought this area and had planned to keep this area as it was. He wanted no one to destroy it. This was the first parcel he purchased and he bought it for that very reason. He knew that this was a sacred place, and the "owner" had no right to sell it, let alone own it. He had planned to keep it as pristine as possible and give it back to the Snoqualmie tribe.

They moved on and headed toward the house. The weather was warm and the sun was shining. There was no more beautiful place on Earth. Monroe loved his life, loved his wife, and never wanted for anything else.

Over the course of the next month, Samuel and Charlie worked on the house. The four men from Ivan's camp had finished the exterior and installed the windows. Charlie and Samuel had put down the finished floors and when Monroe went into the house, he was amazed.

"Have a look around," Samuel said with a smile.

Monroe looked in the rooms. There was a great room with a fireplace and off to the left was what Monroe decided was the kitchen. In each of the 3 bedrooms was a built in closet and a fireplace for warmth. He had seen this only in expensive houses. Monroe walked through and was proud of the craftsmanship and the layout. Off of the kitchen was a dry good storage area. Outside of the door from the other side of the kitchen was a room that was covered for wood storage.

"What do you think?" Samuel asked. He was interested in Monroe's opinion.

"Where did you get all of these ideas?" Monroe asked.

"Some were mine, and some I had read about," Samuel said. "This room is the one I wanted you to see." He led Monroe to a small room between the bedrooms. "This is the washroom. From the main pump, in the kitchen, we can fill the reservoir above us," he said as he pointed up. "This holds 20 gallons of water. We can then open a faucet and water will run in this wash basin, which has a drain that flows outside."

"Who helped you design this?" Monroe asked.

"Gus helped me," Samuel said. "He was trained as an engineer many years ago. He said running water is a thing that will be in every house, very soon. I don't understand why he's working as a logger."

"Me neither," Monroe agreed. "I guess that's his business. I'm very impressed, Samuel. What does Mary think?"

"She wants to move in now," he smiled. "But we should be done by next week. I have to make a run to Jacob's and get my stove and some other things tomorrow. I want to take Mary with me. She's going to need to know these people. Can Sara go with us? It might make things easier for Mary."

"You can ask her," Monroe said. "She needs to see the doctor sometime soon."

Samuel's house was almost finished and Charlie was ready to move back into his own cabin. He had enjoyed his time in the main house and he and Sara had gotten close during the last few months. Monroe and Charlie had taught Sara the finances and she wanted to make sure that everything was current. Sara didn't like putting things on credit. Monroe had made sure that she had access to his account that was now their account. He had moved his account to the bank in Snoqualmie so things were easier with the business.

That evening at supper Samuel asked Sara to accompany them to town the following day. Her eyes lit up and she quickly accepted. She was anxious to see Helga, and Suzy. She had many things to ask Suzy about the great falls and the area surrounding it. She also looked forward to seeing Emily. She had a soft gentleness about her. Emily reminded Sara of her mother. Sara knew her mother had been dead for some months and she was sad to think that she would never see her grandchild. It was comforting to know that she was watching down on her.

Samuel, Mary, and Sara arrived in Snoqualmie by 9am. They had stopped by Jacob's camp but Helga was not there. They pulled up in front of Walker's General Store as Helga was walking out.

"Sara," she smiled. "It's good to see you again."

"Hello, Helga," Sara greeted warmly. Samuel had helped Mary and Sara from the wagon. "Helga, I would like you to meet Mary. This is Samuel's wife, and my sister."

"Hello," she said as she almost shook Mary's hand off. "I'm glad to meet you. I have to go home, but can you stop by on your way out of town?"

Sara nodded and they went into the store. Sara introduced Mary to Suzy and Jacob. They were both very happy to meet Samuel's wife. They held Samuel and Charlie in very high regard. They knew

Samuel had married but had no idea who she was. The fact that she was Sara's sister and Samuel seemed very happy was enough. Sara left Mary in the store and walked across the street to see Emily. As she opened the door, the room looked different than when she had first seen it. Emily had been busy and it showed.

"Sara," Emily smiled. "It's good to see you, again. How have you been feeling? Has the morning sickness gone away?"

"I feel very good, Emily," Sara said. "Yes, it has gone. Now I eat and just want to eat more. Monroe wants to know what I'm feeding inside of me."

Emily led Sara to an exam room and put her on the table. She lifted Sara's dress and pressed on her abdomen. Sara was already starting to show ever so slightly. This was a little unusual given her height that was about 5' 8". Emily felt the height of the uterus and it was larger than she expected to see. Emily was careful not to alarm Sara with anything. This may be normal for Sara and she would know more next month when she saw her.

Sara lay on the table and enjoyed the touch of this woman. She missed Mary's touch, since her marriage. It wasn't the same with Emily, though. She didn't know Emily very well, but she did enjoy the feminine hands on her. Emily did appear to be taking longer than she did with her last exam, but Sara didn't mind.

"Everything looks fine, Sara," Emily said as she helped Sara sit up. "I still need to get out to your house. Do you think you can draw me a map?"

"Yes," Sara responded with a smile. "Will you be coming by wagon, or on horseback?"

"I'll probably rent a buggy at the Livery Stable," Emily said. "I've not bought a horse yet, although I'll need to soon."

"Why don't I have Monroe pick you up on Saturday?" Sara said.

"Okay," Emily said. "About 5pm?"

"I'll tell him that you expect him at 5pm," Sara said. "This way you don't have to rent a buggy. How's your business? Have you had any of the men come to see you?"

"Very few, but most of the women in town have stopped in," she said. "I'd like to put this place on, somewhat, of a paying basis. I know that will take time, but that's what I have is time."

"Can you walk over to Walker's with me? There's someone I'd like for you to meet," Sara said.

Emily closed the door to her office and put out a sign that said "Back in 15 minutes" not that anyone would notice she joked. Mary and Samuel were coming out of the store and saw Sara. She introduced Emily to them and they talked with her for a few more minutes. Emily said good-bye and turned to wave at Sara before she went into her office.

Sara wanted to talk with Suzy about the falls but knew that Samuel was anxious to get home. They did stop by to see Helga for a few minutes. She had a fresh pot of coffee waiting and Samuel went to find Ivan. He would start marking trees next week and wanted to show Ivan where they could start logging.

"I'm so glad to see you again, Sara," she smiled. "I'm very glad to meet you, Mary. I never really get to see another woman unless I go to Walker's and talk with Suzy. I spend too much time with loggers!"

They talked as they drank their coffee. Mary said very little. She was surprised at her reaction to these people she had met. Sara was learning her way around the white man's world. She knew how to talk to these people and wondered how she learned this. Mary liked Helga, for she was as wide as she was tall and when she laughed, she laughed all over. Her laughter was as contagious as the white man's cold and Mary liked the sound of that laughter with her happy nature. Sara saw them bond and was happy for this. She knew Mary would have to have other female contacts beside her.

Mary was sad when she saw Samuel standing in the doorway with Ivan.

"Ladies," Samuel smiled. "We best get on our way."

"Promise you'll come back soon," Helga pleaded. "Maybe I'll come and see you soon."

"Yes," Mary responded. "I would like that."

They made their way to the wagon and Samuel helped them in. The ride home seemed long to Sara. She would go to town more often, and she would ride her ponies. Samuel said he and Ivan would start marking trees just as soon as he and Mary moved into their house. This would happen in the next few days and Mary couldn't wait. This was her house. Samuel built it for her, and their sons and daughters. Mary wanted to give Samuel children. She wanted a family like she had when she was a child before her parents died.

Samuel took the road that led to the great falls. He wanted to show Mary this special site. Samuel remembers playing and fishing at the base of the falls when he was younger. Sara heard the familiar roar and Mary's eyes grew wide as they rounded the bend and the falls came into view. Mary had the same feeling that Sara had. This was a special place.

"Beautiful isn't it?" Samuel said to Mary. She nodded in

agreement as Sara stood to stretch her back. They could feel the mist hitting their face. They sat and took in the splendor. Samuel turned the team and headed for home. "I used to fish down at the bottom when I was younger. Some of the largest salmon I've ever seen are there."

They got to the house and Samuel went on to his house to unload and install his stove. Mary checked on her seedlings and they were breaking the soil. She had planted these less than a month ago and was pleased at the progress.

"Look, Sara," Mary said. "Our seedlings will be ready to plant next spring in the area that has been logged." She paused and looked over her project. "Sara? How do you feel about this plan that Monroe has?"

"I think it's good," Sara answered somewhat puzzled. "Why, Mary? Are you worried?"

"No," she answered. "That's the funny thing. I know that this is right. Just as I know that marrying Samuel was right. I would have never been here if it hadn't been for you. If I had stayed with our tribe, I would be on a reservation now." She stood up and looked Sara in the eyes. "Thank you, Sara. I love you, my sister." She gathered Sara in her arms and then kissed her gently on the cheek.

Sara watched Mary walk to her cabin. She was pleased and relieved by her happiness. She had hoped that Mary didn't wed Samuel without loving him and now she knew that this was not the case. She loved Monroe and they would all grow old together in this mystical, magical place.

As she turned to go to the main house, a familiar figure stood just inside of the tree line. Her gaze met that of the large hairy creature. For a moment their eyes locked before he slowly turned and disappeared into the dense forest. Sara knew that all was right with the world with the appearance of her large friend. Monroe would never believe that she saw this, and she decided to not tell him. She hoped that one day they would let Monroe see them and be able to explain to him what a privilege it was. She walked into her house, turned to gaze at the forest, and closed the door.

Chapter 5

Samuel was true to his word and they were moving their things in on Thursday. Mary was giving Sara a tour of her home as Samuel and Charlie were setting up the brass beds. Sara liked the house on one level. The rooms were large and open and Mary beamed as she showed Mary her stove and her dry storage area.

"This is wonderful, Mary," Sara said. "You and Samuel will raise sons and daughters within these walls."

"We have our own lodges, Sara," Mary whispered. "We have loving mates to share our lodges with. The Great Spirit has blessed us, Sara."

"I would like to propose that we have a house warming," Monroe said from the doorway.

"What's a house warming?" Samuel asked.

"It's something we used to do in England. We invite people here and share a large meal. Everyone brings something to eat, and sometimes they bring a gift for your new house," Monroe explained. "I could ride into town and let the Walkers, Ivan and Helga, and others at the logging camp know. How does Sunday sound?"

"I will ride with you, Monroe," Sara said.

"That sounds like fun," Samuel smiled. "What do you think, Mary?"

Mary nodded her approval. Sara and Monroe went to saddle their horses for a ride to town. Sara had not ridden for a week. She liked to keep her horses well exercised, but had been too busy this last week. Monroe had been doing a good job with this, and they would get plenty of exercise in the next few months. Samuel asked if he could use them when he went to mark trees.

"We can take the buggy if you like," Monroe said.

"No," Sara said. "I feel like riding today. These ponies are getting fat and out of shape, just like me." She looked at Monroe and touched her growing belly.

"I think you're beautiful, Sara Two Trees," Monroe said.

They mounted the matched appaloosas and headed down toward town. Sara had not taken her ponies into town, but Monroe had done so many times. The noise didn't seem to bother them and they did well on the road to town. Sara felt eyes on her and reined her horse to a stop.

"What's wrong?" Monroe said.

"Very slowly, look to your right," she smiled. As he did so he saw the large hairy creature. Monroe jumped slightly and with that the creature was gone.

"Was that what I think it was?" Monroe whispered.

"Yes," Sara smiled. "I have seen them in this same area, just around the great falls, each time I have traveled to town. This is why we can not disturb the land or trees around the falls."

"My heart is pounding, Sara, yet you seem unafraid," Monroe said.

"You should feel honored," Sara said. "They allowed you to see them. You have been accepted. This is why we can't ruin the land around the falls."

"You have my promise," Monroe said. He would never travel this road again without looking for these creatures. How magnificent it looked. He must have stood 8 feet tall, yet he moved without a sound. Monroe kept thinking 'he' but it may have been a 'she' for all he knew. How could Sara remain so calm? He realized that she had more encounters than he could probably imagine. His eyes scanned the trees for anything.

"You won't see another one," Sara chuckled. "I've never seen more than one at a time. It's as though they have sentries posted. You need to relax and enjoy the ride."

They both started to laugh and continued to talk on their way to town. Their first stop was Ivan and Helga's. Both were excited at the prospect of a party. They would tell the camp and Ivan wanted to come up early so he could roast a pig. He would need to start it early in the morning and would bring all the supplies necessary. He also wanted to invite the new mill owner so they could get to know him better. Their next stop was Walker's store. Jacob and Suzy said they hadn't been to a party since they were married some 10 years ago.

Sara saw Emily coming from her office. Sara stepped from her pony and told Emily about the party on Sunday.

"I would still like for you to share supper with us on Saturday," Sara said. "You can stay at the house Saturday night and join us for the party on Sunday."

"That's a deal! I need to get out of this town for a little while," Emily smiled. "Those are beautiful animals you're riding," she said as she stroked the neck of Sara's horse.

"I've had them since they were born," Sara said. "Monroe will pick you up on Saturday."

Emily went into the store with Suzy trailing behind her. Sara watched her for a moment and turned her pony around so they could head for home. Monroe talked with Jacob for a few minutes more and they started back up the hill to their house.

Monroe arrived with Emily at 5:30 and Sara had a wonderful meal prepared. Monroe showed Emily the guest room and placed her bag on the bed. Charlie, Samuel, and Mary joined them. Mary seemed very much at ease with Emily. Charlie and Samuel were mannerly and enjoyed her stories of life in Boston. Emily was the youngest of 4 girls and followed in her father's career choice. He had been a well-respected physician for many years and was pleased at his daughter's decision.

Emily's father had wanted her to join him and take over his practice after he retired. This was not something she wanted. She found her father's colleagues were patronizing and tolerated her because of her father. She wanted to practice where people needed her and she could earn respect in her own way. She wanted for people to see her because of her ability, and not because they knew her father.

"This must have been difficult for you," Monroe said. "To leave your family and come out here."

"It was difficult, but also exciting," Emily said. "This is such beautiful country, and it's becoming more populated on a daily basis."

"Excuse me for asking, Ma'am," Charlie said timidly. "Where are you living?"

"There's living space above the office," Emily said. "I've leased the entire building, but the upstairs could use some work. It's not very glamorous, but it's adequate."

"I'd be happy to do some work for you, if you needed," Charlie offered. "To make it feel more like home, that is."

"I'd like that, Charlie," Emily smiled. "That's kind of you to offer." She drank from her coffee cup and looked at Monroe. "This is a beautiful house you have Monroe. Did you build this yourself?"

"I have some ability, but it was Samuel and Charlie that put this place together," he smiled.

"I've not seen better craftsmanship in the finest homes in Boston," she said as she looked around the room.

They finished their meal and retired to the living room. Sara felt tired tonight. She had been feeling that way for the last few days. Mary and Samuel said they would clear the table so Sara could talk with Emily. Monroe excused himself and went to his office to finish up the last of the paperwork for the mill contracts. Sara sat down in the winged back chair and watched the fire. Emily joined her in the other chair.

"You have a beautiful home, Sara," Emily said. "Thank you for inviting me." Emily noticed as Sara watched the fire. "Sara? Are you all right?"

"Just a little tired," Sara said. "We've had a busy week."

"Tell me what you have been doing since I saw you on Tuesday," Emily asked. She was trying to figure out if this tiredness was warranted. Sara was only 4 months along, and she shouldn't be experiencing this just yet. Emily needed to put her concerns in check. She listened as Sara told her about finishing up Samuel's house, getting them moved in, getting the contracts for Monroe's new business and her involvement in the financial portions.

"You have been busy," Emily admitted. Sara left her chair and retrieved a book from a small desk.

"Emily," Sara asked. "Can you teach me how to be a true lady? I've read everything in this book, but I feel I'm missing something."

Emily took the book, flipped through it, and she began to smile and looked at Sara as she sat down. "This book is on proper manners in English society. Things are done differently in the United States. I'd be happy to tell you what I know, but the fact is, what's important is who you are inside. You are an honest and direct person. You handle yourself well with strangers and, from what I've seen, in social situations." She paused for a minute to let Sara think about this. "Just be yourself, Sara. Being a lady never got me very far in Boston and I found it was more done for the men than for the women."

"I don't want to embarrass Edmundson," she admitted.

"I don't think you could ever do that, Sara," Emily consoled. "He loves you so very much, and wants you to be happy. Don't try to make yourself into someone else."

Sara seemed relieved. She and Emily talked for the next few hours before Monroe came back onto the room. The mantle clock was chiming and it was 9pm. Emily hadn't heard the Westminster chime since she'd left Boston. This was a comforting sound, for it reminded her of her father's study. He would sit with her for hours and tell her stories of his day and the cases he had seen. He had a way of making it sound so exciting and satisfying, which is why Emily took the direction she did with her life.

"How are you ladies doing?" Monroe smiled. He walked over to put more wood on the fire.

"Good, but I think I'll go to bed," Sara said. "I'm very tired."

"Good night, Sara," Monroe said as he escorted her to the stairway. He kissed her gently on the cheek and said, "I'll be up in a bit. I want to read for a while."

Sara nodded a response and Emily watched as she slowly went up the stairs. She was getting more concerned about her fatigue, and decided to ask Monroe about this.

"May I ask you something, Edmundson?" Emily said. He nodded a response and sat down in Sara's chair. "Sara seems very tired. How long has this been going on?"

"I've noticed it just the last few days. Sara never complains about anything," Monroe said. "I'm sure that's her Nez Perce background. She's quite stoic. Why do you ask? Is there something wrong?" He had a slight edge to his voice.

"I think everything is fine, Edmundson," Emily assured. "Because Sara doesn't complain, you will need to watch for anything unusual. Let me know if this tiredness continues. This is normal later in pregnancy, but not so early on. Sara said that she had a busy week, so I'm going to say that this is why. If it continues, I may want to modify her diet."

"I understand," Monroe said. "I am so thankful that you are here. I want Sara to have the best care available. I don't know what I'd do if I lost her."

"I'll make sure that she's taken care of," Emily said. "I'll make sure that you have a healthy child and wife." Emily stood up and said, "I'm going to turn in myself. I have a party to go to tomorrow. Thank you, again, for your hospitality."

"You're very welcome, Emily," Monroe said. He watched her walk up the stairs and knew that Emily would be true to her word. He would have to keep an eye on Sara. He had never heard a word of complaint from her and this could prove to be a problem if there were problems with this pregnancy. He opened his book but he wasn't reading the words on the pages. He was thinking of Sara and their unborn child.

Emily opened the door to her room and lit the lamp. This room was inviting and the brass bed looked so comfortable. She was tired and wanted to get some sleep. As she undressed, she thought about how fortunate she was to have met Edmundson and Sara. She was feeling so alone until she had met them. They seemed to be important people, and they were kind. They were so different from the society in Boston. These people were cruel and dishonest and the more respected they were, the more cruel and dishonest they were. Emily drifted off to sleep with thoughts of Boston, her train trip across the country, and her new found friends. Her life was good, and she wondered what new things were still ahead.

***

Beth thought about her life as Zack continued to talk. Sara, Mary, and even Emily knew where they came from and their family history. Beth never knew her father and her mother died when she was 6 years old. She remembered that day as if it were yesterday. Her mother had never talked about her father's side of the family. She didn't know how much she knew.

Beth's mother, Rebecca, and her father, Russell met while her father was in the Air Force. He was based in California and she was working as a civilian typist for a commander on the base. It was love at first sight, according to her mother. They were married in a quiet ceremony just a few months later. Her mother said she that she wasn't even sure if Russell had told his mother of his marriage and she always wanted to meet her.

After only six months of marriage, Russell was shipped to Viet Nam. Rebecca wasn't aware that she was pregnant until after he left. She and Russell wrote each other every day. In one of the last letters that Rebecca received, Russell told her he had been informed of his mother's death in December of 1961. He had not seen her in a year and was upset that he hadn't taken the time to see her before he left the country. He couldn't get leave to go to the funeral.

It was Valentine's Day of 1962 when Rebecca received the telegram of Russell's death. His plane was shot down and they had recovered what was left of his body. It would be shipped back to California. Rebecca would have him buried in a local cemetery and would stay with her parents until her child was born.

Elizabeth Maria Monroe was born in September of that same year. Rebecca continued to work on the base and planned to raise her child alone. She found a small apartment just off base and enjoyed her evenings with Beth. Rebecca's mother kept Beth while she worked and life was good.

Beth remembered her time with her mother. It was a vague and distant memory but it gave her a warm feeling. She did remember her mother becoming ill and then she was gone. Beth went to live with her Grandmother, Maria after her mother's death. She didn't understand why she couldn't see her Mother anymore. She would continue to ask her Grandmother why she went to heaven. She was never told about her cancer or the reason for her death.

She had a good life until her Grandmother died of a heart attack in 1970. There were no other relatives to take Elizabeth. She was thrown into the foster care system of California. She was placed with an older couple that had no children in the same area. She didn't have to change schools but she didn't feel at home either. Beth didn't realize it, but she had been lucky to be placed with such wonderful people as Steve and Karen Klump. They treated Beth kindly and wanted to adopt her. They did just that at the first opportunity, but with Beth's permission. They wanted, as did Beth, to keep her name of Monroe. Beth grew fond of these people and after the first year, she considered this house to be home. These people also knew her Grandmother and mother and this was a comfort to Beth. She could talk to Karen about her mother. She and Steve had met her father once but didn't know any background on him.

Beth's teenage years passed without too many problems. She didn't like the wild kids at her school and she didn't get into the drugs. Her focus was on her education and she wanted to go to college. She wanted to be a forest ranger. Something was drawing her to the Pacific Northwest and she didn't know what or why.

Her adopted mother told her that her father and his family were from Seattle, or that general area. Beth gleaned, as much information as she could from Karen, but not too much was known. She wanted to find out about her father. She wanted to know about her family, but the time to go to college came too quickly. Beth was accepted at UCLA and was ready to start her fall quarter. Her search would be put on hold for a few years.

This did not stop Beth from reading everything she could about the history of the Puget Sound area. She did come across the name Monroe, but assumed it was a common name and never thought it might be a relative. She found the area fascinating and couldn't find enough information about it. She started a journal of what she felt was pertinent information and would take down the book, author, and note the page number. She would one day sort everything out but she wanted to finish college first.

***

Emily awoke to noises from the kitchen. She used the washbasin, dressed, and went downstairs to find Sara baking bread for today's party. She looked well rested and had a glow about her.

"How do you feel this morning, Sara?" Emily asked.

"I feel wonderful," she smiled. "I have coffee if you like, or I have some tea."

"Tea sounds good," Emily responded. "Everyone drinks gallons of coffee around here. I miss a good cup of tea." Emily took the hot water from the stove as Sara found the tea can. "Is there something I can help you with?"

"I've got everything under control here," Sara said. "I will join you for a cup of tea, though. I have something to show you when we're finished."

They finished their tea with some small talk about the upcoming party and Sara stood up and motioned to Emily to follow. They walked across the yard to the barn. As Sara opened the door, Emily saw her beautiful Appaloosa ponies in the stalls. She walked to the end stall and the mare turned and nuzzled Sara's shoulder.

"This one is for you," Sara said as she stroked her mane.

"What?" Emily asked. "I can't pay you for her right now."

"You don't pay for gifts," Sara said. "You need a way to get around to your patients and this animal is gentle. I've trained her myself."

"I can't accept this, Sara," Emily said. "This is far too fine an animal."

"I'll not argue this with you, Emily," Sara said directly. "This is my welcome to town gift. I would be greatly insulted if you refused. There is a saddle and bridle that she's used to that goes with her. I'll hear no more about it."

Emily turned to Sara and said a quiet thank you. Monroe had witnessed the exchange in the barn and Sara's kindness warmed his heart. Emily was stroking the animal's neck as he turned and left the doorway. He found Ivan and Gus putting a pig on a spit. They already had a nice bed of coals going and it wouldn't take long to cook the pig.

By ten people had started to arrive. Most of the merchants from town had come with various gifts for the new house, and food to share with everyone. Monroe watched Sara from the corner of his eye. He was concerned about how she would handle this large social situation. Sara saw this as an opportunity to play hostess and to introduce Emily to the people who had not had a chance to meet her.

Sara was the perfect hostess. She showed dignity and grace and directed the activity for the food setup. Samuel and Charlie set up long tables outside of the main house and had moved in some logs so people could sit and eat. Monroe had brought his Victrola and cylinders outside so everyone could hear the music.

By 2pm Ivan announced that the pig was done and everyone could eat. The tables were lined with potatoes, breads, beans, and some things that Sara didn't recognize. Since her morning sickness had subsided, she found she liked to try new foods. Along with the pork, people had prepared chicken and beef. The only other time that Sara could remember seeing so much food was after the buffalo hunt from many years ago.

She spied Mary across the table and gave her a smile. Mary was not as comfortable in this large social event and Samuel was never far from her side. She turned to join him and Sara saw Monroe through the crowd. Their eyes met and a warm feeling came over Sara. How different her life was less than a year ago. She was in her own lodge, but it was nothing like the house she and Monroe shared now. Her clothes, friends, and daily life had changed. She now spent her days reading, and preparing for the birth of her child. She had gained many new friends. These were people she trusted and admired.

From the corner of her eye she saw Emily. How interesting her life must have been back in Boston. Sara was envious of the things she must have seen when crossing this country. Her years in college while studying to be a doctor must have been hard. The books she read, and the long training must have seemed endless, yet she was doing what she had dreamed of doing.

The party went well and most people had started for home by 5pm. Samuel and Mary had received many wonderful gifts for their new home. This included cloth and lace for curtains, dry goods, linens, and canned goods from many of the wives. Samuel surprised Mary with a table and chairs that he and his father had made. Most of the people made their way to the new house to look at it. Mary was pleased to give them a tour of her new home.

Emily found Sara and said it was time that she returned to town. She found her bag and Monroe brought the saddled horse to her.

"What a beautiful animal," Emily said again. "Suzy said I could keep her in the corral behind their store."

"She should be a good pony for you," Sara said. "She has a gentle spirit and is sure footed."

"I'll see you in a couple of weeks for your check-up," Emily said as she mounted the horse. "If you have any problems, you come to see me." She turned and looked at Monroe, "thank you for everything. I'd better get going before it gets dark." She turned the horse and turned to wave as she rode away.

"That was a wonderful thing that you did, Sara," Monroe said as he put his arm around her. "This was your favorite pony. Why did you give her to Emily?"

"She needed a good animal, and I greatly admire her," Sara said.

"I wanted her to feel welcomed here and I feel we will need to see her often when we start the logging project."

"Are you expecting a lot of accidents Sara?" Monroe asked in a joking manner.

"No, but I have an idea," Sara smiled. "I'll talk to you about it later. I want to put my feet up first. I'm very tired and it's been a long day." They walked back to the house and Monroe held Sara's hand. He wondered what she had been hatching in her head. She never discussed ideas with him until she had time to work out the details. He liked this about her and was always amazed at how her mind worked.

It had been 2 weeks since the house-warming party and the work had started for the logging camp. Charlie was going to work closely with the mill owner and make sure that things were going well there. The owner had arranged for him to have a small office right at the mill, which pleased everyone. The owner trusted Charlie and asked if he could help him with some other customers. Monroe, Charlie, and the owner came to an agreement and everyone would win.

Samuel had set out the first area to log. He marked the trees that would stay. He and Ivan set out a schedule and would closely follow the map that Monroe had made. Samuel had it sectioned off and was very specific about instructions for the tree removal. This was something that puzzled Ivan because he had always cut any tree that was available, with no thought of the wildlife or the health of the forest. Ivan had hired a crew of good men and all were willing to try something new.

Ivan had a habit of hiring men that had families and not drifters. He found the drifters weren't as stable as he liked and they had a tendency to be troublemakers because of drinking, brawling, or their frequent trips to the whorehouses. Those with families seemed to show up for work and want to provide for their family. He rarely caught them drunk in the morning or while they worked. The only drifter he had hired was a good worker. Gus had become a valuable member of Ivan's crew and could fix anything.

By April 15th they were ready to start. Ivan's men had been clearing an area to use as a logging road. Samuel wanted to start at the farthest area and work back toward the main camp. Mary's seedlings were about 2 feet tall and she seemed to have thousands of them. Sara and Charlie had set up the books. Charlie would keep daily records down at the mill and make sure that Sara got them on a weekly basis.

Monroe and Ivan had all contracts signed and Sara had the books

ready to go. Monroe felt good, and that everyone knew what needed
to be done. Ivan had hired extra help just for transporting logs to the
mill. These men would make sure the wagons were loaded securely
and take them into town. Ivan anticipated that four runs a day could
be made if the pulley system that Gus had designed worked as he
said it would. Ivan would have the crews start today but they would
not start delivering until May 1st. Ivan was concerned that his crews
were not able to keep up with the transport crew. This way they
could stockpile some logs and he could then hire more men if this
was the case.

It had been raining for the last month, but the sun was shining
brightly today. Monroe took this as a sign and set out on horseback
to the first site. Sara and Mary headed out to the logging sight
around ten just to survey the area. The ponies needed to be exercised
anyway. What they saw upon their arrival was unlike anything they
had ever seen. There were men in the top of a tall fir getting ready to
drop the top section.

"Timber!" a voice cried out. All on the ground looked up and saw
the top slowly tilt to one side and then with a loud snap topple over
and fall to the ground. What was left standing was 80 feet tall. All
of the branches had been removed and the rest of the log would be
brought down a section at a time. Sara looked to the right and saw
where some logs had already been placed. There were men working
their way up three other trees. On the ground a crew was stripping
the large branches and putting those into another pile.

"Amazing isn't it?" Monroe said as he walked up to Sara. "The
branches will be saved for firewood. Ivan said that we could sell that
on the side if we wanted. The way Ivan logs takes more time, but
there's not as much waste, and the land is left cleaner."

"There's very little waste," Sara smiled. "I'm happy to see that.
Ivan is a good man."

They walked back to the ponies and Monroe watched as Sara and
Mary rode away. He heard another "Timber" from the treetops and
watched as another top crashed to the ground. He was still surprised
that this was really happening. He and Ivan had tried to foresee any
problem that might arise and resolve it. Not everything could be
predicted, as he would soon discover.

Chapter 6

Two weeks had passed and it was time to start delivering to the mill. The transport crew had been busy cutting up the branches for firewood. They had around three full cords already and many more branches to cut. Ivan had decided to not hire more loggers and to keep the transport crew busy doing this if they had slow time. This would not come for a while with the speed at which his crews were working.

Charlie had estimated the board feet from each load, and after they were processed found his estimates to be right on the money. The mill owner was pleased that Ivan and Monroe were delivering more logs than agreed upon. The call for milled lumber had increased and the price was going up. There were so many areas that were building and the demand was great. Charlie was helping the mill owner with many other things, but his first order of business was to make sure that Monroe and Ivan were paid according to their contract. The mill owner was an honest and fair man so Charlie's job was easy.

One Friday Monroe arrived at the mill after the last load for the week was delivered. The mill owner calculated the amount and wrote a check out for Monroe. He was surprised at the amount. He walked over to the bank and deposited the check in the business account. Sara already had the list of Ivan's employees and was ready to make ready their weekly wages. Ivan had handled this in the past and asked Sara if she could handle this. Much to Monroe's surprise she agreed. She would keep Ivan informed about all of the finances and he would control and have access to all the books.

Sara had come into town with Monroe and needed to stop by to see Emily. She stopped at Walker's to order supplies and Suzy met her with a smile.

"How are you, Sara?" Suzy said as she hugged her. "You look wonderful."

"I feel good," Sara smiled. "I've missed seeing you. We've been busy with the business and I haven't been able to get into town very often."

"Jacob said your business is booming," Suzy said. "There's so much building going on."

"Too much building I think," Sara smiled. "Here's a list of things I need. I need to see Emily and Monroe should be back with the wagon soon. Thanks, Suzy. I'll be back shortly."

Sara walked into Emily's office. Emily looked up from her desk and smiled.

"How nice to see you, Sara," she smiled. "You are looking radiant."

"It looks as though Charlie has been here," Sara said as she looked around the office. She could see newly installed bookcases, furniture, and some new doors. "When has he had time to come here?"

"Sometimes it's early in the morning, and sometimes over the weekends," Emily responded. "He's a master with a hammer and saw. Enough about the office, let's take a look at you." She escorted Sara to the exam room. She was surprised at how much larger she had gotten. Sara was not a small woman and Emily had a suspicion as to why Sara was getting so large so quickly.

"Sara?" Emily asked in a calm voice. "Do twins run in your family?"

"My mother and her sister were born on the same day," Sara said. "Is that what you mean?"

"Yes," Emily said. "Did they look alike?"

"Many in our village could not tell them apart," Emily said. "I could, though."

"I think you may be carrying twins, Sara," Emily said.

"I would like to give Monroe two sons," Sara with a broad smile.

"I won't be sure until later in your pregnancy, so let's just keep this between us for now," Emily said. "I do want you to make sure you let me know if anything bothers you, or you don't feel well." Emily paused, "Promise me this, Sara."

"I promise, Emily," Sara said as she squeezed her hand. "There's something else I would like to talk to you about." Emily sat down next to Sara as she continued. "We have many people working in our business. We have loggers, and they have families. I know that these people only go to doctors when they are ill or hurt. I want to make sure that these people feel that they can come to you when they need to."

"Okay," Emily said in a puzzled voice.

"What I mean by this is, we as a business will pay for their visits to you," Sara said. "This is something that I have been thinking about, but you'll have to agree."

"They can come here any time they wish," she said still puzzled.

"That's the problem," Sara said. "These people rarely get out of the logging camp two miles down the road. Is it possible to go there once a week? Helga said she has a small cabin behind their house that you could use as an office. This might encourage them to see you more. I wanted to see if this was possible before I talked with Monroe."

"Yes, it's very possible," Emily smiled. "That's a good idea. I could spend Wednesdays out there and the rest of the week at my office in town. What made you think about this? What gave you this idea?"

"I watched so many of my people die. The Shaman could only do so much because she didn't understand the white man's diseases," Sara said. "I don't want the families of the loggers to suffer from sickness when we have someone here that can help them. These families are the backbone of this town, and if we continue to grow, there will be many more."

"This is an exciting idea," Emily smiled. "There's nothing like this back in Boston, or anywhere in the nation, that I'm aware of."

"You can submit a bill on a weekly basis," Sara smiled. "Get it to me, or send it with Charlie."

Emily and Sara talked for a while longer. Sara saw Monroe pull up to Walker's in the wagon and stood up to leave. Emily walked with her over to Walker's and Monroe met her with a smile.

"How's my wife, Doc?" Monroe asked.

"Doing nicely," she replied. "Sara tells me that business is good."

"At first look, everything is better than we had hoped," Monroe said. "Ivan is beside himself."

They chatted for a few more minutes and Monroe and Sara started back home. They stopped at Ivan's house so Sara could tell Helga about Emily using the cabin starting next week. Helga had agreed to talk to all the families in the camp and let them know that a doctor would be available for them every Wednesday. Monroe was talking with Ivan about the check he had received from the mill.

"Even after everyone is paid, we have a lot left over," Monroe said. "How did that contraption that Gus put together work?"

"It worked like he said it would," Ivan boasted. "He said that one man could load a wagon with logs, and he was right. I wonder if we need to have him put together another one. We could make twice as many transport runs."

"If we do that it won't be until we secure another contract in 2 years," Monroe said. He saw Ivan's puzzled look. "The price of lumber should be higher and I'm making arrangements to buy another 5000 acres east of what I already have. This deal is being kept pretty quiet and I want it that way. This is government land, and it's cheap."

Ivan's eyebrows went up and he smiled. He nodded his head in agreement. Monroe had not lied to him or misled him in any way. He didn't believe that he would start now. They walked onto the house to find Sara and Mary drinking coffee and laughing about something.

"You'd better tell Monroe about your plans," Helga said.

Monroe looked at Sara and she told him about Emily being at the logging camp one day a week. He thought this was a good idea. She then said that the business would pay for the visits to Emily. Monroe looked at her and almost spilled his coffee.

"Why would we do this?" Monroe asked.

"It's the right thing for us to do," Sara said. "Without our help, they wouldn't feel that they could afford to see a doctor. Healthy families are happy families. This makes for happy workers."

Monroe looked at Ivan and looked back at Sara. "That's a good idea." Monroe knew there was more to this than Sara was willing to say in front of Helga and Ivan. They said their good-bye and headed for the house. They met Charlie on the road and all rode home together. After reaching the house Mary and Samuel said that they had supper ready and they sat down to a wonderful meal.

The next couple of months saw things going smoothly. It was now July and the weather had turned very warm. Sara was growing large and her feet and ankles were swollen. Emily had suggested that she put them up whenever she could. This heat didn't help. Monroe wanted to have the loggers and their families up to the house for a 4th of July party. Sara didn't understand what the meaning of this date was. Monroe had given her a book on the history of the United States so she could learn about it. Ivan wanted to do his traditional roasted pig and all of the loggers would bring dishes to pass. Monroe didn't want any added strain put on Sara so he invited Emily to spend the day with them. She could provide Sara with some company and keep an eye on her at the same time. He had seen how her ankles had swelled and didn't know if this was normal or not.

He had elicited Suzy and Mary's help to minimize the stress on Sara. They agreed to handle many things but to not let Sara know that she was being helped. Mary had this art form down to a fine science and Sara was none the wiser. When the 4th finally arrived, there was little for Sara to do. Charlie and Samuel made sure the tables were set up, Mary had taken care of dishes and cups for coffee, and Monroe had made sure that everyone coming was bringing food. He had even secured some fireworks for the crowds' enjoyment later in the evening.

Emily had arrived early and had made a decision to stay close to Sara but not let her know. She knew Sara would be irritated if she knew that she was being watched. Sara never complained about anything. This was the problem. Emily knew that she would be having twins and to carry them the full 9 months would be difficult. Sara may surprise her, but Emily didn't see this happening.

It was a glorious day, and the weather had cooled. The hot muggy weather had given way to 72 degrees with sunny skies. Ivan was getting the pig started and in a few hours it would be cooked and ready to eat. Sara loved Ivan's roasted pork as did most of the camp. Everyone was in a festive mood because the business was going well, there was plenty of work, and the wages that Ivan and Monroe paid were better than most. The added bonus of being able to see a doctor when they needed to was paying off.

Even the loggers had seen Emily for cuts and scrapes they sustained working. Emily had become an important part of this business. She had gained a respect for these men, their families, and they had gained respect and trust in her. Even Helga, who did most of her own doctoring, had consulted Emily on a few issues.

There was much to celebrate today. Monroe surveyed the area around the house and smiled. He saw Emily and Sara sitting on the front porch, Mary and Samuel taking with Ivan and Helga, and children playing, and all seemed right with the world.

By late July the heat had returned and the temperatures reached over 90 degrees. Ivan knew how hard and how hot it got in the woods. He changed the hours that they worked. He had them in the woods by 5am. It was cooler and he could let the men go home by 2pm. The hottest part of the day was 4-6pm and the heat wore out even Monroe. The transport men could work the same hours and not have to be transporting logs in the heat of the day. It was too hard on the horses. The cutters had stockpiled a good many logs and, much to Ivan's surprise they could keep ahead of the transport men. There were piles of logs waiting to go to the mill. Ivan still wanted to hire more transport men, but Monroe was hesitant to do this. They were exceeding their contract obligations and the mill owner was urging Charlie to get more. Monroe didn't like Charlie caught in the middle, so he and Ivan would meet with the mill owner to settle this once and for all.

The land deal wasn't settled yet and the promise of more volume would come back to haunt them if they weren't careful. Monroe agreed to set up a meeting on Friday at the mill. He had tried, to no avail, to explain this to Ivan. Charlie understood Monroe's position but was not able to fully explain this to the mill owner. Monroe would do this on Friday. On Thursday he went into town and wanted to telegraph the man from the government to find out the disposition of their arrangements. To his surprise, a telegram from this same man was waiting for him. Monroe opened the telegram and read, "PAYMENT RECEIVED. ALL PAPERWORK IN PLACE AND SIGNED. THE LAND IS YOURS."

This was better than Monroe had hoped for. He could now go into this meeting with some relief. That's just what he did, without showing his hand. The mill owner wanted a new contract. With this new contract was a new price for the logs, and no minimum that they had to meet. The cutters could not have to worry about stockpiling for the months when the weather was adverse. The new contract was to take effect on August 1st.

Monroe returned home and told Sara the good news. She was happy about the prospect. She was happier that Monroe was happy. Charlie was ready on his end and Ivan was ready to hire more men for transport, and possibly another cutting crew. Monroe wanted to wait on this until the first area had been cleaned up and re-planted. Mary couldn't plant the trees alone and Samuel was uncomfortable with her doing this.

"What if I could get her some help?" Jacob walker asked Samuel.

"That would be great, but from where?" Samuel asked.

"Some of Suzy's people are looking for work. They were born here, and have always been one with the land," Jacob said. "What about hiring Indians to work with Mary?"

This was an interesting idea and Samuel couldn't wait to talk to Monroe about this. When he did, Monroe told Samuel to hire 3 good people for replanting. This would go quickly, but Monroe would keep them to help with area clean up for the crews. He talked to Ivan, and he had no objection and was happy for the help. Ivan also wanted Monroe to think about hiring a cook for the logging crews.

"Just like a cook they have on cattle drives," he explained. "The men can have a hot meal which we'll need when the weather turns cold."

"We could set up an account with Jacob for supplies," Monroe added. He looked at Jacob and smiled. "Did you ever think that this logging operation would turn into this?"

"I can't believe where we are, and where we were just a few months ago," Ivan answered. "This is making more money than I though possible, and we are trying so many new things; things that have never been done before."

"I feel the same way, Ivan," Monroe said as he shook his head. "Helga said that there's a steady stream of people to see the Doc on Wednesdays. Charlie has been doing right by the mill owner, and the mill owner is elated. The people we hired for the replanting are working out well. Mary has them starting more seedlings during their spare time, and they love it. Samuel has done a good job on selecting the trees to stay." He paused for a moment and looked at the ground. "Did you realize that we are the largest employer in the area? People are constantly asking the mill owner if we need help."

"We are going to need more help," Ivan said. "Especially with the 5000 extra acres you just bought."

"I don't want you to hire more than one more crew," Monroe said. "That's 6 men. I don't want them to log this too quickly."

Ivan looked at Monroe strangely. Monroe went on to explain about the growth cycle of the trees. They could only log every 40 years and he wanted to stretch the first cut out for a while. This would insure work for some years to come. If they logged 200 acres a year, they wouldn't be ready to start over for 40 years. Ivan didn't see this as a business anymore, but as a legacy for future generations. He looked at Monroe and finally understood and Monroe knew he now understood. Monroe wasn't looking at getting into the history books as much as he wanted everyone who worked with him or for him to respect the land. It would provide employment for many years to come if all was carried out as he had planned.

***

Beth had remembered reading something about the Zembruski/Monroe logging company when researching the history of the area. She couldn't remember too many specifics but did remember that the article said that they were pioneers in the logging industry that had been copied by such companies as Weyerhaeuser. She had no idea that this was her great-grandfather and would have to go back to the library and find this book. She had only skimmed the article the first time.

"What are you thinking, Beth?" Zack asked. She looked back at him and explained that she had read something about this in the history books.

"I have to find that book at the library, again," she responded.

"Everyone thinks that the big companies thought up forest management," Zack said. "What the masses don't know is that it was a small company with Native American visionaries."

Beth's eyes met Zack's and he felt those long dead feelings come alive. She looked so much like Anne that it was spooky. Zack remembered looking into her blue eyes that were so intense and feeling that they were the only two people on earth. He couldn't remember when he first realized that he loved her. He didn't commit that moment to memory, but he did remember the first time their lips met.

***

It was July 4th, 1928 and the weather had turned hot. Most of June had been rainy and Zack wondered if summer would ever come. He had seen Anne a few times in the weeks since her mother's funeral. Anne had a house down by the Cedar River just outside of the city of Renton. She didn't grow up in this house, but this was her primary residence. She had spent more time out in Snoqualmie since her mother had passed. She knew the house needed some repair, but was still a handsome place. Her father had built it to last and Samuel had made sure that it was structurally sound. Right after the turn of the century, Anne had encouraged her mother to convert one of the rooms to a bathroom. Sara didn't want to change anything in the house, but Anne convinced her that most people were enjoying this modern convenience.

Anne wanted to continue the tradition her father had started many years ago and have a 4th of July party. With her mother gone, some of the passion for the party was lost. Anne decided to ask Zack if he would like to attend. His excitement seemed to renew some enthusiasm in Anne. This party was a far cry from the first one that Monroe had planned. It was a social coup to be invited. An invitation was never turned down and to be invited one year and not the next meant that you have done something to piss off Sara Monroe or the local tribes.

Anne had left the particulars to a group of planners, as she had done for the last few years. When the day finally arrived, Zack put on the only suit he had and awaited the car that Anne was sending for him. The ride out to the estate seemed to take forever. The driver stopped at the huge falls so Zack could see this wonderful site.

"I had no idea this was so beautiful," Zack said to the driver.

"Miss Monroe wanted to make sure I stopped here," the driver replied.

Zack stared at this power, the mist, and listened to the roar of the water. He was awestruck at this sight. He didn't want to leave, but when the driver cleared his throat, he knew it was time to move on.

The house was just a few minutes away and his excitement about seeing Anne was building. They got back in the car and started winding through the trees. The driver stopped at a large iron gate that sat between two large stone pillars. As they passed through the gate Zack was taken back by the sight of the house, the garden, the fountains, and Anne standing on the front porch. She looked like a queen and, although Zack didn't know it, she was waiting for him.

"What a beautiful place," Zack said as he stepped from the car. He climbed the stairs and joined Anne on the porch. "You look beautiful, Anne."

"You look nice yourself, Zachary," she said with a smile and took his arm. "Let me give you the grand tour while the rest of the guests arrive." They walked into the main entry and Anne gave Zack the history of the house. He learned that Samuel's father and Anne's father had built the house before he and Sara were married. She told him the story of when they met and their journey to this place from the original Nez Perce tribal grounds in eastern Washington. As they walked through the house, Zack noticed the pictures.

He recognized one of the people as her mother. She was so beautiful and the man standing next to her must have been Anne's father. He paused and picked up the picture and looked closer. The gentle way he had his arm around her shoulder and the look on his face said so much. Zack recognized the porch to be the same one he had just walked across. Anne came to his side and brought him back to reality.

"They always looked good together," Anne said as she put the picture back on the mantle. She took him up the staircase and showed him the sleeping rooms. She stopped and entered one of the rooms. "This was my room," she said as she looked around. "I've read every book in here many times. This room was Mary's when she and my mother first came here." She took one last look around and turned to go out. Zack noticed the dolls, and handmade toys in the room. He could see Anne, as a girl, spending hours lying on the brass bed as she read her way through this library.

He turned and left this room that looked like it had remained unchanged and followed Anne into another room. This, too, was filled with books, but most of them were medical textbooks.

"This room belonged to Dr. Emily McLaughlin," Anne said. "She and mother were the best of friends, and she lived here until she died about 10 years ago." Zack looked at the picture on the wall. It was, apparently, of Emily seated on a beautiful Appaloosa. "That's her in front of her first office." They turned and left that room and

G.J. Woosley

entered what Zack believed to be the master bedroom. The blending of Indian and English cultures in this room was unlike anything that Zack had ever seen. This was a woman who broke through the social boundaries of her heritage and succeeded in the white man's world, while never forgetting her heritage.

"Wow," Zack whispered.

"Father never asked mother to forget where she came from," Anne said. "He supported her and loved her with all his heart." Zack noticed a look of longing come over Anne as she looked around the room. He then noticed the pictures. Numerous photographs of Indians in large and small groups, Indian children in front of schools, and there were some of Anne as a girl with two older boys. Zack wanted to ask who they were, but didn't want to intrude while Anne was in such deep thought.

She turned to face him and he saw a tear in her eye. "I'm sorry," she said. "There's so much history here. There are so many memories and they come flooding back when I come in here." She paused and took another look around. "I've not changed a thing since mother died. I haven't had the heart. Every time I think about cleaning things out, Mary talks me out of it."

"It's not easy to do, Anne," Zack said as he took her hand. "It was the hardest thing I ever had to do after my mother and brother died. I'd be happy to help you when you're ready."

"I don't know if I'll ever be ready," she said.

"You will be ready, some day," Zack said. "It's best to take your time."

"Thank you, Zachary," Anne smiled. "You're a kind young man." He looked deep into her eyes and he was very aware of the intense feelings he had for her. He gathered her in his arms and kissed her gently. She didn't pull away and he didn't want to stop. The tenderness of her lips and the warmth of her body excited all of his senses. Her sweet smell and taste was more than Zack had ever dreamed of. He stepped away from her after that stolen kiss and could feel himself blushing.

"I'm sorry, Anne. That was wrong," he said.

"No, Zachary," she said in a whisper. "You did it exactly right." She came to him again and pulled his head to hers. This long, slow, wet kiss was gentle at first and then more forceful and passionate. Zack held her tightly in his arms and delighted in the way her body molded to his. This kiss seemed to go on forever, but forever didn't seem to go on long enough for Zack. He wanted Anne in every way that a man could want a woman. He never wanted anyone more.

70

Some of the girls he dated when in high school never stirred him like this and that was the problem. They were girls, and Anne was cultured, mature, exotic, and more sensual than she could ever know.

He thought back to Mary Kate Murphy. She was one of the few girls he could tolerate for any length of time. She was bright and intelligent and at one time he thought he might like to marry her. They had so much in common, but he had no real feelings for her. They had planned to go to college together, but that all changed with the accident. Mary Kate never stirred anything in him, even during their stolen private meetings.

When the kiss was finished, Anne looked into Zachary's eyes. She had not had any feelings for any man. This was new territory for her. She had always been closer to women, and preferred them to men. She had spoken with her mother about this on several occasions. Her mother understood the confusion in Anne. She explained her feelings for the woman in her past. Sara would always tell Anne how these feelings never went away. After all the years she had been married to her father, the desires to be with a woman remained. It wasn't sexual, but being with the person. It was an intimacy of the soul that so many people failed to understand.

"This doesn't mean that I love your father less," Sara would say. "The Shaman said I had the gift of seeing both worlds. I have given that to you." Anne never felt that this was a bad thing, although polite society thought differently. Her thoughts came back to Zachary. He was so very young, but wise beyond his years. Why did he stir her the way he did? What did he have or do what no other man did for her? She had only felt this with other women. She looked into his blue eyes. She raised her hand and gently stroked his cheek.

"We should get back downstairs. More guests will be arriving," she said. "Let's go enjoy the party," She took his arm and they went down the back stairway.

***

Zack came back to reality and was still looking into Beth's blue eyes. He had so much he needed to tell her. Her entire family history was in his head, and he didn't think she realized it. Talking to her about her great-grandmother was easy. Zack didn't know how he would tell her about her grandmother. Those words would have to be chosen carefully. He had to make sure that she fully understood how her grandmother thought, her intentions, desires, and the weight of the legacy that Anne had inherited.

His ultimate goal was to make Beth understand and accept the importance of her heritage. She had to understand what it meant to Sara, Anne, and what it should mean to her.

Chapter 7

July was unseasonably warm and Sara was miserable. Emily came to the house daily to check on Sara. Mary had taken over many of the duties because Sara had grown too large to stay on her feet for any length of time. Between Monroe, Mary, and Samuel there was a single goal. They kept an eye on Sara while Monroe was gone, and they took over all of Sara's chores, except for the bookkeeping. Sara wouldn't allow anyone else to do this.

Helga even made visits a couple of times a week. She always brought baked goods and Monroe would accept them without question. Monroe had a real addiction to Helga's sweet breads. By the middle of August Monroe had gained 10 pounds and Sara was on total bed rest. Emily was spending each afternoon at the house. She had posted a sign on her office door letting people know where she was. She was still working at her other office at Ivan and Helga's but only in the morning.

Monroe wouldn't leave the area around the main house. He didn't want to be far from Sara if something should happen. Mary would organize the re-planting crew in the morning and spend the rest of the day at the main house. She had turned a lot of the planning and planting over to a Snoqualmie Indian woman who was about 40. She had a gift with the land and her two sons were part of the re-planting crew.

Ivan made sure the crews were busy. Samuel would go out twice a month and mark trees. He and Monroe would be very precise about where to log, and how much to log. Ivan's crews followed his instructions to the letter. None of them wanted to work for anyone else. They couldn't make the money or provide for their families this well anywhere else. Recently there had been many men that had come to Ivan for jobs. He screened them very carefully but hired very few.

He would send them to the mill and between the owner and Charlie they could find them jobs. The millwork was growing by leaps and bounds. The mill owner was getting ready to open a second site. He needed good men and many of them because he was planning to put on another shift to keep the mill running 24 hours a day. Several small logging companies had sprung up over the last couple of months. The mill owner was delighted with the work. Charlie had voiced a concern about the new logging companies not wanting to sign a contract. They wanted to be paid in cash as they brought in the logs.

The mill owner didn't see this as a problem, but Charlie's gut feeling was that they would destroy the land for the profit. He discussed this at length with Monroe and Ivan.

"We can't tell other companies how to do business," Monroe said. "We can only control what we do with our land." Monroe paused and thought for a minute. "I'm afraid that they'll incite anger in the local tribes and then there will be trouble."

"I agree," Ivan said as he shook his head. "Is there any way to stop this?"

"I don't think so," Monroe said. "We have to know what the tribes might do."

"What about the woman who works with Mary on the re-planting crew?" Charlie said.

"How could she help us?" Monroe asked.

"If she can get to her tribe, she can ask the questions," Charlie said.

"And she can let us know what the feelings of the tribe or tribes are," Ivan said.

"The town isn't going to listen to a local Indian woman," Monroe said.

"But they will listen to Sara," Ivan said. "Would she work with this woman on this?"

"Yes," Monroe answered quickly. "She doesn't want to see the land ruined any more than the local tribes. She has the advantage of my name and she is well respected. They'll listen to her."

Monroe knew that Sara could do nothing until the baby came. He couldn't wait for this time. He had always wanted children from the day he met Sara. He didn't care if it was a boy or a girl. He only wanted a healthy baby and a healthy wife. He was comforted by Emily's presence. What he didn't know was that Emily was as nervous as he was, especially with the thought of multiple births. She had been staying in the house for the last week. Monroe had given her a bedroom just down the hall from his and Sara's and she would spend time with Sara in the evening.

Monroe could hear their voices and the quiet laughter that came from the room. He was pleased that Sara felt so comfortable with Emily, and this gave her someone that could challenge her intelligence. Emily would ask Sara to explain why the Indians felt a certain way about things. Sara had a gift for clearly defining and explaining things. This was the reason why Monroe thought Sara was the one person to get involved with the local tribes.

Monroe was listening to the soft voices when Emily called to him. As Monroe walked through the doorway he could see the sweat on Sara's brow.

"I need for you to get Mary and start some water boiling," she smiled. "This baby wants to be born." Monroe stood and stared at Sara. He went over and kissed her on the forehead and turned to get Mary.

Mary went up the stairs but not before she started water boiling. Samuel came in to keep Monroe occupied. Monroe paced and Samuel knew that he needed to get his father. Within minutes he returned with Charlie, who brought in a bottle of bourbon. Monroe looked at Charlie and started to laugh.

"Have a drink," Charlie said. "This may take a while. When Samuel was born I almost wore a hole in the floor. Babies will come when they're ready. Sara is in good hands with the Doc." Monroe seemed to calm down and couldn't begin to imagine what his wife was going through.

Sara was wasting no time. Emily was surprised at how Sara was handling her contractions. There wasn't a sound or a complaint. What a difference between her and the other woman she had seen during her training. They screamed, cried, and moaned. Sara was dignified and stoic. Her contractions were close and strong. Sara was starting to push. Mary was ready with clean towels and blankets. Sara had not told anyone about the possibility of twins. Emily wasn't really sure about this either.

The baby was born about 45 minutes later. He was small and weighed about 5 pounds. Within 10 minutes the second baby was born. He was a bit larger, but not by much. Both boys had great lungs and Mary cleaned each baby with towels and then wrapped them in a blanket. Emily finished with Sara who was the perfect patient. Mary put a baby in each of Sara's arms. She looked at her sons looked up at Emily and Mary and smiled.

Mary went to get Monroe. She did not tell him the surprising news and that was Sara's only request. Monroe opened the door and saw Sara holding his sons. Emily thought he was going to fall on his face.

"Come to meet your sons, Monroe," Sara said in a tired voice. Monroe walked to the bed and sat down. He took his sons from Sara as Emily noted the time of birth for Sara's records. They were beautiful. Both had a head of dark hair and looked the same. Monroe couldn't tell them apart. He had never loved anyone like he loved Sara and now he had these two small boys. "What will you name your sons?"

"I don't know, Sara," Monroe said. "What would you like to name them?"

"That is the father's job," Sara smiled. "Indian woman don't name their children."

"In the white man's world, both parents decide," Monroe said. "I want to know what you want."

"I want our first son to be named Edmundson Joseph Monroe," Sara said. "I name him for his father and my chief. You need to name our second son."

"I would like to name him William Charles Monroe," Monroe said. "William is for my father and Charles for my mother's family name." Monroe looked at his sons and never thought he could love anyone as much as he loved their mother.

The babies started to fuss and Emily took the boys. She wanted to make sure that they had all of their fingers and toes. Mary returned with some warm water and would bathe each of them. Sara would then feed them. Her breasts had grown large in the last 24 hours and as Edmundson began feeding Sara was glad her breasts were full. Soon William was ready to eat.

Emily sat down and watched Sara. What a beautiful sight. Sara had done well; the babies were healthy even though they were about a month early. This was the first time she had seen twins being born. She was suddenly very tired and couldn't imagine how Sara was staying awake.

Monroe went downstairs to smiles from Samuel and Charlie. Mary had told them of both babies. Charlie had planned to build a second cradle for William.

"How is Sara?" Charlie asked Monroe.

"She is doing great," Monroe said. "The boys were hungry, so she's feeding them."

"You're a lucky man Edmundson. You have two beautiful sons," Charlie said as he poured everyone a drink.

"Pour me a small one will you, Charlie?" Emily said as she came down the stairs. "It's been a long day." Charlie handed a glass to Emily. She raised her glass and said, "This is to a wonderful couple and two new lives that came to us tonight." Emily drank down the bourbon in one gulp and almost choked herself. She poured herself a second drink, much larger than the first, and repeated the process. Monroe started to laugh, as did Samuel.

Emily talked with them a bit longer then said her good night and started back up the stairs. She wanted to check on Sara one more time before she retired. The stairs were a little hard to navigate between the bourbon and her fatigue. She walked down to Sara's room just as Mary was putting baby William in the cradle. Both babies were fast asleep. Sara had gotten out of bed and was getting ready to wash up. Mary turned and gathered the sheets from the bed and put on clean sheets and blankets.

"How are you feeling?" Emily asked. "You shouldn't be up so soon."

"I've been in that bed for the last month," Sara said. "After I clean up, I'm going downstairs and get some air on the front porch."

"Sara, you need to be in bed for a week," Emily cautioned.

"That's nonsense, Emily," Sara said. "It's best to get up and move around. My people have done it for years and no woman was harmed by this practice. I'll be fine, Emily." Sara had removed her gown and cleaned herself with the rest of the warm water. When she had finished and put on a clean gown she looked over at Emily. She noticed that Emily had sat down in the chair. "Are you all right?" She went over and could smell the bourbon. "You had a drink with Monroe, didn't you?"

"Two," Emily said. "I already regret it. My head is swimming and I need to go to bed." Sara walked over and helped Emily out of the chair and walked her to her room. She sat Emily on the bed, "You've just had two babies and you're helping me to bed. I feel like a fool, and I feel embarrassed."

Sara sat down on the bed next to Emily. She put her arm around her shoulder and said, "I've been in bed for a month and I didn't have any bourbon. You've been busy taking care of me for the last few months. Thank you for everything." She kissed Emily gently on the cheek. Emily looked into Sara's eyes and kissed her tenderly on the lips.

Emily looked into Sara's eyes again as Sara smiled, loosened her dress, and got her into bed. She got up and walked to the door. Sara turned to look at Emily before she left the room. She made her way downstairs to find Monroe sitting in the den.

"What are you doing up? You should be in bed," he chastised.

"I'm not going to fight with you about this," Sara said. "I already had this discussion with Emily before I put her to bed. The bourbon got to her."

"I'll bet it did. I watched her try to navigate the stairs and thought I should probably go and assist her," Monroe laughed. "Why are you down here?"

"I wanted to get out of that room, and get some air," she said.

"Would you join me on the porch?"

Monroe and Sara sat in the cool night air and talked about the babies, the business, and the future. Monroe discussed the situation with the logging companies and asked Sara to get involved with the local tribes. Sara wanted to talk to Suzy Walker first. She knew the tribal members. She would take this on with pride. Monroe helped Sara back up the stairs and put her into bed. He kissed her tenderly and told her how much he loved her. He sat next to his sons and watched them sleep.

Emily awoke with a splitting headache and to the smell of coffee. She stayed in bed until she could get her eyes to focus. She got up and used the washbasin, got dressed and went down the hall to find Sara feeding the boys. They had only been up once during the night.

"William is very impatient," Sara said as she held him to her breast. "Edmundson is willing to wait his turn." She looked at Emily squint her eyes. "How are you feeling?"

"I'm in serious need of coffee and I feel foolish," Emily said. "I don't know why, that's a lie, I do know why. I drank," she admitted a bit sheepishly. She paused and looked at the floor. "I didn't know how things would turn out with you. I always had a more experienced doctor that I could turn to in the past. Last night it was just my training I had to rely on. I was scared." Emily suddenly had the vision of her kissing Sara. She was concerned she had crossed a very crucial line and didn't want to talk about it, but she needed to. This was one of the reasons she left Boston. She never wanted to marry and had no interest in men. *The bourbon, the God damn bourbon*, she thought.

"Emily," Sara said bringing her back to the present. "What's on your mind? I know it's more than being scared. You can be honest with me." Sara knew what was eating at her. She also knew how this was viewed by polite society. Indians felt much differently about these things. The white world never really understood and she doubted they ever would. Sara put William in the cradle and picked up Edmundson. He nuzzled at her breast as Sara sat down on the bed.

Emily looked up from the floor. God she was beautiful. Sara was a wife, mother, and a patient and a good friend that Emily didn't want to lose. "I did something last night I shouldn't have, Sara." She looked at Sara and continued, "I shouldn't have kissed you."

"Why?" Sara asked. "You showed me how you felt. What's wrong with that?"

"I don't want to lose your friendship," Emily said.

"Emily," Sara said in a comforting voice. "Mary and I were 'close' long before I married Monroe. I still have desires for a woman, and Monroe knows this. They never go away. This has nothing to do with my love for Monroe." Sara paused to let this sink into Emily's brain. "If this is what you think is so wrong, I'll have to disagree with you."

"You weren't offended by my kiss?" Emily asked.

"Not at all," Sara said. "You showed me how you felt. You let down your guard, with the help of some bourbon, and you kissed me. I feel honored that you feel that way. I have always felt that way about you."

Emily just looked at Sara. There was nothing more to be said right now. Emily watched as Sara moved the baby to the other breast. They continued with some small talk but they avoided any more talk about the feelings they both held deep within.

When both babies had eaten and were fast asleep Sara and Emily went downstairs. Mary had fresh coffee and Helga had stopped by with more sweet bread. Her main reason was to see the new arrivals. Mary offered to take her upstairs and Helga followed without hesitation. She had always wanted children, but was never able to conceive. Emily drank her coffee with the hope that it would clear her head, but it wasn't just the alcohol that made it fuzzy. She had a lot to think about and sort out.

Ivan was out on the porch with Monroe. They were discussing some business and the situation with the tribes. He was glad that Sara was taking on the task as liaison. Monroe knew it would be more than just a liaison. He knew Sara would take this personally, especially when it involved saving the land.

Helga came down the stairs with Mary and couldn't stop talking about those two sleeping angels. Samuel arrived and Charlie soon joined them. He was preparing to go out and mark another section of trees.

"Not today, Samuel," Monroe smiled. "We are going to take the whole day just to spend with our families. Take Mary on a picnic, go for a horseback ride, or sit on your porch and do nothing. Today we will do no business." Samuel and Charlie looked at each other. Charlie decided to start the new cradle for the baby and Samuel found Mary so they could go home.

Helga and Ivan said good-bye and Emily thought it was time for her to head back to town. She went to her bedroom and was putting things in a bag to take back with her.

"This will always be your room," Sara said from the doorway.

"It's yours whenever you want to stay, which I hope will be often."

"Thank you, Sara," Emily said. "This feels more like home than my place in town. It's peaceful and quiet. It's getting noisy in town with all the people."

"Then why don't you move in here?" Monroe said from behind Sara. "You can easily get to your office in the morning with a short 10 minute ride." Monroe put his arm on Sara's shoulder. "I would love for Sara to have the company."

"Thank you for the offer," Emily said. "I'll think about it, if that's all right." Emily wanted to say yes immediately but thought about jumping too quickly. She didn't think Monroe was aware of what he was offering. Emily didn't know how long she could hide the feelings she had for Sara. Incurring Monroe's wrath was not what she wanted for she respected him too much and valued his friendship. He was becoming a powerful businessman and was well respected in the community.

Monroe nodded and went to see his sons. Sara stayed with Emily and walked her out to the porch as Samuel brought her horse around. He handed the reigns to Emily and turned to go home. Sara gathered Emily in her arms and hugged her long and hard. She stepped back and looked into Emily's eyes.

"Thank you for everything," she whispered. "Have a safe ride home. I love you."

"You're welcome, Sara," Emily replied. "I love you, too." They hugged one more time and Emily kissed Sara on the cheek before mounting her horse for the ride home. Neither knew that Monroe was watching from the window. He knew that Sara had feelings for Emily. He knew it was the same feelings she had for Mary when they were married. He knew he should have been jealous but he wasn't. He loved Sara understood that love to her wasn't based on sex. It was based on the bonding of souls. If this meant sharing her with a woman and satisfying those needs that he couldn't satisfy, then that's what he would do. He couldn't really be the kind of man he wanted to be to her. He, somehow, knew that Emily felt the same way about Sara. He could tell by the way they looked at each other. It was the same way that his aunt looked at her 'friend' of so many years. He only wanted them both to be happy. Emily was too important to drive away for any reason. She had become an important member of the town and its potential growth. He held his namesake as he slept.

"Life is going to be good for you," he said to the sleeping child. "You and your brother will be happy and healthy. You have parents who love you, dearly." He held him close and kissed his forehead.

Sara could hear Monroe's soft voice as she walked down the hall. She stood in the doorway for a moment and watched this man. She did love him, she loved her sons, and she loved Emily.

"Let's take them downstairs," Sara whispered. "I'll get William and take Edmundson from you. You can bring the cradle."

It was three weeks before Emily came back to the house. The boys were growing like crazy and she was delighted to see how well Sara had regained her strength and shape. During those weeks away, Emily stayed late in the office and did almost anything to stay away. She thought of Sara all the time and was trying to find a way to deal with this. She was spending more time with Suzy in order to learn more about Indian culture. Suzy was happy to tell stories of how she grew up.

It was now the middle of September and the leaves were starting to get some color. It was still warm during the day, but cooled down at night. Emily wanted to check on the boys and she was pleased with their growth.

"I'm giving them bottles along with the breast milk. They seemed to be hungry all the time," Sara told her. "Since I started doing that they seem more content."

"Are you boiling the milk before you give it to them?" Emily asked.

"Helga gave me a recipe for a formula that her sister used to use," Sara said. "Some doctor in Chicago gave it to her because she couldn't make enough milk for her child. The boys seem to like it, but I enjoy feeding them at night."

"I'm glad you're doing that," Emily said. "It's hard enough to feed one baby, let alone two."

"Monroe likes to feed them," Sara said. "He's different from Indian men. They would never do this because they felt it was woman's work." Sara paused and smiled, "I guess it is woman's work. Men don't have breasts."

Emily shot her a glance and turned red. They both laughed as Monroe came in. He smiled at them both and they laughed even harder. They went to see the babies. Emily picked up Edmundson and saw his eyes were still blue. She found this a little unusual with his dark hair. She opened his blanket and looked at the umbilicus. It had healed nicely, and he was well filled out.

William was a little irritated when his blanket was unwrapped. He let you know that he didn't appreciate certain things and this was one of them. His umbilicus had healed nicely and he was filled out. Emily looked at him and noticed his eyes were almost black. This was a striking difference.

"When did his eyes turn brown?" Emily asked.

"He was 3 days old," Sara remarked. "Edmundson's eyes will stay blue, like his father's."

"You could be right, Sara," Emily answered. "They're very healthy and very beautiful." She put William back in his cradle. "It looks like Charlie worked his magic. This cradle is as beautiful as the first."

"I thought that he made them too big at first but I see that I was wrong," Sara said. "If they keep growing like they are, the cradle will be useless in 6 months."

"Their growth rate will slow down," Emily said, "especially when they start crawling." Emily followed Sara into the kitchen and watched her make some tea. "How are you feeling, Sara?"

"I feel wonderful," she replied. "I still get tired, but that is happening less and less. Mary has been a great help to me. She treats those boys like they're hers."

"Does she want children?" Emily asked.

"She and Samuel have been trying, but with no luck," Sara said.

"She still has plenty of time," Emily said. "She's still young."

"I think that she's decided that with me having two babies, she won't need one of her own," Sara responded. "I'm grateful for the help. They are a handful."

"Does Monroe help you?" Emily asked yet quite certain she knew the answer.

"He's up every night so I can sleep," Sara said. She saw the surprised look on Emily's face. This wasn't the response she was expecting. She respected and cared for Monroe, but Emily was under the assumption that Monroe would leave the nurturing to Sara. "You should see him with these boys. He shows that side that only I know about. He's loving and affectionate with the boys."

"He's a wonderful man, Sara," Emily said. "There are few like him around, so hang on to him."

As wonderful as Emily thought Monroe was, she still had no desire to find a man of her own. It wasn't what she wanted. She knew, or thought she knew what she wanted and it was right in front of her. She remembered a younger version of herself just as she started college in Boston. Another girl in her class was from a poor family in Boston. An anonymous donor was paying for her school and she didn't even know his identity.

Claudia was bright, beautiful, and intelligent. Emily's heart was in her mouth by her mere presence. After a few weeks, she mustered the courage to talk to her and from that moment on they were inseparable. She lived at the dorm at the college and Emily would spend a great deal of time with her as they studied. Everything came easily for Claudia, while Emily had to work very hard. It was Claudia who helped Emily more than her father or any tutor she could have had.

The work paid off with them graduating in the top 5% of their class. This was quite an accomplishment at the time. Claudia left for New York to finish her residency. Emily stayed in Boston to work with her father. The day the Claudia left was one of the hardest days of Emily's life. They promised to stay in touch, but Emily knew that each would go on to other things. Just before Claudia boarded the train she held Emily closely then kissed her gently on the lips. With that final act she turned and boarded the train.

Emily stayed and watched as the train left the station. She wondered if Claudia would have stayed if she had told her of her feelings. What if? Why didn't she tell her? What was she afraid of? She drove herself crazy with these questions for the next few months. Emily had received several long letters from Claudia in the next year. They started to get shorter and less frequent by the end of the second year. The final letter she received said she had gotten married to another doctor and they had planned to open an office together in upstate New York. She didn't hear from her after that.

Emily knew she didn't want to remain in Boston. She hated the snobs and the society. She just wanted to be someplace new, rugged, and growing. It seemed to be a stroke of fate that she stopped at Snoqualmie. Her first week in town and she met Sara and Monroe. She didn't know if it was fate, destiny, or some divine retribution, but she loved her life in this wilderness.

Monroe walked into the kitchen and brought her back to reality. "We've not seen you for a while, Emily. Where have you been keeping yourself?"

"Trying to keep the town healthy," she teased. "I figured I'd spent so much time here, before the babies were born, that you were probably sick of me."

"Never," Sara responded quickly.

"She's right," Monroe chimed in. "We've missed you." He paused as he poured himself a cup of tea. "Have you given any more thought to moving in here with us?"

"I have, but I haven't come to a decision yet," she said. "I don't know what I would do with the apartment I have above my office if I moved here. I suppose I could rent it out or use it for storage, or something. It's really not costing me anything to leave it empty."

"I have a few ideas, but we can talk about that later," Monroe said. "I talked to Sara about the fact that I need to spend more time in Seattle. I'll be gone more and I would like to have someone here to keep Sara from doing things she shouldn't be doing."

"I guess there's nothing left to think about," Emily said. "I'll start moving things this week if it's all right."

"I can send Charlie into town with the wagon so you don't have to make so many trips," Monroe offered.

"That would be fine," Emily said. She wondered if Monroe really knew what he was doing by having her move in. She didn't want to do anything behind Monroe's back, but telling him that she in love with his wife wasn't an option. This was very private and very personal to her. She wanted it kept private. She looked at Sara and the smile on her face said everything would be all right.

Monroe was true to his word and he accompanied Charlie into town with the wagon. Emily didn't really have all that many things. Most of the cargo she brought out from Boston was for the office. She did want to move her desk, which Monroe and Charlie moved without incident. It was a small roll top that belonged to her grandfather. He had moved it from Ireland in the early 1800's. Charlie looked closely at the desk and the craftsmanship.

After an hour they were ready to go. Emily looked around the empty room. She wasn't sad about leaving this place. She was always afraid about staying here alone. It had gotten noisier and noisier on the streets and there were more people she didn't know walking past. Jacob and Suzy kept an eye on things, but they had to sleep too.

She tied her horse to the back of the wagon and climbed up next to Monroe. Suzy ran over from the store and said her good-bye. She was happy that Emily was going. She didn't think a woman in town alone was safe. They chatted a few more minutes and started for the house.

"I was thinking about the upstairs space in your building," Monroe said.

"You said you had some ideas," Emily said. "Tell me what you're thinking."

"What about a small hospital?" Monroe said. Emily looked at him with a puzzled look on her face. "The town is growing and we have no place for people who you may treat that can't go home right

84

away. What do you think about that idea?"

"I don't know," Emily said. "I couldn't really run it alone. I'd need to hire a nurse to help with some things. I couldn't be there 24 hours a day."

"I know this but I may have a solution," Monroe said. "I've been talking to Moe Hawkins over at the bank. He hired in some help because of the growth around here. The man he's bringing in is from San Francisco is married to a woman who was trained as a doctor but has only practiced on a part-time basis. She would like to continue to practice. What do you think?"

"I think the idea has merit," Emily said. "I'm finding that I'm working longer hours than I want. I'd welcome the help. I seem to have a great following with the woman, but the men are still a little reluctant to come to me. I usually only see them when they're bleeding."

"It would be the same way even if you were a man," Monroe laughed. "We don't like doctors and I don't think that will ever change."

"When are these people supposed to arrive?" Emily asked.

"Moe said they should be here by the middle of October," Monroe replied. "They want to beat the snow. Can I tell Moe that you'll talk to this woman?"

"Definitely," Emily said.

Emily got settled in her room again. Charlie made sure her desk was carefully placed in her room. Samuel looked closely at the desk also. It looked beautiful in her room. Sara had placed some freshly cut Lavender in a vase and put it in Emily's room. The scent was heavy but not overpowering. Charlie and Samuel left as Sara entered the room.

"Welcome, home," she said.

"Thank you, Sara," Emily said as she turned to look at her. "It does feel like home. It always did." Sara came over and started helping her unpack. Emily was glad for the closet. She didn't have the benefit of one since she left Boston. She heard a baby fussing in the other room.

"That has to be William," Sara said. "He's not happy unless he's around people." She left the room and returned with him. She propped him up on the bed and he settled down. His black eyes followed them everywhere. Mary appeared in the doorway and saw William on the bed.

"I thought I heard him," she said. "He doesn't like to be alone, does he?" She moved close to him and he smiled. "Dinner is ready, whenever you two are. I'll take him downstairs with me." She gathered him up in her arms and left the room.

"I'll get Edmundson. Let's have supper," Sara said.

By mid October Emily had settled into a routine. She was up by 6am and would leave for the office by 7:30. She enjoyed the leisurely ride into town. She normally met men riding out to the logging sights and the planting crew workers were always on their way to Samuel and Mary's house. She would stop and talk with them and enjoyed their easy going way, and they always greeted her with a smile.

She had devised a way to get messages from people. There was paper and a pencil so folks could write her notes, or they could tell Suzy and she would get a message to her. She arrived that morning to find a note from Jack Regan. He was running a logging crew just north of Snoqualmie. The note said nothing more than he would be by to see her. She had met him a couple of times but didn't like the man.

He was in his early thirties and looked like he had lived a pretty hard life. It didn't detract from his rugged handsomeness, though. He tended to be condescending and patronizing, but could be quite charming when it suited him. Suzy had no time for him at all, so Jacob usually waited on him. Everything was a cash basis with his business and he threw enough around town. He thought this would give him the respect he wanted in town. All it did was to make people wonder where all the money came from and question his motives.

He tended to hire drifters and was, ultimately after as much money as he could get as quickly as possible. Emily didn't trust him. She usually would see him was usually in Walker's and he would come up behind her. She hated that because she would get startled. Suzy would usually rescue her by wanting to show her something in the back. Suzy had heard rumors that he came out of the Civil War with a lot of cash. He fought with the Rebel army and anyone who came out of the war with money usually got it under questionable circumstances. He was a long way from Georgia, which is where he said he grew up. He always presented himself as a southern gentleman, but something under the surface bothered Emily.

She had met many men like him in Boston society. Men who came with good names and cultured backgrounds, but beneath the surface were cruel, manipulative liars. It had been her distinct displeasure to be involved with one such bastard during her days in medical school. He was already a doctor who worked with her father. He came from a good Boston family with financial holdings up and down the eastern seaboard.

Emily's father thought he was well suited to match up with her. They had gone to some functions as a couple, but during the quiet moments, he would show his true nature. He expected a wife to be a showpiece and know her place. He preferred the company of his whores, who he paid well to be discreet. When they threatened to expose him, they would disappear. Emily had no proof of any wrong doing, but ended the relationship as soon as possible. Much to her father's dismay, Emily never gave an explanation. She only sighted a difference of opinion for the separation.

She didn't know what was on Jack's mind. Maybe he had a health concern, but she somehow doubted that because he looked pretty healthy. She had let her paranoia get the best of her. "Jesus, Emily," she said to herself. "Find out what the guy wants before you get defensive." She went about her business and opened the office.

Chapter 8

Emily had been busy for most of the morning. She had seen several people with dysentery and found out it they lived in a logging camp just north of town. This was one of the logging camps that Jack Regan ran and was probably the reason for his visit. She found out that they had been taking water from the small creek. She also calculated that there wasn't the best of conditions at the camp. Dysentery usually occurred when human waste came in contact with drinking water.

She saw no children that morning, and very few woman. There were no 'families' at this camp. It consisted of a group of drifters and a few whores who were looking for a better life. She needed to inspect this camp to see if she could make things better for these people. Her meeting with Jack was taking shape and if she could persuade him into taking her to the camp, maybe she could make suggestions on how to improve conditions. This would be under the guise of *public health* concerns and not something personal.

She went over to Walker's at noon to see if some supplies she had ordered had arrived. She was running low on things for the office. Suzy retrieved her package from Boston when Emily told her about the note she got from Jack.

"I hate that man," Suzy said. "I don't trust him, and you shouldn't either."

"I'll treat him with the same respect that I have for a rattlesnake," Emily smiled.

"I think I trust the snake more," Suzy replied.

Emily spent the rest of the afternoon unpacking and storing supplies. It was almost 5pm and she had decided that Jack wasn't coming. She was locking her office door and turned to find him standing behind her. She jumped slightly and saw him smile.

"I apologize for having startled you, Doctor," he said with his smooth southern drawl. "You get more beautiful every time I see you."

"Thank you Mr. Regan," Emily said. "I was just heading home." She finished locking the door. "What can I do for you?"

"I wonder if you would do me the honor of escorting you to supper." Jack said.

"I appreciate the invitation, but I must decline," Emily said. "Was this the only reason for your visit?"

"Yes, it was," he said. He seemed a little rejected and humbled.

Emily decided to work this.

"I would like to talk to you about something else," she said as he perked up. "Let's go over to the hotel and we'll have some coffee."

"After you, fine lady," he said as he pointed toward the hotel. They found a table in the dining room and he held her chair like a perfect gentleman. Emily drank coffee and he drank bourbon. She began by telling him of the people in her office this morning. He seemed unconcerned until Emily expressed her desire to ride out to the camp and see if she could help.

"We could probably avoid these things in the future if we act now," Emily said. "Your men would stay healthy and be able to better do their jobs."

"I had no idea my men were ill," he said. "When could you go out there?"

"The sooner, the better," Emily said. "If the conditions out there need improving, I'll need to educate them." Emily paused and was pleased yet distrustful of his spirit of cooperation. "Today is Friday, and I'll like to get this done. Can you meet me at my office at 10am tomorrow?"

"I would be honored," he said. "We shall ride out together."

Emily left the hotel and headed for the house. It was nice to know that someone was waiting for her. It made her feel like she belonged somewhere. She hadn't had that feeling in a long time. Emily talked to Monroe about her visit she would be making tomorrow. He had a concerned look on his face.

"Don't push him too much, Emily. You may get more cooperation from him if he feels he's not being pushed," Monroe said with a smile.

"I agree," she responded. "I get the feeling he cares nothing about the welfare of his employees. He's only interested in the money he can make. I got the feeling he was doing this as a favor to me."

"I've heard the place is deplorable," Monroe said. "Don't be too shocked by what you see." He paused as he thought, "maybe I should go with you."

"I don't think that's necessary," Emily said. "I don't want to scare him off and if changes need to be made, it needs to be done quickly. It's going to start getting cold."

"Yes, it is," Monroe agreed. "That reminds me, Emily. I need to go to Seattle for a few of days. Charlie, Samuel, and Sara are aware, but I hadn't told you yet. I'm looking at some new equipment for the business. Ivan has a list to things to get, so Gus is going with me."

"I have asked Monroe to bring me some material for dresses,"

Sara smiled. "Is there anything you would like?"

"Nothing I can think of," Emily responded.

"I'm also supposed to meet our new banker and his wife," Monroe said. "They are scheduled to arrive on the 10th or the 11th. I'm going a day early so I can get the things that Ivan and Sara want and then ride out with them from Seattle."

The rest of the evening was quiet. The boys had eaten their fill from the bottles. Sara didn't make enough milk to feed both boys. She was slowly moving them to bottles only. This pleased Mary because she could feed them and not have to rely on Sara's presence. Mary had become crucial for taking care of the boys. Along with her duties of the re-planting crew, she made sure that she helped Sara with the maintenance of the house.

Monroe was thinking about hiring someone to do housekeeping and cooking. He knew Sara would be busy in the near future talking with the local tribes. Mary couldn't keep up the pace either. He thought about placing an ad in the local newspaper, but he hadn't talked with Sara yet. Having Emily in the house help to ease his concern about the health of his children, but that wasn't enough.

The following morning Emily rode out to the camp with Jack and was appalled! These people had nothing and lived in squalor. They had no clean water source, which was the main problem. Emily suggested several things of minimal cost. Jack, much to her surprise, wrote everything down and put a man at the camp in charge of overseeing the completions of Emily's suggestions.

Emily couldn't decide if Jack was being agreeable out of concern for his people, or to please her. It didn't matter what his motive was. What did matter was that some things would change in the camp. As long as she was there, she followed up with some she had seen in the office yesterday. They were feeling better, and the Laudanum eased the cramping. Emily didn't like using the mixture of opium and alcohol. In severe cases she would utilize it on a very limited basis. The chance of addition was too great.

Jack watched as she talked with her patients. He was greatly impressed with the response she received from his men. They seemed to respect her. Her bedside manner was excellent, and he saw a talent in her he had never witnessed in any woman. The women he grew up around were the society of Savannah. These southern 'ladies' were useless. They could be wined and dined, but to have anything more outside of marriage was not permitted. He preferred the company of the women in the whorehouses. They may not be polite members of society, but they were alive. You could talk to them and they had opinions, they had brains, and they had drive. The socialites sat on their verandas waiting for Sherman to blow them up.

He knew, many years ago, that he would not be saddled with one of the southern belles. He wanted a woman that was alive, intelligent, and worth something. He saw all of this in Emily McLaughlin. He wanted her from the first day he saw her standing at Walker's Store. Her auburn hair and green eyes caught him and held on to his soul. He knew, if he only accomplished one thing in life, he must win her. She needed to see he was a good man.

"I'd like to come back in two weeks," Emily said as she untied the reigns of her horse. "These people are feeling better, but I want make sure no one else becomes ill. They know that they can come to my office if that happens."

"I'll make sure all the changes are made by then," Jack responded as he helped Emily mount her horse. He talked to the man he put in charge before getting on his horse. They rode back to town and Emily stopped in her office.

"Thank you for taking me out to the camp," she said. "I would have never found it."

"I appreciate your diligence in this matter, Ma am," he said with an air of sincerity. "I hope you'll allow me to see you safely home."

"Thank you for the kindness, Mr. Regan," Emily said as she caught Monroe standing in front of Walker's. "I'll ride home with Mr. Monroe."

"Then I will bid you adieu," he said as he reeled his horse and rode away.

An air of relief came over her. He was the perfect gentleman. There was not a time that he said or did anything inappropriate. Monroe waved to her as she came across the street. "You were right. Conditions were deplorable, but Mr. Regan seems to want to change that."

"You believe that?" Suzy said.

"I have no reason not to believe him, right now," Emily said. "I'm willing to believe that he's true to his word, until he proves otherwise."

"Do you want to ride back with me?" Monroe asked.

"No," Emily responded. "I need to take some things to Helga's. My supplies came in from Boston, so I'm going to stop and re-stock before I come home."

Emily went back out to Regan's camp two weeks and all the suggestions she made had been completed. Jack accompanied her and when she was pleased, he was too. With winter coming on, the men were doing some much-needed repair to their tents. They weren't really tents as much as canvas buildings. Their idea had come from the large military tents used during the war. These would house four to six men and would accommodate a Franklin stove.

One thing that was now in the middle of the camp was a well. Jack had asked if a clean water source could be used by all was possible. This well was the answer. Emily's reaction from the women was one of gratitude. They didn't have to boil water before drinking it. They had clean water for washing clothes. This smattering of five tents had, what they considered, a modern convenience and they were thrilled.

"The well was a great idea, Mr. Regan," Emily said as they made their way to town.

"Please call me Jack," he said. "Every time I hear Mr. Regan, I look around for my father." He saw Emily smile. "I can't take the credit for the well. My man at the camp suggested that and I told him to go ahead."

"I wish I would have thought of that Mr., excuse me, Jack," Emily said.

They talked until they got back into town. Emily found him to be well educated and well spoken, when he wasn't trying to impress other men around him. He quoted from Shakespeare a few times and Emily teased him.

"I've always been a great lover of his work," Emily said. "I haven't read any since I left Boston."

"I have some of his work," Jack admitted. "I'd be happy to lend you some if you like."

"I would like that, Jack," Emily smiled.

As they rode on he asked, again, if he could see her home. Emily paused before she declined. Although she had seen a different side of him, a softer side, something about him made her uncomfortable. The time she spent with him was not unpleasant and he allowed her to see the gentleman he was bred to be. Monroe came into town with her and picked up Gus before leaving for Seattle. She was going to keep the office closed on Monday and Tuesday. Mary was looking tired and she wanted to give her a break so she could rest.

Monroe had said that Charlie would be moving in with Samuel and Mary. He had hired a Snoqualmie woman, Sally, to be the housekeeper and cook at the main house. She and her sons, who worked on the planting crew, would live in the cabin. Samuel had been trying to get his father to move into his house since it was built. Charlie didn't want to intrude in his son's life, but missed him horribly.

When Monroe discussed the possibility of hiring Sally and having a place for her and her son's to live, Samuel saw the opportunity to get his father in his house. Charlie was busy packing a wagon with his personal things. Samuel already had a bed in his father's room. The furniture in the cabin would stay in the cabin. Sally and her sons would bring their things on Sunday and be ready for work on Monday.

This would give Sara the opportunity to learn as much as she could about the local tribes and the important people to talk to at each tribal council. With Sally leaving the re-planting crew, Monroe put Sally's eldest son, Joseph One Feather, in charge under Mary. He was a strong and responsible young man. He was a year younger than Samuel, but just as responsible. He was the silent leader of the crew, and had been for some time. His mother had taught him about the land and the best way to plant trees.

When Monroe first told Mary that he had hired Sally, she felt like she had done something wrong. He knew she would feel this. He explained that he was pleased that she had such love for his children and his wife. He explained that she couldn't do everything. By putting Sally on at the house, she would not have to work like the re-planting crewmembers. Her life would be easier. It would make it easier for her and Sara to learn about the local tribes so they could work with them.

Mary understood after he explained. "I have important things to do," she responded.

"Absolutely," Monroe answered. "You have many important things to do."

Sally and her sons loved their new home. She felt uncomfortable living there without paying some sort of rent. After Monroe explained that the job included 'room and board' she felt better about it. Monroe took her to the main house and made the introductions. Sally took instantly to the boys. She had never seen a house like this one. It had a peaceful warm feeling inside of these walls.

Sally reminded Sara of the mother she had not seen for so long. She knew that she was in the spirit world now, but she felt she got a piece of her back in Sally. Monroe left the house as the women talked. Sally's sons Joseph and Daniel were fine young men. They were respectful and hardworking. Samuel had nothing but praise for these young men. Their English was not as refined as Sally's but they could understand the language perfectly. Samuel had asked Monroe if it was all right if he taught the boys to read.

"You must ask permission of their mother," Monroe answered. "These are proud people and they fear the loss of their native language."

"It would make life for them so much easier," Samuel responded.

"I know that, but don't push the issue unless Sally gives her permission," Monroe explained. "You still have to convince Joseph and Daniel. That may be harder than you realize."

"I understand," Samuel said. "I'll take it slow."

Gus appeared with the wagon. He and Monroe would be leaving for Seattle this morning. They would be gone for the next four days. This would be the first time that Monroe and Sara had been apart since they were married. Monroe was glad that Emily was at the house. He knew the feeling Sara had for her but that didn't matter to him. Monroe waved to Gus and went into the house to grab his bag. Sara and Sally were still talking.

He went over to the boys and picked up each of them and kissed them gently. Sara joined him and walked out to the porch with him.

"Four days should see me back," he whispered. "If there's a problem, I'll send a telegram and let you know. I love you, Sara." He kissed her and hugged her close.

"Have a safe trip, Monroe," she replied.

"I'll get him back to you safe and sound, Mrs." Gus smiled.

She watched as Monroe and Gus disappeared into the trees. She returned to the house to find Sally looking at the kitchen. Sara knew she would take the rest of the day getting Sally to feel comfortable. Emily arrived in the kitchen to the smell of fresh coffee while Sara made the introductions.

"Is Monroe gone?" Emily asked.

"Just a few minutes ago," Sara said. "What are you doing upstairs?"

"I'm trying to catch up on my reading," Emily said. "I got some new medical journals with the things I received and I wanted to stay abreast of the new things. It seemed like a good day to do this."

"It's cool today," Sara said. "Would you like a fire in your room?"

"I've already started one," Emily answered. "Thanks for the offer, though." She disappeared back up the stairs. Sara spent more time with Sally and then sent her home. The boys were screaming to be fed so she helped with that before going out the door.

The boys were fast asleep and Sara built a fire in the large living room. The rain had started to come down at a heavy steady pace and Sara knew that it would rain for the next six months. She thought about Monroe traveling in this. She was glad that Gus brought the Conestoga wagon. That would protect them a little. She dosed off in the leather wingback while she watched the fire.

It was just she and Emily at dinner. Sara had some fresh salmon that Charlie had caught that afternoon. Emily baked some biscuits and grabbed some green beans from the pantry shelf. Sara decided to light the candles instead of the lanterns. There was a warm glow from the fireplace in the living room and the soft candlelight in the dining room. The house was quiet and Emily loved looking across the table at Sara. She was talking about some of the articles she had read, and Sara tried to follow what she was saying. She knew nothing about Emily's form medicine, and never pretended to. Emily realized what she was doing and stopped talking and started to laugh.

"I'm sorry, Sara," Emily said. "I get so engrossed in this stuff and I forget that you could care less."

"That's not true, Emily," Sara said in a serious tone. "If it's important to you, then it's important to me, even though I don't understand it." She paused for a moment. "Teach me about it. All I ever really knew were the things my mother taught me about using herbs for healing."

"If you teach me about the herbs, I'll teach you about what I know," Emily said. "Is it a deal?"

Sara nodded her head and they continued their meal. They sat and talked until William made everyone aware of his hunger.

"I'll clean up. Go ahead and take care of William," Emily said. "I'll come in and help when I'm finished here." Sara cleared the table and heated water so she could wash up the tableware. She heated water for tea and made a pot before joining Sara in the living room. She was holding a baby to each breast and never looked more beautiful.

"I think they're ready for a bottle," Sara said. "I don't have enough milk for them."

"I'll take Edmundson," Emily said as she took him. "Hello, little man. Let's fill your tummy." He looked at her, smiled, and started to kick his feet.

Sara watched Emily with her son. She was such an amazing woman. Sara had never met anyone like her. She had never been drawn to any other woman as she was to her. What could she possibly see in her? They had nothing in common and no similar interests. Why did she agree to move into the house? Was it a sense of family she missed or was it something more? Only time would tell.

Edmundson and William had emptied their bottles. Sara changed their diapers and they were down for the night. Emily watched Sara put more wood in the fireplace. They sat quietly in the leather chairs and watched the fire.

"I'm tired," Emily said as she yawned. "I really didn't do anything today so I shouldn't be this sleepy."

"We need days like this," Sara smiled. "I think I'll turn in."

They walked up the stairs and Sara stopped and kissed Emily at her door. She watched as she walked through and closed the door. Sara went to her room and looked at the empty bed. She turned and went back downstairs and checked on the boys. They were sleeping soundly in their cradles. She sat and looked at the fire for a while. She wondered if Emily was tucked in and asleep already. Why was she hesitant about going in to join her? She didn't want sex, just the closeness she missed lying next to a woman. She missed the soft roundness she had with Mary.

It was like a coupling of two kindred spirits. She wanted that with Emily, and believed that Emily wanted that, too. Sara took a book from the shelf and started to read. She was having trouble getting into the story. Her mind wasn't on this story, although it was one she had read on several occasions. An hour had passed and she decided to go back to her room.

As she passed Emily's room she saw a light coming from under the door. She put her hand on the doorknob and turned. She opened the door to find Emily trying to read. Sara entered the room and closed the door.

"I want to stay with you tonight," Sara said. "Is that all right?"

Emily stood up from her chair and walked up to Sara. She took her hands in hers and looked into her eyes. "I would like that very much," she said in a whisper. "I didn't want to presume that you felt the same way. I did have hope, though."

"I somehow knew the first time that we met," Sara said as she held her close. She stroked her hair, kissed her forehead, and took her face into her hands. She kissed her long and passionately. It was as wonderful as she had imagined it would be. The meeting of their tongues, for the first time, made Emily's knees weak.

Emily had never had anyone kiss her like this. She had dreamed about this with Claudia, but never thought it could be better than she had imagined. Sara had more experience with these things. Emily had never slept with any other woman, not even her sister. They never shared a room. She had never shared a bed with another human in her life. This was not because she didn't have the desire, but because of circumstance. Emily didn't know what was about to happen and preferred it that way.

That long, slow, wet kiss had finished and Sara turned down the covers on the large brass bed. She extended her hand to Emily who joined her. Sara blew out the lantern, crawled in beside Emily and gathered her in her arms.

Sara awoke to the sound of William pitching a fit. She got out of bed and looked back at Emily. She was still sleeping soundly and Sara quietly closed the door. It was cold in the house and as Sara went downstairs she saw Sally pick up William.

"What's wrong, little one," she said. He looked at her and smiled. "You're soaked through and you're probably cold and hungry."

"You're probably right, Sally" Sara said. "I'll heat some bottles if you want to change some diapers."

"I have already done that, and there's fresh coffee," Sally smiled. "Little William let's you know what he wants."

Sara changed Edmundson and fed him his morning bottle. He was so much like his father in his nature. He was calm and patient. He rarely fussed. Sara thought that he had decided that his brother fussed enough for both of them. She looked over at Sally and watched her with William. She was so good with him. She would look at him and he would smile. The only person who could get a smile from Edmundson was his father, Emily, and occasionally, Mary.

"How long have you been here, Sally?" Sara asked.

"I came over after the boys left with the re-planting crew," Sally said.

Sara realized that it was around 6am when Sally came in. She should have been up but she and Emily had talked late into the night. Edmundson had finished his bottle and she put him back into his cradle. She went back upstairs to get dressed. She paused for a moment at Emily's door and then walked past. She wanted to crawl back into the warm bed and snuggle in close to her, but decided to let her sleep.

She used the washbasin in her bedroom and changed out of her bedclothes. She began to experience a cramping low in her abdomen. She saw the spot of blood in her gown and realized that her monthly cycle had started. This was her first since the boys were conceived. She had never had this kind of pain before during her bleeding periods and was afraid that something was wrong.

She finally got dressed and sat down on the bed because of dizziness. She was starting to perspire as Emily walked into the room. She looked at Sara and got a serious look on her face.

"What's wrong?" Emily asked with concern.

"I don't know," Sara said. "I've started my monthly bleeding and I have pain."

"That's not unusual," Emily reassured. "This sometimes happens after having children, especially with the first cycle." She sat down on the bed next to Sara, picked up her hand, and gently kissed it. "Why don't you lie down for a while? I'll go downstairs and help Sally with the boys." Sara nodded a reply and stretched out on the bed. Emily went to leave and turned around and walked back to the bed. She bent down and kissed Sara gently. "I'll check on you later."

***

Beth remembered her first kiss. As Zack told the story she could picture that face that was so close. She remembered that feeling of excitement, weakness, and desire. Jenny was like a whirlwind. She had turned Beth's world upside down. She was a political activist while they were in college. Beth was drawn to her high energy, intensity, and tenaciousness. Jenny made no secret of her sexual orientation. Beth hadn't completely left the closet she hid in for those years growing up. She didn't know how accepting Steve and Karen would be about this.

Beth had learned, in recent years that you're born with this orientation. Learning the history of her great-grandmother made her aware of this fact. It had to have been hard for Sara. Beth knew that society still didn't respond well to these things. Jenny had tried to change some of this thinking while they were in college. Even with organizations and rallies, there was still open hostility for the gay population.

Jenny was drawn to Beth because of the way she looked. Her dark flowing hair and her blue eyes were in such contrast. As soon as their eyes met, Jenny was hopelessly lost. Beth never knew this, and Jenny was not willing to admit this. She had found a way to meet this beauty after one of her rallies. From that time on they were inseparable, at least while at college. Jenny had invited Beth to her home one weekend. Beth liked her parents. It was a though they had never left the 'sixties'. Their clothes, demeanor, and attitudes had not changed in 20 years. They even had the Volkswagen van that was orange and white.

It was that weekend that Beth and Jenny had made love for the first time. Beth had been with men, well boys really, but had never had this experience or intimacy with any of them. She never wanted to leave her waterbed, and didn't for the better part of the weekend. Jenny was skilled and tender. Beth felt clumsy and awkward at first. This finally passed and Beth started to relax and savor the things happening to her, and desired more.

The weekend passed very quickly. She invited Jenny to her home on their next long weekend. Her parents were so different from Jenny's. They seemed stuck in the 'fifties' like June and Ward Cleaver. The street where she grew up looked like a scene shot for "Leave It To Beaver". Beth looked at her street and started to laugh. Jenny was right.

She introduced Jenny to her parents. Jenny was polite and pleasant. She did nothing to embarrass Beth. She realized how 'straight' these people were and understood Beth's hesitance to admit her orientation. Jenny never pushed the issue with Beth. Everyone has his or her own timetable with these things. She never believed in 'outing' someone for political gain. After dinner they walked down to Baskin-Robbins for some ice cream. Beth though Jenny may think that this was lame.

Much to Beth's surprise, Jenny enjoyed the walk with her parents. She thought it was great that they still wanted to continue traditions they had started so many years ago.

"You should feel lucky, Beth," Jenny told her. "You could have ended up with way worse people than this. I've heard horror stories about the foster care system and the adoption system."

"I know I'm lucky," Beth agreed. "The only bad thing is that all of my records are sealed, which is so stupid. I lived with my mother until she died, and then my grandmother until she died. It's not like I was abused and removed from my home."

"How much do you know about your parents?" Jenny asked.

"Just what my mother and grandmother told me," Beth said. "Karen knew my mother and grandmother so I'm pretty well aware of my maternal side of the family. My father died before I was born, and I know nothing about him or his family."

"Do you know when and where your parents were married?" Jenny asked. Beth nodded her head. "Then we can check in the records to find out some things. It's a good starting point."

Beth remembered the focus that Jenny had about finding out

about her father's family. She was great at research and for the next two years she and Jenny worked to find out as much as possible. She and Jenny had planned to find work in the same area after college. They both wanted to live in San Francisco. They had planned a trip to Seattle after re-locating to follow the trail of her family.

Chapter 9

Beth said good-bye to Steve and Karen. She would miss these people. They were kind and loving and only wanted the best that life had to offer her. She still hadn't mustered the courage to tell them about her relationship with Jenny. They did seem glad that she wasn't going to brave San Francisco alone. They had given her a new car for her college graduation. This was something completely unexpected and greatly appreciated by Beth.

She had rented a small U-Haul that she could pull behind her car. The girls didn't have a lot but didn't want the car stuffed full of clothes and stereos. They stopped at Jenny's parent's house on their way out of town. Beth was surprised that Jenny didn't have the emotional good-bye that she had shared with Steve and Karen.

"I know my parents love me, but I never seemed to be important enough to have boundaries set for me," Jenny said. "Do you understand what I mean?"

"Not really," Beth said as they headed north on the Interstate.

"I'm sure that Steve and Karen had rules," Jenny started. "You know, rules like 'don't go there because you may get hurt', or 'be home by 9' or even the simple ones like 'no jumping on the bed'. My parents didn't do that. They didn't want to inhibit my creative side. They didn't think that rules were necessary because the rules just reminded them of the 'establishment' they fought so hard against in their youth. By doing this, I felt like they didn't care where I was or what I did. I didn't think they cared about my welfare. I didn't think they cared about my safety. I didn't think they cared about me."

"I thought you were the luckiest person I had ever met," Beth said. "Being able to do what you wanted, when you wanted would have been the best way to grow up. I never thought about it the other way." She picked up Jenny's hand. "I'm sorry you feel that way. I'll trade parents with you for a while." They both laughed.

The rest of the day they traveled toward San Francisco. Beth's car handled the U-Haul and the highway well. They found a decent hotel to spend the night about two hours south of San Francisco. They knew they would not make the city in one day. They wanted to enjoy the scenery on the way. They wanted to arrive when they had time to locate the apartment they had found and secured through the help of Beth's employer.

There was a small restaurant across the street from the hotel so

Jenny and Beth walked over there for a bite to eat. There hotel room was spacious and new. After dinner they sat and talked over coffee. They had so many plans, dreams, and things to do in their lives. It was at that point that Jenny surprised Beth.

"I want to be with you always, Beth," Jenny started. "Will you marry me?"

"Yes," Beth said quickly.

"You're sure," Jenny said. "You don't want to take it back?"

"No," Beth said. "I want to be with you always. We can't legally be married, but we can make our own vows to each other."

They walked back to the hotel, got into a hot bath together, and talked about where they wanted to make their promises to each other. They decided that the best place would be right under the Golden Gate Bridge. This would happen this coming Saturday. They could get settled and have their ceremony before Beth started her job on Monday.

There hotel room had two queen size beds in it. Jenny and Beth used both of them at different times throughout that night. Beth was so in love with Jenny and could never imagine being with anyone else. She didn't want to be with anyone else, and now she would never have to be. They would be together, forever.

They arrived in San Francisco by 11am. Beth stopped and got a detail map of the city. They found their apartment and the older woman who managed the place greeted them before they could get to her door.

"Which one of you is Beth?" she asked. Beth stepped forward and introduced herself. "Your first month and deposit were paid by your company. Come with me and I'll show you the place."

It was on the top floor, but the view of the bay was great. There were two large bedrooms, a fireplace, all the modern conveniences, and it had personality. Personality was great, but they had no furniture. Mrs. Austin, the manager, gave them some tips on local places for furniture and where the closest U-Haul location so they could return the trailer.

"You may want to hang on to it so you can move your own furniture up here instead on waiting on delivery men," Mrs. Austin suggested. The girls took their things out of the trailer and drove down to the local used furniture store. Beth browsed and found a queen brass bed for $30.00, a small dining table and two chairs for $20.00, and a love seat for $30.00. The whole time that they were in college they worked and saved whenever they could.

Neither of the girls would go out to drink and party. That was a straight girls' game, or so they rationalized. When they decided to go to northern California together, they saved even more. Jenny found a double bed for the other bedroom, some end tables and lamps for the living room, and a large chest of drawers for their bedroom. This place even had new mattress and box spring sets for very reasonable prices.

They loaded all of their stuff into their U-Haul trailer. It would have made no difference in the price if they took it back at 2pm or at 4pm. Mrs. Austin's nephew and his friend were visiting and she told them to help the girls unload their trailer. Beth felt a little uncomfortable and apologized to Bret and his friend Steve. Between the four of them they made short work of the trailer.

Jenny and Bret put the beds up while Beth and Steve carried up the mattresses and box springs. She heard Jenny start to laugh about something when Bret returned to the living room a wonderful shade of red.

"What's so funny?" Steve asked.

"You know gay men can't handle tools," Bret said. "She's right, we can't. Hey, how would you and Jenny like to go to a club with us on Friday?"

"I guess we could," Beth answered.

"They know their way around here," Jenny said from the bedroom doorway. "I thought they could help us get acclimated."

"Great by me," Beth said.

They watched as they left the apartment. Beth still didn't know how they knew that she and Jenny together. Jenny admitted that she told them. She knew Bret and Steve were together. She even asked Bret if his aunt knew about him. He didn't hide from anyone because life was too short and his aunt was extremely supportive and told him about the Lesbians upstairs.

They returned the U-Haul and found a store for linens nearby. They didn't have sheets or blankets for their bed. They found a pizza place and got one to go. They arrived back at the apartment and Beth unlocked the door. She opened the door to her and Jenny's new home. This was their place. They would start their life together here. They could live and love freely. Jenny looked out the window.

"Look at the sunset on the bay," she said. "Have you ever seen anything more beautiful?"

"Yes, I have," Beth responded as she wrapped her arms around Jenny. "You're more beautiful." They made love most of the night. They didn't have to worry about anyone walking in on them, or being afraid about leaving the door open. Jenny could be as noisy as she wanted to be. Their apartment was the only one on the third floor. They had windows on all four sides of the apartment. No one next to them, no other buildings close to them and a view from any window.

Whoever found this apartment needed to be thanked. She would find out on her first day of work. She wanted to find her office and see how long it would take her to get to work on Monday. She and Jenny would do that tomorrow. Tonight they would enjoy each other and their newfound freedom and newfound life.

Beth found herself back in the present and the sound of Zack's voice.

***

Sally had fixed breakfast and Emily made up a tray and took it to Sara. She was very pale and sleeping. She didn't want to wake her but she needed to eat. She set the tray down and Sara woke up.

"Are you feeling any better?" Emily said softly as she sat on the bed.

"Yes, I am," Sara responded. "That smells good."

"I hoped you'd be hungry," Emily said as she put the tray on Sara's lap. She loved taking care of Sara. She made her feel needed and wanted. They chatted as she ate her breakfast and then Sara decided to go downstairs. She had bookkeeping to do, and didn't want to fall behind on it. Emily decided to go into the office for a while. She had left a note that she would not be into the office, but wanted to take some of the information she had received with her. She had a nice little medical library started and was anxious to add to it.

Sally asked if she could pick up some things at Walker's. It was more than she could carry on her horse, so Sara helped her hitch the wagon. Sara watched as Emily disappeared into the trees. It was still raining and damp. She thought about the night she had spent with Emily. They were not intimate with each other besides snuggling close and kissing. There was nothing more last night. She wasn't sure how ready Emily was for more.

Emily rode through the rain and thought about Sara. She had never been intimate with another woman, but she liked what she had last night. She wanted the whole experience, and she wanted it with Sara. It would come in time, and she needed to be patient. The trip to town seemed to take forever today. She pulled up in front of Walker's and found Jacob. She gave the list to him and walked over to her office.

There was a note from Jack. He thanked her for all of her help at

104

the logging camp and would like to take her to dinner sometime soon. Emily opened her door and left the note on her desk. After about an hour she went back to Walker's and Jacob had finished loading the supplies. She headed back to the house and was home by 3pm.

Ivan was in talking with Sara. He wanted to slow down on some of the cutting because of the weather. He was also going to stop the work on Saturdays. He would still be able to meet the terms of the contract and it would give the men more time with their families. Helga came from the kitchen with William and Mary had Edmundson.

"You two are going to spoil those boys," Sara said with a smile.

"I can't believe how they've grown," Helga said as she kissed William. "Any time you want someone to watch them, you let me know. I'd love to watch these babies." She hugged the baby again. "You may not get them back, though." William kicked his feet and smiled.

Ivan excused himself to go back and see Samuel and Charlie. He wanted to give them the new schedule and see how far ahead of the cutters Samuel was. He'd not been back to the new house since the house warming. Sara had large areas of seedlings going and Samuel had built a small building for her to do the potting. Sally's boys had done well with the re-planting crew to the point that Mary rarely went with them.

Samuel would inspect the few jobs that had done at first and was pleased with the outcome. He didn't even inspect anymore. Mary had two young women from the re-planting crew that helped with caring for the seedlings. Ivan noticed a large container on legs and was looking at it when Samuel walked up.

"What's that for Samuel?" he asked.

"That was Gus's idea," Samuel replied. "It catches water from the house and makes it easier to water the seedlings during the dry season. He's actually working on the same kind of system to get running water into the house."

"The man's a genius," Ivan said. "We're going to not work Saturdays until next spring. It's dangerous to work in the rain at times. The trees get very slippery."

"I've got the next parcel marked," Samuel said as they walked to the barn. "It's this section here." Samuel pointed to a large map on the wall.

"That should hold us through the winter," Ivan said. "Let your father know the change in schedule. He won't have to go to the mill on Saturday anymore, unless the owner is willing to pay him for his time."

The next couple of days passed quietly. Emily was enjoying her time away from the office. She did go down to Ivan and Helga's for her normal Wednesday morning. She only had 3 patients to see that morning. Everyone was fairly healthy, except one of the logger's wives. She had Consumption, which was a fancy word for TB, cancer, or any of the other maladies that plagued society and seemed to just eat away at the body. Gracie had TB and probably wouldn't last for two more years. She had worked in a whorehouse when Geoff met her and wanted to marry her anyway.

"I really didn't love him," she admitted. "He was kind and gentle and wanted to show me a better life. He has done that, and for that I'm thankful. I suppose maybe I do love him in many ways." Emily wondered what would make a woman, an attractive woman, make a living in that way. She was well spoken and appeared to have some formal education. Emily would like to find out someday, but didn't want to push. She was getting ready to go home when the door flew open.

"Emily," Helga said breathlessly. "There's been an accident out at one of the logging camps. Suzy said they're bringing three men into town now."

"I'll get down to the office," Emily said as she picked up her bag.

"I'll come down and help," Helga said. "I've patched men up for years. Now I'll get a chance to see if I've been doing it right."

They arrived at the office about the same time as the wagon. There were three men in the wagon covered in blood. Jack Regan was right behind the wagon and seemed to show genuine concern for his men. He and the two others carried the men into the office. Emily triaged their injuries and started with the worst first. Helga cleaned wounds and bandaged the small things.

"What happened?" Emily asked one of the men.

"Choker chain broke," the man on the table said. "Log bounced back and got all of us. It got Zeke the worst." He let out a moan as Emily put a splint on this arm. "Is he okay?"

"He's going to be fine," she said. Emily looked over at Helga as she changed the bandage on this head. The bleeding was slowing down but some stitches would be needed. She gave her patient some Laudanum and moved on to Zeke. "We're going to need to put in some stitches here, Helga. Have you ever seen that done?"

"No, but I'm ready to help," she said. Emily got the material she needed and stitched up Zeke's bleeding head. Helga was amazed at the precision at which Emily's hands worked. He would have a scar across his forehead, but the bleeding had already stopped.

"I'll need to take those out in 10 days," she said to Zeke. "Don't take them out yourself."

"I'll make sure he comes back, Ma am," the man with the broken arm said.

"Good," she said. "I'll want to see you again, too. I want to make sure that arm is healing straight." She turned to the third man and continued, "You may as well come back in, too. I haven't lost a patient yet, and I'm not going to start with you."

"I'll make sure they're all here, Ma am," Jack said. He motioned to the men to load them in the wagon. Emily had given them instructions on keeping the wounds clean and to rest for the next couple of days. Helga left and went back to her house after Emily had thanked her for her help.

"Is there anything else I can do for you Mr. Regan?" Emily asked.

"Would you share a cup of coffee with me?" he said. Emily accepted his offer and they went to the hotel. They sat and talked quietly when he finally admitted that he felt worthless as he watched her apply her trade. "You are an amazing woman, Emily. I would like to get to know you better."

"If you mean get to know me better socially, then the answer is no," Emily said. "I'm not interested in anything more than friendship. I'm not looking to get married."

"I'll accept that," he said. "I don't want marriage or children either. It would be nice to have dinner, occasionally, with a lady. Can friends do that?"

"Yes, Mr. Regan," she said. "They can."

Sara had expected Emily much earlier and was worried. She was relieved when she saw her at the barn. She told Sara about the accident at Jack's camp and the injuries that the men sustained during dinner.

"He's lucky one of them wasn't killed," Sara said. "I'm glad that Helga was there to help."

"I think she has the makings of a good nurse," Emily said. "I'd have her at my side anytime." She paused and looked at Sara. "I really felt useful today. I stitched wounds, set and arm, and bandaged scrapes. I felt like I was a doctor again."

"You didn't feel like one before?" Sara asked quietly.

"I've been seeing runny noses and dysentery. That really isn't the same as emergency things," she explained. "It's an experience when minutes count. I like the excitement of it. I miss the excitement of it. We would get these cases often when I worked at the hospital." She pushed her food around on her plate. "I couldn't enjoy that feeling when the boys were born. I was scared I might make a mistake and I didn't want to lose either of the boys, or you."

"Emily, you're a good doctor," Sara said. "You proved it when my children were born, and today you proved it to yourself." She reached over and held her hand.

"I was thinking, on the way home, about the things I didn't have today," Emily said. "I need to get some equipment for accidents like I had today. I think I'll write my father and see what I can get from him."

"Monroe should be back no later than Friday," Sara replied. "Maybe that banker's wife has some idea of where to get equipment out here."

They finished dinner and spent the rest of the evening with the boys. They were awake in the evening and sometimes fussy. William just wanted to be entertained. Edmundson was happy just being held. He was very easy natured and was aware of everything. He had his father's blue eyes and temperament. Emily had never seen Monroe angry or heard him raise his voice.

By nine the boys had been changed, fed, and were almost asleep. Emily had retired to her room to read. She and Sara had only been together that first night. She wanted to walk down the hall and crawl into her bed several times each night, but hesitated. She put Sara out of her mind and got into "Hamlet". Jack had left it for her at the office. He was quite the gentleman when he was around her. She smiled as she opened the leather cover. It always took her some time to get into the iambic flow of the words, but once she did, they seemed to dance off the page. Why didn't she take some of her classic literature when she came out here? She would write to her Mother and have her ship them out.

"Would you like some company?" Sara asked. Emily didn't even hear her open the door.

"Sure," Emily said with a smile. She put down her book and slid over. Sara got into bed beside her. "Sara, what would Monroe think about you being here?"

"Monroe knows how I feel about you," Sara said matter of factly. "It's one of the reasons why he wanted you to move in. He needs to travel more and has some things going on in Seattle. He doesn't like to think of me here alone and he trusts you."

"He trusts me even though I'm in bed with his wife," Emily said in a confused way.

"I'm very honest with Monroe. We've never had any secrets and never will," Sara said. "Monroe knew this would happen when he asked you to move in."

"Monroe doesn't care that I'm in love with his wife? I'm very confused," Emily said.

"He knows that. He also knows that I love you and I also love him. That's how he knows that we would never hurt each other. That's what's important to him. I'm not sure if I'm explaining this the way I need to. It's not about sex. It's about a bonding of spirits. Monroe and I bonded when I was 5 years old. I knew the minute I looked into his eyes, just as I knew we would someday be right here the moment I looked into your eyes."

Sara sat up and blew out the lantern. She gathered Emily into her arms and kissed her slowly and passionately. She slowly unbuttoned her nightgown and caressed her breasts. Emily stiffened slightly.

"What's wrong," Sara whispered.

"I'm a virgin," Emily whispered back. She was glad the light was out because she knew she was blushing. "I've never been with anyone. I never wanted anyone like I want you." She found Sara's mouth again and played with her tongue. She was aware of the wetness and the throbbing desire she felt. "Make love to me, Sara."

Sara found Emily exciting and willing. She was slow and methodical as she removed what was left of her clothing. Emily did the same for her and loved the feel of her naked body next to hers. Sara kissed every part of the sleek beautiful body. She could see her in the light from the fireplace and the glistening beads of perspiration on her forehead. She brushed the hair from her face and threw back the covers.

Emily had read about sexual climax in her medical journals, and had even imagined what it would be like. She had also read that a woman's first experience was painful, but this must be with men. She had not expected it would be so wonderful. It was like you died and went to heaven but you could come back. This was her first sexual experience. She held Sara close and didn't want this feeling to end. She was afraid to breath, move, or break the silence with conversation. Sara kissed her forehead, cheeks, and then gently touched her lips to Emily's.

They spent the next few hours exploring each other's bodies before they drifted off to sleep. Emily awoke early in the morning and looked at Sara's beautiful face, full lips, and high cheekbones.

She never imagined that being with someone was like this. She gently touched Sara's face and thought about all the things she had learned about her own body and how to give that same pleasure to someone else. Sara stirred and opened her eyes. She looked at Emily and smiled.

"Good morning," she whispered. "It's very early, why aren't you sleeping?"

"I don't know," Emily said. "I do know that I will never want to wake up with anyone but you ever again." She bent to kiss Sara and they made love until the sun came up. They were cuddling close when they heard the front door open. They knew Sally had come in and heard her starting a fire in the cook stove. Sara knew that it was 6am. The boys would start stirring in another hour.

It was cold in the room and it felt good to stay under the covers with Sara. Her body was warm and inviting. She could stay her forever, and the world could be damned. Her hands found Sara's breasts that were full of milk and starting to seep. She still was breastfeeding the boys once a day. Emily had always wondered what human breast milk was like. She took her finger and wiped a drop of the fluid. She put the fluid to her lips and tasted it. The sweetness surprised her.

"It tastes like cantaloupe juice," Emily said and smiled. "I always wondered."

"I'm glad I could be of service," Sara replied. "We should get up. I can smell the coffee." Sara got up and found her robe. "Will you go for a ride with me today?"

"Yes, as long as I can stop by the office to pick up my messages," Emily said as she started to dress. Sara nodded her head, kissed Emily, and left the room.

They rode to the falls. Emily had always marveled at its beauty. There was a light misty rain falling and the spray from the falls made the trees heavy with moisture. They tied their horses and walked next to the falls. Sara saw a movement from the corner of her eye. She took Emily's hand in hers.

"I want you to, very slowly, with no quick movements, look to the right," she said in a quiet tone. Emily followed Sara's instructions and saw the 8-foot beast standing next to the tree. Her heart gave a start, but the beast didn't move. She stood there in awe and mesmerized as he slowly turned and disappeared into the forest.

"What the hell was that?" Emily asked in a whisper.

"Sasquatch," Sara said. "That's the Indian name. The whites call them Bigfoot. They have lived in these forests for many years. They watch over the forest and over some of us. This area around the falls is their special place."

"I had heard stories and even read some literature back in Boston that mentioned them," Emily said. "I thought it was a myth."

"Monroe has seen them, and now they have let you see them," Sara said. "They trust you and they will watch over you. Never be afraid when you are in the forest alone, they will always be there although you may never see them again."

Sara told Emily of her history with this mythical creature. She told her stories of life when she was a young girl living with her mother. She told her how she first met Monroe and of their trip to this side of the mountains. To see the amazing woman that Sara was and knowing where she came from impressed Emily even more. She had grown up with culture and education, and Sara learned to read while crossing this country on horseback. She had become every bit as sophisticated and cultured as the girls she grew up with. She had one quality that they didn't and never would possess. She was honest.

They left the falls and walked back to their horses. Their hairy friend made one more appearance. Emily looked at Sara and smiled. Emily was still holding Sara's hand. She didn't want this time to end and she didn't want this feeling to end. Sara stopped just short of the horses and was very silent.

"Listen," she whispered. "Can you hear the whispers in the mist?" Emily listened intently and began to smile.

"I do," she whispered back. "I heard this the first time I came to the falls. I can't make out the words." She held Sara's hand and continued to smile. "I love you, Sara," Emily said as she stopped beside her horse. "Love is too small a word to describe what I feel for you. I've never felt this way about anyone, ever."

"We have a lifetime ahead of us, Emily," Sara said as she held her close. "I love you, too."

Sara kissed her in the light rain. Emily's lips were warm and inviting. She was a passionate woman. She was more passionate than Mary had ever been. She showed her pleasure during their lovemaking, when Mary was always very reserved. Sara knew when Emily was satisfied and knew what she liked. Sara wanted a lifetime with Emily, but she didn't want Emily to pass on an opportunity to marry and have children. She would need to discuss this with her at some point in time, but would approach the subject carefully. Emily was just discovering who she really was, even though she was 10 years older than Sara.

They rode into town and checked for any messages. Suzy and Jacob were happy to see Sara and they were amazed at how quickly she had gotten her shape back. They talked as Emily walked over to her office. There were no messages so Emily went upstairs to get some articles she wanted to read. She looked around the empty space and could envision a small hospital. There was enough space and fairly easy access. She looked at what she may need to do to make this happen. She could get Charlie or Samuel to build in some storage for linens. There was room for 6 beds with ample room to move around them in comfort.

Sara touched her on the shoulder and she jumped. "I'm sorry. I didn't mean to startle you."

"I was thinking of Monroe's idea about making this a hospital," Emily said. "It wouldn't be that hard. I was thinking of enlisting the help of the community and that new doctor coming in. What do you think?"

"I think it's a good idea," Sara said. "Will you take Indians?"

"That's a strange question," Emily said almost insulted. "Of course I'll take Indians. I'll take whoever needs medical attention." She paused for a moment, "How can you ask that?"

"It was not meant as an insult," Sara assured. "I've seen the Indians not have the opportunities that the whites have. If we are to grow as a community, we must include all of the community."

"I agree with you," Emily said as she understood exactly what Sara was saying. "It will be for all."

"The community may not be so willing to 'help' if they know that it not whites only," Sara said. "The biggest business in the area, my husband's, will be a supporter."

As they walked to their horses, Moe came out of the bank and told Sara he had just received a telegram from Monroe.

"It looks like he wouldn't be back until Monday," Moe said. "There was some delay with the Eichorns getting out of San Francisco." Sara looked a little puzzled. "That's the new banker and his wife the doctor."

"I never knew their names," Sara said. "Thank you for telling me."

"I was getting ready to send a rider out to tell you, but I saw you," he said with a smile. "You look wonderful. How are your sons?"

"Growing like crazy," Sara said. "Thank you for the message, Mr. Hawkins." They turned to mount their horses and headed back to the house. They rode in silence for a while. Sara broke the silence.

"I hope this weather clears a bit before Monroe starts home. I hate to think of him coming all the way from Seattle in the rain."

"You miss him don't you?" Emily asked.

"Yes, I do," she said. "His sons miss him." Sara knew what Emily was asking. "I need to explain something to you, Emily. Monroe and I are not intimate very often. He was injured many years ago when he was a boy. His doctor told him that he would not be able to have intimacy or ever have children. The times we have had relations has been hard on Monroe. He says it's painful because of the old injuries, but having the boys was worth it."

"Why won't he let me examine him?" Emily asked. "Maybe I could help."

"He has seen many doctors over the years, Emily. They have all said the same thing," Sara said. "Even those in Seattle gave him the same answer. I guess he proved them wrong, didn't he?" Emily nodded her head in agreement. "This is why he wanted you in the house. He knows I have healthy sexual desires. He's never been able to satisfy these, especially with my preferences at times. He isn't jealous about this, but I know he would kill any other man that would approach me."

"I'm starting to understand," Emily said. "He really is an amazing person. I, somehow, knew that the first time we met. I've never known a man who was so unselfish, honorable, and kind. You are a lucky woman, Sara."

Samuel met them at the house and took their horses. Mary was in playing with the boys. Sally was cooking something that smelled wonderful. Sara went to the kitchen and came back to the living room.

"Why don't you, Samuel, and Charlie join us for dinner this evening?" she said. "Monroe will not be back until Monday. Mr. Hawkins got a telegram from him today."

Mary nodded her head and put Edmundson back into his cradle. She went to talk to Samuel, who would wait for Charlie. It would a couple of hours until dinner and the boys had been fed. Sara said she was tired and wanted to take a nap. She looked at Emily, smiled and went upstairs.

Emily took the article she had brought home and sat down next to William and started to read. He began to fuss, so Emily started to read aloud. This quieted him down as he heard her voice. Sally came in and smiled.

"He likes the sound of voices, Miss," she said. "I will come in here and sing old Snoqualmie songs when I am cleaning. He likes that, too. He and his brother are very different. They will have great fights when they get older, I think."

"You may be very right," Emily responded. "I've never seen twins that were so different." Sally left the room and Emily continued reading aloud. Edmundson dropped off to sleep and William not far behind him. She looked at the sleeping babies. These children were indeed miracles. They were never supposed to happen, and they were the first lives that she had brought into the world on her own. She left the living room and went to her room and opened the door to find Sara waiting in her bed sleeping soundly and she didn't want to disturb her. She quietly slipped off her skirt and shirt and slipped in next to her. Sara stirred slightly and Emily snuggled in close and went to sleep.

Sara shared Emily's bed every night until Monroe got home on Monday. They spent their evening hours in quiet conversation and lovemaking. Emily was learning quickly and wanted only to please Sara. Sara wanted to make it clear that Emily needed to be able to relax and let someone please her. When she finally let it happen, Emily finally understood the beauty of a loving woman. She also found that having the lamp on increased the sensuousness of their lovemaking, for she could see Sara's body writhe with pleasure.

She loved Sara's beautiful, shapely body, her mind, and her soul. She was a decade younger than Emily, and even after two children, she was a beauty. She could understand how Monroe would want to endure the pain to make her happy. She still didn't understand his willingness to share her with someone else so she would be happy. This is a level of love she didn't quite understand because she didn't want to share her with anyone. She was here, Sara was here and that's all that mattered. She could live the rest of her life on these last few nights. Monroe would be home tomorrow and she didn't know when they would be together again. She looked at her as she lay sleeping. Her nude body that had been covered in perspiration was now dry. She covered her and kissed her forehead. "I love you," she whispered. Sara stirred slightly and moved close to her. How was she going face Monroe after he arrived home? Emily couldn't think about that now because she was too happy.

Chapter 10

Zack continued to tell his story. He knew that Beth's mind had wandered a couple of times but he never stopped. She needed to know everything, the good and the bad. He had to get her to understand about her roots. She needed to understand the great gift she had been given by her heritage. She looked so young to him. He must have looked the same way to Anne when they first met.

He could never understand what she saw in a kid of eighteen. She was twice his age, but she kept saying something about fate. He used to wonder why she never married, although he never had the courage to ask, she told him eventually. He remembers looking around Emily's room and seeing all the pictures and medical journals. He found it unusual that Anne or Sara hadn't changed the room since Emily's death.

The moment of that first kiss in her mother's room was when her very essence permeated his nostrils and never left. He never wanted anything more than to be with her always. This sleek, beautiful, cultured woman seemed so unattainable.

"We'd best get downstairs," Anne reminded him.

"Yes, Ma am," he said. Anne led him through a back hallway to the new section of the house. There was a secluded stairway that led down to the huge kitchen. There was a flurry of activity going on in the area. There must have been ten people preparing various dishes. Zack happened to notice that half of them were Indian. He was expecting to see Negroes. Most of the cooks and butlers back in Chicago were Negroes.

He followed her out a side entrance to a beautiful private garden. There were flowers of every kind in bloom. It was manicured and meticulously arranged. The aromas were sweet and hung heavy in the air. Anne told Zack that Mary had planted and designed the garden. It was her passion. She walked through another entrance that took them past an office.

The house was like a maze, but he followed Anne until he recognized the large foyer. There was a large portrait of Anne's parents. Her father was a handsome man, with those same blue eyes that Anne had. He stopped and stared.

"This was done the summer after I was born," Anne said. "They were a handsome couple, weren't they?"

"Striking," Zack said. He looked at a smaller portrait of Sara and another woman. "Is this Emily?"

"Yes," Anne said. "It was done the same year by the same artist. There's one in the drawing room of Emily alone, but I like this one better."

"She and your mother must have been close," Zack surmised.

"Very close," Anne said with a smile.

They went back on the porch as people started to arrive. Zack thought it best that he fade into the background while Anne greeted her guests. Anne had other ideas and asked him to stay close and help her greet the arrivals. She introduced Zack to everyone that arrived. He met local businessmen, politicians, and even the Governor. The same old couple that was close to Anne during her Mother's visitation arrived. She gathered the small woman in her arms and held her close. The old man hugged them both.

"Zachary," she said as she held the woman's hand. "This is Tom and Kathleen Eichorn. Tom runs the bank, and Kathleen and Emily built the clinic and hospital in this town."

"It's nice to meet you both," he said as he shook their hands. Both smiled at him and Anne stayed close to this couple the entire day.

He was never far from Anne's side, even during dinner. He paid attention as those at the table spoke of the direction of the country, the economy, and the growth they saw coming to the Northwest. Zack noticed that there were representatives from the local Indian tribes seated at the main table. They spoke openly about the need to preserve the land and to carry on the work that Anne's mother had started.

Anne was well spoken and respected. The Governor had asked her opinion several times throughout the course of the meal. Zack didn't get the impression that he was being polite. She, as her mother, held a great deal of power and, without her consent this area would not be developed peacefully. She could get the buy in from the local tribes and their help if presented properly.

The fireworks were nothing like Zack had ever seen. He sat next to Anne on the porch and as the explosions were going on overhead, she took his hand. When the display had finished guests started to make their exits. They made it a point to find Anne and thank her for a lovely day. No one left without a word to her and many still offered condolences about the loss of her mother. From the corner of his eye Zack saw a handsome man and woman approach. Anne turned and a smile came to her face.

"Caleb," she said as she hugged him. "I didn't know that you were here."

"We got here just before the fireworks," he said. "I found Mother and Dad and you know how that goes."

"I'm so glad you could make it," she said. "Angelina, how wonderful you look. How is your father? I heard he was ill."

"He's much better," she replied. "Thank you for asking."

"I would like you to meet Zachary McGill," Anne said. "Zachary, this is Caleb and Angelina Washington. Caleb is Samuel and Mary's son."

"Very nice to meet you," Zack said.

"We'll be here for the next few days," Caleb said. "I don't need to be back in San Francisco until the 15th."

"That's wonderful," Anne said. "We'll get together here. I'm staying out here for the next few days." They nodded as they left and Anne watched them walk away. "Caleb and I grew up together. He's like another brother."

Most of the guests had departed and the staff was in the process of cleaning up. Anne led Zack to a small library and offered him a drink.

"I'll take some coffee, but I don't drink," Zack said quietly. "My father let alcohol ruin his life and I swore I would never do that, and I made a promise to my Mother."

Anne put away the brandy and joined in with a cup of coffee. They sat quietly and talked. She told Zack the story of her mother and father. He listened for hours and he heard the clock chime 2am.

"It's late," she said. "I can have someone take you back to town, or you can stay the night if you like."

"I'd like to stay," he said. "I don't have to be to work until Monday." Anne escorted him to a guest room in the new section of the house. It was elegantly decorated and had a private bath.

"Sleep as late as you like," she said. "I'll see you in the morning." Anne paused and then looked into Zack's eyes. "Thank you for staying with me today. This was the first year I had to do this without my mother. I was a little nervous. You were the perfect host."

"It was my pleasure, Anne," he responded. "I met some interesting people today. I met some powerful people, also." He took her hand and kissed it gently then looked into her eyes. She fell into his arms and they kissed slowly and gently. This turned into a passion that Zack had problems controlling. "Stay with me tonight, Anne," he whispered as he kissed her ear.

She pulled away from him and went to the door. She turned and looked at him, and Zack felt he had ruined everything with that single question. She turned away and closed the door, locked it, and returned to his arms.

As they made love that night, Zack didn't know if he was dreaming or he was awake. He had never done more than feel a woman's breast before. He had never had intercourse, and now he was lucky enough to be naked in this bed with a goddess. God was certainly smiling down on him. Anne schooled him in patience, foreplay, and pleasure. She told him what she liked and how he could give something to a woman so many men were afraid to try or learn.

Their bodies molded perfectly to each other's. Why had she not married? Why did he care? He was here, and she wanted him here. He never wanted to leave this room, this bed, or her side. When she was finally asleep in her arms, he kissed her forehead. He thought of whispering 'I love you' but something stopped him.

"I love you, Zack," she whispered as she snuggled in close to him. "I love you."

***

"Mr. McGill?" Beth asked as she brought him back to the present. "My great-grandmother was a Lesbian?"

"I think the proper word is bi-sexual," Zack said.

"You seem to understand and accept these things," she said. "What I mean is, well."

"For someone my age," Zack smiled. "Your generation thinks that you were the first ones to think up 'these things' as you put it. Society during the 1890s and the early 1900s was more open minded than your generation is now."

"I suppose I should read my history books," Beth said a little embarrassed.

"Your generation makes everything so political," Zack said. "When we can accept and love people for what they are, and leave the politics and religion out of it, then the hate in this country will stop." He stopped and Beth saw a tear in his eye. "That is my greatest dream for your generation. You need to do better than we did."

"Working the political arena is one of the few ways that we can get people's attention," Beth said defensively.

"Most folks only pay attention to what affects them directly," Zack said. "Do you think some farmer in Iowa cares about homosexuals in San Francisco dying of Aids? As long as things don't touch their lives, they remain blissfully ignorant."

"You're a very wise man, Mr. McGill," Beth said.

"I've had years, and experiences you can hardly imagine, Beth," he said. "When you reach my age, you'll have that, too."

***

Beth thought about Jenny and how quickly she got involved with the group from Berkley. Bret and Steve had introduced them to many of their friends. Steve was taking a few classes at Berkley and they had joined Beth and Jenny under the Golden Gate Bridge for their commitment ceremony. Beth started her job and the PR firm and Jenny found a job at Berkley. She was working for a Professor that taught Political Science. The money wasn't that good, but the networking opportunities were unlimited.

They got into a nice rhythm in their lives. They had a large circle of acquaintances, and some close friends that they could depend on. Bret and Steve were dependable and reliable. They knew their way around the city, and Steve had political contacts. He and Jenny had gotten involved with a group called "ACT UP" who made a statement about Gay issues at every opportunity.

Bret and Beth were concerned about this. This group, even though their intentions were good, would have run-ins with the police. On two separate occasions they had to bail them out of jail. Jenny and Steve thought this was bringing their cause to the forefront. What it was doing was irritating some important people and some of these actions had come to the attention of the White House, but Ronald Reagan chose to ignore it.

"The man thinks he's making a movie," Steve said. "He hasn't acknowledged that there's something killing the gay population. He won't admit it until it bites him in the ass."

Jenny kept pushing Beth to look for her family. She would spend nights and weekends at the library looking at history of the northwest. She read so many things about logging, Native American rights, and some of the political movements, but never really connected the dots. She had read the name Monroe several times, but had no idea that this was her legacy. She wouldn't know this for a few years. She only knew that she started looking for her roots some 5 years ago.

She kept in touch with Steve and Karen, who were doing their own networking to help Beth in her search. They were going to stop in San Francisco on their way back from Seattle. They had friends that they were going to visit and wanted to see Beth.

"It's time you told them, Beth," Jenny said. "It's time to stop hiding."

"I guess you're right," Beth said as she sat in the bathtub with

Jenny. She poured them both some more wine and leaned back. "It's my life, and I'm happy. I should tell them, and I will tell them. They said they would be in around 6pm tomorrow."

"It's time, Beth," Jenny whispered.

Steve and Karen did arrive, and at 6pm. They had always been very punctual. It was good to see them. They looked wonderful. Beth had made reservations at one of her favorite restaurants for dinner. The reservations were for 8pm so they would have time to rest a bit.

Jenny arrived about 6:30pm and said her hello to the Klumps. She knew that Beth had not talked to them yet and didn't know when she had planned to do that. Jenny decided to not push the issue. Beth would have to do this in her own time. Jenny got cleaned up and they left for the restaurant at 7:30pm. The food was excellent, the night was warm and beautiful, and Beth told them over dessert.

"Well," Steve said. "I was wondering how long it would take you to tell us."

"I never wanted to hurt you," Beth started.

"We only want you to be happy," Karen said. "I knew the first time we met Jenny, and if she makes you happy, that's all we ever wanted for you. We love you Beth, we always have loved you, and always will."

The rest of the evening Beth finally relaxed. She talked about her job and Jenny talked about all of the things going on in politics.

"Beth," Steve said as he took an envelope from his pocket. "I have something for you." He handed the packet to her. "Before you open it, let me tell you how this came to be. I have been corresponding with some businessmen in Seattle for some time. I asked them if they could do some investigation for me on your family. What's in the envelope is what I have so far."

Beth opened the envelope and found the name and birth dates of her grandmother and great-grandmother. There were also directions on historical museums to check into for more information. "Steve, Karen, I don't know what to say. Why did you do this?"

"It's important to know your roots," Karen said. "I have a feeling that there's a lot there. It appears as though you have a rich family history. You really need to learn what you can on your own. What is in this packet is your starting place."

Beth looked at Jenny. She was in shock over the information. She finally realized that the Klumps did love her. They knew she had a burning desire to learn about her family and they used their resources to help make that happen. They went back to the apartment and talked into the night. After coffee and breakfast the next morning, Steve and Karen left. Beth watched them drive up the street and turn the corner. She began to cry. She wasn't sad, but extremely happy because she realized how lucky she was that they found her.

***

Four years had passed since the twins were born. They grew up happy and healthy. Edmundson was quiet and reflective, and William was precocious and inquisitive. The boys followed their father everywhere, adored their mother, and always obeyed their 'Missy Sally' without hesitation. As Sara had predicted, Eddy's eyes stayed blue. He was his father through and through. Will was always playing and creating things. He liked Gus and would ask him a million questions when working on logging equipment.

Emily started the hospital with Tom Eichorn's wife, Kathleen. Helga worked with them everyday. She even got some formal training from Emily and Kathleen as a nurse. Their Clinic/ Hospital drew people from 20 miles away. Emily and Kathleen worked well together and Kathleen had connections in San Francisco for supplies and equipment.

Jack Regan was still in the area. He had, with the urging of Emily, cleaned up his logging camps. He had proven to be an honorable gentleman. Emily had accompanied him to dinner on several occasions. Edmundson and Sara had even joined them. After Jack learned to relax and let his true nature show, he found he could learn about the logging business from Monroe. He had started to work with the local tribes to save the land. The money didn't seem as important to him as everyone thought it was. He was still hopelessly in love with Emily, but knew that this would never develop into anything. Jack had cleaned up some of his crews and had required a better code of conduct with his employees. He had even asked Sally's son, Joseph to help him put together a crew for re-planting. Joseph decided that Daniel was the one to do the job. Jack was pleased with the men he had hired and the job they were doing.

The only problem was the seedlings. Jack bought these from the stock that Mary had put together. The added work was more than Mary could handle. She had talked with Suzy and with the local tribe's help, the seedling operation was moved. The Snoqualmie tribe would start, care for, and sell the seedlings as a tribal business. Charlie and Mary would maintain their seedlings for re-planting of this land.

The Snoqualmie tribe had the land, personnel, and needed the income. Sara worked with them and with Jack and a war between the logging community and the tribe was averted. Monroe was amazed at her power of persuasion and when she finally got all the interested parties together in one room, this was when Monroe saw her skill. Local politicians, tribal elders, and businessmen came to an agreement where everyone got what they wanted.

"Your wife is an incredible woman, Edmundson," Jack told him after the meeting broke up. "She looked at every point of view and with a compromise from everyone, worked out a plan where we could all win."

"She is incredible," Monroe agreed. "I knew that the first time I met her. Jack, she may need your support in another venture." He waited for Jack's response. He nodded his head and Monroe continued. "She wants to build a school for the local Indian children. She knows that the whites don't want them in the same school, but they should be educated in the same manner."

"I honestly agree with you," Jack said. "That was one thing I could never understand back in Georgia. They freed the slaves after the Civil War, but wouldn't allow them to get an education. How could they ever hope to make a life for themselves without it? She'll have my support."

"You're a good man, Jack," Monroe said as he shook his hand.

Emily and Kathleen were in the process of patching up a saloon girl who had been severely beaten by one of the patrons. Upon questioning, the man who assaulted her worked for Jack Regan. This man had been in other altercations since coming to Snoqualmie, and had spent time in the local jail. Burt Travers had arrested him again for drunk and disorderly, but was unaware of the assault.

"Let's keep her here tonight," Emily said. "I'll stay here with her."

"No," Kathleen said. "You go home. Katie, from the saloon, said she would stay. If there's a problem, I'm just down the street. You've had a long day, Emily. You need to talk with Monroe about this incident. We need to make sure these girls stay safe, no matter what their profession is."

Emily checked on her patient before she left. As she left the office she got angry. Why did men feel the need to hit, beat, and abuse women? Is it something they learn growing up, or were they just assholes? As she rode toward the house she saw Jack Regan riding toward town.

"Emily," he smiled. "How nice to see you, let me accompany you to the house."

"Thank you, Jack," she said. They arrived back at the house to find Monroe sitting on the porch with Sara and the boys.

"How nice to see you again so soon, Jack," Monroe smiled. He looked at Emily and knew she wasn't happy about something. "Boys, why don't you go ask Missy Sally when dinner will be ready." They went into the house. "What's wrong, Emily?"

"Kathleen and I patched up one of the saloon girls," she said. "It was the work of one of your employees, Jack."

"Don't tell me," he said. "It had to be Bobby Palmer."

"You got it," Emily started. "He's in jail right now for drunk and disorderly. The sheriff is not aware that he almost beat this poor girl to death."

"Let me know what her bill comes to, Emily," Jack said. "I'll pay for this, and he'll be fired as soon as I can get back to town. I warned him about his drinking. When he drinks he gets nasty and I told him the next time he gets into trouble, he's gone."

"Thank you, Jack," Emily said. "I hate this kind of behavior."

"I do to," Monroe said. "I'm glad you're taking care of this. We need to stick together on this. We have to let the logging crews and the sheriff to realize that this kind behavior will not be tolerated."

"Would you join us for dinner, Jack?" Emily asked.

"I'd be honored, Ma am," he said.

They enjoyed a wonderful meal. Jack was amazed at how well the boys behaved. They were quiet, respectful, and ate without being messy. Sally, Emily, and Sara cleared the table and the boys got ready for bed. They went to the study and kissed their father good night and scampered up the stairs. Jack watched these two in wonder. What had he missed not having children?

"You're a lucky man, Monroe," he said. "You have a wonderful family. You know I never wanted children or to be married. But spending time around here is making me rethink my decision." He stood up and shook his hand. "I'd best get home. I want to stop at the jail and talk to the sheriff before I go back to the hotel and I'll deal with Bobby."

"I know you'll do what's right, Jack," Monroe said. Emily and Sara joined them in the study. They said good night to Jack as he left. They chatted for a while and Emily excused herself to go to her room. Sara knew that these things upset her. She spoke with Monroe and said she would spend the night with Emily. He kissed her gently and told her good night.

Sara could read Emily's moods and knew she needed her tonight.

Sara needed her also. She knocked on the door, and entered her room. She had been staring out the window and Sara put her arms around her. She held her closely and kissed her hair.

"I feel so bad for this girl," she said. "She was hurt pretty bad, and for what? This girl could have died because some guy couldn't control his drinking or sexual aggression. It makes me angry."

"I know, honey," Sara comforted. She removed Emily's dress, brushed her hair, and tucked her into bed. Emily grabbed her hand. "I'll be back in a minute. I want to make sure the boys are asleep." Sara walked down the hall and saw both boys snug in their beds. She grabbed her sleeping gown from the bedroom and went back to Emily's room. She quietly opened the door and closed it behind her. She removed her dress and was ready to put on her sleeping gown.

"Leave that off," Emily smiled. Sara blew out the candle and slipped between the sheets. Each time with Sara was better than before. She never tired of her and the excitement never diminished.

Sara awoke to find Emily gone. She put on her robe and went downstairs. The mantle clock was chiming 5am and Emily was sitting by the fireplace. She did this when she had things on her mind. She seemed to find answers in the flames. She turned and saw Sara and smiled.

"Women have no rights," Emily said quietly. "If I had told the sheriff about his assault on this girl, nothing would have been done. Why should they do anything? She's just a whore. She sleeps with men for money so why should they be treated any better than an animal?"

"One thing at a time, Emily," Sara whispered. "Most people thought and still think that the Indians are no better than animals. Little by little the businessmen, loggers, and politicians are recognizing their worth and their gifts with the land. It will be some time before women are given the rights that belong to them. We will have to fight for them. We will win, but it takes time."

"Monroe and Jack will not let this man go unpunished, will they?" Emily asked.

"They will do what they can, within the boundaries of the law," Sara said. "Are you taking about punishment or revenge?"

"I'm taking about justice," Emily said. Sara heard the front door open and saw Sally.

"Everyone is up early today," Sally said with a smile. "You all right Miss Emily?"

"Yes," she smiled. "Just couldn't sleep, but thank you for asking. I think I'll go get dressed. I want to get into the hospital to check on my patient." Sara followed Emily upstairs.

"Don't let this eat you up inside, Emily," Sara said as she closed the door. "Is there more to this than what you're telling me?"

"No," she responded flatly. Emily looked into Sara's eyes and knew that she couldn't lie to her. "It brings back some memories from my days in Boston. It brings back some of the violence I saw men do to women. It was hard to see then, and it's hard to see now." Sara kissed her gently, hugged her closely, and then left the room.

Emily rode into town and was at the hospital by 7am. She saw Kathleen was already there and that concerned her. She hoped Kathleen hadn't spent all night there.

"How's our patient?" she asked.

"Well, it was a rough night for her," Kathleen said. "But I think she'll be all right. I don't want to let her go, yet. I'd like to keep her here for another couple of days."

"That's fine," Emily said. "I'll let the saloon owner know that she'll be out of commission for the next few days. Jack Regan said he would pay the bill for her medical care. He also said he would fire Bobby Palmer."

"The less men like him around, the better," Kathleen added. Helga came in the door and suggested they go get some breakfast at the hotel. They both agreed that the suggestion was a good one. They left the hospital and walked across the street. Randolph Murphy saw them walk in.

"Good morning, Doctors," he said. "You're in early today. I hope everything is all right?" They nodded a response. "Can I bring you coffee?"

"Yes," Kathleen said. "Is it too early for breakfast?"

"No," he replied. "Tricia will come out and take your order."

Emily was picking at her food when she saw Jack Regan walk in. He saw her and tipped his hat. He spoke with Randolph for a few minutes and then walked over to their table.

"May I join you ladies?" he asked.

"Please," Kathleen said.

"I just got back from the jail. Bobby Palmer no longer works for me," he said. "I suggested, strongly, that he clear out of town. I paid him his wages through yesterday and told him not to set foot in any of my camps." He drank some coffee. "How's the girl?"

"She'll be okay, but won't be able to work for a while," Emily said.

"I'd like to see her," he said. "May I?"

"Sure," Emily said. "We can do that now. I'm finished here."

"You didn't eat much, Emily," Kathleen said. "Are you feeling all right."?

"I'm fine," she replied. "Just didn't sleep well. Don't have much of an appetite."

They walked across the street and entered the office. Helga was waiting and said she had changed the patient's bandages. Emily took Jack upstairs to see Maggie. He approached the bed and removed his Stetson.

"I'm Jack Regan," he said. "I'm sorry for what Bobby did to you. I'll be taking care of all your medical bills."

"Thank you, Mr. Regan, but I don't want to be in debt to anyone," she said. "I'll take care of my own bills." Emily was surprised at her response. She was surprised at her clear and concise English, the way she could express herself, and how adamant she was.

"Can you read and write, Maggie?" he asked.

"I may be a whore, but I've finished school," she said. "I'm not stupid."

"I meant no disrespect, Ma am," he apologized. "I'm looking for someone to help me at my office. I'll pay you a fair wage and it will get you out of the saloon." He paused and looked at her. "That's no place for a lady." Emily looked at Jack totally surprised by his actions.

"I'll take the job, Mr. Regan," Maggie said. "I must warn you that many of your loggers are my regulars. This all stops here and now. I'll need your support on this point."

"You'll have it. What is your last name?" he asked.

"Thompson, Maggie Thompson," she replied.

"You can come over to my office when you're well Miss Thompson, and I'll show you what you need to do for me," he said. "Get better soon. I need the help."

Emily walked downstairs with Jack and was still surprised with the turn of events. He explained that he had needed help for sometime, and this way everyone would win. Jack didn't admit to Emily that he had seen Maggie from afar and found her attractive. He had given up whores when he met Emily in the hope that she would allow him to get closer. He knew that this was not going to happen and now was thinking about finding someone to spend the rest of his life with. Maggie was attractive and she was alive. She spoke her mind and he liked that. He knew she could handle his loggers without much help, but somehow wanted to protect her. He couldn't explain this. He'd not felt this way before.

"You did a wonderful thing, Jack," Emily said. "You never cease to surprise me."

"I sometimes surprise myself," he said as he left the office.

Emily spent the rest of her day seeing patients. She saw Samuel and Mary in town. She had gone into her office and then heard the door open. She heard Helga start to laugh and came to the waiting room in time to see Helga hugging Mary.

"Hi," Emily said. "What brings you here today?"

"Will you take a look at Mary?" Samuel said. "We're hoping she's pregnant."

"Absolutely," Emily said. "Come back with me Mary."

They walked into the exam room and Emily confirmed what Mary and Samuel had hoped for. She was indeed pregnant, and from Emily's calculations around 3 months. She was still suffering some morning sickness, but not as bad as Sara had experienced. Samuel hugged Emily and Helga.

"Hug your wife, Samuel," Helga said. "Congratulations to you both." They left the office and it looked like they were floating on air. Emily was so happy for them. They had wanted children from the moment they were wed. Emily looked across the street and saw Suzy hugging Mary and Samuel. She was so animated so Emily assumed that she had already been told the news. She told Kathleen that she was going to head back home around 4pm. She had been tired all day and wanted to go to bed. All was quiet at the hospital, and Maggie would be all right tonight. Katie from the saloon said she would be in to sit with her again.

"Are you feeling all right, Emily?" Kathleen asked again. "You look a little pale."

"Stop being a doctor for a while," Emily smiled. "I'm just tired."

Emily walked across the street and told Samuel that she would be home a little after 4pm. They asked if she wanted them to wait.

"No," she replied. "I'll be an hour behind you. Go spread your happy news." She went back across the street and spoke with Kathleen a few minutes. She told her about Mary and Samuel. She had hoped that was the reason for their visit. She checked in on Maggie, grabbed her bag, and it was such an effort to mount her horse. She was feeling queasy but decided she had nothing a good night's sleep wouldn't fix.

She headed out of town and had the feeling she was being watched. It wasn't the same feeling she had when Bigfoot was near. It was different. The hair on the back of her neck seemed to tingle. "Jesus, Emily" she said aloud. "Get yourself together, and stop being paranoid." She rode on and was about a mile from the house when Bobby Palmer appeared in her path. He grabbed the reins to her horse and pulled her off. She hit the ground with a thud and had the wind knocked out of her. She felt a sharp jab in her side.

"You bitch," he yelled. "You got me fired!"

"You got yourself fired, Bobby," she said as she struggled to her feet and tried to free herself from his grip. She could smell the bourbon. She knew she was in trouble and didn't know what to do. She stopped fighting him hoping he would relax his grip. "Bobby, this is going to solve nothing."

"After I finish with you, I have a little score to settle with Maggie," he slurred. He drew back and hit her in the face, which dropped her to her knees. She was trying to shake off the blackness that was starting to take her over when he caught her in the left temple with another blow. This put her on her back in the middle of the road, but still not completely unconscious. She could feel him begin to tear at her clothes as she still tried to fight him off. She did manage to scratch his face before he hit her one more time. After that she heard, felt and saw nothing.

As Bobby pulled out his knife and was going to make short work of Emily's clothes. He had planned to carve on her a while when he heard a rustle in the bushed behind him. He turned to see a large hairy figure that grabbed him and threw him about 15 feet. The creature stood over Emily and Bobby decided to mount his horse and leave with all haste. Emily's horse had taken off for the house.

Samuel saw Emily's horse standing by the barn and thought that she was home. He took the horse back into the barn and figured she went to the house already. Sara had a funny feeling while she was talking to Monroe.

"What's wrong?" he asked.

"I don't know," she said as she walked outside. She stood on the porch and looked slowly around and spotted the large creature. She met his eyes and he didn't look away. He walked for a bit and never looked away from her. Monroe saw this, too. "We need to follow."

He was never more than 50 yards ahead of them. As they turned a slight corner, they could see another creature standing over Emily. They stopped and Sara bolted toward her. The creatures disappeared into the woods. After reaching the spot where Emily lay, Sara saw she wasn't dead. The blood was coming from a split lip and she could see the bruising already starting over her eye.

"Oh no, Monroe," she said as she kneeled over Emily. "Get the wagon, and some blankets. I'll stay with her."

Chapter 11

Monroe and Sara got Emily into town. She hadn't regained consciousness at all. Sara held her head in her lap. He yelled to Helga as they went by Ivan's. She came out and got into the wagon.

"My God," she said. "What happened?"

"I don't know, but we need to get Kathleen as soon as we can," Monroe said.

"She may still be at the clinic," Helga said. She could see the light on in the office and Helga ran to get the door. "Bring her in here," she motioned to Monroe and Sara. Kathleen appeared from the office and saw Emily.

"What happened?" Kathleen asked.

"All I know is that her horse came home without her," Sara said.

"Was she thrown?" Kathleen asked as she started to remove Emily's torn dress.

"I don't think so," Sara said. "This looks like a fist imprint on her face."

"I think you're right, Sara," Kathleen agreed. "Why don't you wait outside and let Helga and I treat Emily."

"No," Sara said bluntly. "I will stay and help."

For the next hour Kathleen took extreme caution with Emily. She had a broken wrist, and some bruised ribs. Her face was swollen but nothing else was broken beside the wrist. Kathleen was concerned about her not waking up. She was afraid of a concussion or a skull fracture. With the way her dress was ripped, Kathleen was concerned that she may have been sexually assaulted. She performed a full exam and found no evidence of this.

Kathleen had finished her exam and Sara wouldn't leave her side. She helped put a clean gown on her and wash her up. Kathleen went out and talked to Monroe and asked him to help move her to a bed that they had downstairs just beyond the treatment room.

"I'll stay here with her tonight," Kathleen said. "Why don't you both go home and get some rest."

"No," Sara and Monroe answered in unison. "I'm not leaving her side," Sara said. Kathleen knew better than to fight her on this.

"I'm going home for a bit," Kathleen said. "Come to get me if there's any change or if she wakes up. I'll be back in an hour."

Sara sat next to Emily for the next four hours. Monroe went over to the hotel to get a drink. It was 10pm when Emily started to stir. A low moan came from her as she tried to move. Sara stood over her as she opened her eyes. Emily had problems focusing at first and then Sara's beautiful face came into view.

"Where am I?" she asked.

"You're at the clinic," Sara responded. "Monroe and I found you, with the help of our friends. One came to the house to get us. We followed him to where you were being guarded by another."

"Did Bobby rape me?" Emily asked.

"No," Sara replied. "Kathleen checked everything. Did you say Bobby? You mean Bobby Palmer did this to you?"

"Yes," Emily answered. Kathleen appeared in the doorway and smiled at Emily.

"How you feeling?" she said as she sat down on the bed. "Watch my finger." She did a quick check and watched her eyes. "It looks like you have a broken wrist and some bruised ribs but that's all. The bruises on your face are ugly but not terminal. They will turn several colors before they heal."

"Sara, where's my horse?" Emily asked. "She got home before you did," Sara said. "She's safe and sound in barn. Don't worry about that right now." Monroe poked his head in and then came around the corner.

"Thank God you're okay," he said as he bent down and kissed Emily's forehead.

"Why don't you all leave us for a few minutes," Kathleen said. "I want to talk to Emily for a few minutes." Kathleen sat down on the bed as they left. "Watch my finger again, honey." Emily did as instructed. "I think you have a concussion. I'm going to make sure you are awakened every hour tonight. There's nothing else we can do accept wait the next 24 hours."

"What time is it?" Emily asked.

"I've got 11pm," Kathleen answered. "From what I could get from Sara, they found you around 5:30pm. You've been unconscious for the last 5 hours. You're not to leave this bed. If I find out that you have, I will beat you severely myself. Now, tell me what you remember." Emily told her what she could remember of the incident.

As they left the room, Sara started talking quietly to Monroe. She told him that Bobby Palmer was responsible for this. He attacked her where they found her.

"I think he meant to kill her, but was stopped," Sara said. "I found this lying next to her when we found her." Sara pulled the knife out of her skirt. "It doesn't belong to Emily, or me."

"Our friends kept him from killing her," Monroe said. "I'm going to find Jack first thing in the morning and get Burt Travers to find this guy. He's dangerous and must be stopped."

"I'm staying with Emily tonight," Sara said. "Mary has the boys. Sally is close if she needs help."

Kathleen came from Emily's room and said it would be best if she stay the night. Sara sent Monroe home and stayed by Emily's side.

"I thought he was going to kill me," she said weakly. "I don't know why he didn't. I couldn't have stopped him."

"He was stopped by our large friends, Emily," Sara said. "They were watching out for you as I said they would." She held her hand. "Go to sleep Emily, I'll be here if you need me." She nodded off to sleep and Sara thought about what life would be like if she had lost her. When she saw the crumpled heap in the road she was praying to the Great Spirit that she wasn't dead. Sara, for the first time in her life, was angry enough to kill. She wanted Bobby Palmer dead, but she wanted him to suffer first. The tears of relief and anger started to fall. She leaned forward and put her head on the bed and went to sleep, too.

Kathleen sent Emily home the next day and told her she didn't want to see her in the office for at least a week. She would ride out to check on her in a few days unless someone notified her sooner. Monroe brought the wagon into town and before they left for the house, Jack stopped in. Monroe had found him in the hotel and told him about Emily. Jack was getting ready to get Maggie who was also ready to go home.

"Looks like Bobby keeps this place busy," he said. "I'm sorry, Emily. Is there anything I can do for you?"

"Keep an eye on Maggie, Jack. I remember Bobby saying he had a score to settle with her, too. I fear for her safety," Emily said. "Get Burt to find this guy."

"Already done," Jack said. "He's put a $500.00 bounty out on him. Monroe and I are going to ride with the posse."

Emily slowly stood up and the room started to spin. Jack picked her up and said it would be easier if she were carried to the wagon. It was a sunny warm day and there was a mattress and blankets in the back so Emily could travel in comfort. Jack carefully put her into the wagon. Sara got into the back with her and Charlie slowly pulled away.

Jack and Monroe went over to the sheriff's office and left with the posse. The ride home jarred Emily's ribs and seemed to take forever.

She was glad when the wagon stopped. She was queasy to the point of vomiting, but knew that would hurt too much. Samuel, Mary, and the boys greeted Emily as the wagon stopped. Sally had set up a bedroom downstairs so Emily wouldn't have to climb stairs for a few days.

Charlie carefully helped her sit up, carried her into the house, and to the room he had once occupied. The boys came in to see if "Auntie" was okay. Eddy gently touched her bruised face.

"Hurt?" he asked.

"Yes, Sweetie," she said. "A little bit."

"Daddy will find the bad man, Auntie," Will said. "Eddy and I will take care of you."

"Let's leave Auntie rest, boys," Sara said. "You can see her later."

Will said good-bye and left the room. Eddy gently kissed Emily's cheek and followed behind Will. Sara looked at Emily and smiled. She got Emily into some comfortable clothes and tucked her into bed.

"Are you hungry?" Sara asked.

"Starving," Emily said after the nausea passed. "I didn't get a chance to eat last night."

"I'll fix us some breakfast," Sara said as she left the room. Emily watched as she left. Sara's face was the first thing she saw when she woke up from this nightmare. It was the only thing she wanted to see. When Bobby was hitting her and ripping at her clothing she wanted Sara to save her. In a way she did. Her relationship with the Sasquatch spared her life. Emily could hear Will's chatter outside. She could see the tall trees outside of the window and with everything that happened this was still the only place she wanted to be. The only thing missing was Sara's body close to hers.

Emily was getting tired of lying in bed by that afternoon. Her stomach had been upset since breakfast. She felt getting up would maybe settle her stomach. Sara helped her get up and took her outside for a short walk. They went to Mary's house. She saw them walking down the pathway and came to greet them.

"I'm glad you're okay, Emily," Mary said.

"I'm fine, Mary," Emily said as she leaned on Sara. "I wanted to know how you are feeling. Has the morning sickness gotten any worse?"

"I didn't have any this morning," Mary said. "Samuel is like an old woman. He thinks pregnancy is a disease and I should stay in bed for the next 6 months."

Emily started to feel a little weak so they sat for a while on Mary's porch. Samuel arrived and said he just saw Monroe and Jack arrived at the house. Sara decided to get Emily back to her bed. Samuel walked on the other side to help support Emily. He was anxious to see if they found Bobby. Emily's pace was slow and cautious. By the time they got back to the house she was winded and pale.

"Let me sit on the porch for a while, Sara," she said. Monroe and Jack met them and helped Emily up the stairs.

"You shouldn't be out of bed, Emily," Monroe scolded.

"You may be right, but the fresh air has done me a world of good," she said.

"We found Bobby Palmer," Jack said quietly.

"Is he in jail?" Emily asked.

"No," Monroe said. "We found what was left of him because it looks like he met up with a bear or mountain lion sometime last night. He was about a half mile from the falls."

"I wish I could say I was sorry," Sara said. "But I'm not. He got what he deserved."

"I got Maggie settled in the hotel this morning," Jack said. "I'll let her know that Bobby is not someone to worry about anymore. Thanks for your help, Monroe. Emily," he said as he tipped his hat, "let me know if you need anything. Take it easy and get well." With that he turned, mounted his horse, and rode away. About that time the boys came up on the porch and joined Emily.

"Will you be all right out here for a few minutes?" Monroe said to Emily.

"I'll stay with her," Eddy said as he held Emily's hand. "I can take care of Auntie." Emily gave Monroe a smile and he and Sara went into the house. They went to the library and Monroe closed the door.

"Sara," he said quietly. "I don't think that it was a bear or a mountain lion that got to Bobby."

"What do you think killed him?" she asked.

"Our 'friends' I think," he said. "Sara his one arm was torn from its socket, and his neck was broken." He looked at Sara. "Everyone in the posse decided it was a bear, but I know it was something else." He paused and looked out the window at Emily. "If the community would get a hint of this they would hunt them down and kill them. I don't want this to become a sporting event or a blood bath. I never want anyone to know about this."

"I think you're right, Monroe," Sara agreed. "We must never say anything to anyone, especially to Emily. She would feel responsible, although justice was imparted."

"Have you ever heard of them taking revenge?" Monroe asked. "Were there any stories from your tribe about this?"

"Some, many years ago," Sara said. "Remember, Monroe, they are very protective of us and this area. We will have to watch and see what happens."

"I'm glad they're our friends," Monroe said. "I'd hate to think of what they would do if they didn't like us. Let's get Em back to bed. She looks very pale."

She was ready to go back to bed. She had gotten very pale and the nausea hit again. Monroe picked her up and she put her head on his shoulder. The walk tired her out and she stayed in bed for the rest of the afternoon. Eddy never left her side. He played quietly in her room even though Will was urging him to come outside. He just shook his head and continued to play in Emily's temporary room. Sara would check on her every hour or so and Eddy would whisper, "She's sleeping, Mommy." He would then smile.

Sara woke Emily at 6pm for dinner. She wasn't hungry and had started to run a fever. Sara knew this wasn't good. She was still pale and complained of nausea. Monroe sent Samuel into town to get Kathleen Eichorn to come to the house. Within an hour Tom and Kathleen had arrived.

Kathleen did a quick exam and Sara wouldn't leave her side. Emily had rebound pain in her lower right side.

"This has nothing to do with your recent injuries," she said. "You've got Appendicitis. We need to take it out."

"What timing. Can you do that at the office?" Emily asked.

"I have all the equipment, and the training, but need an extra pair of hands," Kathleen said. "I'll get Helga to help. Hope this kind of stuff doesn't make her sick."

They loaded her into the wagon and headed back to town. Sara was thinking that she should have never let her get up. Emily explained that this had nothing to do with the other. It would have happened whether she was injured or healthy. Emily explained to Sara how these things work and it could happen to anyone. She also was glad that Kathleen had been trained as a surgeon.

This was one time when Sara couldn't stay. Helga followed Kathleen's instructions to the letter and boiled all of the instruments. She carefully laid them out in the order that Kathleen instructed. Kathleen was ready to put Emily to sleep and asked Sara to wait with

Monroe. She kissed Emily tenderly on the lips and walked out of the room.

"Be very careful with the Ether, Helga," Kathleen said. "Don't put too much on the mask because it can cause burning in the nose and throat. Be careful not to breathe it, or you will go to sleep, too. Think of a clock, drip, drip, and drip, about every couple of seconds. If you see that the mask is soaked, wait to add more."

Helga started the Ether and within a minute Emily was asleep. Kathleen's hands worked quickly and expertly. Helga expected to see more blood and was fascinated by the process. Kathleen talked to Helga and explained everything that she was doing. By doing this she was training Helga and also making sure she completed each step in the surgical procedure.

"Here's our little culprit," she said as she showed Helga the Appendix. "See how it's dark red and swollen? It had not burst yet and that's a good thing. People can die from the infection after it bursts." She tossed it into a metal dish, irrigated the area, and carefully closed each layer of muscle she had cut through. She had finished the last of the external stitches and asked Helga to rinse the Ether mask and open a window.

She placed a bandage over the incision and put a gown on her. She then started to gently rub her face to wake her.

"Emily," she said. "Come on, open your eyes." Slowly she started to make noise, woke up, and coughed. "Everything went well. It hadn't burst and you'll be fine. I'm going to get Sara, okay?"

Emily nodded her head and Kathleen went to the waiting room and let everyone know that she would be fine. She told Sara she could see her. Monroe and Tom came in to transfer her into the same bed she just left that morning.

"I can't seem to get rid of you," Kathleen chuckled. "You're going to be here for about a week this time. Better make yourself comfortable." She turned to Sara. "I'll stay with her tonight. Helga can spell me around midnight. She'll sleep most of the night, but I'd like you to come by in the morning to give Helga a break. Is that possible?" Sara nodded a response. "Get some sleep, Sara. Emily is going to have a rough day tomorrow, and that's when I'll need you."

Sara talked to Emily a bit before she went back to sleep. The ride home was quiet. Monroe knew that Sara was worried about Emily, but she had complete confidence in Kathleen. When Sara did speak she wondered why this was happening to Emily.

"Sometimes there's no explanation, Sara," Monroe said as he put his arm around her shoulder. "We can't ask ourselves why or how. We have to accept what the Great Spirit gives to us and hope it makes us strong. Emily is strong and is meant to be with us for a long time. The Great Spirit sent us Kathleen Eichorn for a reason. We must continue to see all the good things and not concentrate on the bad." They continued up the path to the house. When they got home, Sally had fed the boys and Eddy was waiting patiently on the porch. It was past his bedtime, but Sally let both of them stay up until their parents got home. They told them that Auntie had gotten sick and that Doctor Kathleen had made her better.

"I should have taken better care of her," Eddy said and started to cry.

"Oh, son," Monroe said as he picked him up and hugged him. "This is not something you could have stopped. You did a wonderful job of watching Auntie."

"She will be home in a few days," Sara said. "You boys need to go to bed. Come on and I'll read you a story." Eddy had stopped crying so Sara and Monroe stayed with them for a while. They loved their bedtime stories and would always ask many questions. They had both gone to sleep before Sara had finished. She kissed each of them, as did Monroe, and blew out the lantern.

Sara arrived at the clinic at 8am. Kathleen was right and Emily had a horrible day. The Ether had caused her to vomit a few times and this was difficult with her bruised ribs. The Laudanum helped with the pain and by the afternoon Sara got some tea and toast in her. This settled her stomach down a bit and Emily could sleep. Kathleen watched Sara deal with this situation and admired the patience she had.

By her fourth day, Kathleen was pleased with her progress and said she could go home the following day. She would remove her stitches the next morning. Emily had already been up and slowly walking around the office. She had visits from Jack, Samuel, Mary, and Monroe even brought the boys in one day. Jacob and Suzy came over daily to check her progress. Patients had brought her bouquets of wild flowers that she placed around the clinic.

She had even received a telegram from her father asking how she liked being a patient. She didn't know how he found out, but Monroe confessed to sending her father a telegram that she was ill. He didn't mention the other little accident, which she was thankful for. Included in this telegram was the fact that her father would be visiting next spring. He was on his way to San Francisco to a conference and wanted to visit is daughter. "LOOKING FORWARD TO SEE WHAT YOU HAVE BUILT. LOVE, DAD" was the last line.

Kathleen removed Emily's stitches. Her incision looked good. Kathleen was an artist with a scalpel. There was very little redness and it was smaller than she had seen other surgeons use. Sara had brought the wagon and the boys with her. Eddy was still feeling very protective about Emily and he rode in the back with her. This first life she had ever brought into the world and he was taking care of her. There was something poetic about it.

Once she was home, she wouldn't hear of not using her own room. She told Sara the stairs would do her good to climb. She needed the exercise. Within two weeks she was back to her old self. Her wrist was the only thing that still cause her some discomfort. Her face had healed nicely and the bruising was gone.

She and Eddy would go for walks every day. Sara would join them most times, but on this day she was busy with her accounting and told them to go ahead. They walked toward the falls and Emily caught movement from the corner of her eye. Eddy had stopped and waved to the large creature. He looked at both of them and turned into the trees.

"Eddy," she said quietly. "Have you seen them before?"

"Yes, Auntie," he said. "I see them all the time."

"Did you know that they watch out for us?" she asked.

"Yes, they showed me and Will how to get home one day. We got lost and Willie got scared but he took us home," Eddy said.

"Did you tell anyone about that?" Emily asked.

"We told Mary, but she said we shouldn't tell any white people because they sometimes don't understand about things," he said.

"She was right Eddy," Emily said as she squeezed his hand. "Some white people don't understand. But I do. You can tell me anything."

They walked all the way to the falls. Eddy loved to watch the water and he loved the thunder. Emily sat under a tree and talked with Eddy. He was a combination of Sara and Monroe. He had his father's gentle caring spirit and had his mother's understanding of the spiritual things. He seemed to innately understand things without being told. He seemed to know when you were sad, angry, or in pain.

He would refuse Will's urging to get into trouble and would sometimes talk him out of doing things that he knew would anger his parents. Will was precocious and inquisitive. He loved to be with

Gus who was always looking to develop new or improve old equipment. Will was already a whiz with tools and could take anything apart. He hadn't mastered putting them back together yet, but was learning.

She heard a rustle from behind her and saw Jack riding up to them. Eddy turned and looked at him and smiled.

"What are you two doing way out here?" he said as he dismounted his horse.

"We went for a walk and we ended up here," she answered. "Eddy loves it here and so do I."

"You look like you're feeling good," Jack said.

"I feel great, but Kathleen wants me to take one more week off," Emily said. "I'm about to go stir crazy, so I take walks everyday. We never miss a day, do we, Eddy? We're ready to head back. Would you like to come with us?"

"Yes," Jack said. "There's something I want to talk to you about. You want to ride, Eddy?" He smiled and Jack put him in the saddle. "Emily, is there any chance we would be more than friends?"

"No, Jack," Emily answered honestly. "I consider you a good friend, but I feel nothing more."

"I had to ask," he said as he watched the ground. "I see men like Monroe and I begin to feel like I'm missing something. When I look at Eddy and Will, I know I'm missing something. I'd like to marry and have children. I know that's not what you want, but I have found someone that I would like to spend the rest of my life with."

"Maggie," Emily smiled.

"How did you know?" Jack asked.

"I'm not stupid or blind. I saw the way you responded when she talked to you," Emily said. "I assume she's working out at your office?" He nodded a yes. "She's had some rough spots in her life, but I don't think you can hold that against her."

"I don't judge women that harshly," Jack said. "She's a good person, Emily, and I just wanted you to know my intentions so there are no misunderstandings between us. I will admit to you that I have been in love with you from the first time I saw you. I know you don't want the things that I want, so I will love you as a friend. It would wound me deeply if I ever mislead you."

"Why, Mr. Regan," she said in a southern drawl. "What a gentleman you are."

"I have to admit Ma am," he said. "I didn't used to be. I have you to thank for that. You made me look at myself and I wanted to be someone you could respect. I did it at first to win your love, but, hopefully, I've won your respect and that's more important. Thank you, Emily."

"You're welcome, Jack," Emily responded.

By next spring all had returned to normal. Mary was heavy with child and Emily was awaiting the arrival of her father. She'd not seen him in 5 years and was nervous. She felt like she was 12 years old again. She and Kathleen and added more equipment after Emily's surgery. They wanted to make sure that they could handle anything that might come in. Emily was finishing the last of her day when the door opened. She looked up and saw her father.

"Pretty as ever," he smiled. She ran to his waiting arms and he hugged her tightly.

"You look wonderful, Papa," she said. "I've missed you." Kathleen appeared from around the corner. "This is my partner, Kathleen Eichorn."

"Nice to meet you Dr. McLaughlin," she said as she shook his hand. "Would you like a tour?"

"Yes," I would. "I'd like to see how you two manage so far from civilization." They started with the treatment room and their small surgery room. He was impressed with the equipment and the layout. They showed him their two exam rooms and then took him upstairs to the 6-bed ward they had developed. Each bed had a lantern, washbasin, storage for linens and a supply area for bandages and other medical needs.

Henry McLaughlin was impressed with the use of space. He noticed all of the built in cabinets and the craftsmanship that Charlie had put into them. He looked at the supply area and noticed that each was set up exactly the same. There would be no need to look for something. It would be in the same place in each cabinet.

"Helga is a stickler for consistency," Emily smiled. "She helps us around here. She has turned into a pretty good nurse."

"You girls have built a real modern facility out here," he admitted. "I know offices in Boston that aren't this organized or equipped."

"We've had to prepare for everything Dr. McLaughlin," Kathleen said. "We never know what's coming in the door and we don't have the luxury of having a large hospital just across town. The closest is in Seattle, and that's 40 miles away."

"Do you see many logging accidents?" he asked.

"Some," Emily said. "Not as many accidents as there used to be."

Kathleen said her good-bye and left the clinic. Emily walked out and locked the door behind her father. She showed him to a buggy that was waiting and they headed for the house. She had arranged with Monroe for him to stay with them for the next few days. She did stop by the falls before they went to the house. Her father was awestruck.

"It's so beautiful, Emily," he said. "I can see why you won't come back to Boston."

"I never want to be anywhere else, Papa," she said. "The people, friends, and my work are all here."

They arrived at the house and were greeted by the boys. Emily introduced Eddy and Will and they escorted them into the house. Monroe and Sara met them in the living room and said dinner was ready. Henry talked about the things happening in Boston and San Francisco. Monroe let Henry know about the political climate in Seattle. They even talked about the growth in this area in the last 5 years.

"Will you send your children to school in Seattle, Monroe?" Henry asked.

"No," he answered. "They will be schooled right here in Snoqualmie."

"What about college?" he asked.

"That will be their decision," Monroe said calmly. "I will neither force them nor deny them. What they want to do with their lives is their business. I can only guide them."

"From the time that Emily was 5 she was playing Doctor," he said as he patted her hand. "I don't think she ever wanted anything else."

They were finishing their coffee when Samuel came in breathless.

"I think it's time, Emily," Samuel said. "Mary wanted me to get you."

"Let me get my bag and I'll be right there," she said.

"Hi, I'm Samuel Washington," he said as he shook Henry's hand. "My wife is having a baby."

"Hello, Samuel Washington," Henry teased. "Congratulations."

"Want to lend a hand, Papa?" Emily asked. He nodded and smiled.

They got down to the house and Samuel had already started boiling water. Sara had brought towels and blankets for the little one. Mary was already working hard. Her water had broken and she wanted to push. Emily was surprised at the speed that this baby made her appearance. They had a beautiful baby girl. She was about 8 pounds and had lungs that could wake the dead. Henry did an exam on the baby while Emily finished up with Mary. Sara bathed the baby and wrapped her in a warm blanket.

"Here's your daughter, Mary," Sara smiled. "She's beautiful." Samuel walked in the room and looked at his daughter. "Come see your daughter, Samuel."

"She's so tiny," he said as Mary handed the bundle to him. "I'm afraid I'll break her."

"Name your daughter, Samuel," Mary said.

"Victoria Joy Washington," Samuel said as he kissed her. Sara noted the name, date, and time of birth in their Bible. Sara told Emily she would stay with Mary for a while and she could spend some time with her father. They gathered their things and walked back to the house.

"You're very good at what you do, Emily," he said. "I'm very proud of you. You didn't act like you were nervous at all. How did you know everything would go well?"

"I've seen Mary every month since she first got pregnant," Emily said. "This way, there are no surprises. I do this with all of my pregnant women."

"That's a good idea," he said. "What gave you the idea?"

"Sara," she said. "I suspected she was carrying twins and didn't want any other surprises. I found it works well with all women. I can see any problems that may arise during the pregnancy."

Emily checked on Mary and Victoria before she went to the office. They were doing beautifully. Samuel was the proud father, and Charlie the boasting grandfather. He was holding the baby when she arrived. She imagined how he must have been with Samuel. Victoria had Mary's light skin and Samuel's dark curly hair. Every baby she delivered seemed more beautiful than the one before.

She left the Washington house and went back to pick up her father. He and Monroe were deep in conversation about something. They saw her and smiled.

"Ready to go?" she asked her father.

Emily was sorry to see her father go. She sent her love with him to give to her mother. He hugged her long and hard before boarding the train. He turned as the train and waved as the train pulled away. She wasn't sure, but she thought she saw a tear in his eye. It was three weeks from the day he left that she got the telegram of his death.

A letter from her mother followed a few days later. He didn't go to a conference in San Francisco. He was seeing a doctor about his cancer. He didn't want her to know he was ill. He wanted to make sure that she was happy and living the life she had dreamed of. He seemed comforted in his final days that she would be all right. Enclosed in the letter was a draft for her share of his inheritance. She looked twice at the amount.

"My goodness," she said quietly. Monroe looked up at her. "My father left me this."

"Looks like you can add to the clinic now," he said as he looked at the draft for $75,000.00.

"I don't know how to handle this kind of money," she said.

"Talk to Tom," Monroe said. "He'll help you with that. He's a wise man."

"I was actually thinking of building a new clinic and hospital," she admitted. "I'd like everything on one level. I got the idea from Samuel's house. Gus has been talking about running water inside. That would be a benefit."

"There's a new builder in town you may want to talk to," Monroe said. "I've seen some of his work in Seattle, and it's very good." Emily paused for a minute and thought about the last time she saw her father. She remembered seeing him talking intently with Monroe.

"Did you know my father was ill?" she asked directly.

"He told me," Monroe confessed. "He asked me to not tell you. He wanted to spare you the worry." Monroe gave her a quick hug and left the room.

Emily talked to Sara at length that night. She was making plans and wanted to put the money her father had given her to good use. She told her what this would mean to the community and the future of the area. She went to sleep in Sara's arms. She had dreams of her childhood, her father, and her future. Some of the dream was clear and concise, but some of it was hazy as though she was looking into fog. She tried to find something in the fog but didn't know what she was looking for but continued to search just the same.

Chapter 12

A year had passed and the clinic was finished. There was a grand opening and everyone in town came in for a tour. Everything in the clinic was state-of-the-art. Kathleen had enlisted help from her friends in San Francisco on the latest and greatest equipment. Emily was proud of what she had accomplished. . Emily had formally trained nurses to staff the hospital for 24-hour coverage, if needed. Her father would have been proud. She still had a large piece of the money her father left her safely in her account.

Gus had designed a system for running water he had heard about. He made some modifications and the system worked well. He was getting requests from other places in town to help them with this modern convenience. He had also read a great deal on septic systems that were being used overseas. He hadn't tried any of these yet, but had hope.

Sara had been busy the last year working with the local tribes and started a school for the local tribes. She found teachers with Indian heritage, which encouraged the tribal members to send their children to school. Suzy and Sally had been instrumental in opening discussions with the tribal elders. They would keep their culture alive while still teaching the students all that they would need to survive in the white man's world.

Eddy and Will were getting ready to start school. Eddy had a fascination with books and could sound out some words. He had a great mind and could remember stories. Monroe used to leave out paragraphs to see if he would catch the omission. When he did this, Eddy always would tell him to read the whole story.

Will's forte was numbers. He had a good grasp of mathematics, which came from working with Gus and his uncle Charlie. Gus had worked with him and had taught him how to take things apart and put them together bit by bit. He taught Will how to lay things out in a pattern so they went back together the same way.

Life was good in Snoqualmie. Monroe's business was steady and consistent. All, including Ivan and Helga, were benefiting from the organization originally laid out 6 years prior. Samuel and Mary were happy and healthy as was little Victoria, who had just started to walk. She loved to be with her Grandpa and she was the light of his life. The big news around town was the upcoming marriage of Jack and Maggie.

They seemed destined to be together. Her work in Jack's office had proven to be exactly what his business needed. She had organized his books, bank accounts, and his life. He was finishing up a house just outside of town about 2 miles from Monroe's place. He was now ready to start his own family and so was Maggie. She saw the good qualities in Jack. Emily had witnessed some of these on brief occasions, but when he was with Maggie, he seemed to glow.

Kathleen and Tom were expecting their first child. Kathleen had been through a rough pregnancy and Emily had concerns about how well she would do because of her petite frame. They both decided that this child would be born in the new clinic/ hospital. Emily had purchased a birthing table and with Kathleen being so close, it seemed logical.

"A time will come," Kathleen said, "that all women will have babies in hospitals. Home births will become a thing of the past, but I don't see this happening for many years."

"We're just ahead of our time," Emily said. "We always have been."

Jack and Maggie wed with the whole town present. He was taking her to Seattle for their honeymoon. She had never been there and he wanted to show her the sights. They left in their decorated carriage that Monroe took charge of. He, graciously, put on the JUST MARRIED sign and tied the tin cans to the axle.

Tom found Emily before she left for home and told her that it was time. Kathleen had looked uncomfortable at the wedding, but being past one's due date will do that to a woman. Tom had taken her to the hospital where Helga was waiting.

Monroe kept Tom occupied in the waiting room while Kathleen was in labor. She was working hard but not progressing as well as Emily had hoped. By the next morning Kathleen was getting close to exhaustion.

"You're not progressing, Kathleen," Emily said. "The baby's heart rate is still good, but your water broke yesterday and still we have no baby. I'm going to give you one more hour. If this baby doesn't come, I'm going in to get it. Is that okay with you?"

"Yes," Kathleen said breathlessly. "I trust your judgment, Em."

Within 45 minutes Kathleen had started to progress and they had a fine baby boy in 2 hours. Emily could see why she was having some trouble. This boy had to weight 9 pounds and Kathleen was a small woman. She had some tearing that Emily needed to stitch and Helga cleaned up the little guy.

The birthing table worked well and made life easier on the doctor. It was a rather cold atmosphere to bring a life into the world, but Emily was glad she had all of her equipment available just in case. Helga handed the baby to Kathleen and she saw his head of red hair.

"He looks just like Tom," she smiled.

"Let me finish washing you down and we can let him in," Emily said. "This table is great."

"You didn't have to lay on it for the last 12 hours," Kathleen said. "Maybe we should let the labor happen in a bed, and move them to the table just before delivery."

"Point well taken," Emily said.

Helga showed Tom in to meet his son. There was no hesitation with him taking his son from Kathleen and holding him close. He kissed his red hair and wrinkled forehead.

"Don't you like to see men with babies?" Emily said as Monroe and Sara came in.

"It's the most beautiful thing in the world," Sara said.

"Have you decided on a name?" Emily said as she noted the date and time of his birth.

"Benjamin Lucas Eichorn," Kathleen said. "Tom and I pick out a boys name and a girls name so we could be prepared."

"We agreed on the boy's name, but the girls name was still under some debate," he smiled. "So, Emily, can I take my wife and child home?"

"Not today, Tom," Emily said. "I'd like for her and baby Benjamin to stay here a couple of days. I want to make sure that everything is okay with everybody. We have nurses to help with the baby and let Mom rest for a few days. You can stay as long as you like, though."

Everyone left the room and Helga took the baby. Kathleen had brought some gowns for him and some blankets. Emily helped Kathleen sit up, which made her dizzy. She grabbed Emily to steady herself.

"Just sit for a minute and get your bearings," Emily said. "This is normal. It usually helps to get some fluids into your system, too." She helped her get into a clean gown and walked her to her bed. She was the hospital's first patient. Emily got her tucked into bed and Helga placed the baby in a cradle next to the bed. He would start fussing any minute to eat and Helga would help Kathleen with that.

As Emily left the room she turned and looked at Kathleen. She was 29 years old and had her first baby, and last so she said. She was exhausted and happy. Emily was glad that all turned out well.

She hadn't taken a baby by C-section in many years and didn't want to start on her friend and partner.

The town was still and quiet. Emily looked at the growth, the new buildings, and the additions on businesses. How things had changed in 6 years. How happy she was with her life and her accomplishments. She had a home, a family, and someone she loved and loved her back. She saw Sara across the street and waved.

"I waited so I could ride home with you," she said.

"Great," Emily smiled. "I'm ready to go."

***

"Sounds like everything was working out well for everyone," Beth said to Zack.

"It was going very well," he said. "The area grew like crazy between the 1880s and the 1900s. The logging industry was booming and the lumber from these same forests got shipped all over the United States."

"What it must have been like then," Beth remarked. Her mind wondered as Zack went to make coffee. She thought about Jenny and how her life was perfect and made sense, once. Her job in San Francisco was going well and within two years she was traveling to Seattle to meet with a client. Jenny saw this as a good time to do some research on her family. She took a few days off from Berkley and accompanied Beth to Seattle.

"Look at the mountains, Beth," Jenny said as they started to make their descent to Sea-Tac airport. They landed and had a cab take them to their hotel. Beth had the rest of that day to do some research and had meetings with clients set up for the rest of the week. They found a library and started to research history on the logging industry and looked for the name Monroe. They found the name of Sara Monroe in many of the articles about Native American history, but never realized who she was.

Jenny came across the Zembruski – Monroe logging company and started to read about its history in the Snoqualmie Valley. Jenny had made several notes about this company and had planned to go out to Snoqualmie when Beth was meeting with her clients. On their way back from the library they stopped and rented a car and got a map.

"I'm going to check this place out, Beth," Jenny said. "I may stop by the city of Renton and see if I can find anything there." They talked about what they may find over dinner. Beth had been thinking about her family for the last 7 years. She wondered if she would ever find anything other than a name on a line in the hall of records.

"We probably should go to the courthouse and look for my

father's birth certificate," Beth said.

"If you give me his full name and date of birth I'll go there first," Jenny said. "It may give me some more names to trace back."

"Make a copy of anything you find, will you?" Beth said. "I don't want to lose any of the information we find."

Beth took a cab to her meeting and Jenny headed for the courthouse. She found Russell's birth certificate and his mother's name "Anne Elizabeth Monroe". The father's name was listed as "Unknown". Jenny thought that was strange. Beth's father was illegitimate. She found a marriage records for Anne Monroe but didn't make a copy of it. She looked back at the birth record and read *Born Snoqualmie Valley Hospital on 3/9/1930.* This gave her a starting place. There may be more information out at the hospital itself, but how would she get the information?

She followed the map and drove out of town on Interstate 90. What a beautiful area. She saw the signs that said 'Snoqualmie' and then saw the sign that said 'Snoqualmie Falls'. Jenny had to stop and investigate. She went to the falls first. How pristine this area was. There were walkways and a tourist area, but the view of the falls was breath taking. She had to bring Beth here. If her father grew up in this area, why would he ever leave?

Snoqualmie Valley Hospital didn't exist anymore. According to the history museum, it hadn't existed for many years. The history museum was quite fruitful as far as information. The woman who ran the museum was a wealth of knowledge about the area. She said that her relatives were part of the local Snoqualmie tribe. She said her great aunt and her husband ran a dry goods store. Their name was Walker. She talked about the Zembruski – Monroe Logging Company and how they opened up this area and were here long before anyone was.

"I'm looking for some history on Anne Elizabeth Monroe," Jenny said. "Do you know who she was?"

"Yes," the woman smiled. "I knew her and her son, Russell."

"Would you know who her parents were?" Jenny asked.

The woman opened a book and showed Jenny a picture of a handsome man and Indian woman. "This is Sara and Edmundson Monroe" she said. These were Anne's parents and Russell's grandparents. "Sara and Edmundson died before Russell was born. What do these people mean to you?"

"I'm helping a friend," Jenny said. "This friend is Russell's daughter, Beth."

"I never knew that Russell had a daughter," the woman said. "I heard Russell died in Viet Nam back in '62."

"He never knew he had a daughter," Jenny said. "He died before she was born. Beth's mother died about 6 years later but knew nothing of the family history. That's what she's searching for."

"You've come to the right place," the woman said. "You should have her come here."

"Are you open on Saturday?" Jenny asked. "It's the only day that she can come out here."

"I'm not open, but I will meet you here around noon," the woman said. "I'll let her look through the documents and pictures. I can tell her whatever she wants to know, or she can talk to Russell's father."

"You know Russell's father?" Jenny said. "His birth certificate didn't list the father's name."

"Anne did that to protect the man who fathered Russell," she said. "Everyone knew who it was but the hospital respected her wishes."

"I was going to make copies of this stuff, but I think I'll let Beth see this and hear this for herself," Jenny said. "Thank you for your help, and I'll see you Saturday."

Jenny was so excited and couldn't wait to tell Beth what she had found. Beth's grandfather was still alive and in the area. How pleased she would be to find out she's not alone in the world. The traffic coming in to town was awful. Jenny hated driving in San Francisco for that very reason. She was heading west after passing the town of Issaquah when the setting sun blinded her. She never saw the truck she ran into.

Beth remembered being called from Harbor View Hospital and by the time she got there Jenny was gone. The only thing she had was the jewelry, watch, and a brown envelope that contained her father's birth certificate. She was so young and beautiful. She was so full of life and Beth died inside also. She made all the arrangements and phone calls then she flew back with Jenny's body and she was buried in Los Angeles. Steve and Karen came to give Beth the support they could offer, but she would grieve in her own way. Steve and Bret came down and some people that Jenny worked with at Berkley.

The service was beautiful and Beth stood at the graveside and talked to Jenny. "I'll never forget you. I'll always love you. You have given me something I didn't think possible. You made me believe in myself and have the courage to love. You died trying to bring me my family. Thank you for sharing my life."

She went back to her apartment in San Francisco a few days later. When she opened the door she could smell the fragrance the Jenny used to wear. Her feet wouldn't move. She looked around and everything she saw reminded her of Jenny. She tucked the envelope, which she never opened, away with the other saved memorabilia from their life together.

***

"You seem deep in thought," Zack said as he brought her back to the present.

"I am," she said as she blew her nose. "I was thinking about someone very dear to me."

"Where is this person now, Beth?" Zack said softly.

"She died a few years ago," Beth said fighting back the tears. Zack sat next to Beth and put a comforting arm around her.

"I'm so sorry," Zack reassured. "Sometimes life isn't fair, especially with those that we love."

Zack held her close and she let him comfort her. He remembered holding Anne when her mother had died. It seemed so long ago, but holding Beth brought the moment in time back. He had spent the next few days after the 4th of July party at the estate by the falls. Anne felt she was ready to clean out some of her mother's things. Zack was in the bedroom when she started. She opened the closet and stared at the clothes.

She fingered them and then closed the door. She started to cry. Zack walked over and held her close. "Let's leave this alone for now. Let's leave everything as it is," he encouraged.

"I think that's a good idea, Zachary," she said. "Let's walk to the falls."

They left the house and walked the mile to the falls. Anne stood and stared at the water for a long time. Zack didn't want to disturb her while she was deep in thought.

"I used to come here as a child to think," she said. "This place holds such mystery for me. There's a comforting here that I haven't found anywhere else. It's a mystical and spiritual place according to legends of the local tribes."

"It's never been logged, has it?" he asked.

"No," Anne said. "My father owned all of this and then he gave it back to the Snoqualmie tribe. He didn't think it was right for a white man to own their holy place."

"I wish I could have known him," Zack said. They walked back to the estate and Zack held Anne's hand. He remembered the sweet passionate love they had made the night before. He wondered if it was a one-night stand. Later that afternoon, he realized it wasn't. Anne was very uninhibited during their sexual encounters. She told Zack that she loved him again, that afternoon.

***

It was during that three-day period that Anne became pregnant. She told him during the first week in September. Zack was overcome with joy and fear. His good Catholic upbringing and Catholic guilt weighed heavily on his young shoulders. He started pressing Anne to get married but she declined. He didn't feel it was an obligation, because he truly wanted to spend the rest of his life with her.

"Anne," he said as he held her close. "I love you, and want to share the rest of my life with you."

"I know you do, Zachary," she said. "I love you, too, but you're half my age. This doesn't matter to me, but it does matter to other people. My business reputation in this town is good. My personal life is something I've always kept very personal. No one has ever known of the people I see or don't see. I want it kept that way."

"Does that mean that you don't want me involved in the baby's life?" Zack asked.

"Absolutely not," she said. "You need to be as involved with this baby as I am. But I won't marry you for my own reasons."

Zachary accepted that. He wondered if he was simply a means to carry on the family name or if she really did care for him. He couldn't imagine his life without her, nor did he want to. She was having his child. In October of that same year, Anne decided to sell her house in Renton and move back to the estate. It was in need of some work and Samuel was busy with his own place.

Anne said she wanted her child to grow up in this place. It was away from the city and the entrapments of that life. Zachary knew that it would be a hardship to get out to the estate very often and was afraid that their relationship would fade away due to absence. As they were having dinner one night Anne looked at Zack.

"What would you think of moving in here?" she said.

"It would be hard to get to work from here, but I suppose I could manage," he responded.

"I could use your help with this business," Anne said. "I could offer you a job right here."

"Doing what?" he said anxiously.

"Mother sold the logging business years ago, but there are still residual payments that come annually. Samuel and Mary now have their son run the business for the seedlings and he ships them all over the state. What I need is someone to get this place back up to its original glory," she said. "I need for you to work with the bank and contractors to get some work done out here. I would like for you to handle the maintenance for this estate, just for starters. Is that something that interests you?"

"Yes, it does," he said with a smile. "I'd like to let the Mortuary know what my intentions are. I don't want to leave them high and dry."

"You would be paid a monthly salary out of the estate fund that my mother set up many years ago," Anne said. "There's more money there than I can expect to spend in 5 lifetimes."

They talked for hours about the plans that Anne had for the estate. Zack was glad that she was thinking of him and now he would be a part of her life. He would talk to Bill on Monday and let him know that he was changing jobs. They spent the rest of the weekend talking about the list of contractors she had used in the past. She let Zack know whose work she liked and who made her feel like she had been taken advantage of.

"Most of these men like to be paid in cash," Anne said. "I never understood this but I pay them as they ask." She walked Zack into the original living room. "Close the door behind you. I want to show you something that only 2 other people on this estate know exist." He followed her to a knotty pine wall and from inside of the built in bookcase she pushed a button and he saw the wall move. She pulled the bookcase out and told Zack to follow her.

"A secret passage way," he said. "I always dreamed of one of these, and used to read stories of castles, a maiden fair, an evil queen and the knight on the white horse that would save the day."

"My but aren't you the romantic," she said as she kissed his cheek. "I suppose you think I need saving?"

"Why, yes, I do, fair maiden," he quipped back.

"The servants know about this passage way, but they don't know about this," she said as she slid a pocket door into the wall. This exposed a small room. Zachary followed her into the room and she turned on a small light. In this room was the largest safe he ever seen. "My father was always a little paranoid about banks. He used to take some currency and gold and put it into the safe. It used to drive my mother crazy, but she let him put this in when they built on the addition."

"She also let him buy this big safe," Zack said.

"Yes," Anne said. "It was the only thing my father really insisted on. The bank in Snoqualmie had been robbed a few times, and their lack of security really annoyed him. He always trusted Tom Eichorn, though." She opened the safe. "If the workers want to be paid in cash, take it from here. If they'll take a bank draft, then write one

out. I'll make sure that you have signature privileges at the bank."
She swung the heavy silent door open. It was large enough for two
people to walk into. There were stacks of money on one side, and
gold bars on the other.

"Jesus Christ, Anne," he whispered. "I've never seen so much
money in my life. Not in my wildest dreams have I imagined this."

"There's around a million in gold," she said as she ran her hand
over the gold bars, "and at least that in cash. Zachary, this is how
much I trust you. There are three keys to the pocket door that opens
this room. There are 4 people that know of this room. Samuel,
Mary, you, and I are the only ones who will know the combination
and you will possess one of the three keys. Never lose, misplace, or
lay it down." She handed him the silver key and kissed him gently.
They left the safe and Anne made sure that he knew the combination.
She made him try it a couple of times before they locked up the
room.

They left the passage way and came out in the formal living room.
Zack's head was still spinning. He couldn't believe that someone
would keep so much money in a house. The economy was so good
and the banks were doing well. Why not just move it all? He decided
not to question any of it. This is the way Anne wanted it and this is
how it would be. He would follow her direction to the letter.

Zachary was shown the suite that he would call home. It came
with its own sitting room and private bath. Anne's room was just
down the hall, but she said she would be spending most of her time
in this room. Giving him is own suite would assure the servants
wouldn't chatter as much. They would still talk, but not as much.
This was the same room where their child was conceived. Anne said
that anything he wanted to move into this room he could.

"Will you be selling your house?" Anne asked.

"I don't think so," he said. "It's a nice little place with a lot of
charm. I think I'll hang on to it for a while. The payments are small
and I may rent it out."

"That's a good idea," Anne said. "I should probably do that with
my house in Renton, too. I think I will. It never hurts to own
property."

"I guess it's my Irish blood," he smiled. "The Irish are big on
owning land. They think it's the only thing worth keeping."

Anne went to the window and looked at the trees. Below she
could see the garden that Mary took so much pride in. Zack came up
behind her and put his arms around her waist. She laid her head on
his chest as he rocked gently.

"I always wished I could have seen this place before Dad put on the new addition," she said. "Mother said it had a rustic charm about it. It was warm and homey. There was love everywhere." She turned around and looked into Zack's eyes. He kissed her gently and held her close. She slowly removed Zack's jacket and unbuttoned his shirt.

They made love with a tenderness that Zack had never experienced. Anne's passionate inhibition gave way to a slow easy tenderness. Zack had learned to take his time and give Anne the erotic foreplay that she loved. In the quiet afterglow, Anne told Zack the story of her parents, Samuel, Mary, Emily, and how the town came to be. She talked to him about the Indian history and her mother's work to keep the culture and tribes together.

This woman he had put into a coffin 4 months earlier was a visionary. She didn't care what polite society thought, but lived her life as she pleased, and loved who she pleased. Zachary had trouble understanding about the relationship between Sara and Emily. It was something he had heard of only of men, never of women. Anne enlightened him about many things that night. She held back some information, though. This would come to light later. Anne didn't want to overwhelm him.

Zack had moved in and had gotten settled before the end of the month. He had decided to keep a part-time job at the cemetery. He was going to be the caretaker. He would need to maintain the graves in the Monroe corner of the cemetery. This may take him 4 hours a week. He would maintain those of the family, and the friends that had joined them over the years.

On Monday October 29th, 1929 the financial structure in this country crumbled. The stock market crashed and people lost millions overnight. There were runs on banks that closed their doors. Loans were called in and the country was in shambles. Anne's finances were in good shape. Tom Eichorn, and his junior officers, had some tense moments at the bank, but they prevailed and made it through the day without closing their doors.

Anne's father still had a small account in a bank in London that wasn't affected. There was also the large cash horde in the house. Zack told Anne that she was lucky, and her father was a genius. Monroe had tried to plan ahead for his entire life. He wanted to make sure that his family would never be cold or hungry. There was no way he could have foreseen this event, but he planned for it just the same.

Anne was still fighting with morning sickness which should have passed by now. She had lost weight and was looking pale. She had been to see Ben Eichorn at his office and he said that the baby was fine, but this sometimes happened. He recommended eating small meals 6 times a day, preferably bland and with no spices. He would also talk with his mother, who was well into her seventies now, regarding her case. She was a wealth of knowledge and experience and Ben had taken advantage of it on several occasions. As Ben was walking Anne from his office he opened the waiting room door to see his mother sitting there.

"Mother," he said. "We were just talking about you."

"I'm like a bad penny," she said as she smiled. "Annie! How nice to see you. You're not ill are you?"

"Now Mother," Ben said. "You're not supposed to ask those kinds of questions. But as long as you're here, can you come back here with us?" There was no one waiting so the timing was good. He took Anne back to an exam room and talked to his mother outside before he sent her in.

"Annie," Kathleen said as she walked in. She was still very professional. "First, let me congratulate you on your new arrival." Anne smiled slightly, but Kathleen didn't get the response from that remark she had hoped for. "Why don't you lie back and let's see what's going on." Her hands were checking Anne's abdomen. They were different from Ben's hands. "It appears as though everything is okay here." She helped Anne sit up. "Annie, I brought you into this world. I loved your mother dearly. I need for you to be honest with me, okay?"

"I always have been," Anne said.

"How happy are you about this child?" Kathleen asked bluntly.

"I'm very happy, Kathleen," Anne said with surprise.

"I know what your head says, but what about your gut?" Kathleen responded.

"I remember Mother and Mary talking about how wonderful children were," Anne said as she started to cry. "I guess I didn't think it was going to be this hard. I didn't expect the morning sickness or the fatigue. I'm 40 years old and I've been thinking that this probably wasn't the best time to have a child." She paused and regained her composure. "I'm scared, Kathleen."

"That's what I thought," Kathleen said as she hugged her closely. Anne let herself cry. If she ever needed a mother it was now. "You'll get through this, honey. You're so much like your mother. You're strong and determined. Being scared is all right. I'll be available if you need me, because I love you as much as if you were my own daughter."

"Thank you, Kathleen," Anne said as she wiped away the tears. "Could I ask a favor of you?"

"Sure," Kathleen said.

"Would you consider delivering this baby? Would you help one more Monroe come into this world?" Anne asked almost pleading.

"You know, Anne, I'm seventy-five years old. I'm retired and Ben has taken over the practice," she said. "My license is still current and," she paused and smiled. "I would love to deliver one more baby. Let's get Ben in here and I'll break the news to him. He can let me know when your appointments are, because I want to follow you all the way through."

Anne was thinking that Ben may not be happy about this, but he was excited. It had been many years since he worked on the same case with his mother. He seemed to see a spark in his Mother's eye that had not been there for a while.

"Your father will not be happy about this," Kathleen said to Ben.

"That's his problem," Ben remarked. "He still goes to the bank everyday. But that doesn't matter. What does matter is that Annie has a healthy baby, you get to bring one more life into the world, and I get to be there with both of you."

"Get out of here for a minute will you Ben?" Kathleen said as she opened the door. "I want to talk to Anne." He left and Kathleen closed the door. "Listen, honey, will you tell me who the father is? And does he know about this baby?"

"Well," Anne said. "I, well, yes he does know about this baby. And really wants to be part of this whole pregnancy."

"But you don't want to marry him," Kathleen said.

"I actually do, but it wouldn't help him out at all," Anne said. "Kathleen, he's only 19 years old. I don't think he should be saddled with an old woman and child at his age."

"Don't you think that should be his decision?" she asked. "I think Zachary McGill would make and excellent husband and father."

"How did you know?" Anne asked.

"Honey, I put your first pair of diapers on you," Kathleen said. "He's the only one of the male persuasion I've seen you show interest in. I knew it the first time we met him at the 4th party. I know that Ben was, and probably still is, in love with you, but that's not what you wanted. Your tastes always went another direction. You are so much like your mother in this respect. This young man must be something very special. Don't lose it, Annie. Don't throw it away by trying to be noble. Don't spend the rest of your life alone. Screw noble, and be happy for a change."

Anne hugged her close. Kathleen made her promise to bring Zack in for her next appointment. She promised she would think about marrying him, but not until the baby came. They had made an arrangement regarding the birth certificate that Kathleen couldn't talk her out of. The father would be listed as 'Unknown'.

Chapter 13

Anne kept her word and brought Zachary along for her next appointment. Kathleen fell in love with him herself. She told him what to expect during a pregnancy and how he could help Anne get through it. Her morning sickness had subsided and she was feeling better. Thanksgiving was just around the corner and Anne invited Ben and his wife, Kathleen and Tom, and Samuel and Mary to join them for dinner.

She wanted to start the holiday season out with friends and people she trusted and with people who knew who Zachary was and how important he was to her. She wanted to put some life back into this house. She gave the servants the day off and she and Zack prepared the entire meal. He was a wiz in the kitchen and she had forgotten how much she missed cooking.

Dinner was a success and Mary and Samuel cleaned up after dinner. Zack lit the fireplace in the original living room, which seemed so small now, and they sat and talked.

"I remember the first time I saw this house," he said. "You weren't even thought of yet, Ben, and we were invited to dinner right after we got into town. Emily showed us the way out here, and took us by the falls first."

"She looked so beautiful that day," Kathleen said in a misty voice. "I can't believe she's been gone for 10 years."

"She and Mother built the hospital," Ben said. "Did you know that Zack? These two women doctors built a hospital in the middle of logging country. The original was in the late 1870's wasn't it? "

"And you were the first baby born in the new building, Ben," she said. "I didn't think you'd ever get here. Emily had faith, though, and you finally made an appearance. She made me lay on the damn birthing table for 12 hours."

"Mother said it was strange, in those days, to give birth in a hospital," Anne said. "Most of the deliveries were at home."

"That's right, Anne," Kathleen said. "I told Emily that it would change in the future and I was right."

They sat for hours and talked about the past and told stories of those who had long since passed away. They talked about the 4th of July parties that started in 1875 and a year was never missed. They also got some history on Zack and his life. He openly talked about his mother and father. He talked about his brother, Kevin, and his desire to go to medical school, which seemed a lifetime ago.

Kathleen realized the reason why Anne was so taken with this young man. He was articulate, loving, handsome, and possessed the qualities of Anne's father and her brother, Eddy. He even resembled them in many ways. He seemed old beyond his years. When he stood next to Anne, she could see Edmundson and Sara. She wondered if Anne would ever marry this young man or she was replacing her father or brother with him. She knew that people around town would talk about the difference in age, but Anne was not one to worry about what people said.

When the guests had left, Anne sat down in her mother's favorite wingback chair and watched the fire. The leather was soft and comfortable. Zack sat in the other one and they talked quietly.

"I remember sitting in here with mother and Emily," Anne said. "Emily always found answers and comfort in the flames from this fireplace."

"Are you looking for answers, Anne?" Zack asked. "What are the questions?"

"You make me happy, Zack," she said. "You make me happy in ways I never expected or received from any other man. When I thought of sharing my life with anyone, it was with a woman." She stopped to wait for his reaction. She didn't know how he would react to this sort of information, but she needed to know. If their relationship was going to progress, she needed to be completely honest with him.

"I understand what you're saying Anne," Zack said. "You are your mother's daughter, and this doesn't make me love you any less. This is who you are."

"Zack," Anne continued. "I was in a serious relationship with a woman for the 10 years. I thought that I never could stand to be away from her, but she left and found us a place in Seattle. She died before I could join her. That was, well, over 12 years ago. I miss her. I miss her touch, I miss her warmth, and I miss her kiss. I never thought I wanted anything else, until you came along."

"What happened to this woman?" Zack asked.

"She was living in Seattle. She was teaching at a school there when it caught fire," Anne said. "Eighteen students and four teachers died. Amanda was one of them."

"I'm so sorry to hear that, Anne," Zack said. "How did you two meet?"

"We grew up together," Anne said. "Her parents ran a logging company around Snoqualmie, too."

They talked about things that Zack could only imagine. He

wanted to know how you know about sexual orientation. How do you know someone else is feeling the same way you feel? He wanted to understand more about this. This was a part of Anne he felt he needed to understand. What he didn't know was during this conversation she had decided to marry him. She wouldn't bring this up until the baby was born. It may be selfish, but she needed to carry on the family name. Zack's family was large and many had relocated to the Chicago area. He had aunts, uncles, and cousins by the dozens. She was the last of the Monroe line. Without this baby, it would end.

***

After Jenny's death, funeral, and tying up the last of the loose ends, Beth went back to San Francisco and tried to go back to work. Her zest for her job, and life, had disappeared. She went through the motions, but she was dead inside. Steve and Bret tried to get her out of the apartment and meet some new people. This they couldn't accomplish. Even Mrs. Austin was concerned about Beth. Finally one night there was a knock on Beth's door. She opened it to find Mrs. Austin standing there with a bottle of wine.

"I need to have a serious talk with you, girl," she said as she walked in. She sat down on the couch, opened the bottle of wine, and poured the two glasses she had brought with her. She handed a glass to Beth. "I'm going to talk to you like your mother, or at least a stern aunt. You need to get on with life, kid. If there are too many memories here, then move. If there are too many memories in this city, then leave the city. If you need to move back to LA, then do it. Don't go through life as a zombie." She emptied her glass and poured more from the bottle. "What happened to Jenny was a tragedy. You're still alive, but only physically. You're too young to be dead emotionally."

"I don't know what to do," she said flatly as she looked in her glass and then drank the contents.

"Then find a good therapist, work through this, and get on with life," she said. "I have some cards for you to look at. These are good people and know what their doing. Call one of them."

"Do you think I'm crazy?" Beth asked.

"No," Mrs. Austin said. "I think you're in a great deal of pain and you need to grieve. I think you lost someone you loved deeply and you need some professional help to work through this. That's what these people are trained for. Good God girl, use them. You're too young to be dead inside."

With that she picked up the empty wine glasses, her bottle of wine, and left the apartment. Beth just sat there and looked around. She wasn't quite sure what had just happened, but she knew that Mrs. Austin was right. She couldn't go on like this. She had thought about quitting her job, but didn't want to make any decisions of this magnitude without seeing someone first and decided to call a woman down the street the next day.

Beth had no idea what to expect when she entered the office of Joan Rushforth. She had never had any experience in this arena. Joan wanted to get to know Beth so she had a fairly standard list of questions she asked. Beth liked this woman. She was forty, and had a calm but confident nature. Her voice was quiet and melodious, which relaxed Beth.

Joan ascertained very quickly that Beth was suffering from abandonment. Mother and Father were dead, no idea about any other family or her family history, and now the love of her life gone.

"I feel that everyone I love dies," Beth said. "I'm afraid to love anyone else, or they will die, too."

"Beth," Joan assured, "these people didn't die because you loved them. They died because of circumstances beyond your control." She wanted to get back to the grieving process that Beth still hadn't gone through. "Tell me about Jenny. Why was she so special?"

Beth spent the rest of the session talking about Jenny. She told Joan how they met, their life together, and their promise to be together always.

"She died doing research for me on my family," Beth said. "I should have made her wait for me, but I had to see a client."

"Why?" Joan asked. "She was doing this because she wanted to."

"But I sent her out there all alone," Beth cried. "I didn't go with her. If I'd been with her, maybe, she wouldn't have died. I was always afraid that something bad was going to happen to her. She took so many chances in her life. She died alone and surrounded by strangers. I wasn't there."

"What makes you think that you both wouldn't have died?" Joan asked. She waited for a response but Beth said nothing. She was dealing with abandonment and guilt. "Let's stop there this week. I'm going to make this your standard appointment time, every Thursday at 4:30pm."

Beth left the office and returned to her apartment. She had messages on the recorder but didn't return any of the calls. She decided the office could wait and she could talk to Bret and Karen Klump another time. She wanted to be left alone. She locked her door, shut off the phone ringer, and started to cry. It had been 2 months since Jenny had died and she kept all the tears inside.

By the time she let herself go, she was like a dam that had burst. The next few hours she wept uncontrollably. It was like a purge that was long overdue. After 3 hours she was tired and her eyes and face was swollen, but she felt better. She even had an appetite. She'd not eaten much in the last couple of months because Jenny usually cooked. Beth was more of the frozen pizza, or out of a can type of cook. She found some eggs and bread and made a light breakfast at 8pm at night. As she sat and ate she looked at her plate and smiled. This is something Jenny would do because she always liked pizza for breakfast and breakfast for dinner. Somehow this gave Beth comfort.

After a month of sessions with Joan, Beth began to get back to her old self. Her co-workers had noticed a favorable change and Beth was starting to enjoy being around people again. She still had no desire to go out and look for someone new and didn't know if she would ever be ready for that.

Joan made Beth work during her sessions. They worked every issue that Beth would bring up. The only issue that Beth really didn't want to discuss was her family history or lack thereof. Joan felt the only way that Beth would feel like she belonged was to look at her family history. It took Joan the next 5 months to convince Beth to consider it. It was almost as though she was afraid to find out. Joan finally decided to ask her directly.

"What are you afraid you'll find?" Joan asked.

"I'm afraid I'll find nothing," Beth finally said. "I'm afraid that I'm nothing more than the child of a name on a line in some obscure record." She paused for a brief moment. "I'm afraid of coming from nothing and ending up as nothing. Most of all, I'm afraid to go back to Seattle."

She and Joan spent the rest of the session working on this very topic. Beth promised to think about starting her search again. Not really the starting part, but the thinking. She found she was thinking about it a lot. She sat in her office and her manager came in and offered her something that would save her, although she didn't know it at the time. She wanted to make no decisions until she talked with Joan, and with Karen and Steve.

"Hi, Karen," Beth said.

"Oh, honey," Karen said. "I was just thinking of you. How nice it is to hear your voice."

"My boss wants to know if I want to transfer to our office in

Renton, Washington," she said.

"What have you decided?" Karen asked.

"I don't know," she said. "I wanted to get your and Steve's opinion."

Karen was silent for a moment. When they began to talk it was clear that she wasn't happy about the distance to the Seattle, but she knew that Beth's life would end up there. Beth said she still hadn't decided when they ended their conversation, but she would let them know.

Beth saw Joan on Thursday and talked about relocating to the Northwest. Joan seemed to take this as a sign that Beth was ready to begin her search.

"Maybe it will prompt me to take the next step," Beth said. "I think this is my first step with getting over Jenny. I need some closure, and I think this might help."

"I agree, Beth," Joan responded. "I have some colleagues in that area. I could give them a call and refer you if you like."

"I think I'd like to take a break for a while," Beth said. "Can you give me their names? I could call them when I was ready to see someone again."

Joan was hesitant but agreed to that. She knew Beth wasn't really ready to stop the therapy process but relocating would somehow be good for her. Facing demons is not easy and she hoped she wouldn't wait too long before calling someone. This transfer wouldn't happen for another month, so they still had time to get some closure on things. She would make sure that Beth knew that she could call her anytime she needed to.

***

"Let's get back to life at Snoqualmie," Zack said bringing Beth back to reality. It was time again for the 4th of July party. This had become the social event of the season. Monroe had hired some help for this the last few years. It was more than Mary, Sara, or Emily could handle. Some of the original traditions still remained. There was Ivan and his roasted pig. This was always the hit of the party.

Victoria was now 8 years old and had a little brother named Caleb, who was the delight of her life. Samuel and Mary were happy and healthy and she had all but quit working with the seedlings for replanting. She managed the process, but didn't have the long hours. She and Samuel had encouraged Jack Regan to get his supply from the local tribes so they could replant his land. This business was found to be very profitable for them.

Charlie was still working with the mill owner and was now a

partner. He was well respected with the logging companies for his honesty. He had become a consultant for the builders in the area and was gaining a reputation as far away as Seattle. Contractors would even consult with him on construction techniques. They would look at the work in his office and question how he did this kind of work.

Emily was still living with Monroe and Sara. She felt like this was home and never wanted to leave. She and Kathleen had built a wonderful clinic and hospital and they had some medical students working with them on a routine basis. The nursing staff had grown, but Helga still managed the day-to-day activities. She was a master at scheduling the activities at the hospital. She had become an irreplaceable asset that Emily couldn't live without.

Eddy and Will were 13 years old. They had distinguished their distinct personalities when they were born. Eddy loved school and did well. Will did well, but liked to challenge the teachers with some of his behaviors. He was still Gus's shadow and would get articles on the new things and equipment available. Eddy was in love with Emily. It started when he was 4 and his feelings hadn't changed. He and Emily had a special relationship that neither of them could understand.

He would talk to Emily about things on his mind. He could confide in her and he would wait at the clinic a couple of nights a week so they could ride home together. When weather would permit, they would stop at the falls. This was a special place for Eddy. He said it made him feel at peace with the world.

Monroe and Sara were happy and healthy. Sara watched Victoria and Caleb and longed for another child. Monroe was now 51 years old and they had not been intimate in some time. His old injuries made this very difficult for him. He seemed to be able to read Sara's mood and brought the subject up the night before. It wasn't so much for him, but for her.

"I'd like to give you another child, Sara," he said. "What do you think about that?"

"I know how difficult it is for you, Monroe," Sara said. "I want another child. I want Eddy and Will to have a little brother or sister."

"Then let's see if we can do this," Monroe smiled.

Sara talked with Emily that night. Emily said that she thought it was wonderful and told Sara that she should watch her cycle for the next month. She told her to count her days from the end of her cycle to have more success in conceiving. It seemed as though everything was set. They talked about the party the next day.

The whole town turned out. There wasn't anyone missing. Jack and Maggie looked wonderful. Jack talked with Emily at length and was concerned about why Maggie hadn't conceived a child, yet. He wanted children so desperately.

"Could you check her out?" Jack asked sheepishly.

"I can," Emily replied. "Have her make and appointment. Or she can talk to me today if she wants."

"I'd greatly appreciate it," Jack said. "I'll tell her to find you." He left and Emily watched him walk away. She was feeling guilty about misjudging him so many years ago. He was a good man, and a decent man. He loved Maggie with all his heart. His gentleness when he was near her was visible. It was as though he needed a friend and she was his first. These friendships led to Monroe, who he respected and admired. Jack's way of doing business had changed. He saw that cutting corners and only being interested in making money didn't pay off in the long run.

The weather held and the fireworks, that Monroe had arranged, were the finale to the day and evening's activities. The explosions, above the trees, were a sight to behold. Tom, Kathleen, and Ben sat with Monroe, Sara, and Emily on the porch. Will was playing with Ben and Eddy was close to Emily.

For the last few years Monroe had hired people out of Seattle to set off the fireworks. He knew nothing about these things, and knew they could be dangerous. Will was fascinated when he watched the setup. Gus was with him and made sure he didn't get in the way, but could still watch how they set up the fuses. Gus made Will promise that he stay on the porch with his parents while they set them off.

Ivan and Monroe had hired a manager for the company. Monroe wanted to add to the house. He had plans drawn up for an expansion. Sara didn't care, but she knew it was important to Monroe. He had some very specific things he wanted to do. He had secret passageways and a blind room added.

"I remember reading about these things in castles in England and Germany," he smiled. "I always wanted something like that in my house."

"Why didn't you put it in this house," Sara asked.

"Well," he stammered. "I thought it a little childish when I built this. Now that I have the money to do what I want with this house, it seemed like a good idea." He looked at Sara and blushed. "Okay, it's a childhood dream." He looked down at the floor.

"Edmundson," Sara said in a stern voice. She always called him that to get his attention. "I think this whole idea is wonderful. You deserve to have fun with this, so do what you want."

"Monroe?" Emily chimed in. "Will you put a tower and turret in for me? I always wanted to be a damsel in distress." They all laughed as the explosions went off above them. Jack tapped Emily on the shoulder and she turned to see Maggie standing on the end of the porch. Emily excused herself and took Maggie aside.

After all the guests were gone, Monroe poured over his plans for the house. Jack and Maggie hung around for a while. Sara, Emily, and Maggie sat in the living room and talked about the growth of the town.

"I hate the fact that we have no say or a way to express our opinion on things," Sara said.

"Like what, for example?" Emily asked.

"Like the schools," Sara said. "We have a school for the 'white' children and a separate school for the Indians. Why are they being educated differently? Don't they all have to live in the same society? Why would it make a difference if the white children knew about and understood some of the Indian customs?"

"You think we should integrate the schools?" Emily asked.

"Yes," Sara said, "especially the high school. By that time they understand the customs of their culture. The Indians have no high school to attend. After 8th grade they are done. This is wrong and we're doing them a disservice."

"I think you're right, Sara," Maggie added. "Why can't they have a higher education if they want? Why can't they go to college?"

"I see your point," Emily said. "How do we do anything about this?"

"How did you and Kathleen build a hospital?" Sara said. "All it takes is money, and talking to the right people. Monroe has contacts in Seattle and Olympia." She paused and looked at the women. She was focused about this subject and had thought about it for a while. "We must change this for the good of the area. If we are going to live in harmony we all must have the same opportunity whether you are Indian, White, Chinese, or Negro."

Emily looked at Sara and wondered what set her off about this. She would ask her later, but in the mean time she would help her any way that she could. She would also ask Kathleen, who had contacts in San Francisco. Jack came in and asked Maggie if she was ready to leave. She said her good-bye and told Emily she would see her on Thursday. Monroe was still pouring over his plans. Sara was still deep in thought when Emily said she was going to bed. Sara accompanied her, but not before she told Monroe good night.

"Where has this come from, Sara," Emily asked after they had made love.

"I was told," Sara began, "that Victoria would need to attend the Indian school."

"Who told you that?" Emily asked.

"Eddy," Sara said. "Their teacher said it would be best if she attended with 'her kind' before they left for summer vacation." She paused and then got angry. "What did she mean 'her kind'? Is it the Negro she doesn't like or the Indian?"

"Sara," Emily said in a calming manner. "This is the first time you've faced discrimination isn't it?" There was no response. "Will and Eddy were welcomed into this school because of their white blood and light skin. They were also the sons of a powerful man. Victoria has no white blood and she's beautifully brown. What we need to do is ask Mary and Samuel what they think. Maybe, they won't have a problem with this."

"That's beside the point, Emily," Sara snapped back with tears in her eyes. "It's not right."

"I know, honey," Emily said as she held her. "But she's their child. If they don't have a problem with this, then we have to respect that." Sara nodded her head in agreement. "If they do have a problem with it, then we can fight this fight with all the resources we have available." Emily stroked her hair gently. "Have you told Monroe about this?"

"No," Sara admitted. "I wanted to handle this alone, but I do need to tell him what I'm planning."

"What are you planning, Sara?" Emily asked not liking the way Sara had put her last statement.

"I'll talk to you about it later, Emily," Sara said. "I haven't worked out details, yet."

Emily knew that Sara was one to plan well. She usually never made a move until she had looked at all sides of an issue. Emily's concern was that she might not be thinking clearly because of the emotion involved with this issue. Her next concern was that Monroe was clueless about this. It was not her place to tell him, but she may have to if Sara decided to move on something.

She held Sara in her arms. She had dropped off to sleep while Emily was still wide-awake. She didn't want Sara to be in any danger, and this is an area where surprises can blindside you. She kissed Sara gently and whispered, "I love you" as she held her close.

Chapter 14

The month of July was cooler than normal. The clinic had been busy with people with Pneumonia. Kathleen and Emily were working some long hours because of this. The strange thing was that most of their patients were adults. The children were healthy. By Wednesday Emily was working at the cabin behind Ivan and Helga's when Ivan came in the door.

"I don't feel well," he said breathlessly. "I had the chills last night and Helga did her best to get my fever down."

"Let me listen to your lungs," she said as she placed the stethoscope on his back. She knew the air was not moving in his lower right lobe. He was perspiring and fatigued. Ivan was not a young man. He was close to 60 and Emily feared he might not get over this. "Ivan, I want to take you to the hospital. I think you've got Pneumonia."

"I've got so much going on," Ivan said. "I'll have to get in touch with Monroe to take care of a few things." With that statement he grabbed a basin and vomited. This was a sign of Pneumonia. She helped him afterward sit upright on the table.

"I'll see him in a couple of hours," Emily said. "Let's get you to the hospital."

Emily took him in the wagon and helped him in the door. Kathleen saw them arrive and was there to lend a hand. She could tell by the look on Emily's face that this was serious. Helga came from around the corner and saw her husband. They got him to a bed and Kathleen talked to Emily about his treatment.

"I don't like his color," Kathleen said. "Are his lungs wet?"

"Very," Emily said. "We need to make sure he's on a wedge. It'll help him breath. He's been vomiting, so we need to get fluids into him."

"I'll stay with my husband," Helga said. "I'll get you if he gets worse."

About that time Sara and Monroe came into the clinic. Emily took the opportunity to talk to Monroe. She sent him in to talk to Ivan. This way he could rest without the worries of the business.

"I'm worried about his fever," Emily said. "Helga is going to try cool baths to bring his body temperature down."

"My mother used to use a tea made from the bark of a willow," Sara said. "It seemed to work on the children of our village. It may work on adults."

"Are those trees around here?" Emily said with nothing to lose.

"Yes," Sara replied. "Let me find you some. I'll be back shortly." With that she left and asked Monroe to wait for her. Ivan talked about all the things that he had left to do, and asked Monroe to talk to the mill owner, Gus, and Samuel. By the time that Sara returned, Ivan had drifted off to sleep. She used the water that Helga had just boiled and made a strong bitter tea.

"How much should we give him?" Emily said.

"Mother used to use a half cup with children every 4 hours," Sara said. "So I would think a cup every 4 hours would be good. I'll make sure that Helga has enough for the rest of the night."

Emily gave Helga the instructions for the tea and decided she would stay with Ivan. She started to put up a fuss but it didn't last long. I think she was afraid for her husband, and was relieved when Emily insisted she stay. Sara said she would stay also so they could take turns sleeping.

Monroe sent word with Charlie to have Sally stay with the boys. He didn't want to leave his lifelong friend. They had set up a vigil at the hospital. Monroe went to the hotel restaurant to bring food back for everyone. The willow bark tea seemed to work for a few hours before Ivan's temperature would go back up. During the times it was down, he felt better and Helga could force water, and broth into him. It was a long night, but by 5am the sun was coming up and Ivan seemed to be better.

"Monroe?" Ivan said in a feeble voice. "I'm hungry."

"You're hungry?" Monroe smiled. "Let's see what the doctors have to say about that."

"I say we feed him," Emily said as she rounded the corner. "I've got some chicken soup and we'll start with that."

"I'd like a steak," Ivan said. "I'll settle for the chicken soup if there's chicken in it. The broth from last night didn't give me anything to chew."

"Let's start slow, Ivan," Emily said. "We'll work to more from there."

It was a week before Ivan could go home. Kathleen concerned that this would weaken Ivan's lungs for future illnesses. They would have to keep an eye on him, and no one, more than Helga, would watch out for him. Kathleen wouldn't let him go back to work for another week. She made sure that Helga was with him, so he wouldn't sneak out to check on his crews.

"You have someone to do that, Ivan," Helga scolded. "Let the man do his job."

Emily checked on him when she had her Wednesday clinic. He looked and sounded good. She was firm about Kathleen's orders. Ivan was driving Helga crazy with his pacing around the house. Emily suggested he go for a walk and talk with Jacob and Suzy down at the store. This would give him some exercise and get him out of Helga's hair. She watched him walk into town and realized how close she came to losing him.

Ivan, on the other hand, had no idea how close he came to death. Everyone seemed to know it accept him. He found Jacob and started to talk. Suzy knew that Jacob would be worthless as long as Ivan was there. It was slow in the store so she really didn't care. Jacob was talking to Ivan regarding his need to expand his current store. There were so many people moving into town that he needed a larger inventory. He had contracted a builder to add on to the back.

"How much will that cost you?" Ivan asked.

"It won't be too bad, Ivan," Jacob said. "I've been anticipating this for a while and have put aside more than enough to add about 1000 square feet of storage space. I talked to Charlie and Samuel and asked them if they could do some custom work inside. They agreed to do that when the weather turns cold."

They continued to talk the afternoon away. Ivan helped Jacob move some supplies from a wagon and felt tired but good afterward. He met Helga on her way to the hospital. She couldn't stay away for very long. She loved working there. She loved making the money that she did. It wasn't much, but it was hers and she got a satisfaction from the work and from having a paycheck with her name on it. She seemed to find validation of her worth in this.

August turned unusually hot. Ivan's crews were working early in the morning and stopping by 1pm. Monroe had started his expansion plan. This would not get done this year. There was marble that was being imported. The main construction would be completed, but the finish work could take the full year. He had a look that he wanted. He wanted function with elegance and a dash of mystery.

He would walk Sara around and show her how this would come together. She still had no concept of what he was trying to do.

"The appearance of the house will change completely," Monroe explained. "The new areas will be built all around the existing structure." He saw that she was still confused. "It's like taking a newer and larger teepee and putting it over the old teepee."

"I understand," Sara said as she nodded her head. "When this is finished, we won't recognize our own house." She looked at him and smiled.

"Well," he stammered. "Sort of, but the original house will still be inside. We're just going to have some upgrades."

"What kind of upgrades?" Sara asked. "Explain what you mean."

"Running water," Monroe smiled. "Gus is talking with the contractor now about septic systems and drain fields. I have no idea what all that means, but the contractor is excited and has done some of these in Seattle. We won't need chamber pots or outhouses. We'll have everything indoors, including bathtubs, and wash basins."

Eddy and Emily arrived at the house. He had ridden into town to accompany her home. He did this almost on a daily basis. She enjoyed it and he felt like he was protecting her. Will was off with Gus and the contractor. Monroe had never seen him so excited. The contractor had hired him for clean up around the construction sight, and he couldn't be happier.

"How's the construction coming?" Emily asked as she stepped from her horse. Eddy took both animals to the barn to groom.

"I'm trying to explain things to Sara, but" he said.

"I understand what you're doing," she replied. "I still don't understand why. But that's okay, because I just want you to be happy."

"I can't believe how hot it is," Emily said as she wiped her brow. "It must be at least 95 degrees, and there's no air moving."

"Its not rained in almost 30 days," Monroe cautioned. "I told Ivan to let his crews know that they shouldn't light any campfires in the logging areas. If a fire starts, we'll never get it stopped."

They went to the house for dinner. Sally had fixed a wonderful variety of fresh fruits and vegetables she had found down in the valley. It was too hot to cook or eat hot food. Will was late, as usual. He tended to eat when he was done following Gus around. It was sometimes just before he went to bed.

Monroe wanted to talk to Will since his announcement that he didn't want to go to high school. Eddy was looking forward to school, but Will had always been too impatient to sit in a classroom all day, especially since what was being taught didn't interest him. Monroe snagged his son and Sara so they could discuss this.

Will gave his reasons, which were logical and well thought out. Monroe discussed opportunities that might not be available to him without the schooling. Will's grades had always been high. His reading, writing skills, and mathematics knowledge were excellent. He liked working and making his own money. He liked the contractor and learning this trade. Gus had given him a good basis in mechanics and machinery.

The discussion ended with Monroe resigning himself to the fact that William would not be attending high school. Sara knew the decision was his. She was glad that he wasn't quitting because he wanted to sleep all day. Will had never been lazy, and he wasn't a student of books. Eddy, in contrast, always had his nose in books. He had read everything in the house and some more than once. Eddy would go on and finish his education and he respected Will's decision.

"How did it go?" Emily asked as Sara joined her on the porch.

"Will is not going to continue with school," Sara said.

"I think that's best for Will," Emily said. "He seems to love working with this contractor and he's learning a good, decent trade."

"How could I have two sons that are so different?" Sara smiled. "I guess we knew that when they were born, didn't we?"

"It seems like yesterday that I was sitting out here waiting for you to deliver," Emily said. "That was thirteen years ago. I think it was really hot then, wasn't it?" Emily paused as a cool breeze hit her face. "I wonder what your next son will be like."

"One can only guess, Emily," Sara smiled. "I wanted to ask you about some pain I've been having."

"What pain?" Emily said in a serious tone.

"It hurts here," Sara said as she pointed to her lower left abdomen. "It hurts now, but last month it was on the other side."

"Remember I told you about counting the days from when you finished your bleeding cycle?" Emily inquired. Sara nodded a yes. "I'll bet you'll find that this pain begins the same number of days following your cycle. The pain you feel is your ovary expelling eggs. This is your fertile time, and the best time for you to get pregnant, Sara."

"Why didn't I feel this pain when I was younger?" Sara asked.

"Things change with a woman as she ages," Emily said. "It's sometimes more dramatic after a woman has children. Remember your first bleeding cycle after the boys were born?"

They both laughed and talked about past events. Monroe came out of the house and joined them. He was still not happy about Will's decision, but would respect it. Emily saw Eddy down at the barn grooming the rest of the horses. He would do this when things were on his mind, but only Emily seemed to know this. She got up from the porch and walked to the barn. He looked up and saw her and smiled.

"It's too hot to be down here, Eddy," Emily smiled as she stroked her horse's neck. "What's on your mind?"

"Will," he said.

"What about Will?" Emily said.

"He's lucky," Eddy said. "He knows exactly what he wants to do with his life, and he's doing it."

"Yes, he is lucky," Emily said. "I think he's known since he was 4-years old and started to follow Gus around."

"I wish I knew what my destiny is," Eddy said. "I sometimes feel a little lost."

"You're just turning 13 Eddy," Emily said as she touched his arm. She saw his eyes fill with tears. He never cared if she saw him cry. She gathered him into her arms and he held her close. He was already taller than Emily's 5'4" frame. "Is there something else, Eddy? I get the feeling that this is more than Will's decision."

"I guess I'm feeling a little alone," Eddy said. He had finished up his work in the barn. He started to walk back to the house with Emily at his side. "Will and I have always done things together. Will has chosen a road of his own and it will be strange to go to school without him."

"I never thought about that," Emily said. "You can always ride to town with me in the morning. You can keep me from riding alone." They reached the house and Monroe and Sara had retired. They sat on the porch for a while longer.

"Emily, can I ask you a question?" Eddy said in a soft voice. Emily nodded her head in the affirmative. "You and Mother are lovers, aren't you?" His blue eyes met hers and he didn't look away. "You always said I could talk to you about anything."

"Yes," Emily answered. "I'm not going to hide who I am. Your mother has never done that, and I have always respected that. We've never openly discussed this with anyone but each other either."

"I understand homosexually, Emily," he replied. "Many of the books I've read about it say it's a mental defect, or illness. I don't think that's right. I favor the Indian culture that says it's a gift. Do you love my mother?"

"More than my own life, and I can't imagine life without her," Emily said quietly.

"I'm happy for her," Eddy said. "I'm happy for you. It's good you found one another. The Great Spirit must have been watching over you both."

"How did you get so wise?" Emily said as she held Eddy's hand.

"I pay attention, Auntie," he replied with a smile as he squeezed her hand.

By October Sara was getting concerned that she wasn't with child. She and Monroe had spent the last couple of months together without results. Emily told her to be patient. Victoria had started school, and to Sara's surprise they had no problem with her attending the Indian school. She left the situation alone at Mary's request. The larger problem with society still ate at her.

The teacher at the Indian school was adequate but not progressive about her material. All of her students could read and write, but she didn't push them for more. Basic mathematics was all that was taught and Sara thought it was a crime to not teach them more. Monroe had heard of members of the Cherokee nation that had their own colleges for advanced learning. Sara decided to open a dialogue with them. Maybe they would have suggestions about what could be done at their school. She felt that she needed to do something to spark the interest of the children that attended the Indian school.

By the end of October it had snowed lightly. Monroe was glad that the addition was weather tight. Will was doing very well and seemed to anticipate the contractor's next move without any discussion from him. He had a logical knowledge of how this whole project would come together, and wanted to see every bit of it. The contractor would send Will into town for supplies when they ran short. He had become a favorite among the workers.

There were Medical students at the hospital and Helga kept them busy. Kathleen would spend mornings at the hospital and Emily would meet her there. They would go to the office around 9am and close at 4pm. It was getting dark early and Emily didn't cherish riding home in the dark. Eddy usually waited for her, and that was comforting. Kathleen was close behind her on most nights.

Monroe asked that Will join the family for dinner nightly. This was his only demand. He saw him miss many meals during the summer and the table didn't feel right without him. He knew that there were always things to do, but he would break, clean up, and be seated at the table by 6pm. Whatever time he went to bed, was his business. Will was considerate enough of Eddy to be quiet when he came in.

Will's body was showing the signs of his physical labor. His shoulders were getting broad and he gained definition and bulk in the muscles in his upper arms. He and Eddy were both getting taller. They now could look their father in the eye. Monroe was 5 feet 10 inches tall and these boys weren't done growing yet.

For the first few years of their lives Emily thought them to be identical except for the color of their eyes. This was not the case. As they grew you could see the differences in them. She never could decide which one was more handsome. She knew they would break some young girls' hearts in the very near future. Both seemed too busy to be bothered with girls, though.

Emily had arrived home with Eddy and Victoria. Eddy took the horses to the barn and Emily went into the house. She spoke with Sally and was looking for Sara. She had a letter from the head of the Cherokee Indian College she wanted to give her.

"Miss Sara is upstairs," Sally said. Emily walked up the stairs and dropped her bag in the room. She lit the lantern because of the darkness and as she walked out the door, saw the light from Sara's room.

"Sara?" Emily said as she put her head in the door. There was no response. She went into the room and was ready to leave when she saw Sara on the floor next to the bed. She went over and knelt next to her. She found a cloth and dampened it with water from the pitcher and placed it on Sara's forehead. In the next minute Sara started to stir.

"When did you get home?" she asked. "I came in here, lit the lamp, and then that's all I remember."

"I just got home, and it looks like you fainted," Emily said. "Let's get you on the bed." She helped Sara to sit on the bed. "Your color is starting to come back."

"My stomach is doing flip-flops," Sara said.

"Why don't you lie down for a bit," Emily said as she covered her with a blanket. "Did you have your bleeding cycle this month, Sara? You should have had it a week ago."

"No," Sara smiled. "I haven't even kept track. Do you think I'm with child?"

"This is a pretty good indication," Emily smiled. "You can come into the office tomorrow and I'll do an exam."

"Let's not tell Monroe until we're sure," Sara said with renewed energy. Emily gave her the letter from Oklahoma but that waited. Monroe was talking with the contractor when he saw Emily and Sara with smiles. He knew they were up to no good and walked over to talk to them.

"I thought you were going to wait until you were sure?" Emily teased quietly.

"I'm sure," Sara responded. She whispered the news in his ear and looked at him.

"Are you sure?" he asked.

"Mostly," Sara said. "I'll let Emily do an exam at the office tomorrow." He hugged his wife and gathered Emily in the other arm. Eddy watched from the barn and knew his mother was with child. He watched Victoria with Caleb and was envious of her. He loved his family but had secretly wished that there were more. He started to whistle as he groomed the horses.

Sara went into town with Monroe the next day and remembered their first trip 14 years earlier. Emily had just gotten into town and Sara knew no one. How many things had changed, yet the feeling he had remained the same. He dropped Sara off at the clinic and went over to talk to Jacob.

Emily confirmed what they had suspected and Kathleen concurred. By all calculations, Sara would deliver around the end of June. Emily was taken back to the first time she saw Sara so many years earlier. She hadn't aged a bit, but had gotten more beautiful. She seemed to glow today. Kathleen had recognized this, too.

"We'll set up a schedule for you," Emily said. "I want to make sure that Kathleen or I see you every month, just like last time."

Sara hugged them both and went to find Monroe. Kathleen asked if she thought Sara was carrying twins.

"I don't know, and won't know for the next month or so," Emily said. "I didn't see her last time until she was two months along. I could feel the height of the uterus was higher than it should have been. Now I know what to look for, and her history of multiple births helps me."

"I've only delivered one set of twins," Kathleen said. "That was in San Francisco many years ago."

"It scared the hell out of me, Kathleen," Emily confessed. "Sara was a real trooper and she was only about two weeks early. The boys were healthy and alert. I got drunk right after that and Sara put me to bed. She had just given birth to twin boys and she put me to bed. Ask me how stupid I felt?"

"Sara is an amazing woman," Kathleen said. "I know you care for her greatly, Emily. I'm going to ask you a question, but I don't want an answer. I just want you to think about it for a while. We can talk about it later." Emily nodded her head and looked at Kathleen. "Are you too close to Sara to objectively handle her care?"

"That's a good point, Kathleen," Emily said. "I will think about it."

Sara was engulfed in hugs from Jacob and Suzy. They couldn't be happier for them. Suzy pulled Sara aside and started to talk her ear off. Jacob was interested in the house project. Monroe was elaborating on the things going on now and Jacob said he had a telegram from the man responsible to ship the marble for the addition. It wouldn't be in until May of next year. The timing should be good.

The holidays were approaching and Monroe had started to really enjoy this time of year. He would always look for new decorations with each trip he made to Seattle. He and the boys would go out and find a tree a week before Christmas. The first exposure to this was strange for Sara and Mary. They would then look forward to this time. Sara worked all year and made many things for the boys, and Mary's children.

The adults would limit themselves to a single gift and exchange names. This year, however, they decided to buy what they wanted for each other. Monroe wanted this to be a Christmas to remember. He wanted to enjoy the warm embrace of his family before they started to move on. He knew that Will would be gone in the next few years. Eddy would be heading to college soon. Sara was carrying a new life and things would start all over again.

Emily had started to see the changes that would happen. She knew Will would do well in anything he tried. She worried about Eddy. He was bright and intelligent, but he had such a sweet gentle nature. She was afraid the world would be tough on him and she didn't want to lose him as a sounding board. They talked about everything. Eddy talked to her about things he would never discuss with Monroe, Sara, or even Will. She had found a book for him for Christmas. It was the history of Europe. He read all he could on this, but his access was limited. He found England especially appealing because of his father and he loved the legends of King Arthur and the Knights of the Round Table. She carefully wrapped it after she received it so he would be surprised and not find out about it from Sally or Sara.

She had asked Charlie to make a toolbox for Will. He was starting to collect some of his own tools. Sara and Monroe had acquired some tools to add to the box. She had found something very personal that she would give to Sara privately. One thing that Emily had found lacking in Monroe and Sara life were photographs. She had taken the boys to town on several occasions to have them sit for the photographer that worked part time for the local newspaper.

This year the photographer was coming out to the house to do the entire family. Emily wanted to be able to look back on this time when she looked at the pictures. She had asked him to come to the house on Christmas Day, and paid him extra for this. She knew the family would be dressed for dinner, which Monroe insisted on for Thanksgiving and Christmas.

Christmas morning arrived and all had the morning with their families. Mary, Samuel, and Charlie would spend the time with Victoria and Caleb. Sally would spend time with her sons. Monroe and Sara would be with Will and Eddy. The gifts would be exchanged amidst the 'oohs' and 'ahs'. When all was over, Emily stood and looked at this family.

"There's one more gift I would like to give everyone," she said. They all looked at her and in unison said that she had given enough. "Be that as it may, I have arranged for a photographer to be here this afternoon for some portraits. He should be here at 3pm."

"I never thought of getting a family picture done," Monroe said. "Thank you, Emily."

"What about getting Mary, Samuel, the kids, and Charlie up here at that time and have their pictures done?" Sara asked.

"Why not get all of us?" Monroe said. "We'll make it an event and capture this moment in time." He looked at Emily and smiled. "That includes you."

"This was for your family, Monroe," she said.

"You're as much a part of this family as I am," Monroe said. "I'll hear no more arguments about it."

By 3pm the photographer had arrived. He did a family portrait with Monroe, Sara, and the boys, one of the boys only, and Eddy asked that one of he and Emily be done. Monroe had just he and Sara for one and then insisted that he take one of Emily and Sara. By that time Charlie, Mary and Samuel appeared and another set was done of them. Monroe was having a ball coordinating this circus. He had asked Sara to put on the original buckskins she wore when they came over the mountains. He had found his jacket and old musket.

He wanted to remember all the time he had with Sara. He loved the look and smell of her buckskin. The boys had never seen her in these and even Will remarked at how beautiful she looked. He even got the man to take some photographs of the construction. He asked him to come back monthly so he could see the changes in the house.

"I think you've created a monster," Sara whispered to Emily as they watched Monroe.

"I think you're right, honey," Emily said back. "I'm sorry, but I don't regret it. It's nice to look at pictures and remember a day or time. When you look at these pictures in the future you will see the happiness on the faces and remember how you felt at that moment."

They walked back into the house and stood by the fireplace. Emily looked at Sara in her buckskin. She touched the soft leather. She could smell the heavy scent and marveled at how she must have looked when she married Monroe. She looked like a princess in the beaded outfit. Sara took her hand.

"Mother made this for me. Every part is hand stitched and even the beads are handmade," Sara said in a quiet voice. Emily knew she was remembering another time. "It is nice to look at pictures but I have all the pictures I need in my head. I have my life when I wore this, my mother, my life with Monroe, the boys, and with you." She kissed her gently on the lips and then held her close. "These are etched into my brain and I can see them anytime I want."

Chapter 15

The snow hit hard in January. It was so heavy that there were days that the logging crews couldn't get to their site. Ivan made sure he kept them busy for a few hours a day helping the transport crew deliver the stockpile of logs to the mill. This was the reason for doing some of the stockpiling. The loggers had been building houses all over town. This gave them time to work on finishing the work they had started a year ago.

Kathleen and Emily were busy at the clinic. The hospital was empty, which was always their goal. They had finally convinced the population of Snoqualmie that it was better to come in as soon as you got ill, rather than wait. Even Ivan was coming in for regular check-ups. Jack Regan and his crews were using them on a regular basis. Jack had weaned out most of the troublesome employees for more stable personnel.

Maggie had been in that morning and Kathleen was happy to announce that she was pregnant and due around the same time as Sara. Jack seemed to walk on air. Maggie was healthy and happy. She was a different person from the first time Emily saw her. She was self-assured, loved, and now pregnant. She had a sound head for business and was the driving force behind Jack's success.

***

"I think I have those photographs that were taken that day," Zack said to Beth. "I know they're in a box around here. Let me go look for them. Why don't you stretch your legs?" Zack got up from his chair and Beth did the same. She walked outside and lit a cigarette.

"What a nasty habit," she thought. She looked at the smoking tip and remembered when she had lit her first one. She was cleaning out Jenny's clothes and found a pack hidden in one of her jackets. Beth knew that she smoked but never let on. She looked at the package and held it in her hand. It was unopened and she was ready to throw it away but hesitated. She pulled the strip and removed one, placed it in her lips, and struck a match.

She almost coughed herself silly, and should have taken that as a hint. She did like the taste of the Menthol, though, and this was her downfall. She continued to pack up Jenny's clothes and found the envelope that still had Jenny's blood on it. Beth looked at it and put it in a box that was going with her to Seattle. She couldn't open it right now. Most of the furniture was sold at a garage sale, and Beth made more money on the stuff than what it cost her to buy it a few years ago.

She did keep the brass bed that she and Jenny had spent so many happy nights in, the chest of drawers, and the ugly leather recliner that Jenny had to have. Bret and Steve helped her pack the small U-Haul. She could easily pull this with her car. When everything was out, she vacuumed the carpet, washed the floors, wiped the countertops and cleaned the bathroom. Mrs. Austin did a walk-thru with her.

"This place is in better shape then when I rented it to you," she smiled. "I'm going to miss you, Beth." She looked at her and she then hugged her warmly. "You're going to be all right, kid. If you think that you're not, seek professional help." She turned and went back down the stairs. She was never very verbal, but when Mrs. Austin spoke, you listened for it was usually important.

Beth took one last look around the apartment. How quickly things can change in your life. A few short years ago, she and Jenny had opened the door to this place and saw the possibilities. She found love, peace, and happiness here. Now that was gone and it was time to move on. She closed the door and never looked back as she went down the stairs.

"I hate to see you go," Bret said as he opened her car door. "You make sure you call me when you get up there. Don't wait to get settled. I want to make sure that you arrive without any problems."

"I promise," she said. "I'm going to take my time. I want to look at the country on the way up. It was beautiful to fly over when we went up before."

"Maybe we'll be up to visit you soon, Beth," Steve said. "It's been years since I was in Seattle and wouldn't mind going back. It's a beautiful city."

She gave them both hugs and kisses. The tears flowed freely and she was still wiping them away as she drove east. She had decided to drive to Sacramento and then stop for the night. She had never been through the Napa valley and this route took her straight in the middle of it. Mrs. Austin had helped her plan this. Beth thought it was because she was a wine lush, but the scenery was quite striking.

By the time she got to Sacramento the heat had taken over. It felt like an oven when she got out of the car. She was glad for the air-conditioned room and the pool. She left by 6am to avoid some of the traffic. She got on I-5 northbound and her next stop would be Grant's Pass, Oregon. She watched the landscape go to arid, dry grass. She thought that no place could be as hot as Sacramento, but she was wrong. Redding was worse and she was glad to just drive through only stopping for gas. It was 8:30am and getting hot.

She kept heading north to the mountains. She passed through the Siskiyous and realized that the tall trees were calling her. She pulled off the road to a "View Point" and stretched her legs. The view was breathtaking. She felt she belonged someplace like this. She suddenly realized that she wasn't running away from something, but running to some sort of destiny. She got into Grant's Pass and found a cheap hotel. She was hungry and physically tired, but not mentally tired. She felt refreshed. Tomorrow she would arrive into Renton. The company had found an apartment for her. She had driving directions from the freeway. The phone, power, cable, deposit, and first month's rent had been taken care of by the company.

She knew it was a 7-hour trip from where she was in Oregon so she left by 5am so she could get to the rental office before they closed. This would allow her ample time, allowing for traffic, which, seemed to be worse in Seattle than anywhere else. She headed north thru Roseburg and Eugene. It seemed to take forever to get to Salem. She stopped and got some food and stretched her legs.

A few hours later she could see Mount St. Helen's. It was clear and you could see the bowl of the volcano. She would make a trip down here one weekend and drive all the way in. It was impressive. A few minutes later Mount Rainier came into view. It seemed to stand like a large white sentry as you drove north. It seemed to watch out for all of those entering or leaving Puget Sound.

She stopped in Olympia to stretch her legs and fill up with gas. The air was clean and cool. She could see the capital dome from the gas station. It was another hour north before she would leave the freeway, according to the woman behind the counter. It was 12:30pm and she should be in Renton by 2:30pm at the latest.

She had made better time than she had anticipated. She pulled her car in front of the rental office at 1:55pm according to the clock in her stereo. She looked around the complex and was pleased. It was on a street that dead-ended and she had a garage and the units were arranged in a semi-circle. The Manager walked her over to her unit and walked her thru. There was a nice kitchen, dining room, half bath, and living room downstairs. Upstairs boasted two bedrooms and the master bath, which included laundry facilities. The closets were huge and the open floor plan made the place look more spacious than the square footage suggested.

"The fireplace is gas," the Manager said. "You also have a small, private deck and back yard. We maintain the grounds, but there are planter boxes for you, if you desire."

"This is wonderful," Beth said.

"I have a few minutes," the Manager said. "Is there anything in the U-Haul you need a hand with?"

"A recliner, and my mattress and box springs," Beth said. "Anything else I can handle alone. Thanks for offering."

They opened up the trailer door and made short work of it. They had emptied the thing in 30 minutes. The Manager said good-bye, gave her directions to the U-Haul place down the street, and left. By 4pm she was back and started to unpack boxes. She didn't have to be to work until Monday, so she had Friday and the weekend to get acclimated to the area. She knew that she would do a drive-by to find her new office. From what her new boss told her, it was within minutes of her apartment.

She had seen a little pizza place down the block as she was taking the trailer back and went for a walk. It was a quiet neighborhood and was lush and well groomed. She waited for her pizza and walked back to her apartment. She opened the door to see the sun streaming in the sliding glass door. Jenny would have liked this place she thought as she plugged in the TV and connected the cable.

"Welcome to King 5 News at 5," a voice said. "In our top story," the voice continued. She wanted to see what was happening in the world. She sat in the leather recliner and ate her pizza. She would need to get some groceries tomorrow, but for right now this was fine. She also needed to find some furniture. She wanted to find something that matched and presented well. These things never bothered Jenny so Beth let it go, but this time her furniture would match.

She found a furniture store and found something she thought looked good and was comfortable. She had problems, although her credit was impeccable, because of her limited time in the area. They didn't want to take a check from her new account and couldn't deliver it until next week. This was unacceptable. They suggested she try a place down the street. These people were most helpful. She could rent the furniture on a weekly or monthly basis, or buy it outright. She opted for a full purchase and they could deliver that afternoon.

She went back to the apartment to finish unpacking boxes, hang the shower curtain, and get her closet in order. She had the stereo on and found a radio station she liked. She remembered she hadn't called Bret. She picked up the phone, got the familiar dial tone, and punched in his number.

"Hi, Bret," she said into his machine. "It's Beth and I got to

Renton without any problems. It's beautiful here. My phone number is 206-228-1113 if you want to call. I start work on Monday, but should be here in the evenings."

She took the time to call Steve and Karen and went back to unpacking. Within 2 hours she had the kitchen done, and the bathroom done. Her clothes were in the closet, or chest and she even had her shoes lined up. There were just a few boxes left in the bedroom and she had them on the bed when the doorbell rang.

The young men who delivered her furniture were careful of walls and doors. They placed it where Beth asked, had their paperwork signed, and were gone within 10 minutes. She tried it several ways before she hit on an arrangement that didn't close the room off. She stood back, looked, and said "this works for me". She had some laundry going and heard the dryer buzz. She always hated going out to do laundry. Jenny used to take the opportunity to people watch, but Beth saw it as time when she could do nothing else. She folded her laundry, put it away, and opened the last box. The yellow envelope with Jenny's blood on it appeared. Beth picked it up and saw it was sealed. She laid it on the chest of drawers and finished unpacking the box. As she was walking out of the bedroom she saw the envelope again.

"Shit," she said under her breath as she picked up the envelope. She walked to the living room and sat in the recliner and carefully tore open the seal and saw the copy of her father's birth certificate. Her eyes scanned through the information until she found the Place of Birth line. "Snoqualmie Valley Hospital," she read. She grabbed her Washington State Map and found the city of Snoqualmie. That's why Jenny was out there. What else had she found? The desire to found out was now starting to peak again. She would locate the office on Saturday, but she was going out there, too.

***

Zack walked back to the living room and saw Beth outside having a cigarette. He could see her profile as the sun hit it. He could Anne again. She would walk on the porch and enjoy the cool breeze and he would watch her through the window. It was February and she was in her 8th month. She was absolutely beautiful. Zack never thought that it was possible, but it was. Anne had, faithfully, seen Ben and Kathleen Eichorn for all of her appointments.

If it was possible, Kathleen was more excited about this than anyone else. She had a chance to bring one more child into the world, and the child of someone she brought into the world some 40 years earlier. Anne had done well during this pregnancy. Zack still wanted to marry her because of his love for her but she had still not given him an answer.

March had come in like a lion with cold weather, rain, and snow. It was March 8th and Anne had been fighting with a backache all day. When she and Zack sat down for dinner, she started feeling contractions. She remained silent about this until Zack had finished his dinner. As the maid started to clear the table Anne stood up and stretched her back.

"Does your back still hurt?" Zack asked in a concerned manner.

"It does," Anne said. "I think it's time, Zachary."

"I'll bring the car around, and get your bag," he said in a tense voice.

"It could be a long night," Anne said. "I'll call Kathleen and ask her to meet us at the hospital."

The trip took longer than expected because of the blowing snow and wind and Zack made sure he didn't drive too fast. He didn't want to hit a tree on the way into town. He saw the lights and knew that Snoqualmie was just ahead. He crossed the railroad tracks and headed for the hospital. There was a parking place right by the door. Zack parked and came around to help Anne out of the car. Kathleen met them as they walked in. He was never so glad to see anyone in his life. Ben was right behind her and they took her down the hallway. They showed Zack where he could wait.

"I'll be out in a few minutes," Kathleen said before the door closed. All Zack could do was pace. It seemed an eternity before Kathleen emerged. "She's in first stage of labor. It could be a long night for everyone, Zack. I'm not going anywhere and neither is Ben. Why don't you come in and sit with Anne for a while." She escorted him back to a room where Anne lay in a bed. He hated to see her in pain, and knew he was the reason she was here.

"Hi," she smiled and held out her hand. "Come sit with me." Zack sat down and when Anne's back would bother her he would rub it. It seemed to relieve the discomfort of the contractions. Kathleen came in around 2am and checked Anne. Zack was rubbing her back and Kathleen smiled.

"That's exactly what you should be doing," she said. "It helps ease off the pain of back labor. Let's check your progress." Zack started to leave. "Where do you think you're going? You need to stay here. There's nothing under here that you haven't seen before." She looked at Anne and winked then did her check. She put Anne's gown down. "It won't be long, now. You're doing beautifully."

The next hour Anne started to get down to business. When

Kathleen came in at 3:15am, Anne was fully dilated. She opened the door and got the nurse. There was a flurry of activity as Anne started to push.

"Don't do that yet, honey," Kathleen said as she stroked her hair. "Let's get you to the delivery room first." They moved Anne to a gurney and wheeled her down the hall. "Go to the waiting room, Zack. I'll find you afterwards." He watched Kathleen walk down the hall and saw Ben join her as they passed through a set of double doors. He couldn't sit so he paced back and forth. At 4:10am Kathleen appeared and smiled at him.

"Why don't you come with me?" she said.

"Anne's dead," he said.

"Heavens no, lad," she chuckled. She led him through a door where Anne lay with a baby in her arms. Kathleen walked over and looked at the baby and then Anne. "Thank you for letting me do this for you." She gently kissed Anne's forehead. "Come over and meet this fine baby boy, Zack. He's got great lungs, and a head of black hair." He looked at Anne and down again at the bundle in her arms and walked over and Kathleen hugged him then left the room. Anne moved the blanket away from his face and he could see the dark head of hair. He was pink, and beautiful. He had Anne's long fingers and her dark hair.

"Hold your son, Zack," she said as she gave him the bundle. "He won't break."

Zack held the baby close and kissed his hair. He rocked gently and watched the tiny creature. He instantly was in love with this baby. Ben came in the room and looked at Zack, looked back at Anne, and smiled.

"He looks like he's done this before, Anne," Ben chuckled. "He's a natural." He walked over and sat on the bed. "How are you feeling?"

"Tired," she responded. "Your mother was great. You'd never know that she was 76."

"You gave her a gift today," Ben said. "She really hated retiring, and I couldn't figure out why she did. She really is good at what she does." He turned and looked at Zack again. "What are you going to name this boy?"

"I haven't decided yet," Anne said. "I thought I would talk to Zack about it." Zack handed the bundle back to Anne. He had started to fuss and wanted to eat. A nurse entered the room.

"This little one wants to eat," she said. "I'll help you get started."

"I'm going to head home, honey," Zack said. He went over and kissed her gently. "I love, you. I'll be back in the morning."

Kathleen was in the following afternoon to check on Anne. She had done well, despite her age. This baby looked so much like Anne when she was born. Anne was attempting to breast feed when Kathleen arrived. The baby was not latching on, as he needed to. Anne was beginning to get frustrated and the baby seemed to cry more.

"Let me give you a few helpful hints," Kathleen said as she repositioned the baby utilizing an extra pillow that he could lay on. "Keep his head above his stomach. Sit up a little straighter and let him do the rest. You need to relax a bit, girl. Take a few deep breaths and get your shoulders down below your ears." Once Anne did relax, the baby latched on and ate contentedly.

"I don't think I'll ever get the hang of this," Anne said.

"It's too late to think about that now," Kathleen said. "We need to finish the birth certificate. Have you chosen a name?"

"Russell Wesley Monroe," Anne answered.

"Do you still want the father to be 'Unknown'?" Kathleen asked. Anne nodded her head. "I thought you might change your mind about that. Zachary is a fine young man. He'll make a good father, and husband."

"I have no doubt about that," Anne said. "I need to continue the Monroe line. I'm the last and that's the way it is."

"Do you love him, Anne?" Kathleen asked. "The same way you loved Amanda?"

"I don't think I'll love anyone that way ever again," Anne said as she stroked Russell's hair. "I do love him, though. Zachary is different from any man I've known, even with his young age. He's wise, loyal, and gentle."

"Does he know about your past?" she asked pointedly. "Does he know about Amanda?"

"Yes," she said. "I told him many months ago. He said it didn't matter, that was in the past. He still wanted to marry me."

"What's holding you back, honey?" Kathleen said as she took the sleeping baby from her arms. She kissed him gently and looked at him in her arms, then walked over and placed the baby in the bassinette and came back and sat on the bed next to Anne.

"I'm afraid of what people will think," she stated. "He's just 19. I'm twice his age."

"You never cared about what people thought before," Kathleen said as she held her hand. "I'm going to say the same thing your mother would say if she were alive. It doesn't matter what people think. It doesn't change who you are, or whom you choose to love. If he makes you happy, then keep him with you always. He doesn't seem to care about the age difference, so why should you?" She paused a minute. "Did you know that everyone in town knew that your mother and Emily were lovers? Do you know why no one cared? No one cared because your father, your mother, and Emily were okay with it. As long as they were okay with the arrangement, other people's opinions didn't matter. It never hurt your father's, or Emily's business, marriage, or relationship."

"I don't want to hurt him, Kathleen," she said. "I don't want him to be stuck with an old woman when he is still a young man."

"If you're anything like your mother, you'll never be an old woman," Kathleen replied. "Make a decision based on your heart, not your head. It's time, honey. Don't spend your life alone. You'll never find another Amanda. Here's someone right in front of you who possesses the qualities that are so rare to find in anyone."

"You even sound like Mother," Anne said as she fell into Kathleen's arms. She let her hold her as she cried. Kathleen stroked her hair and whispered that all would work out. Her mother used to do the same thing to her when she was a child. She missed her so much, but with Kathleen she felt she had a piece of her back. Kathleen had always thought of Anne as her daughter. They always had a strong bond.

Four days later Zachary took Anne and Russell home from the hospital. He had spent much of the time getting the nursery in shape. He had the maid clean everything and there were new drapes on the windows. He had chosen the room that adjoined Anne's for the nursery. He had purchased diapers, gowns, and a new mattress for the crib. He was having a ball and wanted to surprise Anne.

Samuel and Mary met them at the house and were anxious to see the new arrival. Zachary helped her from the car and into the house. Mary was there to take the bundle from Anne.

"Oh, my," she sighed. "He looks just like Eddy." Samuel came over and looked over Mary's shoulder. He looked at Anne and smiled then took the baby from Mary. He held him close and gently rocked. Mary watched him and thought about her own children. How long ago that seemed to her. "You know he'll spoil this child rotten, don't you?"

"That goes without saying, Mary," Anne replied. Samuel handed the baby back to Anne but not before he kissed him. "I think we both need a nap."

"I'll take you upstairs," Zack said and smiled at Mary. He couldn't wait to show her what he'd done. They entered Anne's bedroom and through the open door she could see the changes. She placed the baby on her bed and walked into the nursery. Zack stood behind her and waited for her reaction. She looked at the crib, the new drapes, the freshly cleaned rug, and turned to look at Zack. "Do you like it?"

"It's perfect," she said as she went to his arms. "It's exactly right. Did you do all of this?"

"Mary helped me," Zack said as he held her. "Annie, please marry me?" There was a long silence. Zack didn't take this as a good sign. She finally pulled away from him and took his face in her hands.

"Zachary," she said. "I have never met anyone who has touched my heart as you have. You are the light of my life. I love you dearly." She paused and looked into his eyes. "Yes, I will marry you."

***

Zack looked again at Beth standing outside the window. He would have to tell her that he was her Grandfather. This would not be easy for him. He felt that when Russell went off to the Air Force and Anne died that he was alone. Yet, outside of his window was the replica of the love of his life. This was the daughter of his only son and he never knew who his father was. Zack was a man who married his mother after he was born. He was never told that he was his father biologically. Anne wanted it that way, and he abided by her wishes.

Beth had no idea about any of this, but all would come to light very soon. Zack would have to explain why he didn't tell her right away. If she were anything like her father, she would be angry. This is why tact was important, but what was more important was how she would play into the grand scheme of things. Beth would have great responsibilities to face in the future. He had no doubt that she was up to the task, but would she want to take it on, or would she rather live her life as she had it planned?

Chapter 16

Zachary and Anne were married in a private ceremony at the house. Anne called on her old friend Patrick Reilly to perform the wedding. The weather the middle of May was beautiful. The garden was blooming and Mary had taken extra care so everything was perfect. Anne was very specific with the invitations. Tom and Kathleen Eichorn, their son Ben and his wife, Samuel and Mary, Peter, and Anne's house staff were the only one's present at this event.

Zack had no one he wanted to invite. All members of his family were in Ireland or Chicago. He had not contacted any of them since he'd moved. Kathleen had hired a photographer to document the occasion. Anne had left this detail out and was glad that Kathleen was thinking. She was more nervous than she thought she was. Zack was a mess. He had entertained the thought of running out the back door until he saw Anne.

"You're beautiful," he whispered. She turned around and let him see her ecru wedding dress. He walked over to her to her and took her hands. "How did I get so lucky?"

"I was thinking the same thing," Anne smiled. "You look very handsome. I hope you realize what you're getting into." They walked down the stairs together. Mary had taken charge of the baby. He was sound asleep and content in his bassinette. They stood together before the old preacher.

"Dearly beloved," he began. As he said the words, Zack remember back to the time when he first saw Anne. Her sadness after her mother died had disappeared. The glow, coming from her, lit up the room. They said their vows and kissed to seal their commitment. Following the ceremony they sat down to a large dinner. Kathleen hadn't seen her happy since Amanda died, but she now had someone who would never leave her or break her heart. She had someone who loved her.

Following dinner the photographer took pictures of Zack and Anne. He also did a photo of Anne and the baby. There were several of the guests. Anne wanted to make sure that she had one with Kathleen and Tom. She had taken over the role of her mother that Anne had placed her in. Zack looked at the two women as the picture was taken. This was the happiest day of his life and he wanted to etch the moment into his memory forever.

***

Beth came back in from the porch. Zack could tell that she was trying to grasp all that she had been told. He wondered if her mind was drifting to another time as his was. She sat down and took her coffee cup. She looked at him and he seemed to be able to swim in her eyes. He smiled at her and she looked into her coffee cup.

"Let's get back to Sara," Zack started. "Your grandmother was about to make an appearance."

It was the day before the 4th of July party. During May and June Monroe had worked on the house. He was hoping that the columns and the marble would be in place. The inside work had gotten finished during the winter. The contractor had promised Monroe that the work would be completed by the 4th. The contractor was doing the last of the clean up today. Monroe walked around the house and was pleased with the outcome.

"Is this what you were going for?" Sara said as she walked toward him.

"Yes," he said a little sheepishly. "I wanted it to look like a palace."

"It's beautiful, Monroe," she responded. "I need to go into town for a check-up. If I don't show, Emily will never let me hear the end of it."

"I'll go with you," he said.

"No," Sara said. "Eddy is going to take me in. He's hitching the buggy now. You stay and finish up." She turned to see Eddy bringing up the buggy. She kissed Monroe and Eddy helped her in.

They rode into town. Eddy tried to miss all the ruts in the road but wasn't totally successful.

"Sorry, Mom," Eddy said. "I'm sure this is a fun ride for you."

"Not as bad as you may think, son," Sara said as she took his arm. "Thanks for coming with me today. Your father wants to make sure that everything is ready for his party, and he wants to make sure the house is done." She looked at the trees as they passed close to the falls. From the corner of her eye, she saw an old friend. "Pull up, Eddy." As he did, he saw the figure.

"Our old friend," he said. "It's been a while since I've seen one. I've missed them."

"Me too," Sara said. "This is always a good sign." He turned and disappeared in the woods. "Did I ever tell you that the only reason that Emily is alive is because of them? Bobby Palmer was ready to kill her."

"I knew that," Eddy said. "Auntie and I used to talk about it. She never remembered seeing them that day, but was grateful all the same."

"I thought I was going to lose her," Sara said quietly.

"You really love her, don't you?" Eddy asked not expecting a response. "I love her, too. You were meant to be with each other. The Great Spirit made it so."

"How long have you known?" Sara asked.

"I think I've always known," Eddy said. "Will doesn't, though. I've never talked with him about it. I have talked to Auntie."

"I love you, son," Sara said as she squeezed his arm.

They arrived at the clinic, and Kathleen came out to greet them. Emily was over at Walker's getting some supplies and hadn't gotten back, yet.

"Let me do your check up and hope that Emily gets back soon," Kathleen said as she showed her to an exam room. Sara was ready at any time. Kathleen listened to the heartbeat and let Sara hear it, too. Her eyes grew wide and she smiled. "Have you had any pain?"

"No," Sara said. "I've felt really good."

"Yes, she has," Emily said as she walked into the room. "She's real close, isn't she?"

"Any day," Kathleen agreed. "But wait until after the party. Tom, Ben, and I enjoy it so much." She smiled, patted her on the shoulder, and left the room. Emily felt her belly and noticed the baby had dropped. Sara placed her hands on Emily's and looked into her eyes.

"I've missed you," Sara said. "Can I be with you tonight?"

"I don't know if that's a good idea," Emily said. "I don't want to do anything to start labor."

"I just want you to hold me, honey," Sara said. "That won't cause any problems."

Emily kissed Sara's large belly and helped her up. She held her closely and then they walked out to the waiting room. Eddy looked at them and smiled.

"So you got doctor duty today, huh Eddy?" Emily chuckled. "If you wait a couple of minutes, I'll ride home with you."

All had arrived for the party and Will was busy giving tours of the new construction. He had been a part of each step and explained how it all went together. Monroe listened to his excitement as he talked about the plumbing pipes, the marble, and the finish work. Monroe realized that Will had found his niche. The contractor knew it, too. He asked Will to stay on as an apprentice. He would be working in Snoqualmie for the next couple of years, but after that he thought about moving his business to Seattle. Will, Monroe, and the contractor sat down and talked yesterday and although Will was only 14, the contractor said he would pay him a full wage and expect the same work he had been helping him with through this last job. Monroe had not told Sara of this, yet.

Sara awoke next to Emily refreshed and happy. She and Emily had made love the night before and it was just what Sara needed and just what Emily needed also, although Emily was still afraid that this would put Sara into labor. Sara talked to her about her conversation with Eddy. She had always felt that her relationship with Emily was very private, and that only Monroe knew.

"Eddy is very observant," Emily said. "He can read people unlike anyone I've ever seen and he is wise beyond his years."

They knew the guests would be arriving early so they made sure they were up early. Monroe met them in the kitchen with coffee. Will and Eddy were already helping Charlie and Samuel with the set up. Ivan had already arrived with his pig. Helga was helping Sally in her new kitchen.

"This place is beautiful," Helga said. "I don't know what half of this stuff does, but it sure looks nice."

"I'm still trying to figure it out myself," Sally laughed. "Mr. Monroe has been very good to me."

"Are your sons coming today, Sally?" Helga asked. She smiled and nodded her head. Joseph and Daniel had both married and were living outside of Snoqualmie. They were great with the business and this left Mary free to supervise. Joseph's wife was pregnant but Emily couldn't get her to come into the clinic, so she would go to the house to see her.

By noon the place was filled with people and food. Jack and Maggie had arrived and she looked miserable. This had not been and easy pregnancy for her. She had prolonged morning sickness, and even in her 9th month, would get nauseated. Jack was patient and long-suffering during this time doing what he could to be helpful.

"Maggie," Sara smiled. "Come sit over here and put your feet up." She had noticed how swollen her ankles were. "I had that same problem when I carried the boys."

"This can't be over too soon for me," she said as she sat down. "This heat seems to make it worse." She looked around at all the changes. "Monroe really did a job on this place. It's wonderful and I'd like to see the rest later."

"Hello, Sara," Jack said. "I'm going to find Monroe darlin'. Are you okay here?"

"Fine," she responded. "The four of us will stay here." She patted Sara's hand and her belly. She saw Kathleen, Tom and Ben arrive. Ben saw Caleb and they were off on some adventure. Kathleen joined the ladies on the porch and Tom headed for the pig pit.

Sara surveyed the grounds and looked at the people. Most of the loggers were the original crews from 15 years ago. They had children, wives, and houses. Their lives had grown with the business. Many things had changed, but many had remained the same. The baby was kicking like crazy and Sara stood up for a minutes. She looked down at Maggie.

"This one is trying to tunnel out," she smiled. "It kicks like crazy. What are you hoping for Maggie? Do you want a boy or a girl?"

"I'd like a boy, just like his father," she said. "Jack is hoping for a girl. He says that boys aren't of any use to anyone and he's proof of that." They both started to laugh. "There are times that I can't fault his reasoning. What about you?"

"I'd like to give Monroe a daughter," Sara said. "He said it doesn't matter, but I know differently."

"I'm glad you have your feet up," Kathleen said as she touched Maggie's shoulder and joined them on the porch. "This is the most miserable time during a pregnancy. Where's Emily?"

"I think she's in the kitchen with Helga," Sara said. "I can show you where it is."

"Stay put," Kathleen smiled. "I'll find it and if I get lost, it will give me a chance to snoop around. I need to get a look at this place."

The afternoon passed and everyone ate until they could eat no more. The children played, men drank, and the women gathered on the cool porch to talk. Sara had noticed Will talking to the daughter of one of the loggers. She was a beautiful girl with long blond hair. Her father was one of Ivan's crew leaders and her mother had been working with Helga at the hospital. This was the first time that she had noticed that Will had discovered the opposite sex.

Emily saw this too, and smiled at Sara. They watched as he walked with her and then saw him take her hand.

"Oh, boy," Emily whispered. "They grow up fast."

"I wasn't much older than her when I married Monroe," Sara sighed, "seems a long time ago, now."

"It seems like yesterday when we sat here and you were carrying the boys," Emily replied. "Now look at them. Will is smitten with Ingrid, Eddy is thinking of going to college, and we're still sitting on this same porch. You'd think we would have made more progress."

The fireworks display was always the finale of the day. No one left without seeing this. As the bursts lit up the sky, Sara looked around at the faces. She loved these people. Some had been with them since the beginning. Samuel and Mary with their children, Charlie, Emily, Ivan and Helga, Jacob and Suzy, were constant figures in their lives. As she looked around her eyes met Monroe's. He smiled and gave her a wink. What a wonderful life he had given her. She knew he was special when she first met him some 24 years ago. Time and age had not changed him or how he felt about her. She looked back at the colorful bursts and saw her mother's face in the lights in the sky. She was smiling down on Sara and the baby started to kick again.

"I miss you mother," she thought. "I think of you every day."

"I know, my daughter," she heard in her head. "I have watched you everyday."

At 3am the morning of the 8th Sara awoke and couldn't get back to sleep. She couldn't get comfortable, but she didn't have any pain. She knew that she would have this baby soon. She went to the kitchen and made a pot of coffee. Emily awoke to the smell at 4am and went to find Sara.

"Are you okay?" she said in a sleepy voice. She put her hand on Sara's belly and felt the baby kick. She moved it to the other side.

"Can't sleep," Sara said. "Why don't you go back to bed? It's very early. I'm going to finish some paperwork that I've let go, and I have to get the checks ready for Ivan." Emily came over and kissed her and went back upstairs. Sara sat at the large desk and finished the payroll. By 6am all was done and Monroe could give them to Ivan.

"You're up early, Missy," Sally said as she came in. "Did the baby wake you?"

"I just can't sleep," Sara said.

"Baby will come today or tomorrow," Sally said as she turned and went to the kitchen. Within 15 minutes Sara could smell bacon. She loved that smell. The combination of bacon and coffee made it, officially, morning. Will came in and poured himself a cup.

"Good morning, mother," he said and kissed her on the cheek. "It's going to be a beautiful day."

"Where are you working, today?" she asked.

"We're doing some work on Moe Hawkins' house," he replied. "It should take us about 3 months."

"You really love what you're doing, don't you?" Sara said

quietly.

"Yes, I do," he smiled. "I'd like to be a contractor someday. Have my own crew and business. To take something and make it better or new is rewarding."

"I'm happy for you, Will," she said as she took his hand. Sally handed him a lunch pale and he stood up. "I love you, son."

"I love you, too, Mother," he said as he kissed her forehead. "I'd better get going. Phil hates people who are late."

"Good-bye, son," Monroe said as he came into the kitchen. "Be careful." He poured himself some coffee and Will went out the back door. "You're up early, honey. Are you feeling all right?"

"Just couldn't sleep," Sara said. "I figured as long as I was awake I'd do the payroll. You can give it to Ivan today. It's on the desk." She straightened up as the baby started to kick.

"This baby beating you up?" he asked as he put his hand on her belly. He could feel the movement, which, always was amazing.

"I'm grateful there's only one," Sara smiled. "Two kicking like this would kill me." She laid her head on his chest. "It will be over soon enough, though. Sally says today or tomorrow."

"Then I'll drop the payroll to Ivan and stay close to home for the next few days," Monroe said. "I want to be here if you need to go into town." He finished his coffee and stood up. "I should be back in an hour."

"Where are they cutting today?" Sara asked.

"We start the section closest to the falls," Monroe said. "The 1000 acres around the falls is off limits as we've agreed." Sally had just pulled some fresh biscuits from the oven and Monroe snagged one before he left. Sara and Sally looked at him and then at each other and laughed. Monroe had always had a weakness for fresh breads.

Emily came in and talked for a few minutes then left for the hospital. Eddy was close behind her. He wanted to get his horses groomed and then he was spending time with Victoria. Mary had asked him if he could tutor her over the summer. Her reading skills weren't very good, and she was having trouble in school because of it. Sara knew that this would happen and still was angry that Mary wouldn't fight to send her to the white children's school

"Mother," Eddy said. "It's their decision. Victoria is their child, so let's leave it alone. She's come a long way in the last 2 months."

"It's still not right," Sara snapped back.

"Right or wrong it's still their decision," Eddy said. "We can't make everything right." He put some bacon on a biscuit and drank a glass of milk. "Sally, you've outdone yourself on this batch." He kissed Sara and went out the back door and met Mary coming in.

"Sara," Mary said. "What are you going to do with this area just outside?"

"Haven't thought about it," Sara said.

"I'd like to put in a garden," she said. "A flower garden if that's okay."

"Anything you would like," Sara said. "Have fun."

"Sally, I'm tired," she said. "I'm going upstairs to rest a while." The stairs seemed endless and when she got to her room, she was winded. "I must be getting old." She fell asleep as soon as her head hit the pillow.

It was 3pm when she awoke. She thought the clock must be wrong. She went downstairs and saw Monroe sitting at the desk.

"Is it really 3?" she asked.

"It is," he smiled. "I checked on you a few times and you were sleeping so soundly I didn't want to wake you. Are you hungry?"

"No," Sara said. "I think I'll get some air." She and Monroe walked out on the porch. Eddy was just coming back from Mary's. Charlie had just stopped with a telegram for Monroe. He opened it and sighed.

"My Mother passed away," he said quietly. "My sister said to expect a letter from her."

"I'm sorry, Monroe," Sara said. "I know you always wanted to get back to see her."

"I did," he said. "I could have gone several times, but there was so much going on with the business and my family. I'm sorry she never got to meet you, or her grandsons." He looked out on the trees. "No use crying about something I can't change." He turned to go inside and Sara took his hand. He smiled at her and walked through the door.

"Miss Emily said to tell you she may be late," Charlie said. "Joseph's wife is having a baby. I need to tell Sally."

"She'll want to be there," Sara said. "Can you take her in the wagon?" Charlie nodded his head and smiled. Sara found Sally and walked her out to the wagon. "Stay with your son and grandchild a few days. We'll be fine here." Sally climbed into the wagon and waved goodbye. Sara joined Monroe in the kitchen and they talked quietly. He was distracted by the news of his mother. He was glad that they had made amends before he came to America. She never really understood him, or his desires for a different life. She never understood the hard life he had chosen. To him, this life wasn't that

196

hard. He, gladly, did without some of the luxuries of the affluent lifestyle he was born into and was glad to get out of the snobbish society in London. He didn't need people who were shallow. What he found in this country was a reality and honesty he searched for. He looked around this house and realized that this was more beautiful than any place the society of London could ever have. He had surrounded himself with people of substance. He found this in the people and the way they lived. These people worked for what they had, and a wife that could never be found in all of the London. His mind went back to the large crystal clock that sat on the mantle of the fireplace. He smiled to himself and looked at Sara. He had heard about half of what she said.

Neither Monroe nor Sara had much of an appetite that evening. Will and Eddy were another matter. There was still food left over from the party and they gladly ate their fill. There was roasted pork, breads, vegetables, and dessert. By the time the boys had finished, it looked like the party all over again. Monroe watched his sons attack the food supply and had to laugh.

"They act like they haven't eaten in weeks," he smiled.

"It's good they have good appetites, and good we had all this food left," Sara said. Eddy started to clean up the mess as Will ran the hot water to wash the plates. Sara was always pleased that they picked up after themselves. Monroe helped Will put the food away, and Sara grabbed a towel to dry the dishes. She was talking with Eddy when she felt the rush of warm fluid run down her legs. She looked down and then at Monroe.

"Looks like it's time we go to town," Monroe said. "I'll go upstairs and get your bag. Eddy, go hitch the buggy."

"Is it time Mother?" Will asked.

"It is," Sara said. "I've got time to clean this up before Monroe comes down."

"No, Mother!" Will answered firmly. "I'll take care of it. You sit down and wait for Dad."

She watched her son clean of the fluid that she had lost. Monroe came down the stairs and saw Will mopping the floor and smiled. He took Sara's arm and helped her outside as Eddy brought the buggy. Eddy took Sara's other arm and put her in the buggy. The labor pains had just started and she paused for a moment. Once safely in the buggy, Eddy put a blanket over her legs.

"I should be back sometime tomorrow, son," Monroe said.

"I'll take care of things around here," Eddy said. "I love you, Mom." Sara smiled at him as they rode away.

Monroe made a quick stop at the Eichorn residence before going to the hospital. Kathleen would be 5 minutes behind them. The nurse got them settled in a room and Kathleen appeared.

"I've been told that your water broke," she said. "Let's see how you're progressing." Monroe left the room and joined Tom in the waiting room. Sara's pains were close together and this baby was going to make an appearance quickly. It was 9:30pm and Kathleen expected this baby in the next 4 hours. "This isn't going to take long, Sara. You're moving quickly."

"Where's Emily?" she asked breathlessly.

"She's still out at Joseph's," she responded. "She said she would stop by here before she goes home." Kathleen knew this didn't really comfort Sara. She had always been more comfortable with Emily than she was with her. She expected this given their relationship and history. "I could send someone to get her if you want?"

"No," Sara said. "I'm just being silly. She'll be here if she can." She looked at Kathleen and held her hand. "We'll do fine."

"Would you like Monroe to sit with you?" Kathleen asked.

"Yes," Sara smiled. "I would like that very much. He missed all the fun last time."

Monroe came in and sat with Sara for the next 4 hours. Sara's labor pains had eased off and she got some sleep. She awoke at 2am and felt the need to push. Monroe called to Kathleen and she and the nurse moved her to the delivery room.

"Now you can keep Tom occupied," Kathleen said. They closed the doors and got Sara onto the delivery table. Sara didn't like this device. Kathleen said it was easier for the baby and the doctor. "Emily and I did discover after Ben was born, that it was best to let labor happen in a bed. I spent 12 hours on this thing." She got everything adjusted to the best comfort level for Sara. "It's time to push Sara."

Sara gave her best and Kathleen told her she could relax. Sara pushed again as the head appeared.

"Don't push, Sara," I need to get the shoulders. About that time Emily came through the doors. "There she is, Sara. I knew she'd be here."

"Started without me, huh?" Emily said as she patted Sara's shoulder.

"I couldn't wait," Sara smiled.

"Okay, Sara," Kathleen urged. "I need one more push." Sara pushed again and the rest of the baby arrived. She heard the cry and the nurse took the baby. Sara turned to look at it her new baby and saw only black.

Emily had taken the baby and was working on it with the nurse. She expected Kathleen to finish up with Sara.

"Jesus," Kathleen said. "Get over here Emily!" She turned to see blood everywhere.

"She's hemorrhaging!" Emily said. "We need to pack everything off."

"That's not going to do it," Kathleen snapped. "We've got to stop this surgically. Grab me a surgical pack from the cabinet, and Emily you start the ether. We've no time to waste."

The nurse moved quickly and Emily started the Ether although Sara had already blacked out. Kathleen's trained hands made the incision and had the bleeding stopped within minutes. Sara had lost a lot of blood already. All she could hope for was that it wasn't too much. Only time would tell. She was young and strong and this was the only thing that was going to save her.

Kathleen finished the last of the sutures and carefully put on the bandage. She looked up at Emily, who was listening to Sara's heartbeat. It was strong and steady. She changed Sara's gown and they carefully moved her to a gurney so she could be taken back to her room. Emily stood over her and stroked her hair. She looked up and saw Kathleen.

"What happened?" she asked.

"Don't know for sure," Kathleen said. "She had a normal labor and normal delivery. I did notice after I got in there, something." She walked over to the basin that held the uterus. "Look, there's another small fetus." She showed Emily the uterus and the tiny body. "It looks as though it was only alive for about 4 months. It's a wonder she got through the whole 9 months. These kinds of things will poison the whole system."

"Thank God you were here, instead of me," Emily said. "Think what would have happened if she delivered at home. We'd have lost her."

"We still may, Emily," Kathleen said quietly. "She lost a lot of blood, and I don't know if I acted quickly enough. The next 24 hours are critical." She paused and took off the bloody gown. "Let's go talk to Monroe. We need to tell him about Sara, and tell him that he has a daughter."

They walked out together. The nurses rolled Sara to a room. Monroe saw both of them and had a bad feeling. Tom stood up with him. Kathleen calmly told him everything and how Sara was right now. He just stood there and looked at her and then at Emily.

"You have a fine, healthy baby girl, Monroe," Kathleen said. "I'll be here all night to keep an eye on her."

"Both of us will stay," Emily said. "There will not be a minute that one of us will not be with her."

"Can I see her?" Monroe asked quietly. Kathleen nodded a response and she and Emily walked him down the hall. The nurses had gotten Sara into bed. She had not awakened yet and Kathleen didn't expect her to for a few hours. He heard the baby and turned to look at his daughter. He walked over and picked her up and held her close. He sat back down on the bed and held the baby in one arm and held Sara's hand with the other. "We have a daughter, Sara, and she's beautiful. She looks like her mother, she needs her mother, and I need her mother. Come back to us, honey. We love you." He bent and kissed her forehead.

Emily turned away. She didn't want to have Monroe see her upset. The bundle in the blankets started to fuss and the nurse took her so she could feed her. Monroe stood up and looked at Sara. He said he would be in the waiting room. He would not leave tonight. As he left the room, Emily turned to Kathleen. Her eyes were filled with tears. She went to console Emily, and maybe herself a bit. Emily had never seen Kathleen this affected by any patient. This wasn't any patient. This was a great woman, and a friend.

"I can't think of anyway we could have seen this happening," she said. "I've gone over every exam, labor, and the delivery in my head. I can't think of anything we missed."

"Stop it, Kathleen," Emily said. "There's no blame to assign. Hopefully, we acted quickly enough, and Sara's strength can get her through this."

"We need to get some fluids into her," Kathleen said. "Let's get a couple of pillows and prop her up so she doesn't choke. We need to do this slowly, but consistently."

It took 4 hours, but they succeeded in getting about a quart of water into her. She was pale and quiet. Her heartbeat was strong, and her breath sounds good. By daybreak, there was still no change. Kathleen left to tell Helga that they wouldn't be seeing patients today. She told her about Sara and then went to check on Monroe. He was still in the waiting room. Will and Eddy had joined him.

"There's been no change yet, Monroe," Kathleen said. "We still have to wait. This is the hardest part."

"Can we see her?" Monroe asked.

"There's no reason why not," Kathleen said. "As a matter of fact, why don't you all bring a chair and you can stay for a while. I always felt it was best to have a patient surrounded by the people that love them."

They all followed Kathleen back into Sara's room. Emily looked at them and then at Kathleen. She smiled and nodded her head. Eddy came over and hugged Emily.

"She's a fighter," Emily said. "Go sit with your Mother. Talk to her and I'll bring in your sister."

"Jesus," Monroe said. "I forgot to tell you boys that you have a new baby sister." About that time the nurse brought the baby in. She had a bottle and the baby was fussing. "I'll take her."

"Can I, Dad?" Eddy said. Monroe smiled and nodded. Eddy took the baby and started feeding her, like he was an old pro. Emily looked at Kathleen and smiled. The tears began to well up in her eyes again but she fought them back.

Will sat on the bed and held his Mother's hand. Monroe was on the other side. Kathleen and Emily decided to leave and let the family have some private time with Sara.

"I thought she'd be awake by now," Kathleen said as she and Emily sat in her office. "I'm really worried." She stared at the floor. "We need to get more fluids into her and I need to check her incision. I'll get the clean bandages."

They went back into the room and the whole family was sitting on the bed. Eddy still had the baby who was sleeping quietly on his shoulder. They hated to disturb them. There was a stirring in the bed and a moan from Sara. She opened her eyes and saw her family with Kathleen and Emily standing behind them. She smiled, slightly, and tried to get up.

"You stay put," Kathleen said. Everyone got up from the bed. Kathleen took the baby from Eddy and kissed her gently. "Meet your daughter, Sara." She laid the baby in her arms.

"I, somehow, knew you'd be trouble," she said weakly. She kissed her black hair, and the nurse came in and collected the bundle.

Will and Eddy kissed their mother. Monroe suddenly looked exhausted and Kathleen suggested that everyone get some sleep and let her and Emily look after Sara. Many more kisses happened before they got the room cleared out. Emily came to the bed and sat for a moment. She looked at Sara and held her hand. Kathleen left them alone for a moment, giving some weak excuse about getting different bandages.

"I thought I'd lost you," Emily said.

"I still don't know what happened," Sara said. "I turned to look at the baby, and then I woke up and everyone was here. To see Monroe, the boys, the baby, and you standing there, made me feel like I was in the spirit world. I couldn't find my Mother, though." Kathleen came back into the room.

"We'll tell you everything in a little later," Kathleen said. "Right now I need to check your incision."

Kathleen and Emily spent the rest of the day taking turns checking on Sara. They told her of the problems after the delivery and why it happened. They also told her that she could have no more children. Sara was sad about the baby that didn't live. She took some comfort in knowing that she was with her grandmother in the spirit land.

By that evening, Sara was tired of lying in bed. She wanted to get up and Emily knew this was a mistake. Emily let her sit up and put legs over the edge of the bed. This made Sara's head swim, and this time she knew she was right. Emily held Sara steady as she sat. Sara put her arms around Emily and held her close. After a few minutes Emily helped her lay down. She sat on the bed and held Sara's hand as she drifted off to sleep.

Chapter 17

It had been a week and Sara had been up walking the halls for the last 2 days. She was ready to go home. Kathleen came in that morning to take her stitches out. She didn't like the look of her incision, not because of any infection, but because she had done it so quickly that night. It wasn't going to be the prettiest scar, and she apologized to Sara.

"I'm alive, Kathleen," Sara said. "I want to thank you for that. I can never repay you."

"You lived, honey," Kathleen said. "That's enough for me."

"Are you ready to go home?" Emily asked as she entered the room. "I've got the buggy, when you're ready. I've brought clothes for the baby and for you."

"Speaking of the baby, do you have a name for her?" Kathleen asked.

"Anne Elizabeth Monroe," Sara said then smiled. "Anne is for my mother and Elizabeth is for Monroe's mother. Maggie and Jack stopped in a few minutes ago and introduced me to their new baby girl. They named her Amanda Margaret. Jack was taking them home, too."

"She was born a couple of days after Anne," Emily said. "I'll be back in about an hour so take your time. Monroe is waiting at the house."

The road to the house didn't seem as bumpy as when she traveled it a week ago. Ivan came out of the house as they passed and talked to Sara and looked at the new arrival. He was glad to see Sara up and around. As they headed through the trees he thought about Monroe. He was having a hard time dealing with Sara's illness. He was beside himself with worry and this was the first time that Monroe showed his temper. He made it clear to Ivan that he couldn't be bothered by business. He needed to concentrate on his wife.

"Can you stop by the falls?" Sara asked. "I want to introduce my daughter to this special place."

Emily stopped the buggy and went around so Sara could hand down the baby. She slowly got out of the buggy and they walked over to the falls. They rounded the bend and saw Eddy reading a book.

"I knew you'd stop here," he said as he stood up. "Let me have this little one."

"I've named her Anne Elizabeth," Sara said.

"Little Annie," Eddy said. "She looks like an Annie, don't you think?" He held and cuddled this small bundle. "Listen, Annie. Can you hear the whispers? You will, my sister, you will." They stayed for a few minutes and they all went back to the house. Eddy helped his mother out of the carriage and up the steps and Emily brought the baby. Sara was still very weak. The trip home had tired her out. Monroe met her at the door and took her arm.

"Welcome home, honey," he said and then kissed her. "I have a surprise for you, but you look a little too tired for one right now. I'll take you upstairs so you can rest."

"Thanks, Monroe," Sara said. "I think I'd like to sit down first." Her knees were weak and she started to perspire. Emily came in and saw an ashen faced Sara.

"We need to get her to bed," Emily said. "Monroe, can you carry her upstairs?" He picked her up effortlessly, climbed the stairs, and carefully put her in bed. Emily checked her pulse, which was strong and steady. She needed some home cooking, and rest. Sally came in and checked on Sara and to get a look at the new baby.

"Welcome home, Missy," she said as she held her hand. "I have a new grand daughter myself. Her name is Angelina."

"Oh, how wonderful, Sally," Sara said weakly. She lay back on the pillows and closed her eyes. "I must see her soon."

"Let's all get out of here," Emily said. "She needs to rest." Monroe kissed her gently and cleared everyone but Emily out of the room. "Sara? Do you have any pain?"

"Yes," she said quietly. "I suppose that's expected when you've been cut open. I'm just so tired. I can't keep my eyes open."

"You go to sleep, honey," Emily said. "I'll come up later and check on you."

The spells of fatigue continued for the next month. Each was less incapacitating than the last. By the time Anne was 6 weeks old Sara was back to her old self. Sara was producing no milk for the baby, so the bottle-feeding continued. Eddy loved spending time with his sister. He loved the smell of her and the way she snuggled into his neck when he rocked her. Since he had started school, he would rush home so he could be with her.

Monroe's surprise for Sara was the addition of a nursery in the new section of the house. There was a door that passed from the original bedroom to the new nursery. Will and Eddy had taken rooms in the new section. Eddy had chosen the room next to the nursery. He could hear Anne in the night and sometimes get her before she could wake Monroe or Sara.

Emily couldn't sleep one night and she went down to the living room. Eddy was sitting there rocking the baby and talking to her softly. The baby looked at Eddy and cooed. She watched him for several minutes and didn't want to disturb them. She turned to leave and Eddy saw her.

"Come in Auntie," he said. "Annie was fussy, so I brought her down here. I've been telling her a long bedtime story, but she's not asleep yet. She wants to play."

"You really love her, don't you?" Emily asked. He nodded his head as he kissed Anne.

"I never want to see her hurt or in pain," he said. "I will protect her always. I want to teach her everything. Look how beautiful she is. She's like Mother. She's happy, perfect, and the ills of the world have not touched her. She's an angel."

"Yes, she is," she said as she took the baby. "She's a miracle and a blessing."

They sat and talked for the next hour. Eddy had his two favorite women all to himself. He was in heaven. Emily noticed a change in him. The sadness he, sometimes had, was gone. This baby seemed to fill a void that he had in his life. He always had a more sensitive side than Will had ever shown. What did this baby have that Eddy found in no other human? Monroe and Sara had always shown a great deal of affection for both boys. William didn't seem to require what Edmundson needed, but never would ask for. They were different from the day they were born. This was even more apparent since Annie's arrival. Will cared for his little sister and would even hold and kiss her, but she wasn't his first priority.

"Let's get this little one in bed," Emily said. She handed Anne to Eddy and he disappeared up the stairs. Emily stayed in the living room and watched the fire. She had hoped that Eddy would get interested in some girl, marry, and start his own family someday. He was so much like his father, but he seemed to be a little lost. Eddy still didn't know what he wanted to do with his life. This would all come in time. Emily had no doubt about that.

Monroe was going to Seattle before the November elections. There was some legislation he had gotten wind of about clear-cutting everything possible. He was going to call in some markers and see if it could be stopped. Sara had rallied support of the local tribes, and although that held little weight in Olympia, it did matter to the

Federal Government.

The man from the Cherokee nation in Oklahoma was set to arrive today. He would accompany Monroe to Seattle, and had already made his contacts in Washington D.C. Eddy waited at the train station after school and would bring him to the house for dinner. Tom and Kathleen would join them and discuss their contacts on San Francisco.

A stand would be taken to preserve this area. If they failed, the health of the area was in jeopardy. Monroe, Ivan and Tom had an alternate plan arranged and silent backers to help make it happen. There were millions of acres of government land surrounding this area and they had the financial backing to buy 100,000 acres so the pillaging would never touch Snoqualmie. This way they could control the logging, and save the land from the scarring that so many companies left. Jack Regan had joined them. He wanted something left to his children and grandchildren. He wanted to preserve the area he had fallen in love with.

Eddy waited at the train station and saw a tall man step off the train. He saw Eddy and smiled.

"I'm Edmondson Monroe," Eddy said as he shook his hand.

"I expected someone older," he replied. "I'm John Young Bear. It's nice to meet you."

"You were probably expecting my father," Eddy said. "He'll meet you at the house."

Eddy showed him to the buggy. They talked the whole trip to the house. Eddy was fascinated by what this man had done. John had been educated at Dartmouth College where he had earned his Doctorate in Education. John had exercised his rights as an Indian and utilized a fund set up in 1775 by the Continental Congress for the sole purpose of educating Indians. As much as Dartmouth wanted him out, he wouldn't or they couldn't get rid of him. After finally recognizing his drive and knowledge, they offered him a professorship at his tender age of 21. He, naturally, declined and left the University on his own terms.

Since that time, he had helped start schools on reservations all over the country. He also had a network of qualified teachers from schools all over the nation. He had even contacted someone to come to this school after Sara had contacted him. The teacher there wasn't doing all she could for the students, which was why Sara had written to him.

"I have a wonderful life," John said. "There's nothing like teaching young eager minds to take charge of their own destiny." He paused and looked at Eddy. "How old are you?"

"I'm 15. I just started high school," Eddy replied.

"To have your whole life ahead you," he smiled. "How lucky you are." He looked at the trees. "What beautiful country. There's something mystical and sacred about this area.

"May we stop for a moment?" Eddy asked. "I'd love for you to see something."

"Absolutely," John said. "I'd love to stretch my legs." Eddy made the turn and stopped by the falls. He had this need to share this with John. He had to get him to understand the importance of the fight he was taking on. John could hear it long before he could see it. When Eddy brought him around the bend, John stopped. "Whoa! This is amazing. I think the Great Spirit must live here. This is what your father is trying to preserve, isn't it?" John said.

"Yes," Eddy said. "We have to." Eddy paused and looked over this area. "There's more here than meets the eye, John."

"Like, what?" he asked.

"We have a creature that watches out for us, here," Eddy said. "Many people think that they don't exist, but they do. I, father, mother, and others have seen them many times."

"Are you talking about the legend of the Sasquatch?" he asked.

"It's no legend," Eddy replied. They talked for a few more minutes and arrived at the house. John made him promise to tell him more when they got back from Seattle. Eddy liked this man, and felt he could trust this man. He gave his promise as they arrived at the house. Eddy played the perfect host and made the introductions. Sara was so proud of him. Monroe was surprised and pleased. They had never seen Eddy take charge like this.

As they sat through dinner John talked about growing up in Oklahoma. He talked about the progress that was being made in the schools on the reservations. He also said that Eddy had taken him to the falls.

"As much as we have done with all the schools," John began, "doesn't begin to compare to what we are trying to do here. You are trying to preserve something so sacred. We've made small bits of progress on the reservations. This is something very big. We're trying to beat the government at their own game, and it's a game they are very good at playing."

After dinner, Sara, Emily, and Kathleen went to the living room. Annie was fussing and wanted her uncle Eddy but he was busy talking to the men. Emily and Sara found this refreshing. They knew that Eddy was quite taken with John. Kathleen took Annie and she seemed to settle down. She got her to eat and then she fell asleep.

"Let me take her to the nursery," Sara said. "I think she's down for the night." She carried her up the stairs and Kathleen looked at Emily. You'd never know that she almost died a couple of months ago. She was rested, healthy, and looked wonderful. She returned and sat back down.

"How have you been feeling?" Kathleen asked.

"Always the doctor," Sara smiled. "I feel good and my energy is what it was before. One baby is so much easier than two."

"I don't know how you did it," she responded. "I had my hands full with Ben."

"Annie only fusses in the evening," Sara said. "Eddy usually can get her to settle down, normally, by reading to her. She seems to love the sound of his voice. Monroe can usually accomplish the same thing. This baby can get anything she wants from her father or brother."

"Eddy seems quite taken with John," Sara said as she looked toward the study.

"He's a fascinating man," Kathleen said. "He's done so much in his lifetime, and he's not that old."

"Eddy told me he was 22," Emily said as she returned to the room. "He's done a great deal despite roadblocks."

The men came back into the room and Tom said it was time that he and Kathleen head home. Eddy quietly asked Emily where Annie was. She pointed to the ceiling and smiled.

"Eddy is going with us to Seattle," Monroe announced. Sara looked at Eddy and he blushed. "A couple of days out of school won't hurt him, and the education he'll get in Seattle will be worth it."

"It's never too early to learn the workings of the Government," John said and then winked at Eddy.

"I think this is wonderful," Kathleen said. "You'll spend some time in the big city and really appreciate what you have out here." Emily smiled and nodded in agreement.

"You'd best go pack a bag, son," Sara smiled. "You'll have a long day tomorrow." He kissed his mother gently and disappeared upstairs.

"I'd best turn in myself," John said. "I'm suddenly very tired."

"I'll show you to your room, John," Monroe said. "Tom, I'll see you in the morning before we board the train. It leaves at 10am."

"I think this is great," Will said. "I wish I could go, but Bill is teaching me about framing and load bearing walls."

"You really like this building stuff," Eddy said.

"So do you, but you want to build in a different way," Will said.

"Will you do me a favor?" Eddy asked. Will nodded a yes. "Keep an eye on Annie, Mom, and Emily. You're going to be the only man in the house."

"I can't do it as well as you, Eddy, but I'll do my best," Will chuckled. "Have a great trip and enjoy the big city."

Emily told Sara she would stop in at the school and let Eddy's teacher know that he would be gone for a few days. Sara made sure they had food for the trip. Monroe said they would be gone only 4 days. He would send a telegram if anything came up. He kissed her gently and did the same with Annie. Eddy was having second thoughts about leaving but a little encouragement from Sara was all he needed.

Samuel took them into town and watched them board the train. Monroe waved good-bye and the train left the station. Eddy was fascinated with the scenery. Monroe and John talked about the people they would see and talk to. When Mt. Rainier came into sight, Eddy got a lump in his throat. He stood and walked down to the door that led to the platform on the railroad car. Monroe followed his son as they looked at the mountain.

"Huge, isn't it?" Monroe teased. "It always looked like a sentry guarding the rest of the mountains to me." They pulled into Seattle about an hour later. For some reason, Eddy thought it would take longer and said this to his father. "It used to take more than a day, by wagon. It was a hard trip back then."

They checked into a hotel on the waterfront and Monroe left messages for the others he was expecting. Some had already checked in and some would arrive later. They would all meet for dinner this evening at 7pm. This is when Eddy's education would really start.

Things in Snoqualmie were quiet and peaceful. The clinic was quiet and Kathleen and Emily decided to take the day off. The nurses knew how to get in touch with them if there was an emergency. The med students could handle anything until then. Emily walked over to Walker's to get some things to take home. She saw Jack Regan, who was looking a little tired.

"How's family life, Jack?" she said.

"Just fine," he smiled as he turned and saw Emily. "Amanda has her days and nights mixed up. We've not had a lot of sleep."

"They can turn your world upside down," Emily said.

"I wouldn't have it any other way, Emily," Jack said. "I'm getting a taste of what Monroe had for all those years. I used to be jealous of him, but not anymore. I'm grateful to him for showing me that life is what you make it." He looked at the floor and smiled.

Suddenly, an explosion rattled the windows of the store. Jack looked at Emily and they ran outside. There was smoke coming from the mill.

"Get Kathleen and get to the hospital, and I'll run down to the mill," Jack said. "There could be a lot of people hurt."

That was an understatement. The three medical students, Kathleen and Emily were kept busy for the next 12 hours. They had a total of 15 people injured. Most were burns, and flying debris from the explosion. 3 of the 15 had died before they got them to the hospital. The nurses and students had done a tremendous job of organizing and working as a unit. By 10pm Emily and Kathleen had a chance to sit down. They had admitted 4 of the injured and the rest went home.

"Did anyone find out what caused the explosion?" Kathleen asked.

"From what the injured said, it was a combination of a jammed log and a motor burning out," Emily said. "That motor got hot enough to catch the old dry sawdust on fire."

"Emily?" Jack said from the doorway. "I need you out here." She and Kathleen both went outside and saw one more body in the wagon. Emily pulled the blanket away and couldn't breathe.

"Charlie," she whispered. "Oh, God, Kathleen, its Charlie."

"We couldn't get him out," Jack said with tears in his eyes. "He was in his office, and the walls came in on top of him. I could see him and I couldn't get to him."

"This is not your fault, Jack," Kathleen said. "Let's get him inside so we can clean him up. Then we'll take him to the undertakers. We can do nothing for him here."

"I need to get home," Emily said. "I have to let Samuel know about his father. I'll help you with him first. Samuel will want to see his father before we move him."

"Why don't you go now," Kathleen said as she put the sheet over Charlie's face. "The nurses and I can handle this. We should be done by the time you and Samuel get back."

"You're not riding home alone," Jack said. "I'm going to run home and tell Maggie that I'm escorting you home and why. Don't leave until I get back."

Emily watched the wagon pull away and sat down on the step and cried. Charlie was gone. Monroe was out of town and wouldn't know until he returned. Kathleen sat next to Emily and put her arm around her. She cried openly for Charlie and for the exhaustion she was feeling. Kathleen held her close and comforted her as best she could. She was still holding her when Jack returned. He helped her on her horse and Kathleen watched them ride off into the night.

They waited on the funeral until Monroe returned. All of the good things that happened in Seattle were overshadowed by this devastating loss. Monroe, Samuel, and Sara cried openly as they laid Charlie to rest. Victoria and Caleb didn't understand why their Papa wouldn't be home again. Eddy had taken the children aside and told them that he is now with the Great Spirit and would watch over them always.

The entire town was in attendance. It was the largest funeral that anyone had ever seen. So many men, that Samuel had never met, expressed their condolences about his loss. A young Negro approached Samuel and said he had worked closely with his father. He was training him in estimating board feet. He had worked with Charlie for about 6 months and had gained a respect that he had for no other man

"When I first met your father, I was angry," he admitted. "I was angry at the white man for the enslavement and abuse of my parents. I was angry with the Government that allowed it and then I met your father. He told me that if we keep looking backward, it clouds our vision, and we can't look ahead. We can't change the past, but we can change our future and the future of our people. He made me think, and when I did that, my anger went away. He was the closest thing I ever had to a father, for I never knew mine. I will miss him, forever." The young man was crying openly. "I just wanted you to know."

He shook Samuel's hand, turned, and disappeared into the crowd. Monroe had heard what was said and the tears welled up again. How he would miss his old friend. His life ended much too quickly and there would be a void in their lives. He could never look at his home without seeing his handiwork. From the day that he found him and Samuel on the mountainside, he was like the brother that Monroe had never had. He touched the life of this young man and so many other people that Monroe knew nothing of. He had a quiet strength and dignity that was so rare and now he was gone, but would never be forgotten.

***

Zack looked at Beth and saw the tears in her eyes. He saw those same tears in Anne's eyes when Samuel passed away. Russell was 6 months old and it was the fall of 1930. Life had been relatively easy at the estate, thanks to Anne's father putting aside all the money that he did. Although they were in a 'depression' the estate was fairly self-sufficient. There was always a large garden, canned goods and meat available.

The lumber crews still were logging and a percentage of this came to Anne on an annual basis. This was the arrangement set out when the logging land was sold. "An annual annuity will be paid to any descendant of Edmundson or Sara to equal and not exceed 2% of gross annual revenues." This 2% proved to be greatly reduced but still more than ample for daily life. Any extras, Anne would use from the safe.

"This depression can't last for ever," she said. "The price of lumber will come up as soon and the economy is back on its feet."

"I know that you're right," Samuel told her. "I just worry about Mary. She had no way to support herself, if something should happen to me."

"I will always take care of Aunt Mary, Samuel," Anne re-assured. "Never worry about that."

"I'm very glad you found Zack, Miss Anne," Samuel said. "He will never break your heart. He's a good man." Samuel was never one to openly display affection, unless it was his wife. He reached over and hugged Anne quickly, turned, and left.

He died that same night. Mary awoke in the morning and Samuel didn't. Anne was thinking about their conversation and he knew he would die shortly. She always wondered how you knew you would die. Her mother knew also. She had told Anne that she wouldn't live to see the morning. She was right, too. For some reason this haunted Anne.

Zack was surprised that Anne had shed tears at Samuel's funeral but not at her Mother's. This he didn't understand at all. It concerned him to the point of finally asking her one night after Russell was tucked in for the night. He never thought Anne was cold-hearted. He had never experienced that when they were together or with the baby. She was so tender and loving.

"Why didn't you cry at your Mother's funeral?" he asked directly.

"I did my crying in private, Zachary," she said. "There was nothing left unsaid between my Mother and myself. We had said our good-bye the night she died. With Samuel, I felt that I never told him how much he meant to me. I never told him how grateful I was to him for looking after my mother after Dad had died and even after Emily passed away. He was always there, watching out for all of us. I loved him for that." She started to cry again.

"Let me tell you what he told me," Zack said as he held her. "He said that you were like his own child. He knew you loved and respected him. He knew you would take care of Mary if something happened. He trusted you with his beloved wife. She was the single most important thing in his life, and he entrusted her to you." Zack looked into Anne's eyes. "What does that tell you?" That question didn't need to be answered.

Victoria came home from Whidbey Island where she had been living for the last several years. She had her husband ran a hotel that they had built from nothing. Caleb and Angelina had arrived from Seattle and were staying with Mary. They wanted to make sure that she was making it through this after 55 years of marriage.

The private cemetery where Charlie had been buried was no more. His body had been moved to a cemetery in Renton and placed close to the bodies of Edmundson, Will, Sara, and Emily. Anne went to the far corner and visited these graves after Samuel's service. Most of her family was here, except her and Eddy. Even Emily was buried in the family plot. She had been a part of that family for over 50 years and when she passed away Sara would have Emily on one side and her husband would be on the other. Her grave was also put next to Eddy's.

Charlie and Samuel were next to each other. There were places for Mary, Victoria and Caleb if they wanted to rest here. Anne looked down at her mother's grave. She wished that she could have met her grandson. He looked so much like Eddy. The past seemed to grab her and she couldn't stop the pain.

"Let's go home, Anne," he said as he put his arm around her. They had their discussion about the tears that night and slept peacefully through the night. The following morning Caleb was knocking on the door very early. Anne and just gotten up and Zack let him in.

"Mother is gone," he said. "She died in the night."

"Oh, Caleb," Anne said as she hugged him. "I'm so sorry."

"I felt this would happen," he said. "I've heard of husbands and wives dying within weeks, days, or even hours of each other. I never expected that would happen to Mom and Dad. Now they can be together always."

"I'll make the funeral arrangements," Zack said.

"I would like it to be quick and private," Caleb said "just Victoria, you, Anne, and the Eichorns. These are the people who truly knew my mother. Is it too much to ask if we can have the service tomorrow?"

"I'll do everything I can," Zack said. Anne took Caleb into the kitchen and Zack got on the phone to Bill. He was amazed at Zack's request. "Money is no object, Bill. I'll pay for it myself if necessary."

"I'll make sure it's done, Zack," Bill guaranteed. "Tomorrow afternoon."

Bill was a man of his word. The only people present were those that Caleb had asked for. Kathleen Eichorn, who was Anne's only link to the past, was in shock.

"Samuel and Mary were so right together," she said to Anne. "I never saw one without the other very close. I don't think they spent a single night apart, even when the babies were born. Samuel lived at the hospital. Any time they were sick he was right there with her. She helped him so much when his father died."

"I never knew his father," Anne said.

"You were just a baby when he died," Kathleen said as she stared off into space. "It was that horrible accident at the mill. Emily and I were up most of the night with the injured. Charlie was the last body brought in. Jack Regan was so upset that he couldn't save him. What I never told Jack was that he was dead before he hit the floor." A tear welled up in her eye. "That seems so long ago."

"Jack Regan brought him in?" Anne asked. This was something that she was never told. She remembered Amanda and how she loved her. She also remembered how they never told her father about their relationship. Amanda said he wouldn't understand. They never told Maggie about their relationship, either. For all they knew, Anne and Amanda were born two days apart, grew up together, and were best friends.

"He was talking with Emily at the store when the explosion happened," Kathleen said. "That's all ancient history, but a large part if the history has been buried in the last few days. Tom and I are the only ones left of the original gang. I suppose we're next."

"I won't listen to that kind of talk," Anne said. "I need you too much."

"Selfish to the end," Kathleen teased. "I have no plans to go anywhere anytime soon."

They met back at the estate and had a late lunch. Anne never understood the need to eat after funerals. Caleb and Victoria talked about what to do with the house and all the things in it.

"I'd like to take a lot of the furnishings up to the hotel," Victoria said. "I won't see them go to some stranger in a sale."

"We still have the house to deal with," Caleb said. "It needs some work, but it's structurally sound. I don't want to see it torn down or break up the estate by selling it. And there's that stand of Redwoods that Dad wouldn't let anyone touch."

"What about renting it out?" Zack asked. They all turned to look at him. "We have people who work here that live as far away as Renton. What if you leased it to some of the help? This way you know the people, and the house can be maintained."

"That's a good idea," Victoria said. "Do you know of anyone?"

"Yes," Anne broke in. "The maid has two children and her husband died. She could use a close place to live and get her kids out of the city."

"Let's talk to her tomorrow," Caleb said. "You can arrange to get a truck here to get the things you want to take to the island, Victoria."

The following day was spent packing the truck. When the house was empty they took one last look around. Anne felt the lump build in her throat. Victoria was in tears, and Caleb soon after.

"I've never seen this house empty," Caleb said.

"Look what I found," Victoria said as she opened a trunk. She pulled out the buckskins that Mary had traveled over the mountains in. She held it up and Anne realized that she and Samuel were married as Mary wore this. It was so similar to her mother's. It had been hand sewn by the same hands.

"May I have this?" Anne asked. "My grandmother made this at least 65 years ago and I like to hang on to it. May I?"

They agreed that Anne should have it. She and Zack left Victoria and Caleb alone to say their private good-bye. Anne held the buckskin close to her. She smelled the leather and it reminded her of her mother. Zack put his arm around her and they walked up the porch.

Chapter 18

Zack came back to the present and watched Beth wipe her eyes. He continued with his story but still couldn't shake Anne's face as he looked at her. He could never stand to see her cry and it was the same with Beth.

***

John Young Bear asked if he could stay until after the November elections. Monroe thought that they had covered everything, but gladly offered him one of the guest rooms. They still had their back-up plan, which John thought was important to get rolling.

"I know you think that you can trust these men," John warned. "They're politicians. They will go the direction of the most money. They don't care about the land. They care about power and their ability to keep it."

"All right, John," Monroe conceded. "I'll talk to Tom and get the ball going. It's going to take some time to put this together, but we can do it by the election."

"Even if it's not done by the election," John said. "The people elected will not take office until January. We can do a lot in a month."

Monroe rode into town and met with Tom and Moe at the bank. He talked about John's fears about the political system. He also said that they would not need the financial backing of any partners. He didn't elaborate anything more because Monroe was always the one who would tell you what you needed to know, but never give everything away.

"I think he's right," Tom said. "This area is going to be real important for growth of the entire nation. People are building houses and cities like crazy and we have billions of board feet of standing timber waiting for someone to take it. The price has steadily increased in the last 15 years. I think we need to get our plans finalized and bid on this land."

"If the elections go as we plan, we won't need the land," Monroe said.

"If the elections go as we plan," Tom said. "Who knows what will happen in 2 years. We could be having this conversation all over again and the land would be out of reach. We could consider it an investment for the future. I'll get in touch with our investors."

"No," Monroe said. "I don't want anyone else to know about this. The Government is willing to part with 100,000 acres for a dollar an acre, right?"

"That was the written agreement," Moe said.

"How much cash can you boys get your hand's on?" Monroe asked. "That's a stupid question. You work in a bank so you can get your hands on all of it." He laughed. "I meant your personal money."

"I can get ten to twelve thousand, without to much of a problem," Moe said.

"That sounds about right to me too," Tom said. "What are you thinking?"

"I have a little bank account in London," Monroe admitted. "There's enough in there to buy three times that amount of land. I'll pay for it outright, and you'll each have a 12th share. You can pay me when you get the money. If you want to put in more, you can. Agreed?"

"Yes," Tom and Moe said together. "Where did you get this kind of cash?"

"Some was and inheritance, investments, and logging have been good to me over the years," Monroe smiled. "I continued to wire drafts and deposit them in London." Moe and Tom looked at each other and raised their eyebrows. "I'll pay for the land outright. You can pay me when it's convenient. At the time you make payment, we can do the paperwork."

"Well," Moe said. "I guess the only thing we need to do is to get the money to the man at the Land Bureau office."

They took care of the last of the details and Monroe left the bank. He met John coming from the hospital and waved to him. He had wanted to see the Indian school and the hospital that Kathleen and Emily had carved out of the wilderness. He was surprised at how well equipped it was. He had not seen this since he left the east coast.

"You're fortunate to have this caliber of facility here, Monroe," John remarked. "These women are ahead of their time."

"They always have been," Monroe said. "It's my opinion that they really don't need us at all. They could take over the world and run it much better than we ever could."

"I gather," John started, "that you're not real supportive of them being able to vote."

"To the contrary," Monroe replied. "I think it's crucial for the success of this country."

Within a week of the elections, Monroe had received the deed to his expanse of land. The men that he had put his trust in got into office, but this didn't mean that they would do what they said they would during the campaign. He found the promises being kept, in any political arena, were the exception rather than the rule, especially where growth, development, and profit were concerned.

There had been 'fly by night' logging companies springing up all over the area. Monroe's next problem was how to keep them out of his land? Many people had easements so they could get into town.

"Fencing is not an option," Monroe told Sara. "This would be difficult to maintain or even build and there are many that have easements to get to their own land. I think we need to mark the boundaries though."

"What about hiring someone to patrol the land?" Sara asked. "He could be like a private policeman and report any problems to you or Ivan. Then the local sheriff could take care of the problem."

"It would take more than one person," Monroe said. "I would like for them to work in pairs just for safety. Four people could handle it nicely but I'll need talk to Samuel first so he can mark the boundaries, or find a surveyor who could." He turned to leave and Sara just shook her head. She had a way of getting him to think, and then he would run with it. He watched the floor as he walked, deep in thought. John had packed his bags that morning and was planning on leaving that afternoon. He was going to have Monroe take him to the station, when Eddy arrived.

"I completed all of my work," he said. "So the teacher let me go early. I'd like to take John to the station if it's all right?"

"I'd like that, Eddy," John replied. "I was hoping to see you again before I left." John found Monroe and Sara and thanked them for their hospitality. "I'd like to come out next summer to check on the Indian school. Would you mind having me around for a few months?"

"You're always welcome here, John," Monroe said as he shook his hand.

They got into the buggy and drove out of sight. Eddy took John passed the falls one more time. There was a light mist falling and the look of the falls had changed. The low-lying fog and mist seemed to obscure the beauty and make it appear menacing. John drank in the scenery, for there was nothing like this in Oklahoma and he considered not going back at all. He had some loose ends to take care of there and would be back out next summer.

"The falls look angry today," Eddy said. "I hate to see you go, John. I've never met anyone like you."

"You're a remarkable young man Eddy," he responded. "I think

I'll miss you most of all but I'll be back next summer. I really love this area and I love the people."

"Me too," Eddy said. "I can't imagine living anywhere else. I don't want to go anywhere else."

"What about college?" John asked. "Have you thought about that?"

"I have, some," Eddy answered. "I want to do something with the land. I don't want to farm or log, but I want to make sure that the land is healthy and cared for. I then want to teach people to take care of the land."

"I can't think of any colleges that offer that kind of program," John said. "It probably would be wise to get your teaching certificate and then go from there." They stared at the falls for a while longer.

"I'll miss you, John," Eddy said as he looked down at the ground. John put his arm around Eddy's shoulder and held him close.

"I'll miss you too, Eddy," John said. "In ways you wouldn't understand right now."

"I understand more than you think I do," Eddy said as looked into John's eyes. "Let's just leave it at that until you come back next summer."

They rode to the station and never stopped talking the entire time. John had so many things he wanted to do next summer. He wanted to do some exploring and get to know the area. He wanted to be more involved with the Indian school and, maybe, develop more in the area. He had so many ideas in his head. He wanted to see this place grow and he wanted to be a part of it, but more than anything, he wanted to spend the time with Eddy. John never thought anyone felt as he did, and still wasn't sure about Eddy. This he would find out next summer.

***

Beth listened to Zack's words and remembered the first time she had driven to Snoqualmie. She stopped at the falls before going into town. Something struck her soul that she couldn't explain. She felt she had been here before, but how could that be? She knew that Jenny had been here. There was no doubt in her mind or in her heart. She read the history on some of the markers located around the tourist center.

She asked for directions into the town itself and left to find it. It was only about 2 miles into the town down a winding road bordered by big trees. This sleepy town lay in a valley. She could see the railroad tracks and a building that said "Museum". As she got to the door she saw the hours posted. It was Saturday, and they weren't open. There was a local library and she thought that she would find what she could on her grandmother.

They had all of the old newspapers on film. The woman at the library helped her get started. She showed her how to find articles on people by name, year, etc. She entered Anne Elizabeth Monroe and found it was on reel 12-61. She loaded the reel and saw the picture appear before her. "Anne Elizabeth Monroe died of a heart attack early this morning. She will be buried in a private service on Thursday and laid to rest at Mt. Olivet Cemetery. Donations may be sent to: Snoqualmie Falls Preservation Committee."

Beth stared at the picture. It was like looking in a mirror. Her grandmother appeared to be in her forties. She looked back at the article. Anne was born on July 9, 1889 at Snoqualmie Valley Hospital. She pulled the name up again and saw 6-28. She found the reel and loaded it. She saw another picture of Anne and also a larger picture of someone named Sara "Two Trees" Monroe.

She read the article. "Sara Two Trees Monroe died on June 14, 1928 and will be laid to rest in a private ceremony on June 17th at 2pm. Public viewing will be on June 16th from 2pm to 5pm. She was preceded in death by her son William, and her husband, Edmundson. She is survived by her daughter Anne, and son Edmundson."

She stared at the page and wrote down the information. The lady at the library saw what she was looking at. She was taken back by Beth when she walked in. She looked just like Anne.

"Can I help you find anything else?" she asked.

"Not really," Beth said only half listening to her

"I knew Anne," she said directly. "My mother worked for her."

"What?" Beth said. "She worked for her?"

"Yes," she said. "Who is she to you?"

"I'm her granddaughter," Beth replied.

"I used to work over at the Museum," she said. "A girl came in several years ago and asked a lot of questions about the Monroe family. She was supposed to come back the next day, and I waited by the Museum, but she never came. Are you the same girl?"

"No," Beth answered remembering Jenny. "That was a friend of mine. She died later that same day, and I never got the information she may have found. I just recently started the search for my family again."

"Who were your parents?" she asked.

"My father's name was Russell," she said.

She and the woman talked for some time. She strongly suggested that she go to the Museum when it was open. There's so much history about the entire family that she could read. Beth thanked her and left. The woman watched her walk from the library. She had the same glide that her grandmother had.

The next week she located Mt. Olivet Cemetery and would go out there and see if she could locate the graves. This would have to wait until Friday. It was the only day that she could get out of the office at a decent time and do any looking around before the sun went down.

The week seemed to drag on forever. By the time Friday rolled around she couldn't contain her excitement. She left her office at 2pm and went home to change. There was a light mist falling and the weather was cold for March. She went into the office and got a map for the grave occupants. An old man in the back heard she was asking about the Monroe graves and only caught a glimpse of her as she walked out to the cemetery. He looked at the woman who had helped Beth and had given her a map. She smiled at him. He followed her quietly and watched as she bent down and brushed away the leaves. Who was she and what did she want? There was a strange familiarity about her. He could feel his heart in his throat as he saw her face.

***

John had been right about the politicians. They changed their direction as soon as they had taken office. Monroe was glad he had purchased the land. He had the upper hand, and despite the telegrams from these politicians, the land was his. He had purchased it now they would have to work with him. This was a Government purchase. The local politicians had little recourse in these situations. The re-writing of state laws would have little effect on Federal issues.

Eddy was working feverishly to finish his 4 years of high school in 2 years. The teacher let him work at his own pace and he was moving quickly. He still spent as much time as possible with Annie. He found that reading to her from his textbooks provided him the opportunity to cover the material and she could hear a story, although she had no idea what he was talking about. Monroe watched him one night from the bedroom and understood how he could cover so much material and still have time with this sister. What a way to make use of your time. He marveled at his son. He marveled at his gentleness with Annie and his desire to finish school early. He was almost driven.

Will, on the other hand, had become a work-a-holic. He was

spending 10 hours a day learning the building trade and this translated to money. He would have worked for nothing with the amount he was learning. He knew he would start his own business in a few years. He would need all the experience necessary for this. He would ask Gus to join him. If anyone could figure things out, he could.

Monroe looked back at Eddy and entered the nursery. Annie saw him and started to kick her feet.

"She wants her Daddy," Eddy said. "I'm a good substitute, though." Monroe reached down and picked her up. She had them both wrapped around her little finger.

"Finish up your reading," Monroe said. "I'll take her downstairs for a while. I don't think she's ready to go to sleep yet." He walked down to the small original living room to find Sara and Emily enjoying the fire. "Annie is ready to play. So I thought I'd give Eddy a break and bring her down here."

"She's trying real hard to crawl," Emily said. "I hate to think what's going to happen when she gets mobile. Nothing will be spared."

"The boys were just as bad," Sara said. "Remember the fireplace wood?" Everyone started to laugh. "Will thought that the kindling was his private stash of building blocks. We couldn't figure out where it was disappearing to, and then we looked in the pantry. He was building his own estate in there."

"Sally just left it alone," Emily smiled. "She wanted to see how far he would take it."

"Until I tripped over it one night," Monroe said. "I almost broke my neck."

"Eddy had pulled all the books on the shelves he could reach out," Emily said. "He never did know how to put them back. He'd open every single book and leave them open all over the floor. He still has his nose in books."

"Annie will pick her own thing," Sara said as she watched her playing on the blanket. "She may surprise us all."

"You girls look tired," Monroe said. "Why don't you turn in? I'll put Annie down, when she's ready. From the look of her, it may be a while."

Sara and Emily said goodnight and went up the main staircase. Emily opened the door to her room and found Eddy had just built a fire.

"It's going to be cold tonight," he said. "Thought you two would like a fire." This was the first time that he had let his mother know that he was fully aware of she and Emily's relationship. Sara felt a little self-conscience. Emily gave him a hug and thanked him. He kissed his mother as he left the room and closed the door behind him.

"How long do you think he's known?" Sara whispered.

"For a few years," Emily said. "He talked to me about it a long time ago. He said he understood and that the Great Spirit brought us together." Emily went to Sara and started to take off her blouse. She softly kissed her neck and nibbled on her ear. "It may have been the Great Spirit, but the desires we both have played a part, too."

Sara took Emily's face in her hands. She looked into her eyes and then kissed her tenderly. Emily's lips parted and Sara's tongue found hers. The fire was going nicely and the heat coming from the fireplace was inviting. They made love in front of the fireplace on the thick rug. Each time they were together was like the first night when the boys were just infants. The anticipation of being together never changed or diminished.

They would spend hours in pleasuring each other, and when it seemed they could not satisfy each other desires, they would fall asleep in each other's arms. Sara awoke in front of the fireplace still holding Emily's naked body. She looked at this woman, and the beauty of her shape. She never wanted to be with any woman other than Emily. She gently stroked her breast and then took it in her mouth as it began to get hard.

Emily began to awaken and moan slightly. She worked her way back up her neck and found her mouth. The whole process started over again. It was 3am before they dragged their tired, sweating bodies into bed. Emily knew it would be a long day tomorrow, but the reason for the tiredness was worth it. She and Sara had given everything to each other. There was nothing held back, and nothing would ever be.

By Spring Ivan and Monroe had decided to hire some people to patrol the expanse of land that was purchased. Ivan decided not to purchase any of the land from Monroe, which came as a surprise. He had started to back off on many of his duties and allowed the foreman to handle the day-to-day organization of the crews.

"I'm thinking about retiring," Ivan said. He saw the surprised look on Monroe's face. "I'm 64 years old, Monroe. I want to relax and travel a bit, if I can get Helga out of that hospital. I want to see some of the country."

"What about the business?" Monroe asked.

"I have no one to leave it to," Ivan responded. "I'll turn all the equipment and crews over to you. We have a lot of money in savings. Helga and I should be all right."

"I won't let you just walk away with just your savings," Monroe said adamantly. "I'll continue to pay you every month. I can cash you out for all the equipment and you can consider it a retirement plan or maybe a consultant fee. I may call on your help at any time. How does that sound?"

"You're a fair man, Monroe," Ivan said. "I've always trusted and respected you. I was never sorry about going into business with you."

"I know that we have always done business on a handshake," Monroe said. "I'd like for Tom and Moe to put this on paper for us. The way the political climate has changed, it would be a benefit for both of us. Everything would be legal and binding. Let's get this done tomorrow. I'll meet you at the bank at 10am."

Monroe watched Ivan leave and felt sad. He had built this business with him and now things were starting to change. He also had some business he needed to take care of at the bank. The timing couldn't be better. Even Tom was unaware of any of this, and Monroe would need his help to make sure that all of his wishes were met. He talked to Sara that night and told her of Ivan's plans. She wasn't surprised when she heard this.

"Helga said he was considering this since he had been ill," Sara said. "He should be able to enjoy life. He's worked hard and has earned it."

"He's going to meet me at the bank tomorrow," Monroe started. "I want to make sure that he and Helga are taken care of. They're like family to us." He told Sara of his plan to continue to pay him on a monthly basis for the rest of his life. Sara agreed that this was the right thing to do. It also meant that Sara's job would increase dramatically. There would be many more accounting things she would have to take care of.

"That means dealing with the mill, too," Sara said. "I'm really not sure how all that was done. With Charlie gone, who can teach me?"

"He spoke very highly of a young man, Barton," Monroe said. "He was at the funeral and maybe we can see if he'd meet with us." Monroe saw the hesitation in Sara's face. He knew this was not a task she wanted to take on. If this were the case, then she would have to tell him. She needed to be prepared to understand all aspects of the business. It would be important for her survival, although she didn't know this yet.

"I understand the payroll, and making sure the bills get paid," Sara said. "I may as well learn all of it." Monroe felt more at ease and would arrange a meeting with this young man. He felt better about this, but was torn about not being completely honest with Sara. He couldn't do that right now. He couldn't tell her of his suspicions or his deepest fears that haunted the back of his mind and caused his recent sleepless nights, until he sought professional help.

The following day Monroe went into town and stopped by Ivan's on the way. His friend suddenly looked old to him. They arrived at the bank and all the arrangements were put into writing and signed by both parties, and witnessed by Moe and Tom. Rather than write a check every month, Tom would automatically deposit the amount in Ivan's account on the first of the month. This way Sara could just deduct the amount the same time every month.

"We'll take it from the logging account," Tom said. "This way, no one will have to write you a check every month, and if you're traveling, your money will still go in. You can draw on it at any time."

Everyone was pleased and satisfied with the arrangements. Ivan left the bank and Monroe stayed behind to talk with Tom. He didn't want Moe involved in this conversation. He trusted Tom completely so he closed the door to his office and returned to his desk.

"What's the big secret?" Tom smiled. He quickly lost his smile when he looked at Monroe's face. "Jesus, Monroe, what's wrong?"

"Tom, I want you to put together my will," Monroe said. "I want to make sure that my family is taken care of and the government doesn't end up with all the money."

"Monroe, you're still a young man," Tom responded.

"If you call 53 young," Monroe smiled. "I'm not sure how long I'm going to be around."

"Are you ill?" Tom asked.

"I may be," he said. "I'm going over to see your wife today. I know that Emily is at the other location today, and I want this kept quiet until I decide to say something. That's why I'm talking to you. I know that Kathleen will probably talk to you about it, and that's okay. I just didn't want you to hear it from her, and not me first."

"Okay," Tom said in a state of shock. "We need to make sure all the paperwork is in order. This includes all deeds to all property and we need to make sure that we get Sara's name on the account in London."

"No," Monroe said flatly. "I want to close that account and move everything here, but I don't want the cash. I want it converted to gold bouillon."

"Gold" Tom said, "why gold?"

"Because gold will not loose its value," Monroe said. "Paper money can quickly be worthless."

"How much are we talking, Monroe," Tom said. "How much do you have in your account in London?"

"Around 250,000 pounds," Monroe said casually.

"That's over a million dollars!" Tom said. He regained his composure. "I'll need to get in touch with a friend of mine in San Francisco about how to do this. After this is done, where do you plan on keeping this gold? We don't have the room here."

"I have that taken care of," Monroe said. "The next time you're at the house, I'll show you."

"Okay," Tom said. "Let me get started on this." He stood up and shook Monroe's hand, "get over to the office and see Kathleen. You may be worrying for nothing."

Monroe walked over to the clinic. Kathleen was the only one there. Helga was working with Emily at the other location and the rest were at lunch. Kathleen smiled when she saw him.

"Emily is at the other office, Monroe," she smiled.

"I know this, Kathleen," he said. "I came to see you." She took him to an exam room and asked him what the problem was. "I'm having pain, deep in my back," he said. Kathleen did her exam and asked Monroe to get dressed. She told him to come to her office when he was finished. She as already made her diagnosis, but wanted to consult some of her medical books.

He came in and sat down and Kathleen had several books open on her desk. She looked up at him and he knew his suspicions were right when he saw her face.

"You have cancer," she said. "It's quite advanced."

"Can you cut it out?" he asked.

"It's too advanced and I'd have to remove more than I could save," Kathleen said directly. "I wish there was something I could do for you. Even if you had come to me sooner, the outcome would probably be the same."

"How long do you think I have?" Monroe asked.

"Maybe a year," she said. "The next 6 months you'll notice small changes. Then the pain will get more frequent and more severe. Your appetite will drop off, and you'll lose weight. I can give you Laudanum for the pain, but toward the end, nothing will moderate it."

"I know exactly how this goes," Monroe said. "My father died of the same thing. That's how I already knew what it was."

"I'm sorry, Monroe," she said. "I wish it fell to anyone else to give you this news. Have you told Sara?"

"No," he said. "I've talked to no one but Tom and you. Tom is getting my affairs in order and I want no one to know until that's done."

"Emily should know about this," Kathleen said. "She can help you through this."

"No," Monroe said. "She will tell Sara, and that's my job. I want no one else to know about this, Kathleen, no one."

"I'll do as you wish," Kathleen said. "I'll help you anyway I can." Monroe rose from the chair and looked at Kathleen. He saw a tear roll down from her face. He went around the desk and hugged her.

"Promise me you'll look after Sara, Emily, and the kids," he said as he held her. "But never let them know. They all have the greatest admiration and love for you, just as I do." She agreed that she would and he turned and left the office. She watched him get on his horse and ride out of town.

Tom saw him leave, too. He walked over to the clinic and saw Kathleen crying. He held his wife in his arms and started to cry, too.

"This is so unfair," Tom said as he held his wife, "why him? How long does he have?"

"He has a year, maybe," she said. "He wants this to be kept quiet. We had better get ourselves together to avoid any questions. We can't tell anyone, and you need to get the things he asked you about in order. Time is something he doesn't have much of and we need to do everything he asks and some things he won't ask. Do you understand what I'm saying?" Tom nodded and hugged his wife again. "Who said life was fair anyway?" Kathleen asked as she laid her head on her husband's shoulder.

Chapter 19

Tom was feverishly working with his friend from San Francisco to get Monroe's affairs in order. Sara and Barton had met and instantly liked one another. He was telling her all the things that Charlie had taught him. Although the mill owner paid him for his work, Monroe thought it might be best if he came to work for them. The mill owner was paying him a menial wage and Monroe knew he could keep him busy and pay him better.

While Tom worked, Monroe had hired a painter to do some portraits of the family. Monroe had given him pictures of them that had been taken the Christmas before. He also had given him a picture of Sara and Emily. The portraits were to be a 4th of July gift for Sara to put anywhere she wanted.

"Sally has moved into the main house since we put on the addition," Sara said. "How about asking Barton if he wants to live in Charlie's cabin?"

"I think that's a wonderful idea," Monroe said. "He cared for Charlie a great deal, and it puts him right out here with the transport crews."

"He can work right out of the cabin," Sara said. Her real reason for this was that she couldn't stand to see the cabin empty. She had always thought of it as Charlie's and now with him gone, and the cabin empty, it was too much of a reminder of the absence of their dear friend. Monroe was thinking the same thing. Barton would make sure that the mill owner would treat Sara fairly and this would be one less thing for her to have to worry about.

By the time of their 4th of July party Tom had gotten everything in order. All paperwork was legal and binding. Everything had been signed with Kathleen and Tom as witnesses. His account was converted to gold and when Tom delivered it they placed it in the special safe that Monroe had built.

"This place is more secure than Fort Knox," he remarked. "How many people know about this?"

"Three, including you," he said as he closed the door and spun the dial. "This is the security for Sara and the kids I wanted."

"You'd get the impression that you didn't trust banks, my friend," Tom said.

"I trust banks, but not some of the people that run them," Monroe said. "I don't mean you. I trust you completely, but I saw a great deal of my father's money disappear when my father died. My mother wasn't knowledgeable of such matters, and they robbed her blind. By the time she died the only thing left was the property. My sister and her husband took that or the bankers would have found a way to sell that off, too. The only thing I got was the crystal clock on the mantle. When my time comes, I want to make sure that Sara is comfortable for the rest of her life and there is something for the boys, Annie, their children, and maybe their children's children."

"I think you have accomplished that, Monroe," Tom said. "You own 108,000 acres of prime country in the Pacific Northwest. This land will continue to earn a profit for many years to come. It's land that you own outright. There's no lean or mortgage. If Dale Carnegie knew, he'd be jealous. Here, help me carry these out. These are the portraits I had done for Sara."

They left the hidden room and came out in the library. Monroe locked the door and they joined their guests. Tom looked at the portraits in the light. They were extraordinary and the people looked almost real and Tom remarked at the excellence of the work.

Sara, Emily, Kathleen, and Annie were on the front porch. Annie was just learning to walk and she was fun to watch. Eddy was never far from her. She was insistent on not wanting help from anyone.

"She is stubborn," Sara said. "She does everything hard. This will serve her well when she gets older. My mother used to tell me that I was the same way. I always had to learn things myself, and usually get hurt in the process."

Monroe sat down next to Sara. He held her hand.

"Come into the house," he said. "I have something I want to show you." He stood and looked at Sara. "All of you come in for a minute."

Kathleen looked at him and he smiled. He looked tired and a bit uncomfortable. She had been keeping an eye on him today, but not letting him know. She and Tom had made a pact that they would stay with him as much as they could. They followed him into the house. Monroe went into the library where he and Tom had put the portraits. Sara looked at the odd things covered with sheets and looked strangely at Monroe. He walked over and uncovered the first of them. Kathleen let out a small 'Oh Monroe'.

"They are beautiful," Sara said. "They're perfect." He uncovered the second one of Sara and Emily.

"Monroe," Kathleen whispered. "They're both so beautiful. They're lifelike."

"How did you get these done?" Emily asked. "I know I didn't

pose."

"I gave the artist the photographs we had done a couple of Christmas's ago," Monroe smiled. "I saw this guy's work when I was in Seattle and I hired him to do the portraits. Good aren't they?"

"They look alive," Sara said. "Thank you." She hugged him and gently kissed his cheek. Emily joined in and kissed the other cheek. Everyone looked closely at the portraits. The brush strokes were smooth and fluid. The coloring was perfect, including the color of Sara's skin. He had captured Emily's green eyes.

"Put them anywhere you want," Monroe smiled. They returned to the porch and sat down again. Monroe was surveying the people all over the estate. Everyone was happy and having a good time. Sara was generally surprised with the paintings and this is what he had wanted. He wanted to capture memories of happier times. He wanted to capture a moment in time where everyone was young, happy, and healthy. He didn't want to think about the tasks he had ahead of him regarding his health, or lack thereof. He wanted to take this one last time to put everything out of his mind and enjoy the company of friends and family.

Ben and Caleb were off on another one of their adventures. Will was with Gus. They talked constantly about the things that Will was learning. They were making plans for Will to start his own business the next couple of years. Gus had agreed to work with him and this pleased Monroe. He knew that Will would be fine. He was bright and intelligent. He had a drive and desire to go after what he wanted, and was planning to make it happen.

Eddy watched over Annie and Monroe didn't know what Eddy would finally do. He had talked about being a teacher, but no solid plans had been made yet. He hoped that Eddy would decide before he had to leave this world. Of all of his children, he worried about Eddy the most. Annie would be all right. He could see that even as a small child. She was tenacious and stubborn. She was so much like her mother. He felt a lump form in his throat and looked over the estate.

About that time a man on horseback rode up. Monroe stood to greet the arrival and saw his face as he walked toward the house. It was John Young Bear. Eddy turned to see him and rose to greet him.

"I hoped I would make it in time for this party," John said as he shook Monroe's hand. "Hello, Eddy. You've gotten tall and I believe more handsome." He shook Eddy's hand and said his hello to everyone. He even bent down and picked up Annie. She giggled and squirmed to get down.

"When did you get in?" Sara asked.

"About an hour ago," John said. "I rented a horse from the livery and rode straight out here. I stopped by the falls before coming to the house. It's as beautiful as I remembered."

"Let's go see how Ivan is doing on his pig," Monroe said to John and motioned to Tom. They walked down to the pit and Eddy watched, wanting to join them. His heart was in his throat when he saw him. He was here for the summer and they would plenty of time to talk. Annie was rubbing her eyes and Eddy knew that she was sleepy.

"I'm putting her down for a nap, Mother," she said. "If we don't we'll pay for it later."

"Thank you, Eddy," Sara said. He always knew what to do before she could say it. She watched him carry her in the house. Within 10 minutes he came back out, and found John. Emily looked at Sara and smiled. Sara knew what was on his mind. Emily was sure about it. He had talked to her, in a way, after John had left before. Emily knew this would be a hard life for Eddy if this is what he chose. Thinking back to her childhood, it wasn't really a choice, it was the way she was born. Only time would tell with Eddy, but she believed he had already chosen his course.

She looked down and saw Will and Ingrid. They were such opposites. Will's black hair and eyes were a contrast to Ingrid's blond hair and blue eyes. Will had, recently, cut his hair and this gave him a less Indian appearance. Eddy had left his hair long and tied it back as his father always had. He looked so much like his father. She looked back at Monroe. Something wasn't right with him and she looked at him more closely. He was looking old, and slightly frail. He'd lost some weight in the last few months. Emily wanted to ask him but didn't want to alarm him or anyone else. There was this feeling in her gut that wouldn't go away. She hadn't even talked to Sara about this. She didn't want to worry her. Had Sara noticed? She would talk to Kathleen and ask if she had any suspicions. She had always been very observant or, maybe, Tom had said something to Kathleen. Emily was making herself crazy about this so she decided to put it out of her mind and enjoy the day.

The party was a success, as it had been every year. Monroe was surprised when some of the newly elected congressmen and senators showed up. Since he beat them at their own game and tied up most of the land in this area, they were now working with him, or more appropriately, kissing his boots. They had plans for development and his cooperation was crucial. He knew he had the upper hand,

and they knew he had the upper hand.

Tom and Moe were amused by they way they followed Monroe around like a puppy. Tom did notice that Moe was speaking with Congressman Banks. Their conversation seemed quite animated, but Moe said nothing when he joined him. This was a special occasion because the Governor even made an appearance. Sara had no idea who he was, or what he did, but she didn't like his smooth suave air or trust him.

"I wouldn't buy a horse from that man," she whispered to Emily.

"He's a politician, Sara," Emily said. "He's going to make the people with the money happy. This is the way it works, so better you understand things, the better you can deal with them."

"Why should I have to deal with them?" Sara asked. "Monroe can do that."

"Monroe is a powerful man, Sara," Emily said. "There may be times when you have to deal with them. He may be out of town for some reason when a decision will need to be made." She looked at Sara's scowl. "Think of it as a game. It makes it fun."

The fireworks were bigger and better this year. Monroe went all out and the guests were impressed. He had joined Sara on the porch. He loved watching the faces of the children during this time. He looked out and saw Will with Ingrid. He scanned the crowd and saw John and Eddy. Even Annie was quiet and watching. He knew he would not be around for another party like this, and there was nothing he could do to change that. He looked over at Sara and knew she would be all right but she would have a great deal of responsibility after he was gone and the weight of the wealth he had accumulated.

Emily would be around to help her. She had a better knowledge of politics and the deception that was inherent within. Tom and Moe would help her navigate these shark-infested waters. He would not see Annie grow up. He would watch down on her from the other world, if such a place existed. He would make the best of the time he had and every minute would have to count.

The explosions around him brought him back to reality. The smoke of the gunpowder hung heavy in the air. When they had stopped, people gathered their belongings and started to head home. All stopped by on their way out and expressed their gratitude. By 10pm all the guests had left and Eddy was showing John to one of the guest rooms. Annie had to accompany him during this time. She was still wide-awake and only he would be able to get her to sleep.

Tom and Kathleen had located Ben. Tom was getting the buggy

and Kathleen was in deep conversation with Monroe. Emily stood back and watched, not hearing what was being said. This was not about social amenities for both of them were very serious. She turned to find Sara.

"You're feeling poorly today, aren't you?" Kathleen whispered.

"The day started out good, but I've run out of steam," Monroe said quietly.

"Have you talked to Sara?" she asked.

"Not yet," Monroe answered. "I'll do that this week. I wanted to make sure that everything was in order before I talked to her. Now that this is done, I can tell her."

"Would you like for me to be there with you?" she offered. "It might be easier if she has questions about the disease progression."

"No," he answered. "I do want to you tell Emily, because she will be able to help Sara understand this. I want to talk to Sara tomorrow when no one is here. If you could talk to Emily tomorrow then she can answer any of her questions. Can you do that for me?"

She agreed and said goodnight. She realized as she got into the buggy that this was the last 4th of July party that Monroe would have. How stupid of her to not remember that until now. She wished she could help him. All of her knowledge, skill, and years of schooling were useless and she would have to watch him die slowly and painfully and there was nothing she could do. The only thing she could do was to give him enough Laudanum to keep him comfortable because for him to become addicted to the opium was of little consequence at this point.

Emily left for the office and noticed that Monroe was still in the kitchen. He was normally gone by the time she left for the office. She chatted with him for a few minutes and he told her that he wanted to talk with John before he went to the mill. This was a true statement, but he also wanted to talk with Sara. He needed this off his mind.

Emily enjoyed the ride into town and saw that Kathleen was already at the clinic. She had made coffee and Helga had brought in some of her fresh sweet bread. They had very few patients that day and they decided to close down the clinic early. Helga said her good-bye after lunch and as Emily started to leave, Kathleen stopped her. They sat in the office and Kathleen told Emily of Monroe's illness. Emily didn't seem as surprised as Kathleen thought she might me. She listened carefully as Kathleen laid out the details, and what Monroe had asked Tom to take care of.

"For the last few days I've known that something wasn't right," she said. "He's been losing weight, and he's looking frail. Has he told Sara?"

"He's doing that today," Kathleen said. "He wanted you to know so you could answer any questions that she may ask you."

"Why didn't he come to me when he got ill?" Emily asked. "Did he say? Doesn't he trust me?"

"Quite the contrary, Emily," Kathleen said in a re-assuring way. "He's very fond of you. He wanted to tell Sara on his timetable. He doesn't question your ability to keep things confidential, but given the relationship between you and Sara, could you really have kept this from her? Sara can read you like a book. Monroe felt it was unfair to put you in this position. What he needs from you now is to help Sara, or better still, help each other get through this."

"He was sparing me?" Emily clarified. "He's dying and he's sparing me."

"He's a remarkable man," Kathleen said. "This is such a loss. He doesn't want anyone else to know, yet. He will talk to Ivan and Samuel and Tom has already done the legal things that Monroe wanted."

"How long does he have?" Emily asked quietly.

"Less than a year," Kathleen said. "Six to nine months at most." Emily shook her head. She couldn't believe that Monroe would not be around to see his children grow up and have children of their own. She knew this would greatly affect Sara. She loved him so. She and Kathleen left the office.

"Are you okay?" she asked Emily after placing her hand on her shoulder. "You're going to need to be strong for Sara, Em."

"Sometimes life just isn't fair," she said. "I'd better get home." She walked across the street and grabbed the reins of her horse. She headed out of town and up the winding rode that led to the house. She took the fork that led to the falls. She sat at the edge and looked down at the mist. From the corner of her eye she saw the large figure. Their eyes met and it didn't look away.

"Maybe you could explain it to me," she said quietly and hoping for some response. "Why did it have to be him?" The creature continued to look at her. She searched for answers in his eyes. He turned and disappeared in the forest. There were no answers to life's questions and in all the years of her life, this was the first time she thought about praying. This was her Catholic guilt coming out or maybe just a way to make a deal with God. "You gather all the good ones in and leave the living to those of us who need to still learn something," she thought. She didn't know how long she had stared at the water and decided she needed to head to the house. Her pony knew the way home because she didn't remember the ride to the house. She arrived to find Eddy and John grooming the animals. He took her pony and looked at her strangely.

"Auntie?" he said quietly. "Are you okay?"

"I'll talk to you later, Eddy," she smiled. "Not right now."

A month had passed since that day. Monroe had talked to Sara and as Emily came into the house, she was in tears. Monroe was in no better shape and they both embraced Emily. He met and talked with the boys later that evening. Will, much to everyone's surprise, didn't handle this very well. He was angry and hostile. He didn't understand, and didn't want to. Eddy was the calm voice of reason, although Emily knew he was torn up inside.

Monroe had his wishes all laid out on paper. He explained in detail how to handle everything with the business. Sara would take over everything. It was all legal and binding. Eddy wanted to take on the job of policing the land. He had been thinking about this since his father purchased it. He had been studying the maps and boundaries and knew how to best patrol the area. Monroe was happy to hand those responsibilities off to him now.

He had talked to Ivan and Samuel. Ivan wanted to come out of his brief retirement and help out but Sara disagreed with this. If she had to handle things, it would be best if she did it now, while Monroe was still alive. He could mentor and advise her in all aspects. Samuel was doing the best he could. He had just lost his father, and now the only other man he looked up to, was going to be gone.

By the time the boys' sixteenth birthday came around, Monroe's health had declined dramatically. The severe bouts that used to be weeks apart were now only days apart. Emily had a large supply of Laudanum on hand, but never let Monroe know. He would use it only during his bad times, which lasted a few hours. Annie seemed to know when these times were. She would sit with him and he would read to her to take his mind off of the pain. Sara found her sleeping next to him one afternoon. He was sleeping from the Laudanum and she decided it was naptime. She closed the door and let them alone.

By the middle of October, Emily had arranged for Kathleen and the Medical students to cover the clinic. She stayed home to care for Monroe. As much as she wanted him in the hospital, it would be wrong to deny him the right to die in the comfort of his home. The last few days of October were rainy and cold and Will, along with Eddy, didn't leave their father. Ivan, Helga, Tom, and Moe had stopped by to say good-bye to their dear friend. Kathleen had checked in on him weekly and Emily kept her informed of any changes. He asked Tom to stay and he talked with him privately before he left. Sara had held up well, considering the last few months. Kathleen knew he probably wouldn't last the night. She asked Tom to stay and he agreed.

At 4:30am a quiet calmness came over Monroe. He looked at Sara and she went and sat down next to him. He looked at her, smiled, and picked up her hand.

"Thank you for marrying me, Sara," he said weakly. "I have loved you and we have had a good life. You have many things to do after I'm gone. Depend on your friends. Don't be swayed by popular opinions. Do what's in your heart. Tell my children how much I have loved them and I will watch out for them from the spirit world." He closed his eyes as he held her hand. "I'm ready to go, Sara."

On November 1, 1890, at 5am, Edmundson Monroe passed away. He was 53 years old and was surrounded by his sons, daughter, and wife. Emily, Tom, Kathleen, Samuel and Mary were standing behind his family. The pain he had endured and that showed on his face daily was now gone. He was at peace and would be forever missed.

There was a silence in the room that was only broken by Annie. She walked over to Monroe's bed and kissed his hand.

"Night, night, Papa," she said. "Night, night."

The funeral of Edmundson Monroe dwarfed that of Charlie Washington. There were people that Sara had never seen passing by the coffin. Many were crying and she wished she could ask them how they knew her husband. The political contingent was present. The Governor, State and US Senators and Congressman, the Mayor of Seattle, were a great contrast to the tribal elders from the local Indian tribes. They came in their tribal dress. Sara had buried Monroe in the buckskins he wore when they were married. She would always remember him this way.

Patrick Reilly was back from Chicago and was pleased when Sara asked him do the funeral. He and Monroe had many years of history. They had both help carve this place out of the wilderness. Patrick had learned many Indian languages. Sara was pleased that he had learned the language of her people and said the words honoring the Great Spirit. She had not heard these words for many years and had almost forgotten the sounds.

One request Monroe made of Tom was to be buried on a hill in the town of Renton. Tom never understood why he wanted this. He had assumed that Monroe would want to be buried on the land he loved so dearly. He asked him why before he died.

"This is my last request of you, Tom," Monroe said weakly. "I would hope that this land will stay in my family for generations, but no one can be sure. I have purchased many plots in the new cemetery. This way, if the land goes to someone else, I can still rest in peace. Understand, Tom? I don't want to be dug up in 100 years and moved somewhere else."

"I understand, Monroe," he said. "I'll do as you wish." He came back to the present and listened to the language that Patrick Reilly was speaking. He saw the tears run down Sara's face as she remained dignified and held her head high. Following the service, Monroe would be loaded onto a private train and taken to Renton. The trip would take an hour and another 20 minutes to the cemetery. There would be private graveside services and they would return on the train that evening.

Will, Eddy, Jack, Tom, Ivan, and Samuel were Monroe's pallbearers. Samuel had crafted the coffin from one of the redwoods on the property. There wasn't a nail anywhere. Dovetail joints and wooden pegs expertly joined this work of art. Charlie had taught him well, and here was proof.

The local politicians had brought photographers with them to document their presence. Sara was firm about no pictures. John Young Bear was there to peaceably make sure that this was enforced. No one questioned John's directives. He was a nationally known man and his 6 foot 3 inch stature didn't hurt. All of Sara's wishes were carried out. The politicians and photographers didn't force the issue. They boarded the train and headed for Renton. It was a beautiful trip through the mountains. The afternoon sun glistened off the Cedar River. As the train pulled into the station, Sara could see the waiting wagons for the trip to the cemetery. Sara was exhausted. It was already a long day and it was far from over. She was glad she'd left Annie at home.

They went from the train to the wagons and made the trip to the cemetery. He had picked a pretty spot. He had purchased several plots in the far corner. Sara was very specific about the marker for his grave. A plain bronze plate with his name, date of birth, and date of his death was the only marker. There would be nothing more. Everyone said a few words about Monroe at his grave. They said good-bye the only way they knew how. Sara stood at the graveside for some time after everyone started back to the train. "I will never forget you and I will try to keep everything as we have planned," she quietly whispered. "I will miss you, my husband. I will never forget you and our life. I see you in our children and in every room of our home. You are now with my mother and you will watch our lives." She left the cemetery, boarded the train, and headed back into the mountains.

Emily sat next to Sara and held her hand. She laid her head on Emily's shoulder and cried. She cried because she had lost one of her best friends and the father of her children, she cried for her child who would never really know her father, and she cried because she was tired. Emily had worked all day to remain strong and would for as long as Sara needed her to be.

By the time the train pulled into Snoqualmie, Sara was asleep. Emily woke her gently and John got the buggy to take the family home. They arrived to find Annie still up and waiting for them. There was a light supper fixed and Sara didn't realize she was hungry until she started to eat. Jack and Maggie came to get Amanda. She kept Annie occupied while they attended the service.

Jack walked into the main living room and saw the picture of Monroe and Sara. He openly began to cry. He respected Monroe more than any man he had ever known in his life, and that included his father. He had come to this area because no one knew him and he could do exactly as he pleased. He found that his way wasn't the best way for his crews or the land. These are the things that Monroe got him to understand. He looked at Maggie holding Amanda. If he hadn't seen what Monroe had he would never had married nor had a child. How happy he was with his family, his wife, and his business. He made a vow to Monroe that he would help Sara in any way he could. There were many political vultures circling and they would attempt to land soon. He gathered his family and said good-bye.

The last of the guests had left. Annie and Will were asleep. Eddy and John were still talking in the library. This day, that so many came to dread, was over and Emily stood in the doorway and looked at this woman she loved. Sara turned and smiled at her. Emily pointed up to let Sara know she was going to turn in and she nodded then turned back toward the fireplace.

Monroe's face stared down at her from the portrait. Sara's life would now be forever changed, as it was when she first met her husband. He had taken the time and taught her the necessary skills to be ready for this day, although it came far too soon. She watched the flames and remembered their trip to this land and learning to read and write along the way and it seemed so long ago. She couldn't look backwards anymore. She had to look forward. Monroe would want that because he had left his dream in her hands. She would take that dream and the reality it had become and continue to nurture it.

Chapter 20

Emily and Kathleen had closed the clinic for a few days following Monroe's funeral. Emily's presence was requested at the reading of Monroe's will. He had been very specific about things he wanted to do for certain people. His gift to Emily was a lump some of money for the hospital and clinic. He wanted her to use this as she and Kathleen saw fit. He had left sums of money to each of his children. This could be used for whatever they wanted, but they had to 18 years old before they could touch it. He had left money to the Indian school for a better facility. He had left John in charge of using the money wisely to help the local tribes.

As expected, the bulk of his estate was left to his wife. All operation of the logging camp and company were in her hands and the mill owner would answer to her regarding payment and contracts. She could consult with Ivan if she needed, and Tom was available for any legal issues.

"You need to be aware, Sara," Tom said. "There's close to a million dollars in gold in the vault at your house, $500,000 dollars in your account at the bank, and some cash in the vault. This is a huge estate, Sara. All property is owned outright. There are no liens. This makes you one of the wealthiest women in the country."

"Where did the gold come from?" she asked.

"Monroe had me convert his assets in London to gold," Tom said. "He didn't say why."

"I know why," Sara smiled.

"There's one thing I must caution all of you about," Tom said. "If anyone knew the extent of your wealth and holdings it may cause you problems. There are people who believe that they need to take it away from you or that you should donate to their personal cause. They may be politicians or con men. Promise nothing. Consult with me before any money changes hands. Never use the gold, unless you have to. Convert the gold to cash through me. Let no one know what you have. This is for your safety."

On the way home, Eddy and John decided to stop by the falls. Will was absent and Sara would talk to him later about his father's will. Emily was still surprised at his bequest to her and Kathleen. The first thing on Sara's mind was to meet with all the logging crews. She would ask Samuel, Barton, and Joseph Two Feathers to get the crews leaders together at the house on Monday morning.

Ivan had left word that he would be able to help her with this before he left for California.

Eddy and John arrived later and he wanted to talk with his mother. He had been thinking about going to college, but hadn't made a definite choice.

"With Dad gone," he said. "I'd like to handle the patrolling of the land. I figured we could do it with 2 teams of 2 people each. It wouldn't be good for these people to be out there alone. I've looked at the maps and established a sweep route that repeats every 4 weeks."

"You've thought this through haven't you?" Sara smiled.

"Yes," Eddy smiled. "I want to hire local Indians for this. My reason for this is their desire to preserve the land, and the spirit that resides there. John would like to help me with this. We would check on these teams weekly so we could get any information they may have."

"What kind of information?" Sara asked.

"Tracks in and out of the area," he said, "people they may run across, or any logging that is going on that we don't know about. These teams would work with us and the local authorities when discoveries occur."

"Okay, Eddy," Sara smiled. "The job is yours and you'll have to work with the local sheriff's office and make sure they know the people in your teams. Let me know when you start."

"Thanks, Mom," Eddy said. "I won't let you down."

"You never have, Eddy," she said. "Can I ask you something before you leave?"

"Sure," he replied. Sara went over and closed the door to the library. This made him a little nervous. He was trying to think of something he may have done wrong. Sara turned around and looked at his face and started to laugh.

"You're not in trouble," she chuckled. "Eddy, there's no subtle way to ask you this, so I'll just be direct. Are you and John involved?" He sat quietly for a moment and looked at the floor.

"I love him, Mother," Eddy said quietly.

"Are you ashamed of how you feel toward this man?" she asked as she took his face in her hands. "Never be ashamed of your feelings. John is a wonderful person. Does he feel the same about you?"

"He says he does," Eddy said. "We haven't been physically, together because John wants to wait on that. He said he wants me to be sure about this. He wouldn't do anything to jeopardize our friendship."

"Do you know what you want?" she asked.

"I can't imagine my life without him," he said. "Can you see your life without Emily?"

"Not for a second, son," Sara responded. "Be true to yourself. I'll support you in any decision you make because I love you and want only your happiness. John is a good and decent man." Eddy hugged her long and hard.

"Thank you, Mother," he whispered in her ear. As he left the room she realized how tall he'd gotten. He wasn't much shorter than John. It would be a difficult life for him if he decided to stay with John. It would mean no children, but if he loved someone, it must not matter to him. Emily had made that choice years ago and didn't regret it.

Sara met with the logging crew leaders with Ivan by her side. They all had known her for years and had the greatest respect for her. Ivan made it clear that any problems would need to be discussed with her. He would not act as a buffer, but a consultant to Sara. She had always been fair and honest with them and they didn't feel this would change for they knew that Sara understood the business and that she issued all the checks.

Emily went back to the clinic and asked Kathleen about the best use of the money Monroe had left to them. They both decided that they were well equipped and would keep it in trust until improvements needed to be done. Sara had asked if she would move into her room. She could leave her room for an office. Eddy and Will went through their father's clothes. They kept many of the things he owned. Will could wear his pants, and Eddy his jackets and shirts. Eddy kept his buckskin jacket.

When he put it on, Sara could see Monroe when she first met him. Eddy looked so much like him, just taller. He had his same blue eyes and beautiful smile. Even Emily remarked at the resemblance. He was wearing that jacket the first time she met him, when Sara was pregnant with the boys. It seemed a lifetime ago for her.

Sara had the portrait of her and Monroe hung in the large living room, over the fireplace. It seemed to be the best place for it. She had the portrait of she and Emily put over the fireplace in the old living room, which was now the library. They had spent many happy hours in this room and this seemed the only place it should hang. The eyes in the portrait seemed to watch over all that sat in the large leather winged-back chairs.

***

Zack remembered sitting in that library with Anne and Russ when he was a baby. He would look at the portrait and look into the eyes of these women. They were so beautiful, but only had eyes for each other. He sat in the same chairs that they did so many years ago. Anne had the chairs repaired and re-covered right after Sara had died. She was specific about the color and the type of leather. She didn't want anything stiff or rough. It had to be like what was on them now. Russell had started to walk, and would clear every shelf he could find. The library was a particular favorite of his. He would systematically pull every book within his reach off and move it to the floor.

"Mother said Eddy used to do the same thing," she said.

"Why didn't he come to her funeral?" Zack asked without thinking. Anne shot him a look that made him realize that he had ventured into a bad area. She took a deep breath and regained her composure.

"It took me 5 days to get a message to him," she responded. "By the time he got the message, she was in the ground. I told him that I knew he couldn't attend, but I wanted him and John to know."

"How many years have he and John been together?" Zack asked.

"Since 1892," Anne answered. "So that would make it 38 years."

"That's longer than most marriages last," Zack smiled. "Anne? What are we going to tell Russell when he asks about his father?"

"We'll tell him that you have been his father since he was born," Anne said, "and nothing more."

"I still want to adopt him, legally," Zack said. "I don't want him to think that I didn't care enough about him to make it legal."

"I think that's a good idea," Anne said. She knew that if she put Zack's name on the birth certificate they wouldn't be having this conversation. He knew it, too. He understood her reasoning at the time, but it was getting hazy now. Zack wished he could resolve this in his mind but he couldn't. About the time he was going to start this discussion again, the maid came in with the daily mail. Anne thumbed through it and stopped at one envelope. She looked at it and smiled then opened it. She handed the rest of it to Zack. He opened bank statements, and some solicitations from local vendors.

"Eddy's coming home," she said. "We should see him next week. He and John are taking the boat down from Alaska. They'd like to stay a month, maybe indefinitely."

"I'm looking forward to meeting him," Zack said with a smile. "You said that he was like your father in many ways. I wish I could have known him."

"Me too," Anne said. "I think I'll get a message to Ben Eichorn about Eddy coming home. He was always fond of him."

"Why don't we have a dinner party?" Zack said. "We can make sure that we have all of Eddy's old friends come. We've got the 4th of July party in another month, but that's a little to long to wait."

Anne went into Snoqualmie the next day and stopped to see Ben and Kathleen. Both were pleased to hear about Eddy coming home.

"The boat will get into Seattle on Thursday," Anne said to Kathleen. "I can give them a couple days to rest, so how about Saturday night for the party? Be here at 5pm for drinks and hors'd'ouerves and we can eat at 7pm."

"It will be so good to see Eddy again," Kathleen said. "Is John coming with him?"

"Yes," Anne said. "I think there's a reason behind this trip. Eddy hasn't been home in 30 years. Something must be bringing him back now, especially with an unspecified length of stay. I'm not going to question why he's coming home. I'm just grateful he's coming."

"It's not best to question, why" Kathleen cautioned. "It will be so good to see him again. Does he know about Zack and Russell?"

"Yes," Anne said. "I wrote to him right after Russ was born, and Zack and I married. I'm sure it was a shock, after Amanda I mean. He probably never expected to get news like that. When he wrote back he said he was very happy for me."

"Why wouldn't he be?" Kathleen replied. "All he ever wanted for you was happiness. He didn't care whether it was with a man or a woman. He had always felt it was his job to protect you at any cost, especially after your father died. It broke his heart when he left to go to Alaska. He made me and Emily promise that nothing would happen to you." She looked at Russell and stroked his hair. "Look at his beautiful boy. He looks like your father, Eddy, and Zack all rolled together. Eddy's going to fall in love with him."

"I'll need to check his suitcase before he goes back to Alaska," Anne laughed.

"Maybe he's not going back," Kathleen said. "Maybe that's why he can't give you a definite answer about his length of stay. Maybe he wants to come home, but doesn't know how. If this is what he wants, make it easy for him, Annie. It would be good to have him here."

"It's been my wish for 30 years," Anne said quietly. She hugged Kathleen and left.

As scheduled, Eddy and John arrived at the train station at 4pm.

John stepped from the railroad car and looked very old. She supposed he had a right to look old. He was now 63. He saw Anne and smiled. He was still a handsome man. Eddy was behind him and he ran to Anne and gathered her in his arms.

"It's been so long, honey," he whispered in her ear. "I've missed you everyday. I've thought about you everyday." He held her shoulders and looked at her and hugged her again.

"It's my turn to hug this beautiful woman," John said. Eddy put her back down on the ground. John held her shoulders and then hugged her. "Having kids seems to agree with you. You look wonderful. I could have sworn it was Sara standing there."

"Where are Zack and the baby?" Eddy asked.

"Waiting for us up at the house," Anne said. "Russell is real cranky when he doesn't get his nap."

"This place has really grown," Eddy said. Anne loaded their bags into the car. He stared out the window and Anne drove through town. He had never taken a car to the house. It had always been a buggy or horseback. Within minutes they were at the fork that led to the falls. Anne automatically turned anticipating they would want to stop there before going to the house. "Thanks, Sis."

"I figured you boys would want to stop here," she said. "I'll walk over with you." They left the car and walked around the bend to the falls. It had been dry so the falls didn't have the flow it had during the rainy season. It was still impressive. John put his arm around Eddy and they stood together. She was going to leave them alone, but something stopped her. She stood next to Eddy and saw an old familiar figure from the corner of her eye.

"It's been years since I've seen one," Anne whispered. "It was as though they knew you were back. They waited for you for all those years."

"I've been waiting for them," Eddy said as the creature turned and disappeared into the trees. "This tells me that my decision to come home was right, even though, I never doubted my decision. I'm sorry it took so long." He held Annie close and stared out at the mist.

They arrived at the house and Eddy paused on the porch. Everything was well maintained and beautiful. They entered the foyer and Zack was holding Russell. Anne made the introductions and Eddy took Russell from Zack.

"It's been a long time since I held a baby," he said as Russell giggled. He was squirming to get down. He had learned to walk quickly and Eddy set him down and he bolted for the library. They followed him in and Eddy looked at the picture of his mother and Emily. They were both gone. He had said good-bye years ago, but the pain was still there.

"It feels like I've never left," John said. "Everything is exactly the same as when we left. It's so refreshing." Russell was busy taking every book from the shelves he could reach.

"I thought we'd have an early dinner," Anne said. "I'm sure you're tired."

"I'll have your bags put in your old room," Zack said.

Dinner was quiet and peaceful. Eddy asked Zack a great deal about himself and asked how he ended up here. John and Eddy told of their work in Alaska working with the Eskimos, establishing many schools, but getting qualified teachers had been a challenge. The Gold rush had brought so many bad things to them from changes in their diet to the abuse of alcohol. Eddy had staked a claim just southeast of Nome right after they arrived.

The true gold rush had not started yet and he had no problems filing his claim, legally. As John researched his role in school set-ups, Eddy learned how to pan for gold. He got enough out of the stream for a nice little stash. John even got the 'gold fever' and they worked their claim together. Within a year, the area was crawling with people who were ready to be rich. Eddy and John only took in some dust when they were short of money. This didn't raise any suspicions of any of the locals, and no one tried to jump their claim.

"As far as anyone knew," John said. "We were just a couple of guys just barely making a living from panning gold. No one knew that we had found as much gold as we had."

"We had to keep it quiet because we were being paid by the local tribes to set up their schools which we did," Eddy said. "We panned for gold on our own time and never put off any of the Tribal business to pan. They knew we did this, but they never knew how much we had found."

"How much did you find?" Zack asked being caught up in the story.

"Don't know, exactly," Eddy said as he smiled at him. "We still have most of it in gold dust. The only person I trust to do anything with it is Tom Eichorn. I'll go see him tomorrow."

Zack went to put Russell down for the night. He finally ate some dinner and he was ready to go to bed. He kissed his Uncle Eddy and his Uncle John before Zack took him upstairs.

"He's a handsome boy, Annie," Eddy smiled as he watched Zack take him upstairs. "Will you take a walk with me?"

"Sure," Annie said.

"I'm going to stay behind," John said. "I'll talk to Zack some more. I like that young man."

"You like all young men," Eddy teased.

"You're right," John smiled. "I'm just too old to do anything about them anymore."

Anne and Eddy walked back toward Mary and Samuel's house. He was sorry to hear about them passing away. He wasn't surprised that they went so close together. They shared a life for all those years, and they were united in death.

"I was surprised that Mother lived for another 10 years after Emily died," Eddy said. "I expected her to die shortly after Emily. They were so close."

"Mother still had some things to do," Anne said. "She also had some people she still had to piss off." They both laughed. "She missed Emily so much. She wouldn't let me change her room or take any of her clothes away. I don't remember father dying, but when Emily went, mother almost couldn't bear it. She didn't eat or sleep for days. It took Kathleen, who admitted her to the hospital, to get her to eat and sleep. She spent many hours talking with her and bringing her back."

"Kathleen could always get away with things that no one else could with Mother," Eddy said. "Thank the Great Spirit that she was here."

"I understand that Kathleen saved Mother when I was born," Anne said. "She saved her again after Emily died. Did you know that she came out of retirement to deliver Russell? She said it was the greatest gift I could have given her. What she doesn't know is that I really didn't trust anyone else."

"You always were short on the amount of trust you gave," Eddy said.

"With that being said," she said in a serious voice. "Why did you come home?"

"Didn't wait long, did you?" Eddy smiled. "You're just like Mother. You never approached subjects subtly. John is ill, and will probably die soon. He didn't want to die in Alaska and I didn't want him to die in Alaska. I didn't want to be there without him."

"If he wasn't sick, would you be here?" Anne asked.

"Yes," Eddy said. "I wanted to come home a long time ago. I just didn't know how. I didn't want to have to face what John and I faced before we left."

"Those people are long gone, Eddy," Anne said. "Why did you

care what they said or thought anyway? They were Neanderthals with small minds."

"But," he said. "They were powerful Neanderthals, with connections all over the state. They could have made life difficult for John, Mother, you, and me. I didn't want that to happen to any of you. And John's reputation had never been tarnished. We quietly left the state, the country, really, so they couldn't touch us. The funny thing is, by them insisting, we beat the millions to the Alaska gold rush. We beat them at their own game and have enough money to buy any politician we want. I wonder if some of the 'good ole boys' would dare mess with us today?"

"I never knew why you left," Anne said. "I've been mad at you for all these years thinking that you were being selfish. I didn't know about the political side."

"They were going to use my relationship with John to blackmail Mother," he said. "They were trying to get their hands on the land that Dad bought before he died. Mother blew their plan when she said she already knew about our relationship. When they threatened to go to the newspapers, I decided that we should leave. Mother tried to stop me, but I didn't want her to be hurt. She even had Emily talk to me, but to no avail. The last thing I wanted to do was to leave here, Annie. I loved you and Mother so much."

"I understand, Eddy," Annie whispered. "Now I understand."

"I did learn to love Alaska," he smiled. "There was a wildness there that was disappearing around here. I wouldn't trade the experiences I went through there. The only regret I have is the years I lost with you, Mother, and Emily."

"You're home now," Annie said as she reached for his hand. "The rest doesn't matter." They finally came to Samuel and Mary's house. It looked good. The maid and her children had cleaned up some the overgrown foliage and it looked neat and tidy. Eddy was glad that someone was living there. They continued to walk and talk.

John was asking Zack about life in Chicago. He had not been there for many years and wanted to know how much it had changed.

"The last time I was there was in the 1880s," he smiled. "It wasn't a real friendly place when I was there."

"It was different if you were Irish," Zack smiled. "Irish or not, if the political or organized crime fraction had a beef with you, you would be dealt with. I believe that's why my brother died. He was a believer in prohibition and stated that fact loudly and in print."

"Did you go to college, Zack?" John asked.

"I was getting ready to when Kevin and Mother died," he said. "I had a scholarship to Northwestern's Medical School but came out here instead. Seems like a long time ago, now."

"Not so long, Zack," John said. "You could still go to Medical School if you wanted."

"That's not what I want right now," he smiled. "Anne keeps me busy just maintaining the estate and taking care of the accounting with the Foundation. Russell keeps me busy and I don't want to miss a minute of his growing up."

"Sounds like your priorities have changed," John said. "Are you happy?"

"More than I thought I could ever be," he said and then blushed. "I know that I'm not Anne's first love. I also know that she prefers, well, but we have a bond that I've never felt with anyone. I can't imagine life without her."

"You are a rare young man, Zachary McGill," John said. About that time Anne and Eddy came back in. They found Zack and John in the library and Eddy looked at the picture of his Mother and Emily. He walked over and touched the frame. He hung his head and began to cry.

"I'm sorry I couldn't be here for either of you," he whispered. "Forgive me."

"Emily gave me a message to give to you," Anne said while standing at his side. "She said to tell you that she hoped you and John would have as many years together as she and Mother. She also said to tell you that yours was the first life she brought into the world, and she loved you from that moment on."

"Is Emily buried with Mother?" Eddy asked.

"Yes, she is," Anne answered. "Father is on one side and Emily on the other. I could think of no better place to put her."

"I'd like to go visit their graves," Eddy said.

Saturday morning Anne, John, and Eddy left for Renton. Zack had some work to do at the house and thought it was best to not intrude on this. The road wove through the mountains. Eddy remembered seeing this area the first time when his father had died. They arrived at the cemetery and Eddy found them expertly maintained. He knelt and placed flowers on them all. The markers were all exactly alike.

"Did you bury Mother in her buckskins?" Eddy asked.

"Yes," she said. "I wanted to keep them, but Mother was insistent about it. Mary didn't want that for herself. She left them in a trunk and Caleb let me have them. Our Grandmother made them and I wanted something of hers."

John remembered the first time he was here. Edmundson Monroe was laid to rest that day. He remembered it like it was yesterday. He looked at Eddy and realized that he was just a few years older than his father was when he died. Where had the years gone? Eddy was one of the few people he was completely honest with. He could be himself and let the anger, he harbored for the white man, out. He could talk of the races of Indians that would forever be wards of the Government because they wouldn't allow them to live they way they had for hundreds of years.

The massacre of the Sioux in the plains states was still an open wound to him. The Government gave them the black hills, until they discovered gold on it. Then, as with every treaty, they broke their own word. John was tired to hearing the words, *manifest destiny*. It was another way to steal, rape, pillage, and plunder the land for their personal gain. With their culture destroyed, they turned to alcohol and allowing themselves to be taken care of. The pride of that society was forever destroyed.

John used to talk about Sara and his respect for her. She was lucky to find a man who was willing to help her learn the ways of the whites, but didn't want her to forget her culture. This is why he loved Eddy. He was a combination of his father and his mother. He had the sensitive side of his father and the spiritual side of his mother. He came back to the present and watched Anne and Eddy. They loved each other so much, and they had so many years to make up for. He should have made Eddy come back years ago instead of hiding out in Alaska. He could have been here for Emily and for his mother. He stood and looked at Edmundson's grave.

"Would have, should have, and could have," he whispered, "they don't count anymore. He's home and he'll stay here until he dies. This is as it should be. I can think of no other place that I want to be, either. I'll be joining you soon, and we'll watch over them together."

Chapter 21

Kathleen and Tom were elated to see John and Eddy. Ben and his wife arrived later. Caleb and his wife came up from Tacoma for the dinner. It was good to have everyone he remembered and who was still alive, around him again. Eddy was busy playing with Russell and Kathleen looked at Tom and smiled.

"He used to do the same thing with you," Kathleen said to Anne. "I don't remember a 4th of July party when he wasn't playing with or taking care of the kids. He looks so much like your father and Russell so much like you, it's as though I've flashed back about 40 years."

"I thought I was the only one who felt that way," John joined in. "It's like we stepped back in time."

"Accept we're all old," Tom said with a smile.

Anne looked around the room and felt at peace for the first time in many years. She looked at Zack and smiled. He saw the light coming from her face. She was happy. Everything seemed right with the world. He knew he could never fill that place in her heart that belonged to the past and to her family. He had no right to think he ever could.

***

"Sara had so much put on her shoulders when Monroe died," Beth said bringing Zack back to reality.

"He had prepared her the best he could," Zack said. "He had good people like Ivan and Tom to help her, but she already knew what she had to do. In the background was Emily. She would advise Sara but never push her to make a decision in either direction. She was supportive whenever Sara needed it."

"She also had Eddy, Will, and John," Beth said. "Did they take over any of the operations outside of the patrolling that Eddy was spearheading?"

"Let's get back to the story," Zack said.

***

Eddy and John set up a patrolling parameter and hired local Indians to perform the task. They were intimately knowledgeable about the area. Each team knew where the other team would be at all times. This would be important for their safety. If a team failed to appear at a pre-determined time or place, they would know where to look for them. John and Eddy would spend time with each team and learn their routes. They would set up checkpoints and would meet them on specific days.

They anticipated that they would be gone for about a month. They would work with, ride with, and stay out with these teams until checkpoint facilities could be located. John even suggested small cabins, at these checkpoints, for stockpiling supplies for the teams. Eddy said he could determine that later. The day came when John and Eddy were ready to go out with the first team. Eddy kissed his Mother and hugged Emily. He found Annie and told her that he would be back. He was wearing his father's buckskin jacket. When he rode away, Sara could see Monroe. She smiled as Eddy turned and waved, just like his father used to.

Sara had met with the crews and they were getting reports to her weekly as she requested. The mill owner was sending his reports as she had requested. After the receipt of these she would spend the weekend getting all the facts and figures together. Maggie Regan had helped her get this system in place. It gave an overall picture of what was coming in and going out. She knew exactly where the business was at all times.

Emily and Kathleen were updating some equipment and trying to get another doctor in to help them with the hospital. They wanted an MD on staff to handle just the hospital patients. This would free them up for clinic work. They had solicited in Seattle and San Francisco, but with no response yet. Emily's concern was how to pay whoever they got. Monroe's generous endowment would be a buffer for this. She had finally heard from a doctor in Boston and she should be arriving in a few months. She happened to be a family friend who was educated at Harvard.

A year had passed since Monroe's death. Sara easily saw how quickly the money accrued. She was surprised when Tom told her the value of Monroe's estate when he died. She had more money now than she could spend in 5 lifetimes. Why did she need more? She needed enough to maintain the estate and pay the servants. Samuel and Mary made their own profits from the seedlings. Barton was paid from the business account, as the logging and transport crews were.

Sara set up a meeting with Tom about an idea she had. She had it worked out in her head, but wanted to run the legalities past Tom. She stopped in the clinic and took Emily and Kathleen to lunch. Tom met them in the hotel restaurant and she accompanied him to the bank.

"What's your idea?" Tom asked.

"It's the crews who make this business run," Sara said. "How about we share some of this profit with them? If the company does well, then quarterly they can expect a share of the profits. It's like an incentive program."

"Interesting idea," Tom said. "What made you think of this?"

"When you read Monroe's will," Sara said. "I had no idea there was so much money. Now, as I manage all the books, I see what's coming in. It's more money than I can spend. It's more money than my children can spend, and it grows every week. Why shouldn't the workers share in this good fortune?"

"Did you have a percentage in mind?" Tom inquired.

"All of it," Sara replied.

"I don't think that's wise," he said. "We need to exclude all operating costs and wages. Let's start with 10% of the profit and see what that comes to."

"Why not half?" Sara asked.

"You want to make sure that you have money in reserve for any new equipment or personnel you may want to hire or replace." Sara nodded her head.

They took all the figures that Sara brought with her and then broke down the profit. Even Tom hadn't realized the magnitude of the figures. By the time he finished and calculated the number of employees, he saw that they could expect a nice amount quarterly. Sara was pleased with the outcome.

"I want to start this just before Christmas," Sara said. "We can explain to them that this will come quarterly, depending on the earnings of the appropriate quarter."

"It will be for the quarter before," Tom said. "The payment in December would be for the 3rd quarter, or July, August, and September."

"Yes," Sara said. "This way all the figures are valid instead of estimating then we would know that all bills are paid and equipment are purchased."

"How much time are you spending on your weekly reports?" Tom asked. "How much time are you spending doing payroll?"

"I usually spend the whole weekend on reports, and then I work on payroll during the week," Sara answered. "Why do you ask?"

"Have you considered hiring an accountant?" Tom suggested. "Or do you like spending all of your time on details instead of working on growing the business?"

"It has become a fulltime job. Do you have someone in mind?" Sara inquired. "I wouldn't know where to look for such a person."

"We get letters all the time from people looking to secure a position in a bank," Tom said. "They would be ultimately qualified for something like this. We could give him an office here at the bank and he could handle all of your accounts. The bank and you would split his salary with the company."

"I'd like to get my nose out of ledgers," Sara said. "I have no time for Annie or Emily, and I don't like that. I also want to do more with the Indian school." She paused and looked at the floor. "I think Monroe would agree with you. This is not the life he wanted for me, but he always taught me to pay attention." She paused and looked at the floor while deep in thought. "Do it Tom. Get me the best person you can, because I want him to continue my system. I don't want it changed."

Tom agreed with her and said he would start having Moe look more closely at these letters of inquiry. Sara thanked Tom for his help with this and left the bank. He watched her go across the street to Walker's store and marveled at her idea. She had learned that if the workers were happy and had an incentive, other than their weekly paychecks, they would look after the business for her. Making money was not as important as rewarding the crews for a good job. The business would be stable and would grow with very little effort. Monroe had trained her well to look at the larger picture.

The second piece to this was that the extra money they made would be put into the economy of the town. They would purchase more from the storekeepers and everyone would win. When Sara realized that she had more money than she could spend, she found a way the whole town could benefit, without really knowing it. The only thing that Sara was going to take away was the payment to the clinic for their visits.

After much consideration and discussion with Emily, she found that most of these people had been paying for their visits already. They didn't feel it was fair for Monroe to pay for this. It was a pride that they had. They made good money and could afford this. Emily had submitted nothing in the last few months and her business had not decreased. The whole reason Sara wanted to do this in the first place was to encourage them to seek medical help when they needed it and not when they were half dead. This had been accomplished. Emily and Kathleen were well respected in the community and were making a very nice living.

A month had passed and just before Christmas Sara handed out the first of the profit-sharing checks. The logging crews were elated with this unexpected windfall. Many of the families would have a better Christmas than they had in the past. There was money for the extras that they had saved for all year. Now they could use this for improvements in their homes, or buy the things they used to do without.

Eddy and John had returned from their trip. They talked about the beauty and ruggedness of the land. The Indians they had hired knew the area well and help them acclimate to the area. Annie was overjoyed at seeing Eddy. She ran to him and didn't let him go the entire night. Emily thought about him not having children of his own. Maybe this was his way of being a father when he knew he couldn't.

John said he had finally found his place in the world. He remarked that if he never came out of the woods, he would be happy. He loved the remoteness. The feeling of being alone on the face of the world was a something he had never experienced. He loved the feeling of discovery and the fear involved in relying only on what he knew.

"Until you got hungry," Eddy interjected. "The man can't cook to save his life, can't hunt either. I've never seen an Indian that doesn't know how to hunt let alone use a gun."

"He's right," John laughed. "I would have starved if it hadn't been for Eddy. As far as the hunting, I can't hit the broad side of a barn. I grew up on a reservation, where we couldn't have guns. Everything was provided for us. As soon as I could leave the reservation, I did. I went to college in the East and had never ventured past the Mississippi River until I came out here to help Monroe and Sara."

Will talked about how he and Gus would be starting their own business in the spring. He had so many things he wanted to do, including asking Ingrid to marry him. He wanted to spend his life with her and she said the same about him. He blushed and everyone congratulated him on this. Will had never been forthcoming with personal information like this and Sara was happy to see the change in him.

Sara stood back and watched Eddy, Will, John, Gus, and Annie. There was a new generation making plans in this room. Eighteen years earlier Monroe, Charlie, Samuel, Ivan, Mary, and she sat in this same room and made their plans for the future. They tried to think of every possible problem that could arise and solve it before it happened. They didn't plan on death coming to take any of them so soon. To interject that now would be cruel. They needed to have something to look forward to and work for. Emily came up behind her and put her arms around her waste.

"You're thinking about another time, aren't you?" she whispered.

"I was thinking of the plans that were made in this room, before I met you," Sara said quietly. "We had such hopes and dreams, and they turned out as planned, except."

"Except what, Sara?" Emily asked.

"We didn't think about death," Sara said. "All of my hopes and dreams are for these kids. They want to conquer the world. It's not my place to tell them they can't or shouldn't try."

"We just need to support them," Emily said as she kissed Sara's cheek. "Let's go get a cup of coffee." She and Sara went to the kitchen and sat by the table. They could hear the laughter and talking from the library. They never talked about the future anymore. They knew that they would spend it together with, absolutely, no doubts about that.

By the end of the summer of the following year Will and Ingrid had married. They were living in the original building that Emily had lived in when she first arrived. The upstairs had always been large and spacious and Will used the downstairs for an office for his business. He and Ingrid had planned to relocate to Seattle but Will hadn't been able to secure many jobs. He had more work than he could handle right around Snoqualmie, so he decided to stay.

This delighted Ingrid because she didn't still didn't want to be that far away from her parents. Will didn't want to leave his family either. As much as he led everyone to believe that he was adventuresome, his heart didn't want to stray from this area. He decided to build a house right in town. Eddy, on the other hand, was happy to live at the estate. He and John shared one of the large guest suites and Sara had never seen him happier.

They had a nice life, and John was good to Eddy. Sara's business was growing and Samuel had started marking trees in the new acreage that was purchased. He told Sara that they would never get the logging done on this land in three lifetimes.

"I don't understand why Monroe bought so much," he said to Sara.

"It wasn't for the business, Samuel," she explained. "He wanted to save the land from progress. He never meant to buy it for profit, or for the business. He wanted to keep some part of this area the way he found it."

Five years later things had started to change in the area. John and Eddy had found more bootleg logging outfits and they needed to hire more help to keep them out. These places would go up overnight and cut everything in site and rape what land they could. They could do more damage in a week, than nature could repair in 50 years. The removal of the trees was only one part. With that came the damage of the salmon streams, and wildlife destruction.

Eddy ended up hiring a company they called Pinkerton's to enforce the law. The patrol crews would find these outfits and the Pinkerton's would clean them out. They had the blessing of the local and state authorities. During one raid, they had confiscated horses, equipment and arrested 20 men in the process. Jack Regan was having the same problem on his land.

Some new mills in the area were escalating the problem. They were taking logs from anyone anytime they could get them. They didn't want contracts or ask questions. They were paying top dollar and some of the small companies were going there. The local mill owner was losing business because of this. Barton had visited the mill and came home to tell Sara about some of the things he'd heard. She called a meeting with Jack Regan, Ivan, Samuel, Eddy, John, and Tom for the following week. She had asked Jacob and Suzy to attend with Suzy's connection with the local tribes. They all arrived at noon on Saturday. Barton started the meeting off.

"When I was at the mill last week the owner told me of a trend we know has already started," he began. "We've had some 'fly-by-night' mills and bootleg logging companies in the area."

"We've run out the same group three different times," John said. "They pay the fine and they're back in business the next day."

"Maybe the fines aren't big enough," Jack said.

"I think they're big enough, but I think these guys have backing somewhere," John said. "I think it's from outside of this area."

"Tom," Sara said. "What can you find out for us? Is there anyone in the local or State government you trust?"

"I can think of a couple of people," he said. "I'd need to go to Seattle, but I had planned a trip anyway. I'll send them a telegram and set up a meeting."

"Be careful not to mention the reason for the meeting," Jack said. "Maybe I'm paranoid, but I think our culprit is right under our nose."

"Suzy, can you meet with your people?" Sara asked. "I don't want any trouble from this direction. They may know who these people are, and where the money is coming from. John, didn't you say you arrested the same group on three different occasions?" He nodded a reply. "Were there any Indians with them?"

"No," he replied "they were all whites."

"There was a notice at the mill for a company looking for loggers," Barton said. "Maybe we should get someone on the inside?"

"It can't be one of us," John said. "We're too well known. An Indian would be a little too obvious."

"I have just the person for the job," Jack smiled. "A friend of mine from the war is sending his son out here. No one knows who he is. If he's like his father at all, he's smart. He's to arrive on Monday. I'll tell him what's going on and set him up in the hotel in town. This way he'll have no connection to me. Let's see what we can learn."

"This could be dangerous if he's caught," Tom said.

"I'll talk to him first," Jack said. "If I think he can't handle this, I'll let you know."

"I'll trace the money," Tom said. "I'll need to let the mill owner know and maybe we should involve him. Mills don't spring up overnight. It takes money for the equipment and manpower to run it. If he's losing business because of these guys, he'll want to help."

"We need to talk to the crews," Ivan said. "They hear things from other loggers, especially around town. We can ask them to keep an ear open. You can do the same thing at the store, Jacob."

"I was thinking that," he replied, "and one other thing. I've been moving a lot of dynamite in the last few weeks." John, Sara and Tom looked at one another. "Why and who would be buying dynamite? I'm not aware of there being that much use in logging and these people pay in cash and I've never seen them before. I never see the same person twice."

"I'm starting to not like this," Jack said.

"Let's not jump to conclusions," Sara said. "Let's meet here next week, same day, same time, and find out what we can this week. Jack, if you can bring your friend's son along, he'll need the big picture." Sara paused for a minute and looked at Monroe's picture. "I'll not let everything we've built here be destroyed. I have a feeling this is political and financial. Monroe pulled the rug out from under some powerful feet when he bought this land. I think we should look to Olympia."

The next week passed with everyone doing what they could to gather information. Tom had left for Seattle on Tuesday and would return on Friday. John and Eddy had uncovered another bootleg operation with the help of the patrol crews. John had directed them to not approach or attempt anything without the Pinkerton's. These arrests came at a price. The loggers were armed and there was a gun battle. When everything was done, two loggers were dead and one of the Pinkerton's had been wounded. The equipment taken in this raid was extensive. They had set up a mobile mill to process the logs at the site. John inventoried the equipment and it was all brand new. There was also a stash of dynamite found. This was the same group that had been arrested three times prior.

"What are they doing with this?" John asked Eddy.

"I don't know," he responded. "I think we need to look around the area they were logging and see if we missed something. That case of dynamite had been opened. We need to see what they've been using it for."

They rode back out to the sight. Three Pinkerton's went with them in case they hadn't rounded everyone up. They started a systematic search of the area. With each circle they went further out. About 4 miles from the original logging site, they found the blasting spot. On the side of a blind cliff they could see the tons of rubble at the base. Water had been converted from a small creek. The creek flowed into a length of 3-foot pipe the narrowed to a 2-foot pipe. This pipe ran downhill along a steep grade that narrowed to a 1-foot pipe. As the water picked up speed, it would pick up pressure by going through a smaller pipe. By the time the water reached the monitors the pressure was enough to blast away rock and debris by the tons.

John looked at the damage from the dynamite and water. They were mining. They had even put up a small railway with ore cars and made slues boxes with the milled lumber. They followed the railway and saw where it met up with the main railroad line. This main line was not located on any of the Monroe property, but it was just a few hundred yards away.

"The logging was meant to mislead us," John said. "Once we found this, we didn't look any further. We thought it was just a bootleg logging operation. It was a cover for the mining being done. They must have been here for quite a while. They even have slues boxes built to catch the gravel as it washes down the hillside. It looks like they've taken tons out of here."

"If they found gold or silver, we better have Tom check to see if Dad maintained all the mineral rights," Eddy said. "We need to get the sheriff out here and we'll need to post Pinkerton's. I want this operation stopped. We can physically stop this by our presence, but we need to find the brains behind it."

John asked that the Pinkerton's stay at the mine site, and he would send out a crew to destroy the water monitors and tear out the railway for the ore cars. Whoever was behind this was not going to be happy and this was John's hope. He hoped someone would get angry and shoot his mouth off. John made sure the crew had arrived before he and Eddy headed back to the estate. Will and Gus even accompanied them out to the site. Gus had always had an interest in geology and he could ascertain what they may have found, or were finding. They would not be back in time for the Saturday meeting, but Will would get word to Eddy as soon as they knew something. John and Eddy left for their full day ride back home. They could push it to 8 hours if they needed to, but John never wanted to put that kind of strain on the animals.

They got back to the house by 11pm on Friday night. It was good to sleep in a bed again and both were asleep before their heads hit the pillow. Eddy awoke 5 hours later for no apparent reason. He got up and checked on Annie, who was sleeping soundly. Amanda Regan was spending the night. She and Annie were inseparable. They went to school together, played together, and had many adventures with their vivid imaginations. Eddy quietly closed the door and went downstairs.

He felt uneasy about something. He couldn't put his finger on it. He walked out to the porch and looked around. He could spot nothing but the feeling wouldn't go away. He went to the kitchen and grabbed a snack and went back to bed, but couldn't sleep.

"What's wrong?" John asked quietly.

"Don't know," Eddy said. "Go back to sleep. I'm going downstairs to read a while." He went downstairs to hear the clock chime 5am. He saw Emily sitting in the library and walked in and joined her. "You can't sleep either?"

"I want to get into town early," she smiled. "When did you get in?"

"Late," Eddy answered as he yawned.

"Why are you up so early?" Emily asked.

"Don't know," Eddy said. "I woke up with this uneasy feeling and can't shake it. I checked on Annie and she's okay."

"Amanda is here," Emily smiled, "so all is right in Annie's world." Emily saw Eddy staring at the floor. "Honey, what's wrong?"

"I can't, I don't know," Eddy said. "Something just isn't right and I don't know what it is." He looked at her and smiled. "I'm driving myself crazy, aren't I? I'm going to make some coffee. Why don't you join me?" They retired to the kitchen and Eddy did his best to hide this feeling he had. He kept going to the windows and staring out. By 6am Sally came in and Sara had gotten up.

"Everyone is up early," she said as she kissed Emily's cheek. She went to the other side of the table and kissed Eddy. "When did you get in?"

"Late," he smiled. "Hope we didn't wake anyone."

"I need to get moving," Emily said. "I want to be in town by 6:30. I'll see you all later. Love you both."

Sara looked at her son and knew something was on his mind. They talked over a pot of coffee and Eddy still couldn't sort out why he felt the way he did. She told him how his grandmother would sometimes feel when things happened before she was told. Eddy was convinced that whatever had happened wasn't good.

"Why do you say that?" Sara asked. "If you've never felt this way before, how would you know if it's good feeling, or a bad feeling? We must wait and see and waiting is always hard."

Eddy spent the morning grooming the horses. When he needed to think, they seemed to listen. John watched him from the doorway and smiled. He left him alone to think. He found Sara and told her what they had found, and the damage caused by this mining operation. She shook her head and walked away.

The group started to arrive at noon. Ivan had sent word with Emily that he was running late but not to start without him. Sally had made a light lunch for everyone. Tom and Kathleen arrived with Ben who went to find the girls. Jack and Maggie arrived, followed by Samuel and Mary. By 1pm Ivan and Helga had arrived. Kathleen, Maggie, Helga, and Mary left the library and closed the door. Tom had brought a stack of papers and started filing through them. Sara got everyone settled and then stood from her chair.

"Eddy, John," she started. "Why don't you tell us what you found?"

"We located a mining operation," John said. "The logging was just to throw us off. The real operation is about 4 miles from the logging camp. They've blasted the hell out of the area with high-pressured water monitors. The damage will never be repaired."

"Mining for what?" Tom asked.

"We don't know," Eddy answered, "could be gold or silver. I sent for Will and Gus. They'll look at the operation and let us know, but that's not until next week."

"It has to be gold," Jacob said. "There's been a lot of cyanide coming through the store. That's used to leach the gold."

"Have you followed the money?" Sara asked Tom.

"It leads to Canada," Tom said. "There's some mining company up there who's paying the bills. I haven't found out who owns it yet. It's held by some corporate holding company and that tells me that the true owners don't want to reveal their identities. I will find out who they are."

"My nephew was one of the loggers that got arrested," Jack said. "He made sure that he didn't protest or drop any names. He said that his foreman gave them orders to cut and haul out as much timber as possible. They were bailed out by an anonymous source. He said that they are to go back to work as soon as the area is clear."

"How do they know if the area is clear?" Sara asked.

"They know it's clear as soon as their new equipment arrives," Jack said. "The new stuff arrives with instructions on where to go. There's someone locally who's running this enterprise. I asked this kid to keep his ears open and get me a message as soon as he knew something."

"They seem to be one step ahead of us," Eddy said. "It's time to turn the tables. I'm afraid that this may escalate and get ugly."

"I'm going to be around for a while," Ivan said. "I want to work with Eddy and John on this. I can, easily, watch the train depot. Everything is unloaded with a mile from my house. It's easy to see large equipment coming in."

"No, it isn't," Jack said. "They unload the equipment near the mine. But watching the railcars is still a good idea. It comes on open flatcars and everything else comes in boxcars. If the equipment is being unloaded before it gets into town, you'll see the empty flatcars. Just look for them or any equipment and that should tip us off."

By 4pm the meeting was starting to break up with everyone knowing what the next move was going to be. Emily, Maggie, and Kathleen were informed about some of the things going on and asked to keep their ears open. As they stood in the living room a rider galloped up in front of the house. It was one of the Pinkerton's that Eddy and John had left at the mining sight.

"Mr. Monroe?" he said breathlessly to Eddy. "There's been a problem at the mine."

"What kind of problem?" Eddy asked.

"There was an ambush around 4am this morning," he said. "White men dressed up like Indians. We got most of them, and those we didn't get, ran off."

"Was anyone hurt?" Eddy asked.

"Yes, sir," he said as he looked at the floor. "Your brother Will is dead."

Chapter 22

Gus arrived a few hours later with Will's body. He'd been shot through the head at close range. Gus told the story of what happened early that morning. Two of the Pinkertons, that had died, had been scalped. The attackers wanted the illusion, of this being done by local Indians, to be real. What they didn't expect was the number of people at the camp. They were only expecting there to be three, at most five people guarding the site. They weren't expecting the other 10 men that were there.

"When the shooting started," Gus said quietly, "I tried to get to Will. I was in the mine taking samples. He had just left an hour before to get some sleep." He looked at Will and tears began to fall. "I couldn't get to him. I couldn't save him."

"Gus," John consoled. "If you had gotten to him, you may be dead, too. Don't blame yourself."

"They shot him while he slept!" Gus yelled, "Those cowardly bastards!" He paused and regained his composure. "I got the guy who killed him. He was pleading for mercy before I slit his throat and wouldn't give up who had hired him."

"How many were there, Gus, and what are they after?" Tom asked.

"Near as we could figure, about eight of them," he replied. "We got six of them but two ran off into the woods. Your Indian boys are tracking them, Eddy. If anyone can find them, it will be those two. One of the Pinkertons is with them, so everything is legal. These boys were hired killers. Each of them had a brand new $50.00 gold piece in their pocket." He paused and looked back at Tom. "What they're after Tom is gold. From my preliminary tests, the vein is pretty rich and they've taken a lot out."

"We need to tell his wife," Sara said quietly as she stroked his bloody hair. "I'll go into town and let her know about Will."

"No, Mother," Eddy said. "I'll do that. I'll ride into town with Tom and Kathleen. I'll take Will's body to the undertaker." He looked at Kathleen. "Will you accompany me to Ingrid's, Kathleen? I know she won't take this well."

"I'll go with you, Eddy. We should stop by and get her parents," Kathleen said. "They will want to be with Ingrid during this time."

"Emily," Eddy said. "Will you stay with Mother?" She nodded her head and watched as he left the house. John went with him. She looked at Mary and Helga, who were both in tears. Will and Mary had always had a special bond from the time he was born. Sara turned and went into the library and Emily followed her and closed the door.

"I'm sorry, Sara," she said. As Sara turned and looked at her the tears began to run. "I feel like part of heart has been ripped out. I can't imagine what you're feeling." She held her for a time and they consoled each other.

"He'll be buried next to his father," Sara said as she straightened up and stepped back. "I didn't think one of my children would join him so soon."

"This isn't fair," Emily said.

"Life isn't fair, Emily," Sara said flatly. "I will tell you one thing. I will find out who was behind the death of my son. When I do find out, he'll wish he were never born. We need to clean Will up before Eddy takes him to town. I'll not have his wife see him like this."

Emily had never seen Sara like this before. She was calm, cold, and calculating. She had a single purpose, and that was to find who was behind her son's death. Emily knew Sara well enough to understand that she would not rest until she found out the whole truth. Tom and John removed Will's body from the wagon. Sara and Emily cleaned him up and put clean clothes on him. He still had some at the house that he hadn't moved. John and Eddy put him back into the wagon and before Eddy covered him with a sheet, he kissed him gently on the forehead.

William Charles Monroe was laid to rest near to his father. Ingrid's parents were supporting her through this tragedy. The child that she and Will wanted never came to be. She only had a few years of marriage to remember and a broken heart that she was sure would never mend. There was nothing left of the life she loved and she had moved back in with her parents. She gave his toolbox and its contents back to Sara, for she somehow felt this was appropriate.

Annie stuck close to Eddy the entire day. She wasn't fully aware of what death was, but knew she would never see her brother again. Sara remained dignified and stoic. Emily was a little concerned about the lack of emotion, but knew Sara would grieve in her own way. She was having her own problems dealing with this particular event. She had brought this life into the world. She could still see that infant child in the man that lay before her.

Eddy seemed to feel guilty about asking him to the mine. John had talked with him for hours on end about this. He had always heard that twins had a special bond, and he knew this to be true because Eddy awoke early on that Saturday morning, it was at the time his brother died. This was the reason for the disturbing feeling he had. He seemed even more disturbed that he wasn't able to recognize that those feelings he had that morning were caused by his brother's death. John watched Eddy during the funeral and he was taken back to his brother's death. He closed his eyes hoping to erase the memory. He remembered finding his brother hanging from the tree on the edge of the reservation. He had been beaten to death before he was hung. This was to be an example for anyone before leaving the reservation. It was a different time but the reality of a needless death was before him. Patrick Reilly spoke in his gentle voice and he found the Nez Perce he spoke to be comforting. The train arrived back in Snoqualmie. There were four men waiting for them. The two Indian trackers, the Pinkerton, and the Sheriff Travers were standing inside the station as the train slowed to stop. John stepped from the train and was joined by these men. They began to talk quietly and Eddy, Tom, and Sara soon saw the gathering.

"Emily, will you see Annie gets to the wagon?" she asked. Emily looked at the men and took Annie's hand. Kathleen walked with her as Sara and Tom joined Eddy, John and the other men.

"They found our two runaways," John said. "They're down in the jail."

"I'll tell Emily to go back to the house," Sara said as she turned. "We're going down to the jail for a little chat."

"Mother," Eddy said. Sara turned and the look on her face told Eddy to not test her resolve in this matter. "Okay, John, Tom, and I will meet you outside." She turned again and walked away.

"What shape are these boys in?" Tom asked the Sheriff.

"Cuts and bruises," he said. "They'll live, unless Sara decides to kill them now. I don't think a court in the land would convict her, but I'm holding them for murder. They'll probably hang unless they can tell us what we want to know."

They caught up with Sara and walked down to the jail. The Sheriff opened the office door and then the door that led to the cells. He pointed to the cell on the right, which housed two men that looked no more than 18 years old. They looked tired, and when they saw Eddy and John, they looked scared. Sara walked up to the cell and looked at them. Without being introduced, they knew who she was.

"They gave up without a fight," the Pinkerton said to Sara. "They were tired, cold, and hungry when we finally found them."

"Tell me your names," Sara asked in a soft voice. One of them stood and looked at Sara.

"I'm Martin Carson," he said respectfully. "This is my brother, Peter." The second man stood up and nodded.

"How old are you, Martin?" Sara asked.

"I'm 20, Ma am," Martin answered. "Pete is 19."

"I'm Sara Monroe," she responded. "I've just buried my son and I'd like to ask you some questions about how that happened. Is that all right?" Eddy was amazed at how his mother was handling this situation. He could see that these boys were scared and she playing into that, or was she? Both of the boys nodded their heads.

Sara, methodically and carefully, worded her questions. Once the boys started to open up, they told how they came out west because of the dime novels they'd read while living in Pittsburgh. The romantic illusion created by these novels prompted them to hop a train. They were on their way to California when Martin decided he wanted to see Seattle. After arriving they had done odd labor jobs to raise enough money to get to California. They were spending the money just as fast as they made it just to live.

As they sat in a saloon in Seattle they heard a man talking at the next table about some good money being paid to work a mining operation. They understood mining coming from the Pittsburgh area. They figured a few months on this job would pay their way to California.

"We took the jobs," Pete said. "We didn't know that anything illegal was going on."

"You were working the mine when everyone was arrested?" John asked.

"Not that day," Martin said. "We had the day off and went exploring around the camp. When we came back we noticed everyone was gone and there were guards with guns. So we grabbed what things we could, without getting caught, and came into town."

"Did you talk with anyone here?" Eddy asked.

"By the time we got here," Martin said. "The men we worked with, that were arrested, had been released from jail. They told us to meet them at the livery stable later. That's when we were paid the $50.00, in gold, to clean everyone out of the camp."

"What reason did they give you?" Sara asked. "Did they tell you why they wanted the camp cleaned out?"

"We were told," Martin said then paused as he looked at the floor. "We were told that the owner wanted these men killed because they were claim jumpers."

"Why the Indian disguises?" John asked.

"We were told that if they thought that the Indians killed them," Pete started, "that it would help get them all moved to a reservation, and then the owner wouldn't have to worry about interference from any of the locals."

"When we saw the first man killed," Martin said," Pete and I decided to get out of there. We never fired a shot. We ran as fast as we could." The Sheriff went back to the outer office and came back with the guns they had taken from the boys.

"They're telling the truth," the Sheriff said. "Neither of these rifles has ever been fired. They're brand new."

"I'm truly sorry about your son, Ma am," Martin said to Sara. "We may be stupid and young, but we're not murderers. If we need to hang for this, then so be it. We didn't hurt anyone."

"Do you know who the owner is?" Sara asked quietly.

"No, Ma am," Pete said. "We never met them. A man named Tony Pideza paid us. He said he worked for the owners." Tom's head popped up and he looked at John. Pete looked at Tom and back at Sara. "What's going to happen to us?"

"I don't know, Peter," Sara replied. "That's up to the Sheriff. Thank you for being honest with us." Sara turned to leave the jail cells and before she walked through the door she turned and looked at Martin and Peter one more time. She waited in the outer office until the Sheriff locked the door. He turned and looked at her.

"I don't think we can convict them of anything but being stupid," the Sheriff said.

"Can you hold them for a few days?" Sara asked. "I'd like to know who comes to see them, if anyone. As far as anyone knows, these boys may hang for the slaughter up at the mining camp, and that's what I want them to think. I'm interested to see if the people behind this are going to let them hang."

"I see where you're going with this, Sara," Tom replied. "If anyone comes to see these boys and they tell them that they've talked to us, their lives won't be worth spit. We'll have to protect them."

"I can't believe you want to protect the same people who killed Will," Eddy said.

"Edmundson," Sara said. "These boys were lied to and thought they were protecting the property of the owner. They showed they could be loyal and they were paid a great deal of money. As soon as they saw what was happening, they left. They knew something wasn't right. These are good young men, and we do need to protect them." She turned to Tom and continued. "Can you stay and talk to them. Tell them they won't be charged with anything and tell them to not discuss our conversation with anyone except you. Explain why they are going to be here for a few days. Can you ask Kathleen to take a look at them? They could use some bandages for some of their wounds."

"What about after they get out?" Tom asked.

"I have a few ideas," Sara said. "We'll take care of that in a few days."

Everyone left the Sheriff's office and John scanned the street to see if anyone was watching the jail. The ride back up to the house seemed longer than usual. Eddy drove the buggy and John was on horseback. As they neared the falls road, Eddy looked at John and he rode toward the house and Eddy turned off and headed for the falls. He stopped the buggy and helped his Mother out of the wagon. She tucked her arm in his and walked to the cliff's edge. The mist felt good on her face and she began to cry. How many things had changed since she first stood here with her husband some 24 years ago? The one consistent and constant was the falls. They didn't change or become any less magnificent.

"Mother," Eddy said breaking the silence. "I'm sorry about what I said earlier. I didn't think it through. I saw those boys as the reason for Will's death. I wanted to hate someone, and blame someone."

"There is someone to blame," she replied. "We just don't know who, yet. This may get very ugly. There's a lot of money behind this mining operation. Where there's money, there are powerful people. If these powerful people want something bad enough, they'll figure out a way to get it."

"What do they want, Mother?" Eddy asked as he stared at the water.

"This land," Sara answered. "They will do anything to get it." She put her hand on his shoulder. "Does John make you happy?"

"Yes, he does," he replied. "I never thought I could love anyone as much as I love him. He seems to know what I'm thinking."

"And do you know his mind?" Sara asked. "Does his touch satisfy you?" He nodded a 'yes' and blushed. "That's as it should be."

"My only regret is that we will have no children," Eddy said. "There's no one to carry on the Monroe line."

"There's Annie," Sara said. She stood up and Eddy stood beside her and put his arm around her shoulder. She turned and looked at him. "Don't let William's death keep you from living life to its fullest. He will continue to watch over us with your father and grandmother." She and Eddy turned at the same time to see their large friend looking on.

Kathleen went to the jail to treat and bandage wounds that Martin and Peter had. She was fully prepared to hate these men, but after she saw their innocence, couldn't blame them for Will's death. Tom had not told her what to expect, which he found best. He found Kathleen formed her own opinions regardless of what he told her.

Peter and Martin were polite and grateful for the medical attention she gave them. The Sheriff was keeping track of who was in to see them. Three different men came in on different days and times to speak with these boys. He got a message to Tom, who in the mean time, was tracking down the whereabouts of Tony Pideza. He didn't have to track him long because he was one of the men who visited the boys.

Tom was getting ready to leave the bank and talk with the boys. He looked up and saw Tony standing at Moe's desk. They went into his office and closed the door. Tom decided to stick around and thought he would file some paperwork. He heard the voices start to get loud. He was filing just outside of Moe's door.

"As soon as those boys get out of jail, I'll take care of them," Tony said.

"I don't want to know any of this," Moe said "Do you realized that one of the men killed was Sara Monroe's son?"

"Who gives a shit?" Tony said. "It's just one more, dead Indian."

"Things are getting messy. Clean it up quickly, Tony," Moe replied. "Everything is shut down, and we'll wait till things cool off, if they ever do."

"What's that suppose to mean?" Tony asked.

"Sara has a lot of pull all over the state," Moe said. "She also had the money and political contacts to make life very miserable for everyone involved in this."

"We have some good political contacts ourselves," Tony said. "Besides, Moe my old friend, I have one ace up my sleeve. I think Monroe' squaw may come around to our way of thinking."

"She can't know that I have any part of this, Tony," Moe warned.

"You may be a silent partner" Tony said, "and it would destroy any gathering of information that you could get for Congressman Lawrence Banks. You worry to damn much. You're as twitchy as an old hen and you need to let me do what I do best."

Tom heard the chair slide back and went back across the room to his desk. He sat down and felt sick. Monroe had trusted Moe for years and even offered him a chance to get in on this land when it was purchased. He could never raise the money so he never became a partner. As far as the Congressman, Tom knew that this was the man that Monroe screwed when he bought the added 100,000 acres and who was still fighting to get his hands on it.

The door opened and Moe and Tony walked out. Tony waved a hello to Tom and he smiled back. He wanted to beat the man within an inch of his life. He had never hated anyone more than Tony Pideza, and he had the same sudden hate for Moe. He was grateful that Moe knew nothing about the gold in Monroe's safe. He had not been a part of any of that. He had no idea of Sara's total worth and this was now a blessing.

"Tony and I are going to lunch," Moe smiled. "Would you care to join us?"

"Thanks, but no," Tom replied. "I have some things to finish up here." He watched them leave and looked into Moe's bank account. If he was making money he wasn't keeping it in this bank. Tom didn't think he was that stupid, but he did find a note from a bank in Seattle. About that time the door opened and Emily walked in.

"What's wrong?" Emily said as she saw at the look on his face.

"No time to explain," Tom said. "I need for you to go to the jail and talk to Peter and Martin."

"I was going over there to check their wounds," Emily said. "The Sheriff is going to release them as soon as I'm done."

"As soon as they're released, they'll be hunted down and killed," Tom said. "I don't have time to tell you everything, but we need to get these boys out of town quietly and quickly."

"Sara is over at the store," Emily said. "Let me go talk to her before I go over to the jail."

Emily left the bank and found Sara. She told her about Tom's information and Sara decided the only place the boys would be safe was at the estate. She had the wagon and if they could get out of town she would pick them up at Ivan's house. No one would expect that the Monroe family would harbor these boys.

Emily went to the jail and saw Martin and Peter. She made sure the Sheriff couldn't hear what she was about to say. She carefully told the boys to take the road out of town that led to the falls. They knew the Zembruski house and would wait behind it until they saw Sara's wagon.

"Why is Mrs. Monroe doing this for us?" Peter asked. "We were paid to kill her son."

"But you didn't," Emily whispered. "You knew it was wrong. If anything happens to you, there will be no trail back to the people responsible and that's why your lives are in danger. Do you both understand?" They nodded their heads. "Don't trust anyone. If the Sheriff wants to know where you're going when you leave here, tell him you've got enough money so you're going to California."

"We were told to report to the mill tomorrow morning," Martin said. "Won't they miss us?"

"By the time anyone misses you," Emily smiled. "You'll be safely hidden away. If they come here, the Sheriff will tell them that you boys lit out for California." She turned to leave and looked back at their faces. They were scared and they should be. "I'll see you tonight."

Jacob loaded Sara's wagon quickly and left a spot large enough to carry the boys in the center under the canvas cover. She would keep them hidden until she was well out of the site of any houses. Jacob wished her luck and said they would come to the house tomorrow for their weekly Saturday meeting.

The Sheriff released the boys and they found their way to Ivan's house and found Sara waiting. They quickly got to the wagon.

"Were you followed?" Sara asked as they climbed into the wagon.

"No, Ma am," they said. "We split up and met up here."

"Stay under the canvas until I tell you to come out," Sara said as she headed into the trees. She had no idea how precious the cargo she was carrying was. She didn't know why their lives were in danger, but trusted Tom's judgment without question. When they were well within the trees, Sara told them to come out.

"It's warm in there," Peter said as he crawled out. "Where are we going Ma am?"

"I'm taking you to my home," Sara said. "We can keep you safe there." The boys looked at one another in surprise. "If you want to work, I can find things for you to do and pay you a wage."

"That sounds good, Mrs. Monroe," Martin said. "I want to tell you just how grateful we are, Ma am."

"Everyone calls me Sara," she responded.

The boys got settled in the small cabin that Sally had once occupied with her sons. Barton was happy for the company and they were grateful for the roof over their heads and the work. These boys were not lazy and willing to do the most menial tasks if asked. Samuel had taken charge of their assignments and had a list of things that needed to be done. He found Martin had a good mind for carpentry. The barn and old cabin needed some repair, which he couldn't get done. Peter loved the horses. Eddy had always groomed and exercised them, but gave that duty over to Peter. Both boys seemed happy with their new duties and still had no idea how large a role they played in this political war being waged.

Tom and Kathleen arrived for the Saturday meeting. Tom had told Kathleen none of the information he had found out while standing outside of Moe's office. Ivan and Helga were close behind them. Kathleen saw Peter down by the barn and excused herself. As she walked toward the barn he saw her and smiled.

"How are you feeling, Peter?" she asked.

"I'm just fine, Dr. Eichorn," he responded.

"How do you like it here?" Kathleen asked.

"We have jobs, and place to live, and Mrs. Monroe has been wonderful," Peter said.

"She's given us a home," said Martin as he came down the ladder from the roof. "I hope we don't let her down."

"Sara is a wonderful person," Kathleen said. "She'll take care of you as long as you do your work and be honest with her." She looked at the boys' faces. They looked happy and this was quite a change from what she saw when they were in jail. "You two take care. Stay close to the house for a while."

"Yes, Ma am," Martin replied. "Mrs. Monroe doesn't want us to leave the estate until further notice. We have no problem with that and there's enough work to last a lifetime."

Kathleen walked back to the house and met Eddy and John on the porch. They walked into the house and saw Sara, Tom, and Ivan in the library. Jack Regan had just arrived with Amanda. She and Annie went to the upstairs playroom and Jack closed the library door.

"I've had some interesting developments in the last 24 hours," Tom started. As he told everyone about the conversation he had overheard, they sat in amazement. No one could believe that Moe Hawkins had anything to with this mess. "I found a reference to another bank account in San Francisco that I have a friend checking out. He's not in this alone and he's not the brains behind the operation."

Tom continued to tell everyone what he found out and the name of the Congressman he had overheard Moe talk about. He still had some inquiries out on him with his friend in Seattle and would know something soon. "I've asked to have a meeting in Seattle. I don't want any information going across the telegraph wires. There are too many ears and eyes. We have no idea who was paid off or who's listening."

"Our only link to what happened at the mining camp and these men are there," Sara said as she pointed out the window at Peter and Martin. "They will hunt these boys down and kill them. They won't think to look here, and if they do, we have plenty of protection."

"I have people posted around the house and on the main road," Eddy said. "We'll have ample warning"

"Do these boys know their lives are in danger?" Jack asked.

"Yes," Sara answered. "I talked to them about it and they know that they can't talk to anyone outside of the estate or leave until we get this sorted out. They don't know the magnitude of what they were involved in. They're just a couple of young kids that walked into a bees nest while looking for honest work."

"We don't know the magnitude of this either, Mother," Eddy said. "We don't know how high up it goes."

"Congressman Banks probably thinks that he's untouchable because of his elected position," Tom said. "What concerns me is the comment the Tony made about an ace up his sleeve. Does anyone have any idea what he's referring to?" He looked at the blank stares he was given and that gave him his answer. "Let's keep our eyes and ears open."

"When are we going to tell Martin and Peter the scope of these things?" John asked. "They have a right to know, and not feel like they're being held prisoner here."

"I don't think they feel that they're prisoners, John," Eddy responded. "I do agree that they should be told. They need to know that their very lives depend on their silence and their absence."

"Would you and Eddy talk to them, John?" Sara asked. "Get them now. That way if they have any questions, they can ask us, while everyone is still here." John left the room to get the boys.

"I think that's it," Tom said. "I'll keep everyone informed on what I find out in Seattle. I'm leaving on Monday and should be back on Wednesday. Until then, we need to go about our business as normal. We can't let Moe or Tony suspect that we know anything."

"I'm not sure how much I trust the Sheriff," Jacob said. "Suzy has seen him spending time with Tony. I have no reason to not trust him other than that."

"I'll talk with him," Tom said. "Monroe got him his job, and I can find out if there's any loyalty there."

"There better be some loyalty," Jack said. "He can be replaced very quickly. You're the Mayor, Jacob. You can fire him in a heartbeat."

"I can, but I need to have cause," Jacob said.

"Is being involved in an illegal mining operation cause enough?" Jack responded. Everyone smiled and Jacob agreed. Sara stood and adjourned the meeting and all agreed to meet next Saturday. Eddy looked at his mother and noticed that she looked tired. He looked at the rest of the group and they all looked tired. This situation was taking a toll on all involved. John had returned with the boys and they were given the opportunity to ask anything they wanted. As Tom told them every detail he knew and how the trail was leading to the political arena, their faces were almost ashen. Martin shook his head and looked at the floor while Peter just stared out the window. They now understood what they had stumbled into and were prepared to do what was asked for as long as needed, because their very lives would depend on it.

"We're not in a hurry to leave, Mrs. Monroe," Martin said. "Pete and I like it here, and we owe you for giving us a job, a place to live, and for your son. What we were paid to do was wrong, and I would like to see these men punished." They left the house and went back to work.

"Those are good boys," Tom said.

Sara lay in bed that night and told Emily of everything. She listened quietly and was surprised about Moe Hawkins. Emily and Sara had always used each other as sounding boards, but Emily knew that this was weighing heavily on Sara. This was personal with the death of her son and she wanted to make these people pay, but it wasn't retribution as much as justice. What struck at Sara's heart was the fact the Moe was someone Monroe had trusted for years. He had built this empire with Moe's help.

Sara understood the deception of the white man with the Indians but she didn't think it happened in the white world. This was a rude awakening that she wasn't expecting. She remembered her Mother talking about other tribes raiding the village for the food stored up for winter. She understood fighting for your very survival, but she was new to the political struggles for power or for money.

"You have to understand, Sara," Emily whispered as she held her. "If you have something that someone else wants, people will beg, borrow, steal, or kill to get it. In the white world this is common and most feel the means they use to get what they want is justified. It's a struggle for power to make, change, or ignore laws that are made to protect. I have always asked myself the question, if the law doesn't protect me, why should I obey it? Women have been victims for so many years and not protected. Look at Maggie Regan, who was almost beat to death, and Bobby got a fine and a night in jail."

"I'll never understand that kind of thinking," Sara said. "I don't understand the need for power, but I'm beginning to."

"Whether you realize it or not, you have a great deal of power in the area and, combined with your wealth, your responsibilities are great," Emily said. She gave Sara a chance to let this sink in. "Monroe was a rare man who followed all the rules and his honesty was his special gift, and he was no one's fool. He built a life for you and his children with hard work and foresight. You were lucky to find him."

"He found me," Sara said as she turned to face Emily. "I was lucky to find you." She kissed her softly.

"You didn't find me. You saved me," she whispered. She kissed her passionately and removed her gown.

Chapter 23

By the spring of 1898 Sara along with Tom's help had flushed out all the information they needed to take the owners of the mining operation to task. The trail went to Canada and led right back to Moe Hawkins and Congressman Banks. They had a holding company in Victoria and would run everything through that. From what Tom could find, they were making a great deal of money from several mining operations all over the state.

Tom had found, and got the documentation, thanks to his friend in Seattle, of all the activities happening around Snoqualmie. Tom was ready to get the help of the Governor and the State's attorney to bring these people down. Just before he was set to go to Olympia Moe had come to him with cash in hand to pay his money for the land that Monroe had purchased before he died. Moe didn't have the money at the time, and Tom was glad for this.

"I can't get the paperwork in order before leaving," he said. "I'll get to it after I get back."

"I'll just deposit this in Sara's account and you can do the paperwork," Moe said.

"Just wait on that," Tom said trying not to appear too anxious. "I'll need to authorize the receipt and the deed when the money is paid, and I can't do that right now. All the paperwork is in Seattle. Just hang on to the money and we'll get together when I get back. I'll bring all the paperwork with me at that time."

"Okay," Moe agreed. "This has been weighing on my mind and I want to get this done."

He turned and left and Tom breathed a sigh of relief. If there were any exchange of money, any prosecution would be mute. If he was a part owner, he couldn't be prosecuted for mining on his own land, even though he was just a part owner. While Moe was having his conversation with Tom, Tony had run into Eddy.

"Let me by you a drink," Tony said as he sat down at Eddy's table.

"I don't drink," Eddy responded. "I'll take some coffee, though."

"I noticed your friend, John, doesn't drink either," Tony smiled as he poured a liberal portion into his glass. "You Indians can't stand the 'fire water', can you?"

"What do you want, Tony?" Eddy asked quietly as he controlled his anger.

"Nothing much," he smiled as he poured another drink. "I was just wondering what all of your high powered friends would think if they knew that you liked to fuck men?" Eddy felt his temper flair and began to stand up. "Sit down, Chief. I'm just joking with you." Eddy sat down as the waitress brought him coffee. He regained his composure and sipped his coffee.

"I don't know, Tony," Eddy said. "I don't really care what they think."

"I wonder what you're squaw mother would think?" he said hoping to goad Eddy into a fight.

"I think this conversation is over," Eddy said as he stood up.

"You know this whole area would be better off with all of you were locked up on the reservation or killed," he smiled. "You and your whore wouldn't be a problem, but your Mother would be difficult to get to. If life has taught me anything, it's that anyone can be killed. Your Mother would be an interesting challenge. But I'll make a deal with you. If you and your friend leave town, I'll let your Mother live."

Eddy grabbed Tony by the jacket and put him up against the wall. John appeared behind him and touched him on the back.

"Don't do it, Eddy," John said. "He's drunk and stupid. He's not worth going to jail for." Tony just began to laugh.

"Listen to the little, woman," he said as he chuckled.

"If you ever threaten my family again," Eddy whispered. "I might kill you, but there are things much worse than death." He let go of him and Tony straightened his jacket. "That's not a threat. That's a promise, you piece of shit." He threw a quarter down on the table.

He and John left the hotel restaurant and Eddy was still angry enough to kill. They walked over to the bank and saw Tom was just leaving. Eddy motioned to him and they walked to Walker's store. Jacob showed them to the back room and Eddy told Tom what had happened. Eddy had never admitted to anyone, except his mother and Emily, the relationship that he and John had. Admitting this to Tom was not easy for Eddy. Tom didn't seem surprised by the information at all and he didn't seem to care.

"This must be the ace up his sleeve," Tom said. "I wonder how he found out. Is this why you're so angry?"

"No," John said. "He threatened to kill us, and Sara."

"He was saying that Mother would be a challenge, but he was up to it," Eddy said. "He also said if John and I left town he would let Mother live."

"He threatened her life?" Tom asked in amazement. "Those were his exact words?"

"His exact words were 'anyone can be killed, but your Mother would be a challenge' and then he smiled," Eddy said.

"You'll need to get back to the house and let Sara know what's going on," Tom said. "I need to check with Kathleen before I leave town. I'll let her know about this and talk to Emily. John, make sure that Sara goes nowhere without a Pinkerton and let the rest of the security posted around the estate know the details. They'll need to stay alert."

They talked for a few more minutes and left Jacob's office. Tom informed Jacob of the latest turn of events. He would go and talk with the Sheriff. There wasn't anything that he could do until Tony tried something. Tom left the office and walked over to the hospital. He found Kathleen and Emily talking in the office.

"What's wrong?" Kathleen said when she saw the look on his face.

"I need to talk to both of you," he said as he closed the door. He told them of the encounter that Eddy had with Tony. Kathleen didn't seem to care about Eddy or John's relationship. He explained what Eddy and John were going to do for Sara's protection.

"Eddy and John are in danger, too," Emily said.

"They know this," Tom said. "They are going to be extra careful." Tom kissed Kathleen and said his goodbye. "I'll be back in three days. If there's a delay, I'll send a telegram. Oh, Moe finally tried to give me the money for his share of the land, which I refused right now. I told him we would take care of the paperwork when I returned. I won't, because that would negate any chance of prosecution." He kissed his wife. "Take care of each other."

Emily looked at Kathleen as Tom left the office. She couldn't believe that Tony was so brazen. If he wanted to eliminate all of the Indians, then Annie and Eddy were in as much danger as Sara.

"Emily," Kathleen started. "It's been quiet at the clinic and the hospital. Why don't you stay close to the estate until Tom gets back into town? He should have all of the documents he needs to proceed with the legal action."

"You can send word if you need me here," Emily said. She was ready to leave when she decided to ask the question. "You didn't seem surprised by the information about Eddy and John."

"I guess I've known for some time, as had Tom," Kathleen said. "It makes no difference to us." Emily nodded her head and smiled and turned to leave. "He is his mother's son." Emily looked at Kathleen.

"Meaning?" she asked.

"We've known each other for more than twenty years, Emily," Kathleen said. "I've known about you and Sara for years although we've never discussed it. I know what she means to you and what you mean to her. You can see it on your faces when you're together. I see the same thing on the faces of Eddy and John. Life is too short to judge or condemn anyone for who they choose to love and build a life with. I can't judge people that harshly and never will. Tom has always felt the same way."

"Thank you, Kathleen," Emily said. "Being accepted is been the hardest thing for any of us in this situation. Getting people to understand is impossible."

"Your true friends won't care," Kathleen said as she put an arm around her shoulder. "Now get home before it starts to get dark."

The following three days were quiet. Eddy, John, Sara, and Emily all stayed close to the estate. They kept Annie out of school for the first two days until she pitched a fit. One of the Pinkerton's escorted her to and from school. Sara was starting to feel like a prisoner in her own home. She took solace in the fact that Emily was there to keep her company, but she was edgy and was looking behind every tree when they were outside the house.

"You need to relax," Sara laughed. "You're making me crazy."

"I know," Emily said. "I won't relax until Tom gets back and we can do something legally about this whole situation."

"It could still take some time after he gets back," Sara said. "You need to prepare for that and go back to work if that happens. You can't stay here and hold my hand forever."

***

As Beth continued listening to the story she could see the trouble that everyone was in because of greed and deception. She wondered how everything would turn out, but she knew it would be good because she was here. Zack remembered the first time he heard this story. Eddy and John had come back from Alaska and Zack had asked about some of the family history.

"Anne hasn't told me too much," Zack said.

"She hasn't told you much because there's a lot she doesn't know," Eddy said. "She was just a kid when so much of the stuff was going on. What do you want to know?"

Zack started asking questions and Eddy found it was easier to start at the beginning. He regaled Zack with the story of his mother and father and how they met and the empire they built together. Zack wished he could have lived during that time. He wished he could have met Sara before she died. It was the wee hours of the morning when Anne appeared and suggested that everyone go to bed.

"I'll sleep enough when I'm dead, Annie," Eddy said. "I want to find out more about this young man." Anne looked at Zack and smiled. She kissed Eddy and went upstairs. "It's good to be home."

"How long have you been away?" Zack asked.

"Since the summer of 1898," Eddy answered as he looked around the house. "I never thought I'd see this place again. I should have come home years ago."

"Would have, should have, and could have really don't count," Zack said. "I used to drive myself crazy with those thoughts."

"You're a wise young man, Zack," Eddy said, "and a considerate one. I can see why Annie fell for you." Zack blushed and smiled. "Russell is your son, isn't he?"

"Yes, he is," Zack admitted. "Anne has been very adamant about that not being common knowledge. I don't agree with her on that point, but I have respected her wishes."

"Knowing how head-strong that Annie is, that's a wise decision," Eddy laughed. "It's been Annie's goal to carry on the Monroe line. My brother died before he and his wife could have children, and me, well, that's not been possible." Eddy paused and looked at Zack. "You really love her, don't you?"

"More than life itself," Zack answered. "She stole my heart from the first minute I laid eyes on her."

Eddy smiled and continued to give Zack the family history. Most of the 108,000 acres was now a National forest and still preserved. The growth around the falls had ruined the pristine appearance and this made Eddy sad. He told Zack what it was like when he was growing up. He told how Emily and Kathleen built the hospital and worked with the logging camps.

He told Zack about the first time he saw the coast of Alaska. This was before the gold rush of 1901. He talked about all the work he and John did with the Eskimos in the area. He talked about the schools they built and the gold they panned out of the creek right beside their cabin. They told no one about the full scope of the amount they found. When the rush hit, there were so many claim jumpers. Everyone thought that they had a cabin next to an unproductive creek. They also let them think that there was no interest in the gold being found.

He and John continued to build schools and were paid by the Government to do that. During the last few years, John had found it harder and harder to stay warm during the long winter. He had contracted Pneumonia each winter for the last few years and he had gotten weaker after each bout.

"He wouldn't have survived another winter," Eddy said quietly. "The doctor up there said that he wouldn't have too long anyway. I wanted to bring him back down here and have Kathleen check him out. She is the only doctor I ever trusted, besides Emily McLaughlin." He looked at the floor. "I thought I was in love with her when I was a kid. I wanted to marry her, until I met John. She only had eyes for Mother." He looked up at the portrait of them. "They were beautiful together, weren't they?"

"Yes, they were," Zack replied. "Just as you and John are."

Eddy looked at Zack and smiled. It had been many years since he had talked this way with anyone other than John. All the years in Alaska, and all the people he'd met, had never produced a single person he could talk to about such things. He didn't realize how much he'd miss that until now. He liked Zack and admired his open mind and the love he had for his sister. They talked until the sun started to come up. Zack knew all of the family history and was proud to be associated with these people.

"Now you're part of it," Eddy said. "You must make sure that this is not forgotten. The ancestry and history are important things in the Indian cultures. Your son shares this, and his children will carry on this legacy."

"Have you two gone to bed, yet?" Annie asked from the doorway.

"Not yet," Zack answered.

"I think I'll catch a nap later," Eddy said. "I'd kill for some coffee, though."

"Already brewing," Annie said as she turned and headed for the kitchen. Eddy and Zack followed her.

All of Kathleen's skill and knowledge couldn't repair the damage to John's heart. It was only a matter of time before it would give out. Two weeks later John Young-Bear died peacefully in his sleep. Annie had asked Patrick Reilly to preside at a simple graveside service. He would be buried in the family plot in Renton and Eddy would reside beside him when his time came. The day before he died, Eddy had taken him to the falls. John knew his time was near and wanted to visit this magical place one more time. Eddy knew he was saying goodbye to the land and water. He and John said their goodbye at the same time. Eddy wanted nothing held back and said what had been unspoken between them for so many years.

Patrick had prepared part of his ceremony in Cherokee to honor

John's native tongue. Zack noticed how frail Patrick was and knew he would soon have someone presiding over his grave. Kathleen and Ben Eichorn attended but Tom was not feeling well. He was, after all, 81 years old. He had buried all of his friends and now with John the younger generation was starting. He had helped Zack and Annie manage the finances of the estate and would retire the day he died.

Everyone met back at the estate for drinks and dinner. Eddy asked Annie if he could stay on at the estate. Zack thought that a strange question. It was his family home and why would he feel the need to ask?

"I need to ask because I don't want to intrude on the life that you and Zack have built here," Eddy said. "You have little Russell to think about."

"What do you think, Zack?" Annie asked in a strange way.

"This is your home, Eddy," Zack said. "I would be insulted if you went anywhere else." He couldn't understand why Anne had asked him. Maybe she and Eddy needed assurance about what he felt. The decision was made, and Eddy would live the rest of his life in the house he was born in. All the people that passed before him were still alive within the walls and trees of this estate. It was fitting that he would begin and end his life in the same house.

***

"What information could Tom have come back with?" Beth asked Zack. "How could they stop the politicians from taking what they really wanted?"

"In those days it was easier to get to these people," Zack answered. "You didn't need Senate inquiries, or independent counsels. I'll tell you what Tom did come back with."

Tom arrived back in Snoqualmie accompanied by Federal Marshals with warrants for the arrest of Moe Hawkins and Tony Pideza. There were two Federal Bank examiners ready to look into all of the bank records for Moe and this company in Canada. These people had been working with the Canadian officials regarding the company located there for the last year. They had operations in Oregon and California, which were all illegal. The money was being traced and the account in England and was finally located.

They had never been able to find them guilty of anything more than the fly-by-night operations they had run for the last year. With the deaths of Will and the Pinkerton's, they had the ammunition to shut them down completely. Congressman Banks had been arrested, in a loud fashion, in Seattle two days ago. His name and signature are on all records, along with Moe Hawkins. When they searched his office in Olympia, they found letters talking about the whole situation that led to Will's death. This was the damning evidence they needed to end his career.

Tom and his guests went from the train station to the Sheriff's office. The Federal Marshals showed their credentials and discussed their plan of action for the apprehension of those listed on the warrants. The Sheriff was willing to remain neutral during this process, but would house them until they could be transported to Seattle to stand trial.

"Moe won't be a problem, but I've not seen Tony in about 2 days," the Sheriff said.

"We can probably get that information from Moe when the time comes," Tom said. "We can go over to the bank and get the first one taken care of." They left the office and walked over to the bank. When Tom walked in with his companions, Moe knew something was up. He was arrested without incident and it was a though he was waiting for it. He was also shown a search warrant for his home. They would execute this as soon as he was put in jail.

"You can tell my wife where I am," he said to Tom. The bank examiners went into Moe's office and proceeded to go through every paper. Tom closed the bank early so they could work without interruption.

They questioned Moe about Tony. He said he didn't know where he was. Everyone was ignorant to the fact the Tony had been watching, from behind the saloon, while Moe was being taken to jail. He was unaware of the Congressman's incarceration. He knew that Peter and Martin Carson were at the Monroe estate, but they were not his targets, anymore. What he did know, for certain, is that he was paid $1000.00 to kill Sara Monroe. He had been watching her for the last week without being spotted by the guards around the estate. He knew her schedule and even knew through which window he could see her at certain times of the day. Nighttimes were even better because of the light coming from the windows but decided that it would be too risky for him to make a clean getaway at night. He had chosen his time and place carefully.

Tom had taken the opportunity to hire another man to work with him at the bank. With Moe being in the situation that he was, help would be needed. Tom had located a man he knew in San Francisco who was now in Seattle. This man's son had just finished college and was looking for a position in a bank. Tom trusted this man, and knew his son well. He would arrive on Monday and Tom hoped the bank examiners were finished by then.

He left the bank and walked over to the hospital. Kathleen was coming out the door as Tom walked up to her. She smiled and kissed him. He let her know what was going on down the street.

"If Tony finds out about Moe, he'll run," Kathleen said.

"I hope so," Tom replied. "At least he'll be out of the area. The Marshals are talking to many people in town, trying to get a bead on this guy. They'll find him. Let's go home, because I have to be back at the bank in 2 hours."

"When is Jeremy coming in?" Kathleen asked.

"Monday," Tom answered. "He'll be a welcome addition here."

Jacob and Jack were already aware of the developments because of the Marshal's presence in the store. John had stopped in for a few supplies and they all agreed that their meeting on Saturday could be cancelled. John agreed to tell Sara about this and was relieved at the news. Tomorrow was Friday and they could breathe a little easier.

"We need to keep an eye on everyone until Tony is behind bars," Jack cautioned. "If he feels he's cornered, I think he'll do something stupid, and by stupid, I mean dangerous."

"He'll run," Jacob said. "He's a coward."

John arrived at the estate and told Sara, Emily, and Eddy the news. This was better news than they had ever expected. They thought that Tom may have the papers, but they never expected he would bring the re-enforcements and warrants. Emily had taken the whole week off and she decided she would go back to work on Friday.

Sara thought she might go into town to do some shopping and check on the progress at the Indian school. She felt like she had gotten out of jail and wanted to spend the day away from the estate. Eddy told Pete and Martin, but cautioned them that they needed to still stay close to the house until Tony was caught. They would be primary witnesses against him and needed to keep a low profile.

The following morning was warm. Sara awoke next to Emily and kissed her gently. Emily stirred and Sara got up to make coffee and join Emily for breakfast. She put on her robe and turned to see Emily had dozed back off.

"If you're going to the clinic, you'd better get up," Sara said.

"I'm up," Emily said half asleep. "I'll be right down."

"I'll meet you downstairs," Sara said as she closed the door. She started down the stairs and smelled the coffee. She found Sally, Eddy, and John already eating. "Everyone's up early this morning."

"We've got too many things to do today, Mother," Eddy said.

"John and I want to ride out and meet the security teams." He took another bite of his eggs. "What are you doing today?"

"I want to go into town," Sara said. "We need supplies, and I want to check on the Indian school."

"I don't think you should go alone," John cautioned. "Eddy, we can wait and see the security teams tomorrow. We should accompany your Mother to town."

"Don't be silly," Sara said.

"It's not silly, Sara," Emily joined in from the doorway. "Please, Eddy, don't let her go alone."

"You're over-ruled, Mother," Eddy said. "I'll be ready whenever you are." He and John cleared out of the kitchen and Emily and Sara enjoyed a quiet breakfast. Annie stumbled in about an hour later. She was dressed and ready for school, but not fully awake. She ate, and picked up her books.

"Are you coming, Auntie?" she asked Emily.

"Let me grab my bag, and we can leave," Emily smiled. She kissed Sara and turned to leave. "Stop by the clinic and see me if you're in town. I'll be at the hospital in the afternoon."

Sara found the papers she wanted to take to the school and she had a list of supplies that Sally had put together. She went to the barn to talk to Pete and Martin. She liked these boys. They were hard workers and had wonderful manners.

"Good morning, Mrs. Monroe," Martin said.

"Please call me Sara," she replied. "You boys will be able to leave this place soon. I'm sorry you haven't been able to even go into town."

"We haven't missed much, Ma am," Pete said. "There's nothing we need and we don't like saloons."

"All the same," Sara said. "I'd like you boys to stay on after this is all over. The decision is yours, but we need you here, and like having you here."

"Thank you, Ma am," Martin said. "We'd like to stay on. We think of this place as home."

Sara nodded to Eddy and he hitched the wagon. She walked back to the house to get her shawl and papers. Sally had added more to the supply list, thinking that Sara wouldn't notice. She smiled and pretended not to notice. She had played this game with Sally for years and never let on.

It was almost 11am when they started down the road into town. They had just passed the falls road. John and Eddy were talking about the upcoming trial. They had wondered if the Marshals had

G.J.Woosley

located Tony, yet. Tony was watching through the trees. He couldn't believe his luck because he had all but given up on being able to catch Sara away from the house. Now right in front of him were three targets for the price of one.

"Not a single one of them is worth the thousand bucks I got paid," he said as he cleaned the site on his rifle. They were about a mile from town when they heard a shot. Sara's head jerked back when another shot rang out and then a quick third shot. John grabbed Sara and jumped from the wagon. He cushioned her fall with his body and then rolled on top of her to protect her. She was bleeding badly from her head, but the bullet had just grazed her. Her shoulder wound did not have an exit, and her ribs were another matter. This shot went clean through.

Eddy had jumped from the wagon on the other side, but not before grabbing his rifle. He crawled under the wagon and looked at his Mother. Her head was bleeding badly and John held a handkerchief on it while Eddy tied his handkerchief around her shoulder and kissed her gently.

"Please don't die, Mother," Eddy pleaded. "Did you see anything?"

"No," John said as he pressed on the handkerchief on Sara's head. "I thought I saw a flash about 100 yards up on the right."

"Don't leave Mother," Eddy said. Before John could stop him, he was gone. The wagon obstructed the view and after a few minutes John heard five more shots ring out. He heard Eddy yell and then all was silent. It seemed like an eternity and John was ready to get up and look for Eddy when he saw him walking back to the wagon. He was covered with blood.

"Are you hurt?" John asked as he cradled Sara's limp body.

"No," Eddy answered. "The blood belongs to the late Tony Pideza. Let's get Mother to the hospital."

They put Sara into the back and John drove the horses into town at a full gallop. Eddy held his Mother close and kept talking to her. She never responded and the wound from her shoulder wouldn't stop bleeding. John went strait to the hospital and they met Kathleen as Eddy carried Sara's bloody body into the treatment room.

"John, Emily is still at the clinic," she said. "Get her now." Two nurses and a medical student appeared and Kathleen turned to close the door. Eddy sat down and put his head in his hands. All he could see was his mother's limp body. He closed his eyes trying to blot the vision out when Emily appeared.

"Where's Sara?" she asked. "Are you hurt?"

286

"Kathleen needs you," Eddy said. "Get in there." She went through the door and Eddy sat back down. He looked at his hands and the blood of Tony Pideza was intermingled with his Mothers. He closed his eyes and relived what had just happened. When Eddy came up behind him Tony heard nothing but he was still firing in the direction of the wagon. Eddy grabbed his rifle and spun Tony around and as his rifle went flying but Tony pulled a knife.

"Looks like I got the squaw, now it's your turn," he said in a guttural voice. He swung the knife at him and Eddy grabbed his arm and heard the bones in his wrist crunch. Tony grimaced in pain. Eddy caught him with a right upper cut that set Tony on his back. Eddy jumped on top of him pinning his arms down with his knees and grabbed his knife.

"You don't have the guts," Tony panted.

"That's where you're wrong," Eddy said as he grabbed Tony's hair, pulled his head back and then slowly and deliberately sliced open his throat. He watched him bleed and didn't get off of his body until he had quit moving and his lifeless eyes stared at the sky. "You'll never hurt any of us again." Eddy tried to wash the memory of his pulsing blood pouring from his throat and his eyes that were fixed on him. He watched as he breathed his last breath and started back for the wagon.

"Eddy?" John said as he sat down next to him. "This is one of the Federal Marshals. He asked me what happened, but needs to talk to you."

Kathleen and Emily were having their own challenges. Sara's shoulder wound was not fatal, but they needed to remove the bullet from the upper part of her humerus just below the shoulder joint. The bone was broken but not shattered. It would heal nicely in time. The Medical student expertly stitched the wound on Sara's forehead. She would have a scar, but not much of one. He carefully cleaned and bandaged her head. The wound in her side went straight through without any damage to major organs. It had hit and shattered two ribs and Kathleen had to deal with some bone fragments and getting the bullet from Sara's shoulder. Emily cleaned and bandaged that. Her arm was placed in a sling to keep it immobile. The nurses removed the rest of Sara's clothing and cleaned all the blood from her. They put a clean gown on her and Kathleen went out to find Eddy.

"Mother's dead," he said.

"No," Kathleen said. "None of the wounds were fatal. Her head wound was minor, but it took me a while to get the bullet out of her shoulder. The one on her side went clean through, although it did break some ribs. She's resting comfortably if you want to see her." Eddy got up to go to his mother.

"What happened, John?" she asked. John told her the story and who was responsible. "Where's Tony now?"

"Dead," John said. "The Marshal went out to retrieve his body."

Eddy sat next to his Mother's bed and held her hand. Emily put her hand on his shoulder. He turned his face to her and cried openly.

"Everything is okay, Eddy," Emily whispered. "She's going to be fine. She'll be asleep for the next few hours. Why don't you go get cleaned up? I'll stay right here until you get back."

"I should have never let her go out," Eddy said.

"You couldn't stop her," Emily said. "You didn't let her go alone. If you had, she would be dead. You saved her life, Eddy." She hugged him close as he stood up. "You saved her life."

Chapter 24

Eddy had gotten some new clothes at Walker's and cleaned all the blood off. He didn't realize it until he took his shirt off that he had a long knife wound on this abdomen. He returned to the hospital and found Kathleen. She looked at the wound and cleaned it thoroughly.

"It could use some stitches," she said. "It's too old now, so we'll have to make do. Are you hurt anywhere else?"

"This was all I found," he said. "Don't tell Mother or Emily about this. They've had enough worry for today."

He was by Sara's bed when she awoke. She didn't know where she was and was taken back to a time when Monroe was still alive. Her vision was blurred and she could have sworn that Eddy was Monroe. Her head was pounding as she lifted her head and her vision finally cleared.

"Mother," Eddy whispered. "You're in the hospital. You were shot, but you're going to be fine."

"Who?" she said weakly and put her head back on the pillow.

"Tony," Eddy answered. "He won't bother anyone anymore." Sara nodded back off to sleep with the help of some Laudanum.

She spent the next 24 hours sleeping. She was awake long enough for Emily and Eddy to get some fluids and soup into her. Emily never left her side, and Eddy was there whenever possible. There was a constant line of people to see her, but she never knew. Emily would give everyone reports on her progress, but that was all. By the second day she was more alert and wanted to get out of bed. Emily was not as successful at keeping her there as Kathleen. Eddy was better than either of them. She was allowed to sit up and put her feet over the edge of the bed, but that was all. After 5 minutes she needed to lie down again. She was as weak as a kitten and admitted that to Eddy. He helped her back down and stroked her hair as she closed her eyes.

"Get some sleep," he whispered. "I'll be back in an hour." Eddy met Emily coming into the room. "She's awfully weak, Auntie. Is that normal?"

"After what she's been through, yes," Emily smiled. "She lost some blood and the trauma to the body takes its toll. She'll be fine, if she let's herself heal."

"Keep her in bed," Eddy said as he looked back at her. "I'll be back in an hour. I need to meet with the Federal Marshals. They're getting ready to move Moe to Seattle. I want to talk with him before he leaves."

"Don't do anything you'll regret," Emily said.

Eddy walked out the door to find Tom waiting for him. They both went to the jail as Moe was being escorted out. He looked at Eddy and then at Tom.

"I'm sorry everything had to end this way," he said to Tom. "I never knew what Tony had planned, Eddy. After the mine incident I wanted to get out, but I was too far in. I never meant for any harm to come to your brother or to your Mother. I'm glad she's all right."

"I'm sorry it came to this too, Moe," Eddy said. "My father always thought very highly of you. What anyone thinks doesn't matter. It's in the hands of the court now." The Marshal took him to the train station and the other stayed behind to talk to Eddy.

"I have to ask you one more time, Eddy," the Marshal started. "Did you kill Tony in self-defense?"

"Jesus," Tom said. "How many times do you need to ask this? Isn't it enough that his mother is in the shape that she's in?"

"Tom," Eddy stopped him from saying anymore. "He fired several rounds, and when I found him and disarmed him, he pulled a knife." He lifted his shirt and showed the Marshal the wound on his abdomen. "I had no other choice. He would have killed me."

"I'm satisfied," the Marshal said. "I'll let you both know when the trial starts, unless Moe pleads guilty. I have a feeling he won't. He won't admit to murders or attempted murders he says he knew nothing about." He shook Eddy's hand, and then Tom's. "Take care of your Mother. I'm glad she's okay."

After 5 days Sara was feeling better. Her arm was very tender because of the broken bone, and her ribs hurt with each movement. Her head had healed nicely and Kathleen carefully removed the stitches from her forehead.

"That really looks good," she said. "You'll barely have a scar. Your arm, on the other hand, is going to sport and real beauty."

"How long will this take to heal?" Sara asked.

"A month to six weeks for bones," Kathleen said. "Emily has some exercises for your elbow so you don't loose mobility during that time. Having your arm in a sling can cause some problems. These exercises are going to hurt, and that's normal. Now that's just the bones. You're going to weak for some time. When this happens you need to rest. You've been through a great deal of stress physically and emotionally. It all takes its toll, Sara. Don't push yourself."

"How's Eddy's wound?" Sara asked.

"You're not supposed to know anything about that," she said. "He didn't want to worry you."

"I know," Sara said. "I'm grateful to him for that." She paused for a moment and looked at Kathleen. "I don't think I've ever told you how grateful I am to you. You've saved Emily many years ago you saved me when Annie was born, and now here we are again. I'm so grateful to you and Tom for so many things. I respect you, and trust you more than I can express. I'm proud to call you a friend."

"Thank you, Sara," Kathleen said as she blushed. "Of all the people in the world whose respect I desired was yours. I'm also proud to call you a friend and I will always be that." She sat down on the bed and held her hand. They continued to talk for the next hour. Emily came into the room and smiled at the sight.

"Have you told her when she can go home?" Emily asked.

"We haven't gotten to that yet," Kathleen replied. "How does tomorrow sound, Sara?"

"Good," Sara responded.

"You'll need to take things easy for the next month," she cautioned. "That arm will take a while to heal. The ribs are going to take just as long and probably longer. I'll come out to see you next week, if that's all right?"

"Make sure you bring Ben and Tom and stay for dinner," Sara said.

***

"Wow," Beth remarked. "Sara was lucky that day."

"She was," Zack replied. "Tony had a history of drinking heavily, and was probably drunk, so his shooting was off."

"What ever happened to Moe Hawkins?" Beth asked.

"You're getting ahead of me," Zack said. He was reminded of when he had first heard this story from Eddy. He asked the same questions and would give Beth the same answers. Zack had learned so much from Eddy in the time that he lived with them. From the time he came back Russell thought the world of his Uncle. Eddy spent time telling him stories and reading all the books to him that he had read to Anne when she was young.

In some ways, he was jealous of Eddy's relationship with his son. Russell was never told that Zack was his father, per Anne's wishes. Eddy thought this was wrong, but Anne was insistent. Russell did enjoy Zack, who he called Daddy and they would do many things together. Eddy spent a great deal of time in the stable and was happy to see that Peter was still there. They were about the same age and they were glad to see one another but their time had been limited by John's illness and then death. It had been years since he had groomed horses and was glad to get back to something he loved to do.

"What ever happened to your brother, Martin?" Eddy asked as he worked on the tangles in one of the gelding's mane.

"He got married shortly after you left," Peter said. "He continued to work here, and with Samuel. He had a bunch of kids and died a couple of years ago. I don't see much of his kids. They all moved away from this area."

"I'm sorry to hear that," Eddy smiled. "What about you? Did you ever marry?" Eddy already knew the answer to this question. He knew the answer when he met him more than thirty years ago.

"No," he said. "I'd prefer the company of horses to people. I surely do miss your Mother, though. She was one of the few people on this earth I respected. I always respected you too, Eddy. You were very good to us after Will died, and you had a right to hate us."

"I had no right to hate you, although I wanted to," Eddy smiled. "You didn't do anything wrong. You just took the wrong job at the wrong time. But, thank God, you did, or we never would have stopped that operation."

"I'd like to take a ride this afternoon," Eddy said knowing full well that Peter would understand what he was asking. "Do you want to join me?"

"Yes, I would," Peter smiled. "I'd like that a lot."

Anne was standing at the window and smiling. Zack joined her and wondered what was holding her interest.

"Look," she whispered. "Peter and Eddy found each other."

"What are you talking about?" he whispered back, "and why are we whispering?"

"Peter never married," she replied. "We used to have long conversations when Mother and Emily were alive and I was seeing Amanda. He would confide in us about his feelings, because he could trust us. He was always envious of Eddy and his finding someone. He was envious of his courage to live his life, although somewhat deceptively, as his heart desired. I think they'll be good for each other."

Pete and Eddy were good for each other. They spent time with the horses and Eddy fixed up the cabin and moved in there. It was well built in the 1860's and would stand for years to come. Anne had never seen Peter happier. Russell was now 10 and school was a bore to him. He was still crazy about his Uncle and seemed to understand about his relationship with Peter.

Russell and his Mother didn't always communicate on the same levels. He had started asking questions about his parentage. Anne would never tell him who his father was. Her response to him was always that it wasn't important. Russell and Zack would occasionally have disagreements about the way that he talked to his mother. Zack felt that Anne deserved the utmost respect and would accept nothing else.

The local hospital had closed down a few years ago. There was a great deal of fallout after the depression. There were larger, more modern facilities not too far away. Ben had kept the clinic open. Kathleen Eichorn had lost her husband 6 years earlier. She seemed to remain strong and healthy despite her age. She still lived in the house that she had shared with Tom for all those years. Anne had gotten word from Ben that Kathleen's health was failing fast. She and Eddy made it a point of going down to see her.

"Ben called you, didn't he?" Kathleen teased. "He thinks I'm dying, which I am of course." Anne and Eddy sat down beside her. "I've lived too long anyway." Anne looked at her and there were tears in her eyes. "Now don't start. This is a reason to celebrate. I'm escaping this world to go and join your Mother and Father, Emily, Tom, Mary, Samuel, Charlie, Will, and my husband. It will be like old home week or a 4th of July party. We will all be watching over you from the spirit world."

"I can't tell you what you've meant to us, Kathleen," Eddy said. "You've been part of our family for as long as I can remember."

"More than 60 years, Eddy," she smiled. "God I'm old!" Everyone laughed. "I wonder if I'll ever make it into the local history books. I guess it really doesn't matter. I know what we did here."

"I can't bear the thought of this place without you," Anne said.

"Death is a natural order," Kathleen said as she held Anne's hand. "You'll understand this one day. I'm not afraid of dying. I've done everything I wanted to do. I've loved and was loved. My career was rewarding and you gave me the gift of bringing your son into the world." She looked at Eddy who was also in tears. "I've loved you both as much as I loved my own child. You two need to take care of each other. Take care of Zack. He's a good man. Russell is the future for the Monroe family. Teach him all he needs to know. And Annie, tell him who his father is. Don't let him go through life wondering."

Anne gathered Kathleen's small body in her arms and held her close. She didn't want to let her go. She somehow thought that if she didn't let her go, she couldn't die.

"I love you, Kathleen," Anne said. She let her go, kissed her on her forehead, and left the room. Eddy gathered her into his arms and held her close.

"Thank you for everything," Eddy whispered. He released her and gently kissed her cheek.

"It's been a hell of a ride, hasn't it?" she smiled as a tear ran down her face.

"Yes, Ma am," Eddy said as he wiped it away. "A glorious ride."

Kathleen Eichorn died that very afternoon. Ben had arrived shortly before Anne and Eddy left the house. She simply went to sleep and didn't wake up. Zack, Anne, Eddy, Russell, and Peter attended the funeral service. Eddy looked around this corner of the cemetery and realized that he knew more people here, than among the living.

It was quiet and private ceremony and she was laid to rest next to her husband, and a few feet from Emily. They had worked side by side for many years. They built a hospital and clinic together, and delivered every baby in town for 40 years. It seemed appropriate that they be side by side in death.

***

"Zack, what about Moe Hawkins?" Beth asked.

"Let's see," he stalled in a teasing way. "Where were we? Oh, yes, Sara was just getting out of the hospital."

Eddy brought the wagon into town with blankets to cushion Sara during her trip home. John suggested she sit up on the seat with Eddy because of the spring in the seat. It was easier on her and Eddy took it slow to minimize the bumps. By the time they got to the house she was leaning heavily on Eddy. She was grateful when the wagon stopped.

"John, take care of the horses," Eddy said as he sat his mother upright and got down from the wagon. "I'll take Mother inside." He picked her up and carried her inside. "Upstairs or downstairs, Mother?"

"Upstairs," she said softly. "I want to sleep for a while." He took her to her room and put her on the bed. She let out a small moan as he put her down. He covered her and kissed her on the forehead.

"I'll check on you in a little while," Eddy said. "I'll bring you some food later. You've got to eat."

The week passed and Sara got stronger but she hadn't bounced back as quickly as she had hoped she would. She and Emily would go for walks in the late afternoon. They would try to go a little farther everyday, but Sara tired easily and they hadn't been able to get very far away from the house. The coming of summer was an unspoken agreement of renewal. Sara would drink in the sunshine and warmth as they walked and each night Emily would do exercises to keep Sara's elbow from getting stiff. Kathleen, Tom, and Ben arrived as Kathleen had promised and she wasn't pleased with her progress but did confess to Emily that it was slower than she had expected.

"She's not a kid anymore," Kathleen said. "We shouldn't expect her to bounce back as quickly as she did after Annie was born."

At dinner Sara talked about starting to plan the 4th of July party. This was an annual event that always happened, even after Monroe died. Ivan and Helga had made it a point to stay close to home over the last few months because of the illegal mining situation. He was always home during the 4th. He had never missed a party and this year would be no different. Emily wanted to take on most of the responsibility for the planning.

"The trial is supposed to start on the 16th of June," Tom said. "Martin, Peter, Sara, and Eddy will have to be there to testify along with many others so the Federal Prosecutor would let him know when. They said you people would be first."

"I don't cherish the thought of traveling in two weeks," Sara said. "I'm still not feeling completely well."

"We can't put this off," Tom said.

"What if I went with you?" Kathleen said. "I could use the break. Emily could plan the party, and I could make sure that someone looks after you while you're in Seattle. Besides, I haven't been there in years and I'd like to see what their doing at the big hospitals."

"That is a good idea," Emily said. "You deserve a chance to get away. How long would you be gone?"

"No more than a week," Tom said, "but what about Ben?"

"He can stay here with us," Emily said. "It will be fun."

Two weeks later Emily saw the group off at the train station. For all the years that Sara had lived in this area, she had never been to Seattle. She was surprised at the number of people, buildings, and the dirt. They stayed at a large hotel downtown. It was a short walk to the courthouse. The Prosecutor met with everyone individually. He then called them all together and told them where they were with the case.

"I'm sorry about your son Mrs. Monroe," he said. "I knew your husband very well. I was still in law school when I first met him. My father's firm handled all of his land purchases. I couldn't believe that one man could own so much property and want to own it to save it from progress."

"Thank you," Sara responded. "He was a wonderful husband and father."

"I asked for this case, because I did know him," the Prosecutor replied. "We have these guys buried. All I ask is that you answer the questions honestly and directly. Don't try to hide or mislead the lawyers or the jury. Remember, you're the injured family. Your son and brother died on these people's order. Your land was raped and you were robbed of a great deal of money."

"Will they attack us personally?" Tom asked.

"Probably," he answered. "I'll try to stop that before it starts. Trust me on this."

"What about the judge?" Tom asked. "What do you know about him?"

"Is he on someone's payroll?" the Prosecutor responded. "No, he's a good and honest man. It will be fine. I'll meet you at 8am tomorrow at the courthouse."

The trial had been going on for two days when the time came for Martin and Peter to testify about the man that paid them the money for the raid that William died in. They admitted that they had only dealt with Tony. They then called for Sara to testify and Moe's lawyer went on the attack. The Prosecutor held him in check and the judge cautioned him on more than one occasion. By the time he had finished with Sara, she felt demeaned, insulted, and exhausted. He had questioned her for 2 hours. This man had attacked her ethnic background and the validity of her marriage. He also attacked her business dealings, and the fact that she owned property that should be returned to the Government. Sara remained calm during this whole process, and this was what sapped all the strength she had.

"Don't show your anger, Eddy," the Prosecutor whispered. "That's what this lawyer wants. He wants you to lose your temper. Don't let that happen." Eddy nodded and heard his named called. He stood took a deep breath and walked toward the witness stand. The clerk swore him in and he looked at his mother. She was pale and looked tired. Kathleen sat next to her and had her arm around her shoulder.

The lawyer seemed pleasant at first. He asked Eddy the

circumstances surrounding the discovery of the mine. He then asked about the day his mother was shot and the death of Tony Pideza. Eddy handled himself very well. The lawyer said he had finished with Eddy and was ready to let him leave the stand.

"Just one more question, Mr. Monroe," the lawyer said. "Did you kill Tony Pideza in self-defense or did you kill him because he was going to expose you as a homosexual?"

"Your honor, I object!" the Prosecutor said.

"Over-ruled," the Judge said. "Answer the question Mr. Monroe."

"I killed Mr. Pideza because he had shot my Mother three times. I disarmed him and then he pulled a knife and tried to kill me," Eddy said.

"Are you a homosexual, Mr. Monroe?" he asked.

"I object, your Honor," the Prosecutor said.

"Sustained," the Judge answered. "Move on to another line of questioning."

"I have nothing more for this witness," he smiled. Eddy got up from the chair and saw his Mother had her head on Kathleen's shoulder and her eyes were closed. As he walked back to his seat the Judge announced that they would recess for the day. Everyone stood as the Judge left the courtroom. Sara stood slowly with Kathleen's help. As he closed the door to his chambers, Sara sat back down.

"We need to get Sara back to the hotel," Kathleen told Tom and Eddy. They both put an arm around her and started out of the courtroom.

"I'm sorry about that, Eddy," the Prosecutor said. "I didn't expect that any of this would become an issue."

"I have to get Mother back to the hotel," he said.

"I'll get a cab for you," he said. "Wait here." He left for a moment and came back inside. "It's waiting outside. Tom, you're the only one that has to testify tomorrow. The rest of you need to stay away from the courthouse. Let me know if you need anything for Mrs. Monroe. I have some good connections in the medical field."

They got Sara loaded into the cab and to the hotel 3 blocks down the street. The sun glistened off the water of Puget Sound. Sara could smell the salt air. She had never seen so much water and it was refreshing. The cab pulled up in front of the hotel and Eddy paid the driver.

"I'll get Mother," he said.

"It's all right, son," she responded. "I can walk." She got out of the cab and Eddy caught her before she hit the ground. Kathleen escorted them to her suite and got her into bed. She was tired, and in pain, but she was also hungry.

"How about having dinner right here tonight?" Kathleen said. "We'll order room service. The men can go out if they like. We can eat out on the balcony and watch the sun set on the water."

"That sounds wonderful, Kathleen," Sara smiled. "Will you stay with me a while?"

"I'll be right here," she said as she sat down on the bed. "You need to take a nap."

After Sara nodded off, Kathleen found Eddy and Tom and told them to take Martin and Peter downstairs for dinner. She said she would stay with Sara and have dinner in the room.

"Is she all right?" Eddy asked.

"She's just weak," Kathleen said. "Her injuries are painful and this whole ordeal has taken its toll on her. She just needs to be home and for all of this to be over. You go ahead and eat. I've ordered something for us already."

"Okay," Tom said. "Can I bring you anything?"

"It's been years since I've had a good bottle of wine," Kathleen smiled. "See if you can find one." He smiled at her and nodded his head. Kathleen was serious about the wine. She used to relax many years ago with a glass of wine, although it wasn't highly accepted. She and Tom grew up around San Francisco and there were small wineries everywhere. She had always been partial to white wines, but Tom liked them dark red and heavy. Kathleen stared out the window at the water. She missed seeing the ocean, although the Sound really wasn't the coast, it was still salt water. She could look down the waterfront and see the ships at the piers. She found this interesting but would trade her life in Snoqualmie for any of this.

There was a quiet knock at the door and Kathleen realized that it was dinner. The hour had passed quickly. The waiter rolled the cart in and Kathleen tipped him well. She set the meal out on the small table and lit the candle provided with their dinners. She gently woke Sara.

"Dinner is here, honey," she said. "Let's get you up so you can eat." Sara sat up slowly and saw the food covering the table on the balcony and the lit candle. "I thought we could have some ambiance while we ate. There's not a hint of a breeze outside."

Sara sat down and looked at the food and across at Kathleen. They began to eat. Sara was hungry for the first time in weeks. Her ribs and arm were throbbing, but the smell of the food distracted her from the discomfort.

"This is very good," she said. "This reminds me of dinners that Emily and I used to have when Monroe would travel. We would fix wonderful meals from nothing and light candles for the table. The boys would be down for the night by the time we started eating. We don't do that anymore."

"Why?" Kathleen asked. "You shouldn't let the romance go out of your romance."

"You're right," Sara said. "Does Tom still romance you?"

"Yes he does," Kathleen said. "He will bring me gifts for no apparent reason. I'm always surprised, and he knows just what to get me. It's wonderful to share your life with someone who knows you that well, isn't it?"

"It is," Sara smiled. "I've been lucky enough to find two people like that."

"Sara," Kathleen said quietly. "Do you miss Monroe?" She heard herself say the question. "What I mean is... I don't know what I mean."

"Yes, Kathleen," Sara said. "I miss him very much. I did love him. What I have with Emily is perfect, but what I had with Monroe was perfect also. I don't expect people to understand this. They don't understand that you can love more than one person at the same time, with the same amount of intensity, in different ways. They really don't understand when those two people are the same sex."

"I didn't think I could understand it either," Kathleen admitted. "But I do. I saw you and Monroe, and I see you and Emily, and how right both relationships are. You're a lucky person, Sara."

By the time dinner was finished, the candle was burned down. Kathleen loaded the plates back on the cart and wheeled it out into the hall. Sara remarked that she could get used to room service very quickly. There was no cooking and no dishes. Kathleen joined her on the balcony as the sun was setting. It had to be 9pm and the tiny sparkles on the water were magnificent.

There was a tap on the door and Kathleen got up to answer it. It was Tom and the rest of the gang. Kathleen asked everyone to join them on the balcony. Eddy kissed his mother and was glad she looked better.

"I found a bottle of wine," Tom said.

"Let's all have a glass," Kathleen said. "It wouldn't hurt any of us, including you Sara."

Tom poured everyone a glass and Kathleen told them to not drink it quickly, but sip it. Before everyone took a drink Tom proposed a toast. He held his glass high and looked around the room.

"Here's to good friends," he said. Everyone took a drink and Sara smiled.

"It makes you warm," she said. "It's wonderful."

"It can also become and addictive habit," Kathleen said, "so everything in moderation."

They spent the rest of the evening talking about the past, the future, and hopes for their lives. Eddy was quiet during this time. Tom had noticed it, but no one more than Sara. She knew he had something eating at him and now was not the time to discuss it. Kathleen and Sara wanted to walk around the waterfront tomorrow morning. Kathleen had arranged to visit the local hospital with the Prosecutor's help and connections.

Eddy, Martin, and Peter were going to find the library. He also wanted to find a gift for John, Emily and Annie. He wished John could have come with him on this trip. The Prosecutor said that there was nothing he could add. He was glad that he was there to keep an eye on the estate, but he missed him. Tom left for the courthouse the following day and said he should be finished with all of his testimony that morning. He kissed Kathleen before he left. She and Sara were not too far behind him as they left the hotel. They found so many things in the shops that were strange and unusual. Sara asked many questions as to the origins and the countries they came from.

Kathleen found herself giving history and geography lessons all morning. Sara discovered that these were areas she knew nothing about. She had the desire to find out about them. While Sara was busy looking at some fine crystal figures, Kathleen found the perfect gift for her. It was a large globe that she had paid for and arranged to get shipped to Snoqualmie. She would give it to her on the 4th. She could then get a picture of what the world looked like.

By 11am Sara was getting hungry. They found a little restaurant with fresh seafood. Sara had never tried any of these items and didn't know what to make of the clams.

"They will steam them until they open," Kathleen said. "Fresh clams are great. We'll get a variety of things, and you can try it all." About that time Eddy, Martin, Peter, and Tom appeared. Their timing was perfect.

"I haven't had clams since we left San Francisco," Tom said almost drooling. "You boys are in for a treat."

They had mussels, scallops, shrimp, crab's legs, steamed with potatoes and corn on the cob. There was a seasoning salt that enhanced the taste. Small bowls of melted butter for dipping accompanied their feast. Martin, Peter, Eddy, and Sara had no idea what to eat and were leery at first. They watched Kathleen and Tom and tried each thing. It only took a few minutes for them to realize that this was good stuff.

Peter and Eddy loved the scallops and shrimp. Martin was partial to the mussels and crab legs. Sara found the clams to be her favorite. Eddy kept adding his clams to his mother's plate when she wasn't looking. She finally caught him and smiled.

"I thought those weren't disappearing very fast," she laughed. "Don't you like them?"

"Yes, I do," he smiled. "But you love them. I'm enjoying watching you."

"I can't believe I ate that much," Kathleen said as she wiped the butter from her hands. "There's nothing better than fresh sea food."

"How do you know it's fresh?" Sara asked.

"First," Kathleen said. "The taste is excellent. Second, if you look over there you can see them unloading it from the boat." Kathleen looked at Sara and smiled.

"The only thing you have to do is to look for the boat unloading it," Tom teased. "That's usually the best indication of something being fresh."

They finished their feast and left the restaurant. Sara was ready to go back to the hotel and Kathleen met her escort to the local hospital in the hotel lobby. They would spend one more night here and catch the train back to Snoqualmie in the morning. They all met that evening when Tom received a note from the Prosecutor. Tom read the note and looked at Kathleen and Sara. He shook his head.

"Moe Hawkins killed himself," he said as he crumpled up the note. There was nothing more to be said. Kathleen and Sara just shook their heads. "He was in so deep and couldn't do the time. I'm sure the thought of spending the rest of his life in a Federal Penitentiary was more than he could handle."

"He was a good man, once," Sara said. "Monroe thought so, and so do I. The Congressman doesn't have the guts to kill himself. I'd like to see him hang."

"The verdict is for him to spend the rest of his life in Federal Prison," Tom said. "That's worse than death." Tom looked at Kathleen and Sara. There seemed to be justice for everyone. Moe and Tony paid the price with their lives and Congressman Banks was sent to the Federal Penitentiary.

It was good to be home. John and Annie met the train. They had so much to tell everyone about the plans they had made for the party on the 4th. Emily was coming from the clinic and would ride home with them. The train trip had tired Sara out. She was ready to go home.

"Thanks for everything," Sara said to Kathleen and then hugged her close.

"Take it easy, Sara," she replied. "I'll see you next week at the clinic." She looked at Emily and motioned to her. She took a few steps away from the group. Emily came close. "Sara has had a rough few days. She's still very weak and tires easily. Testifying was hard on her emotionally, on Eddy, too. Take care of them Em."

"I'm glad you were there for her," Emily said. She turned and helped Sara in the buggy and headed to the house. John and Eddy had talked Martin and Peter into stopping at Walker's to get some new clothes. They had been working for the last several weeks with no opportunity to spend any of their wages.

"I could use and upgrade," Peter said as he looked at his shirt.

"Live a little," John said. "You boys deserve it."

Suzy found several shirts and pants for each of them. She was having a ball dressing these boys up. John just looked at Eddy and laughed. Eddy was preoccupied and John saw it. He seemed happy to be home. Maybe, he would talk to him later, when they were alone. He was sure the trial had taken its toll on everyone. Sara looked worse than when she left and maybe that was what was on Eddy's mind.

An hour later they started for the house. Eddy looked at the trees and thought about how much he loved this place. He thought about growing up and all the things that had happened in his life. He a difficult conversation he needed to have with John tonight. He had already made plans and was going to follow through with them. He hoped John would be with him on this, but he also knew that John had his own plans.

They got back to the estate and Peter said he would take care of the horses. Eddy was glad to hear that because he wanted to check on his Mother. He went into the house and found Emily in the kitchen pouring a cup of coffee.

"Is Mother in bed?" he asked.

"Yes," Emily said. "She was exhausted. She didn't talk much about the trial. Tell me how everything went."

Eddy sighed and told Emily the details of the trial. He talked about the lawyer belittling his Mother and insulting her intelligence, questioning the validity of her marriage, and questioned her right to even own property in front of the entire courtroom. By the time he had finished with her, she was ready to collapse but remained dignified.

"Mother was amazing and when he got to me, he wasn't any kinder," Eddy said. He stopped there and Emily knew there was much more to tell.

"Tell me what's eating at you," Emily said as she placed her hand on his arm.

"He asked if I killed Tony because he was going to expose my 'sexual preferences' for lovers," he said quietly.

"You killed him because he was trying to kill you," Emily said.

"I killed him, but I didn't have to, Emily," he whispered. "I could have taken the knife, tied him up, and brought him in to stand trial. I didn't do that." He looked at her and she could see the pain in his eyes. "I didn't do that because I was afraid that this very thing would be brought out at a trial locally. Everyone in town would know, and it's none of their business." He paused and played with Emily's coffee cup. "I didn't have to kill him. I felt it was my duty for William, and for Mother. I cut his throat and watched the life pour out of him."

"Eddy," Emily said as she stood and hugged him. "You are not a cold-blooded killer. You have more patience and restraint than anyone I've ever met. You did what you had to do and you did the right thing."

"Did I?" he whispered. "I'm not so sure."

"Ask John," she said. "He'll tell you the same thing."

Chapter 25

The 4th of July party was a hit. Emily and John had done a wonderful job of planning and decorating the grounds. This was the first for Martin and Peter. They met many people from the community and they were treated well by everyone. Tom and Kathleen brought out the large globe and gave it to Sara. Her hands ran over the countries and she was fascinated by the names of places she couldn't begin to pronounce. Eddy had been distant from the time of the trial and Sara knew something was weighing heavily on his mind, but didn't press him.

After the fireworks were done, and the whole gang was on the porch, Eddy decided to make his announcement. He stood and looked around at all of the people he dearly loved. Tom, Kathleen, and Ben sat near Emily and his Mother. Annie and Amanda were playing on the floor by Jack and Maggie Regan. Ivan, Helga, Jacob, and Suzy sat on the steps and looked up at him. Mary, Samuel, Victoria, and Caleb had just joined them, for Eddy had grown up with all of these people, and the words he had to say stuck in his throat.

"Friends, and family," he began. "I have talked with John, and we have made plans to travel to Alaska to help them set up schools for the Indian children. John has made arrangements to work with a village just outside of Nome." No one said a word, but they just looked at one another. "We have booked passage out of Seattle on the 10th of July, to take advantage of the warm weather." Everyone looked dumbfounded and the silence was deafening.

"Well, Eddy," Tom said finally breaking the silence, "how exciting! I heard that Alaska is an amazing place and I, for one, am envious."

Everyone finally started talking about this to Eddy accept, the person he most wanted to hear from. Sara stayed quietly in the background while Kathleen watched her out of the corner of her eye and could see a tear glistening. John was busy talking Emily's ear off about their new adventure. Sara slowly made her way into the foyer without anyone noticing her, but Kathleen followed her in without attracting attention. She found her heading into the library. As Kathleen walked through the doorway she saw Sara staring into the fireplace. It was too warm to have a fire going, but she stood there as if some magical answer would jump out at her.

"Sara?" she asked quietly. She turned and Kathleen saw the tears in her eyes.

"I should have known this was coming," she said. "He's had things on his mind since I was shot. I should have made him talk to me."

"He's a man with his whole future ahead of him," Kathleen said as she put her arm around Sara's shoulder. "He has to find his own way in the world. You've raised him to think for himself, and his father taught him to plan ahead. He loves you more than life itself. He feels he needs to do this. Show him that you support him. That's what he needs most from you. Now come out and rejoin the party. I won't let you stay in here and stew about something you can't change." Sara wiped the tears from her eyes and followed Kathleen back out onto the porch. Everyone was still chatting away and hadn't noticed their absence.

Eddy found his mother as she was talking with Helga. As he stood there, Helga finished her conversation and said it was time that she and Ivan head home. Eddy stood next to his Mother and felt his heart pounding in his chest. He put his arm around her shoulder and she reached up and held his hand. With that single gesture there was an unspoken assurance that she accepted his decision. The guests were leaving and Kathleen caught Sara's eye. She smiled and winked.

Eddy stayed by his Mother's side until all the guests had left. Emily went into the house and at long last only he and Sara were left on the porch of the suddenly quiet house.

"I wanted to tell you so many times what I was planning," Eddy said as he escorted his mother to the large porch swing. "I just didn't know how and I didn't want to say anything until we had a plan in place."

"You're like your father in that respect," Sara smiled. "He never made a move without thinking out everything detail. It served him well, and he was successful. It will serve you well in your life."

"Mother," he said quietly. "I love this place. I couldn't have asked for a better place to grow up, or spend the rest of my life. So much has happened in the last few months. Will's death, your injuries, the trial have all piled up on me. I need a change of scenery."

"You need to go somewhere where no one knows you," Sara said. "You want to start over, thinking that the feelings you have can be washed away by different scenery. Life doesn't work that way, honey. No matter where you go, you still have the same face that stares back at you from the mirror. Whatever you're trying to run away from will follow you. It's inside you."

"I don't think I'm running away," he responded and paused. "Maybe, I am. Mother, I have to talk to you about something." She sat quietly and listened to him tell about what really happened just before he killed Tony Pideza. "I should have let him live, and let the courts decide his guilt or innocence. It wasn't my place to be judge and jury."

"Maybe you're right," Sara said. "Only you can decide what was really in your heart. You always had a strict sense of right and wrong. You always believed in justice, too. This man had your brother killed, and then tried to kill me. My personal feeling is that you were justified in anything you did, but, that's only my personal feeling. It's never good to take another human life, yet, if given the chance, I would have killed him myself."

"That's my problem," he answered. "I haven't decided if I was justified to take his life. Everyone else seems to know that I was justified, but I don't feel it. I don't feel it in here." He pointed to his heart. He looked out over the estate. Martin and Peter were taking down tables. The torches were still lit and it made a warm glow around the house. "It hurts to leave you, Mother. I hate to think of no one around to take care of you. I don't know how I can get Annie to understand."

"Annie will understand someday," Sara said. "She needs to grow older first. Contrary to what you may think, I can take care of myself." She looked at him and smiled. "I remember when I left my mother. She was ill and I knew I could never see her again. She said something to me that always gave me comfort when I thought of her. I think you should hear those same words from me."

"What did she say?" Eddy asked.

"As your father and I prepared to leave the village she took me into her lodge," Sara said with a quiver in her voice. Eddy put his arm around her shoulder. "We sat together in her lodge. It seems like a lifetime ago, now. In the glow of the fire she said the words that I'm about to say to you." She paused and held his hand. "I understand why you must leave. I loved you the minute you were born and every minute after. It's your turn to not cry for me, but to live for me. Don't look backward, but look ahead. If my eyes never see you again, I'll be with you. Your father and I will be watching over you."

Eddy sobbed quietly and took his Mother into his arms. They were so much like his father's arms and they were comforting. Emily watched them from the doorway and quietly went back into the house. Her heart was heavy with the thought of Eddy leaving. She had always had a special place in her heart for him. He was the first life that she delivered in Snoqualmie. He had a gentleness she saw only in his father. This gentleness was so rare. She was concerned about his safety in the wilderness that he and John were traveling to.

She had made John promise her that he could keep him safe. John vowed to her, as he kissed her cheek, that he would. He said they had a 5-year plan and wanted to come back to the estate to live out the rest of their lives.

"This is a special place, and Eddy's home," he assured. "He can't leave his family for very long. He gets his strength from this place."

"What about you?" Emily asked. "Do you consider us your family?"

"This is the closest thing to a family that I've ever had," he admitted. "My father was a drunk and my mother and brother died when I was very young. I've never known the meaning of the word until I met Edmundson and Sara. Now I'll never hear the word family and not think of them, and of you. You're like the sister I never had, Emily, and I will miss you."

"Promise me, one more time, that you'll take care of him," she said with tears. "And if he ever wishes it, you'll bring him back."

"I promise," he whispered.

The next six days passed far too quickly. Eddy had made the rounds in town and said his goodbyes. He found it very hard to say that to Tom and Kathleen. Tom was like a father to him and it felt like he was losing his father all over again. Kathleen was crying openly and didn't care if anyone knew.

Ivan and Helga were in Walker's when Eddy stopped in. They all wished him good luck and asked him to write if he needed anything. They would find a way to get it to him. Ivan even suggested that he would deliver it. He was dying to see that country, but his health wouldn't permit such a trip anymore. As he and Eddy rode out of town they saw Jack and Maggie coming in.

"Eddy," Jack smiled and waved. "I hoped that we would see you before you left."

"I thought I would see people today," he smiled. "This way there won't be a mob at the train station tomorrow."

"You and John will truly be missed," he said. "There won't be any Monroe men around here, and that's a shame."

"Speaking or that, Jack," he said. "Watch over Mother and

Emily. They're proud women, and a little stubborn. Would you do that for me?"

"I'd be honored, sir," he said in his southern drawl. "You have a long hard trip ahead of you. Stay safe, and best of luck to both of you." He shook their hands and rode into town. John and Eddy gave their horses a kick and headed for the estate. They turned onto the falls road and sat there for an hour. They drank in the sound, the beauty, and as Eddy had hoped, his large hairy friends came to say goodbye.

"I've never seen more than one at a time," he said quietly. "It's like they know I needed to see them."

"They do know," John answered. "Somehow they do know." Eddy watched them and they didn't look away. Something inside of him made him raise his hand as if to wave. They responded in kind. "Look at that, Eddy! They copied your gesture. You truly do have a bond with them."

"When I was little," he admitted. "I used to come here hoping to see them. There was one, a small one, maybe young, I don't know that would wave back to me. This must be the same one grown up. Think of it John, we grew up together in this magical place; two different species with kindred spirits." Just then they turned and disappeared into the trees. Eddy knew he might never see his friend again. He could bare the pain no longer and got up and walked back to his horse.

They ate a wonderful meal that evening and were accompanied by Samuel, Mary, and their children. The dinner conversation was light and everyone talked about everything except the departure of Eddy and John tomorrow. Before leaving the house, Samuel and Mary said their tearful farewells.

"My heart was saddened after Will's death," she said as she hugged him. "Now I fear it will never be the same again. I think of you as my own son. I love you as a son. Always remember where you came from. Remember us and remember the blood of the Nez Perce chiefs runs through your veins." She kissed him gently on the cheek and turned toward the doorway. Even Samuel had tears and gave Eddy a quick hug.

After the house was quiet he joined his mother and Emily in the library. There was a fire in the fireplace to remove the night's chill. He sat on the floor next to his mother's knees and stared into the flames.

"I would prefer that you not go to the station with me tomorrow," he said quietly. He looked at Emily, "neither of you. We'll say our goodbye here in the morning."

"I'm happy to abide by your wishes, my son," Sara said. "I don't think I could bear to see the train pull away knowing that you're on it."

No more was said about this. They spent the rest of the evening talking about times gone by. They talked about Will, Monroe, the start of the business, and the happiness they shared in this room. Eddy wanted to drink in as much as he could. He had no idea when he would return. His plan was for 5 years. It seemed an eternity right now. Annie would be 14 years old by then. The more he thought about this, the more he was talking himself out of going.

He looked at John. He was so excited about this opportunity. He was looking forward to the boat ride up the coast. He heard it was beautiful and wanted to see another wild and unsettled place before he took up the rocking chair. If Eddy backed out now, John would be disappointed. He didn't want to do that to him because he loved him too much. It was starting to get late and Sara said she was ready for bed. She kissed Eddy and hugged John and went to bed. Morning would come too soon as it was.

They agreed to meet for breakfast and it was a quiet meal. Sally had fixed something wonderful but no one seemed to be eating. Annie came down and crawled up on Eddy's lap as she did every morning, when he was at the house. She ate most of his food. He heard the clock chime 8 times and knew they should leave in the next 15 minutes.

"I have something for you," Sara said. She left the kitchen and returned a few minutes later. "I don't know how much cash you have for your journey. This is money that your father left to you, Will, and Annie. William won't need his, so I divided it up between you and Annie." She handed him the fat envelop. "This is, by no means, all of it, but it can get you going."

"Mother," he said. "I can't take it. John and I are okay as far as finances."

"I know you are," she said. "Keep this as an emergency fund. Put it in your shoe, or hide it under a rock once you get to Alaska, but take it please. I would feel better knowing that you have the means to buy what you need."

"Alright, Mother," he said. "I'll split it up with John, so it's safer. That way I can't lose the whole thing." He smiled at her and they walked out on the porch. Peter would accompany them to town and bring back the horses. John hugged Emily and kissed her. He went to Sara and held her gently.

"Me, too," Annie demanded. John picked her up and hugged her tight.

"I'll miss you both," he said. "As soon as we get settled, I'll write."

Eddy held Emily and kissed her. He picked up Annie and whispered something in her ear. She giggled and squirmed to get down. He watched as she went back into the house. He looked at his Mother and gathered her in his arms. He held her for as long as he could.

"I love you, Mother," he said as his voice quivered. He could say no more.

"Stay safe, my son," she replied. "I've loved you, always." They mounted their horses and rode toward Snoqualmie. There was so much that Sara wanted to say. She wanted to beg him to stay, but that would have been wrong. He had to choose his own way. She looked at Emily and she was sobbing. She took her arm and walked her back into the house.

***

Beth was crying as Zack told the story. She excused herself and went into the bathroom. Zack put on water for tea and when Beth came from the bathroom she had composed herself a bit.

"He never saw his mother again," she said. "Did he?"

"No," Zack said quietly. "His 5-year plan turned into 10 years, and then 30 years. He did send letters on a monthly basis, and never missed a month. The money that Sara had given him came in handy. They didn't realize how expensive it was to live there, especially after the big gold strike of 1900. People went to Alaska by the boatfuls, all hoping to strike it rich as soon as they got there. Many were disappointed and died broke."

"I don't understand how you can love someone, as Eddy loved his mother, and leave her," Beth said. "And how could she let him go so easily? I guess I don't understand that kind of love, or maybe I haven't experienced it, yet."

"You will, child," Zack said. "You'll understand if you have children of your own."

"I'm going out for a smoke," she said the Zack. She wasn't ready to tell him that she never planned to have children. That wasn't possible for Lesbians without some serious help from the medical community. Even if she wanted to have children, she wanted to raise them with someone she loved.

Zack watched Beth go out the door and thought about his son. As he aged, he and his Mother grew farther apart. He was very close to his uncle. He spent many nights in the cabin that he and Peter shared. Since John's death, Eddy stayed close to the house. He spent his days with Anne and Zack, and his nights with Peter.

At age 14 Russell started to inquire about his parentage. He was angry that his Mother would not tell him about his father.

"It's only biology, son," Anne said. "Zack has been your father since you were born."

"Don't you know who he was?" Russell finally asked directly.

"Russell!" Eddy said sternly. "That's no way to talk to your mother."

"Why can't she be honest with me?" he pleaded. "Why is it a big secret? Was he a deadbeat or a politician?"

"It's not important, Russ," Eddy said with a chuckle. He regained his composure and took a more serious tone. "What is important is that Zack has been your father, and an excellent one at that. He loves you as a son, and that's what's important. Biology is biology, but it's the day to day things that count." Russell looked at Zack and accepted that answer. He turned and left the room.

"Thank you, Eddy," Zack said. "He's very strong willed."

"He reminds me of his uncle William," Eddy smiled. "He had to do everything the hard way. He was always impatient. Mother used to say he was born that way. Russell is the same way."

"He wants so much," Anne said. "He's bored living here. He wants the excitement of the big city, where there's more things to do."

"You mean more trouble to get into," Zack said. "He's found plenty around here."

"He's not hurt anyone, broken any laws, or destroyed any property," Anne replied.

"No, he hasn't," Zack replied. "He has scared us half to death, though."

"It only scared you to death because you knew about it," Eddy said. "We never told Mother or Dad about half the things Will and I did as kids. They probably would have felt the same way. I do have to admit, that Will was the one who instigated most of our antics."

Russell let the subject of his father go. He had become interested in airplanes and wished he were old enough to go fight in the war. He wanted to see the world, and he wanted to see it from the air. Zack started picking up books on airplanes every chance he got. Russell was excited with each and every book.

Eddy's health had deteriorated over the last year. He had a serious bout of pneumonia over the Christmas holidays that he didn't recover from. He had talked to a friend of Ben's who practiced law and got his will in order. Most of the cash of his estate he left to Peter. He left some to Russell and the land and went to Anne. He made Anne promise to take care of Peter after he was gone.

In the spring of 1947, Russell turned 18 years of age. He announced that he would be joining the Air Force right after graduation. Over the last 3 years he had put his nose in his schoolbooks so he could become a pilot. He knew he had to graduate from high school, and there were certain courses that they wanted to see that he had. He would graduate at the top if his class and leave June first.

"You know what you want to do," Eddy said to him one night. "That is something I never figured out in my whole life. Your uncle William knew what he wanted to do at age 14. He worked toward owning his own business and accomplished that before he died. I was always envious about that."

"I don't want to stay here," Russell said. "I want to see the world, all of it. I may come back here someday, but it will be some years before I come back to stay."

"I don't understand why you dislike this place," Eddy said.

"I don't dislike it, exactly," Russell said. "I never belonged to it the way that you and mother do. It's like you're in tune with the trees, the wind, and the rain. I don't understand that. I suppose it's that I don't want to understand. Maybe the Indian part of my background didn't come through."

"I think you just want different things," Eddy said. "I will miss you, Russ. Watching you grow up was like having my brother back again. I've missed him for all those years. Promise me something, will you?"

"Anything," he said.

"Make sure you keep in touch with your Mother," Eddy said. "She loves you so much. You two are very much alike, which is why you don't get along at times. Don't forget about Zack. He's the only father you'll ever have."

"And he's been a good one, Eddy," Russell said.

"He needs to hear that from you," Eddy encouraged. "More than you'll ever know."

Eddy graduated the end of May and on June 1st boarded a train to Seattle. From there he would travel to California to start his flight training. It was a cold, rainy morning when he said goodbye to Anne, Zack, and Eddy. He hugged his mother, kissed her, and told her he loved her. He then turned to Zack and saw the tears.

"Dad," he whispered. "Thank you for always being there for me. I love you."

"Be careful, son," Zack said as his voice quivered. "Let us know if you need anything."

"My mother gave me something when I left for Alaska many years ago," Eddy said as he hugged Russell. He handed him the envelope. Russell looked inside and his eyes grew wide. "This is for the unforeseen things that happen. Put it in your shoe, or somewhere safe. I know the Government is supposed to take care of all of your needs, but sometimes you may need things that aren't provided. Have a nice life, Russ. Keep in touch with us."

He boarded the train and Anne finally broke down when the train had left the station. Zack put his arm around her.

"He'll be back," Zack said in a comforting tone.

"No, he won't," Anne said flatly. "I'll never see my son again."

***

Zack came back to the present and looked out the window at Beth. Their time and this story would come to a close soon. He would need to tell her who he really was. He hoped she would be happy about the fact that she had a living relative. There were many more surprises in store for her before their time together ended. He hoped she would have the strength to take on the burden of her heritage.

This was something that Russell never wanted. Anne believed she was right that day at the train station. She thought Russell would never did come home. He was being sent first to Korea and then to Viet Nam. The letters he wrote turned into post cards, and then nothing. Zack never knew about his marriage, and Russell never knew about his child. Here she was, after all of these years, coming back to a place that her father ran away from.

Beth came in from the porch. She looked at Zack and smiled. She sat down in the recliner and picked up the cup of tea that sat on the end table. She cradled it to warm her hands.

"That tastes good," she said. "It's cold outside. I think the dampness is worse than the cold temperature."

"It cuts through to your bones," Zack smiled. "I'm sorry I made you sad. Not all in life is happy. We can't appreciate the mountains without the valleys, just like we can't appreciate happiness without the sadness."

"Sara doesn't have either son, now," Beth said. "But she still has Annie."

"Yes, there's still Annie," Zack said.

313

Chapter 26

It was a month before anyone heard from Eddy. He had sent a letter from Anchorage right after they had landed. He talked about the rugged beauty of the coastline and the black and white whales they saw on their journey north. Sara tucked the letter away in a box. It was the only thing in the box, but she expected to have many more in the future.

Over the next couple of years many changes came to the town of Snoqualmie. Ivan and Helga Zembruski had passed away. They died within hours of one another. The strange thing was that Helga died first. Kathleen and Emily believed that Ivan died from a broken heart. Emily always thought that Ivan would get along just fine without Helga. In reality, the opposite was the truth. They had their funerals at the same time. They were buried side by side near all of their friends. This particular part of the cemetery was beginning to fill up.

Loggers from many miles around attended. There wasn't a tree cut within a twenty-mile radius of Snoqualmie that day. To Sara's surprise, Gus showed up. He left Snoqualmie when William was killed and hadn't come back. One of the original logging crew still kept in touch with him and sent him a telegram when Ivan died. It was a sad reason to return, but he was glad he did. He was doing well and was working with a mill farther north. The mill was new and Gus had developed many mechanical enhancements to the existing equipment.

Ben Eichorn had finished school and was going on to medical school. This was his dream, although his mother tried to talk him out of it. His mind was made up and Sara asked if she could help with funding his medical school. Tom and Kathleen didn't want to accept this gift.

"All I ask is that he return and practice in this town," Sara said. "I have more money than I know what to do with. It's one way for me to repay both of you for your lifelong help and friendship. This is his dream, and I would hate to see that dream not come true for him." They decided they couldn't refuse. This was like a gift from heaven. The cost of tuition alone was going to be more than they could afford. Ben was going to have to work and go to school. Now they could cover his books, Sara would pay the tuition, and Ben could concentrate on his studies.

Sara realized that she could set up a fund for just such projects.

Why not use the money that the business still generated, in large amounts, to help graduating high school students fulfill their dreams. There would have to be certain criteria that the student would have to meet before the funds would be available to them. She spoke with Emily about this, and contacted the man who prosecuted Moe Hawkins about the legalities. He was thrilled with the prospect of handling something like this. He had opened up his own law practice in Seattle and was willing to come out to Snoqualmie to meet with Sara about this. Emily and Sara met Tom and Kathleen in the hotel restaurant for dinner that weekend and Sara told them what she was planning.

"I want to make sure that an equal fund is set up for the white school and the Indian school," she explained. "Everyone should have an opportunity to achieve their dreams."

"This is a wonderful thing, Sara," Kathleen said. "This is something that will come back to the community for years to come. There's a word for people like you. Do you know what it is?" Sara shook her head. "The word is philanthropist. It's a wonderful word."

"So David Webster is going to handle the details?" Tom asked.

"Yes," Sara answered. "He's in private practice now, and has worked closely with some of the schools in Seattle. He also knows people with influence. That's always important for what I have in mind."

"What do you have in mind?" Tom asked.

"I want the Indian children to be able to attend any school the white man attends," she said. "It may be an uphill battle with some of them, but money can get you anything. And money I have, and if I'm right, the schools want it."

"You're right about that," Emily said. "I still get letters from my school in Boston asking for donations. I haven't sent them anything in years, but they keep asking."

David Webster arrived two weeks later. Sara met him at the train station and he was surprised at how good she looked.

"The last time you saw me, I was still recovering from some gunshot wounds," she smiled.

"What a pretty little town," he said as he looked around. "If you let me know where the hotel is, I can drop my bags there."

"That won't be necessary," Sara said. "We have several guest rooms at the house. You'll stay with us on the estate. I would like to show you what my husband built."

"I'd like that Mrs. Monroe. I'd like that very much," he answered.

Tom and Kathleen came out for dinner. Afterwards, Emily, Sara, Kathleen, and Tom talked with David about this fund.

"I've been thinking about this," David said. "First we need to form a foundation, and then name it. I was thinking 'The Monroe Memorial Foundation' if that's okay with you, Sara? We would then set up a scholarship fund. There would be a specific amount for each scholarship to be awarded annually at each school."

"I have a few stipulations to the schools," Sara said. "I want to award scholarships only to schools that will take Indian students as well as whites."

"That could be a problem," David said. "There are very few of those in this area."

"That's where you come in David," Tom said. "You know people who could influence the Boards for these schools. If they want donations from this Foundation, they will have to admit Indian students."

"There's nothing that money can't buy," David said. "I'll start making my contacts as soon as I get back to Seattle. In the time that I'm here, we'll get the paperwork in place for the Foundation. We'll also need to set up a specific bank account for the Foundation. How much do you want to deposit, initially?"

"The bank account is set up," Tom said. "There's $50,000.00 in there now. This should cover start-up costs, and your fee, of course."

"I would like to keep you on retainer, David," Sara said. "I would pay you an annual fee to make sure that this is carried out as I wish. Does that interest you?"

"Absolutely," he smiled. "I was hoping you would ask me. I so admired your husband, and you. Tom, are you going to handle the bank account? I mean, are you going to write the checks?"

"I, Sara, and you will be able to write the checks," he said. "You can grease what palms you have to in order to get these schools to agree. I will talk to you about that later. I don't want the same palms getting greased annually. The only thing that Sara and I ask is a strict accounting of who was paid, why, and how much. Make sure that there's a paper trail. We can use this in the future if they get amnesia."

"I understand," he said with a smile.

"I want nothing illegal," Sara said. "If future generations are going to reap the benefits of our work, it will need to be done legally."

"Agreed," David said. "I can't tell you how refreshing it is to do business with someone who wants to obey, instead of usurp the law." He looked around the room. These were amazing people. These were people who looked many years ahead for the betterment of future generations and not to their own pocketbook. "I can't tell you how proud I am that you chose me to be a part of this."

The next few days David worked with Sara and Tom on the paperwork and guidelines for the foundation. Sara was learning a great deal during this process. She learned more about the legal system than she had ever intended to learn. David took things slowly so Sara could get the full picture. She would be heading the foundation, David would take care of the legalities, and Tom, Kathleen, Emily, Maggie and Jack Regan agreed to sit on the board. Together they would decide the criteria for scholarship qualifications, the amount, and the school would have to be put in later.

"It might be easier to give a specific amount," David said. "This way they can use it at any school they choose. Some students may not want to go to college locally."

"I didn't think of that," Sara admitted. "We can do that and still work on the schools to admit Indians."

"Yes, we can," David responded. He leaned back in his chair and stretched his arms above his head. "Let's quit for today. I'd like to see some of the area. We've accomplished a lot in the last few days, and it's time for a break."

"I think that's a good idea," Tom said. "I need to get back to the bank this afternoon, anyway. My wife hasn't seen much of me in the last few days, and I wouldn't mind getting home early and fixing her a nice dinner."

David and Sara spent the rest of the afternoon walking around the estate. Peter saddled a couple of horses and they rode to the falls. David was pleased by the beauty and peacefulness here. He understood why Monroe never wanted to live anywhere else.

"He was a wise man," David said to Sara. "He would have done well in Seattle, but he did very well here. His priority wasn't to make lots of money, but to care for his family. He did that very well."

"He did," Sara responded. "He built something that would take care of future generations of this family. Too bad there aren't any."

"What about Annie?" he asked. "She could carry on the family line."

"It's up to her, I suppose," Sara said. "That will need to be her decision."

Five years had passed since Eddy had left. He was true to his word and Sara's box was filled with letters from her son. He and John had settled into a nice life and they were proud of the work they were doing. He sent things down for Annie and Emily on a routine basis. He would send things to his mother from the villages when he could. These were all handcrafted carvings made from ivory or bone.

One of the local men in the village would give his things to Eddy. It kept him busy during the short cold winter days. Sara always marveled at the detail on these carvings. She had Samuel build her a cabinet with glass front doors so she could display these works of art. His most recent letter stated that he and John were going to stay in Alaska. They had much to do because of the influx of people looking for gold.

Emily returned home to find Sara quiet and distant. She found it best to not ask her questions about her mood. Sara would mull things over in her mind and usually talk to Emily when she was ready. Sara was ready that night to talk to Sara. She told Emily of Eddy's plans to stay in Alaska. Emily now understood her mood. For the last few months Sara had been looking forward to having Eddy home.

"I'm glad he's doing well, and he seems happy," Sara said as she lay next to Emily. "I just miss him, and wish he would come home."

"Write him and tell him that," Emily responded.

"I don't want him to come home because I asked him," Sara replied. "I want him home because this is where he wants to be."

Annie was spending the night with Amanda. They had been inseparable as children and now, as teenagers, it was the same. If Annie wasn't at the Regan's then Amanda was at the estate. They were both 14 years of age and were becoming beautiful young women. Amanda had Maggie's dark red hair and green eyes. Annie looked like her mother. Emily was amazed at how much she reminded her of Sara the first time she saw her in her office many years ago.

Annie and Amanda were starting their own discoveries, both emotionally and sexually. Annie was fully aware of the relationship between her mother and Emily. She knew of Eddy's relationship with John. Ben Eichorn would come home from school and spend time with Annie, but he seemed like another brother to her. She wasn't interested in anything else.

She and Amanda would take horseback rides and had several remote places that they called theirs. They knew the miles of trees around the estate intimately. The only ones who knew it better were the patrols. Some of the Pinkerton's stayed on after the incident with the mine. They would see Amanda and Annie and enjoyed talking with them.

On this particular night, while Sara was talking with Emily about her son, Amanda had taken the initiative with Annie. For the last few months, her hormones had taken over and she found it difficult to be with Annie. She had no idea what Annie would think or if she felt the same way about her, but she needed to know. They were laying in the dark of Amanda's room when she asked the question.

"Annie," she said quietly. "Do you love me?"

"Of course, I love you," Annie said as she rolled over. "You're my best friend."

"That's not what I mean," Amanda whispered. "What I mean is, well." She didn't know how to say the words. She leaned up on one elbow and looked at Annie. She touched her face and bent down and kissed her softly. There was enough light in the room to see Annie's face and read her response when she pulled back. "That's what I mean."

"I didn't know you felt that way," Annie said. "I thought that I was the only one who felt this way." Amanda bent down and kissed Annie more passionately. That first night passed without anything more than kissing and touching. Neither knew the excitement of a previous sexual experience and this was unlike anything they had ever experienced. They made a pact to never tell anyone. It was not out of shame or embarrassment, but it they wanted to share this with no one, but each other.

When Annie and Amanda showed up later that day, Emily saw a glow in Annie that she hadn't seen before. That glow came from Amanda, too. Emily knew why they had that glow. This was something that she had suspected would happen. She knew this as she watched them when they were children. The road for them was not going to be easy, but you can't deny things or tendencies you were born with.

She looked at Sara sitting at the desk in the library and smiled. She had lived and loved in both worlds. They were both getting older. Sara had a few rare strands of gray hair at 44, and hers was more pronounced at 54. She didn't feel old, but she did notice more aches as she got out of bed in the morning. Sara came out of the library and saw Emily. She always had a smile for her.

"What?" she asked. "Why are you smiling?"

"Annie and Amanda just got in," Emily said while still smiling. About that time they walked into the living room. Sara saw their glow and winked at Emily.

"Mother," Annie said. "We're going for a ride. We should be back by dinner, unless there's something you need for us to do here?"

"No," she replied. "Go out and have a nice ride. Take the gelding out, will you? He's getting fat and lazy. A good run through the woods would do him good." They left and walked to the barn. Peter had their horses saddled, and he happened to grab the gelding. Sara looked out the window. "Peter knew he needed exercise, too." She turned and looked at Emily. "Now, what's so amusing?"

"Those two," she said. "You'd think they discovered something new."

"They did," Sara said, "each other, and kindred desires and spirits. There is nothing like discovery within yourself or with new experiences." Emily walked over to her and picked up her hands and was always amazed at their softness and beauty.

"I remember the first time we kissed," Emily said and held Sara's hand to her cheek.

"I'm surprised," Sara said. "You were very tired and drunk, and if I remember correctly, I had to put you to bed."

"I may have been tipsy," Emily teased back. "But the memory lives vividly in my mind. It's right there with the first time we made love."

"And the many years thereafter," Sara said as she kissed her cheek, "and the many years to come." She followed her statement with a long, slow, wet kiss. Even after all of these years, the excitement and passion never diminished.

***

"The Monroe Foundation was started by my great-grandmother. They're known on a national level." She paused and smiled. "My grandmother was a lesbian, too. There's something to be said for heredity."

"So you're," Zack paused," inclined in that direction yourself."

"Yes, Zack," she admitted. "The girl that I thought I'd spend the rest of my life with died on Interstate 90 a few years ago."

"I'm very sorry to hear that," he consoled. "Losing someone you love is always very hard. Tell me about her."

As Beth talked about Jenny, Zack thought about all the people that were lost after Russell left for the Air Force. Eddy died a month after Russell left. He had been ill for some time but never told Anne. He had been seeing Ben and went to bed one night and never awoke. Peter died shortly thereafter; of what Anne felt was beyond a broken heart. They had 10 wonderful years together and Anne was happy for both of them. She buried him with John on one side and Peter on the other.

After Eddy died, Anne didn't seem to be very interested in the Foundation. She turned most of the work over to Zack. They would receive postcards from Russell, and Anne would store them in the box next to the letters that her mother kept from Eddy. The house seemed so empty and cold. There was no life, and no young people. Even the servants had gotten old.

By the mid 1950s Anne's health was beginning to fail. She and Zack still took walks whenever they could, but aging was a part of life. Zack had written to Russell and suggested he come home to see his mother. It was 2 months before they got a response from him, and he was in Europe. He hoped he would be coming back in the next year. That didn't happen as quickly as Zack had hoped. It was, finally 3 years later, in the fall of 1958 when Russell appeared at the door of the estate. Anne opened the door and saw her son, who, was now a mature man standing in his uniform. She fell into his arms and held him close.

"My son," she whispered. "How long I've waited to see you."

"Hello, Mother," he said as he kissed her hair. "I didn't realize how much I missed you until I saw your face."

"How long are you here for?" she dared to ask.

"I've got two days before I head down to Edwards Air Force base," he said as they walked into the house. "I wanted to see you and Dad before I left. I don't know when I'll be back up this way." He saw Zack, smiled and hugged him close.

"You look good, son," Zack said. They retired to the library and talked until dinner. It was nice to be a family again. Most of the hostility that Russell had when he left had subsided. Either the military or maturity had changed the way he looked at things. He seemed, genuinely happy, to be home. He talked about what he would be doing in California. He seemed excited about testing new jets, but Anne was concerned about it being dangerous. He was like his uncle William in that respect.

"This will be a piece of cake next to Korea," he smiled. "No one is shooting at you here. I'll be fine Mother, don't worry."

The next couple of days passed too quickly and before Anne and Zack knew it, he was kissing them goodbye. They watched him get into his car and drive out the gate. He promised to come home over Christmas the following year. Anne seemed to be satisfied that he came home at all. She was counting on nothing more. When Russell didn't come home at Christmas, as he promised, Anne's health started to deteriorate. She had been having problems with COPD for the last few months. She knew she didn't have much time to put off what she had hoped she wouldn't have to do. She needed to update her Will and make sure that things were in order.

She knew that Russell wanted no part of the Foundation and would need to make sure that it would continue running and the funds would be maintained. The Law Firm that David Webster had started many years ago was doing a fine job and they would continue to do this. Zack had been making most of the decisions for the last several years. Anne had given him this authority some time ago and his business decisions were sound, and she never questioned any of them. She knew that Zack would continue to take care of the foundation and the estate as he had done for the last 30 years.

The land, estate, and the monthly stipend that was received would go into a sub-account of the foundation for Zack. This would be for his personal use and any expenses he may incur for the rest of his life. This account could be willed to Russell and his children when Zack saw fit. Sara met with David Webster Jr. and had all the papers drawn up and signed.

For the first time since 1858, when Edmondson Monroe first purchased this land, the safe keeping was being left in the care of someone other than a Monroe. Zack was an honorary Monroe through marriage, but it still saddened Anne to think about this.

Russell didn't make it home for Christmas of 1960 because of some things happening overseas. He sent a letter in August saying he had met someone special. He never gave a name or this person. In November he informed them that he was leaving for Viet Nam. His December 1st departure date made a visit at Christmas impossible. He never mentioned that he'd gotten married. As far as anyone knew, he was still single.

Anne gave up after Russell left the country. She contracted Pneumonia and despite her doctor's best efforts, she died in the early morning of December 12th, 1961. Zack was by her side and it seemed to comfort her that he would be here for Russell. Zack quietly and privately buried his wife near her mother and father. She looked as beautiful in death as she did in life.

Just when Zack thought his heart could not hurt anymore, the telegram from the Government gave him the news about the death of his son. *"We regret to inform you that Lt. Russell Monroe's plane was shot down over the Gulf of Tonkin. There were no survivors."* Zack read the telegram twice before he sunk down into the leather chair in the library and cried openly.

There was a private service held for Russell. There was no body in the coffin, but some of his friends from school did show up. Much to Zack's surprise some of the men he served with in the Air Force arrived. They told Zack that he had gotten married, but didn't know his wife's name. Zack got the Law firm started on tracking down any information on his wife. This went on for months and just when they thought they might have a lead it proved to be a dead-end.

From the information that Zack received he knew that his son married shortly before he went to Viet Nam. There would have been no time to have children. He now had to think about what to do with the property and inheritance that was to be passed on to Russell's children. He would have to make some hard decisions, but that would have to come later.

***

"She had apparently been out to Snoqualmie Falls and the Historical Museum," Beth said. "She was on her way back to Seattle to share this with me, when the accident happened. I put the envelope away for a few years before I opened it. That's when I found my father's birth certificate."

"You've been searching for many years," he smiled.

"I'd lost hope of finding anyone who actually knew any of my family," she said. "How lucky I was to find you at the cemetery."

It wasn't luck that brought him to the cemetery that day. It was coincidental that he was there because that was the only day he, normally spent at the estate. After Russell died, he couldn't live at the estate. It was too cold and empty and he had this house that he had owned since 1930. He had kept it in good repair and had added on to it some 15 years ago. He had moved many of his, Anne's, and Sara's most cherished items here with him.

He kept the estate up, and the servants still lived in the house. The house that Samuel had built for Mary was still standing, but the cabin where Eddy and Peter had resided during their final years, was in great disrepair. The Foundation secretary did work out of the house, and there would be charity events that would happen there every other month or so. The 4th of July party that Monroe had started years ago was still the social event of the season.

They would still have the banquet, and fireworks display. Anne had added a dance to festivities. She would have a stage and a live orchestra. All of those who benefited from the Foundation Scholarship Fund were invited. They would come from thousands of miles away to attend. The new recipients would have theirs' awarded at the party. It had become a real black tie affair in the years before her death. After Anne's death, Zack continued the tradition. There hadn't been a year that was missed since 1874. The planning had begun for this year's party. How nice it would be to have Beth at his side for this party. It all belonged to her anyway.

"I guess it was lucky," he agreed although he knew that luck had nothing to do with it. He had a strong feeling about visiting those graves today and didn't know why until he saw Beth in the office. Some greater power had made him change the schedule he had kept so rigidly and now standing in front of him was the reason.

Chapter 27

"I'd like to take a walk back out to the gravesites," Beth said. "It's a beautiful sunny day and I would like to see the others buried with Sara and Anne."

"I'd like to stretch my legs myself," Zack said as he stood up from the chair. "We can talk as we walk. I will warn you, it's quite a walk." It never seemed that far to him in reality. He walked this route almost daily.

"That's fine by me," Beth said. "I could use the exercise."

They went out the door and walked through the cemetery gate. The young caretaker was mowing grass and trimming around headstones. Beth thought this was a strange way to make a living, but when she really thought about it, it didn't seem so strange. You really wouldn't get any complaints from your clients and you could work at your own pace. Zack picked up his story right where he left off.

***

The Foundation had donated money to many of the schools in the Puget Sound area. Most were willing to allow the Indian students into their program and this pleased Sara. Over the next few years more than 14 scholarships were given to students wanting to major in many different subjects. Sara and David decided to drop the clause that required that they return to Snoqualmie to pursue their chosen vocation. After the first couple of years, it wasn't practical. The town didn't need that many doctors or engineers.

Anne and Amanda had graduated from high school and they, too were off to college. Amanda wanted to be a teacher, and Anne was going to take some courses in business. She needed to be prepared to take over when Sara retired, or died. This was something that she and Emily discussed, heatedly, several times.

"Your mother can't run this forever," Emily said. "There's no one else to handle this."

"What if it's not what I want to do?" Anne replied back.

"Who else is there?" Emily asked. "Eddy is in Alaska and we both know he probably won't be back." The argument would usually end at an impasse because Emily would not give on this and Anne wouldn't either. Emily also knew that this was on Sara's mind. She had noticed how little Anne wanted to get involved in the operations of anything including the foundation.

One day at the clinic Emily had talked to Kathleen about this.

Kathleen listened but gave no support in either direction. She and Anne had always had a special bond. Kathleen thought of her as the daughter she never had, and Anne respected Kathleen as she respected no other woman. In the last year of two, Ben had made advances in Anne's direction, but couldn't convince her to ever date him. Kathleen knew why and convinced him to look elsewhere without ever giving him the real reason.

Just after the girls graduated from high school, Kathleen ran into Anne in town. She invited her to coffee and talked with her about her future.

"We've always been straight with one another, Anne," Kathleen started. "I'm going to be straight with you now. Answer me this, why do you not want to run the Foundation and logging business?"

"I'd have to stay here to do it," she said. "I don't know if I want to stay."

"You mean you don't know if Amanda wants to stay?" Kathleen said directly. Anne's face turned red. "I've known you since the day you were born. I've known your mother for longer than that. I've known about she and Emily, and I know about you and Amanda. You need to make a decision for you. If Amanda truly loves you, she'll understand that decision and all will work out."

"It scares me to think what life would be like without her," Anne admitted.

"I'm sure it does," Kathleen agreed. "Your father built something many years ago so his family would be taken care of. He looked into the future and wanted to make sure that his children and their children's children were left some sort of legacy from this place that he loved so much. Whether you like it or not, it's your responsibility to carry on that legacy. Your Mother has added to that in her own way. The work the Foundation does is wonderful. It benefits people now, but it will touch many in future generations. Is being with a lover worth the risk of losing all of this?"

"I didn't think of it that way," Anne said quietly. "It scares me when I think that I have to shoulder this responsibility alone."

"It's not alone," Kathleen said. "There are plenty of people to help you. If you mean alone, as without Amanda, then it wasn't really meant to be." She looked at Anne while she stared into her coffee cup. She reached over and put her hand under her chin and Anne's eyes met hers. "I love you like a daughter, honey. You're eighteen years old, and society considers you an adult. It's time to make adult decisions." Anne's eyes began to tear. "Don't throw away everything your father built and died for. That would break his heart."

"You're not telling me something I don't already know," Anne admitted. "I've had my head in the sand doing my best to avoid this. Emily has been at me for the last year about this and my mother has a right to know what I'm going to do."

"Your mother deserves a little peace," Kathleen said. "Will's death and Eddy's departure was difficult. Add to that her physical injuries, legal issues, and running a large business have all taken a toll on her. She's a strong woman, but not knowing if all of this work will be in vain is an added stress she doesn't need. She needs to know that this legacy is secure for future generations of Monroe's."

"The future generations of the Monroe family died with Will," Annie said. "I don't think Eddy has any plans for children, and neither do I."

"The future is a funny thing, Anne," Kathleen said as she held her hand. "You can never see all of it."

Kathleen was right, and she was right because of experience. When she and Tom were in San Francisco, she could never have imagined herself practicing medicine in a rural setting. When she and Tom first arrived, she wanted nothing more than to get on the train and head south. Tom convinced her to give it a try. She met Emily and realized that she had a chance to make a real difference in the lives of these people.

The impact she would have here would be felt in all of the town's people. In San Francisco she would be just another doctor in a large hospital. It was easy to fade into the woodwork and remain anonymous. She really couldn't effect any change because of her gender and the established rules. It was different here, and now it was the only place she wanted to be. She hoped Anne would come to this realization, also.

Anne and Amanda discussed the future. Amanda wanted to be a teacher and teach in the Indian school. Her parents thought this might not be the best career for her, but accepted what she had decided.

"Have you decided what you want to do Anne?" Amanda asked her during and afternoon horseback ride.

"I want to take some business courses and I'll come back here and have Mother teach me the logging business, and the work with the Foundation," she said.

"I think that's excellent, Annie," Amanda said. "Your father did some wonderful things for the community, and it needs to be taken care of. Did you know my father had the greatest respect for your father?"

"No," Anne responded. "I never knew my father." Anne only remembered vague images of him. "I hope I can manage the business he built. I'd hate to see it ruined."

"You're smart," Amanda said. "You have some good people to help you, like your Mother."

They were both going to different schools in Seattle, but David Webster had arranged an apartment for them. It was between the schools so neither had far to go. When August rolled around, they left their families and boarded the train for Seattle. David assured Sara and Maggie that he would meet the girls at the station. Ben Eichorn was still in his residency and would look in on them from time to time.

In September of 1907 Anne and Amanda started college. They would be home for Christmas holidays and decided to stay in Seattle the first summer. They both had jobs locally and didn't want to leave them. They had also found some 'kindred souls' that they liked to socialize with. It was nice to meet people their age, with the same sexual orientation. They could talk freely and express their opinions.

During the fall of 1908 a flu epidemic hit the Northwest. It was traveling through the mining and logging camps and the first case hit Snoqualmie in November. Kathleen and Emily had heard that entire families were dying east of the mountains. They set up wards in the hospital to isolate any cases they may get. There had been a great influx of people to the area because of the need for lumber overseas. The railroad was also building new lines, and power companies were starting to string their wires everywhere.

By December, they had seen more cases than they had expected and just before Christmas Amanda and Maggie appeared with Jack. He was weak and pale and Kathleen knew he had contracted this flu. They got him into the treatment room and put him on a gurney.

"How long has he been sick?" Kathleen asked as she listened to his chest.

"Mother said he's been this way for 3 days," Amanda said. "He wouldn't let her bring him in." Emily appeared and helped Kathleen get Jack into the isolated ward. He didn't look good and suddenly looked old. They went back and talked to Maggie who was worried.

"All we can do is wait," Emily said. She gave her a cotton mask. "If you want to sit with him you'll need to put this on. We want to make sure that you don't contract this, too."

"He's so weak," Maggie said. "I should have brought him in whether he wanted me to or not. I should have forced him."

"There's no point is beating yourself up about this," Kathleen assured. "We'll do everything we can."

It was two days until Christmas and Maggie, with Amanda by her side, stood vigil at the hospital. Anne, Emily, and Sara joined them. They all took turns sitting with Jack, who wasn't improving. He was not a young man, but even at 68, was a powerful man. He had just made a deal with a large timber company to sell his business. This would keep Maggie and Amanda in a lifestyle he had given them. They would get a monthly check for the rest of their lives, and their children's lives.

Sara found out that this is why he didn't go to the hospital sooner.

"Amanda doesn't want to run the business, and Maggie wanted us to travel. I don't think that's going to happen unless she goes alone."

"You need to rest," Sara said. "Concentrate on getting better."

"I always respected you and Monroe," Jack smiled. "I wanted you to know that." Jack dropped of to sleep. Maggie and Amanda came in and sat with him. Sara left and found Kathleen in her office. She stood in the doorway and Kathleen looked up from her desk.

"He's not going to make it, is he?" Sara asked.

"No," Kathleen responded in her direct way. She never liked to talk around a subject but she was always cautious to not be cruel. "If he had come in sooner, we could have kept his strength up. As weak as he was when he came in, I'm surprised he lasted this long."

"How long does he have?" Sara asked.

"Within the next 24 hours, is my guess," Kathleen said. "I'd stay close." Sara nodded her head and turned down the hallway. Emily appeared in the doorway looking tired. Neither of them had left the hospital for 3 days. Christmas had come and gone without notice from anyone here.

"You told her?" Emily asked as she sat down.

"Yes," Kathleen answered. "Maggie will need her strength and support. Amanda is going to need Annie." She looked at Emily. "You really look tired. Why don't you catch a nap on my couch? I'll wake you in a couple of hours."

"I'm going to take you up on that," Emily said. She reclined on the couch and Kathleen threw a blanket over her. She closed the door as she left the office and walked toward the isolation ward. She was tired herself and Ben couldn't get back in town fast enough. She expected him in two weeks. He had finished his residency and was coming home to practice with his mother. Kathleen entered the isolation ward and saw Maggie and Amanda sitting next to Jack's bed. He was awake and talking with them.

"All of the paperwork is in the desk in the office," he said.

"We don't need to discuss that now," Maggie urged. She didn't want to discuss business and it was the furthest thing from her mind.

"You need to know these things," he continued. "The deal is set and Tom is aware of all the details." He paused and looked at his daughter. She looked so much like her mother, but had a hint of his mother. He had not seen her in 42 years, and to see her by his bed, reminded him of his mother. "I want to make sure you're taken care of. Let's be honest with one another, Maggie. We've always been honest with each other."

"I've never lied to you Jack," Maggie said. "I never needed to. You always accepted me as I was."

"Then let's not start now," he said. "You know I'm not getting better. I'm not going to leave this hospital in an upright position."

"I know," she whispered. "I just didn't want to believe it." Sara came into the room with Annie by her side. They stayed in the background with Kathleen. Jack dropped off to sleep again. He was burning up with fever, and the nurse was trying to get him to drink. She made several unsuccessful attempts and looked at Kathleen. She motioned her to not try anymore and spoke with her briefly at the door.

"Find Dr. McLaughlin," she said. "She's sleeping in my office. Have her come in as soon as she can." The nurse left and within 10 minutes Emily appeared looking sleepy. "I wanted you to be here." She paused and swallowed hard. "Jack doesn't have too long."

"Thanks for waking me," she said in a tired voice. "I feel like I could sleep for a week." They sat next to Sara and waited. Maggie sat on one side of Jack's bed and Amanda on the other. They each held his hand. The sun was just coming up and it was shining through the window. Jack woke up and looked at his wife and daughter.

"I hoped I could see one more sunrise," he said weakly. "I wanted to see the sun on your faces one more time. I love you both." He closed his eyes and breathed his last breath. A look of peace came over his face. Maggie began to cry and put her head on his chest. Amanda looked over at Annie. Sara, Kathleen, and Emily were in tears as their friend joined those who had passed before him.

In Sara's mind she could see him joining Monroe, Will, Charlie, Ivan, and Helga. They were waiting to show him to the spirit world. He would be there to watch over those yet to come. Emily walked over to the bed and looked down at this man she hated the first time she met him. His genteel southern charm seemed patronizing and shallow but was his way. When he stopped trying to impress people and became his own man, he became a good friend and a good addition to the community. She put the sheet up over his face and put her hand on his head.

"Good night sweet prince," she said quietly. "Parting is such sweet sorrow."

"Shakespeare," Maggie smiled. "He always loved his writing. Thank you for remembering."

Two days later they buried Jackson Jefferson Regan. He had chosen and purchased plots not too far from where Monroe had purchased his. There was no logging on the day that he was buried. Most of the loggers in the area knew Jack and respected him as a businessman. He made sure that the timber company that purchased his business kept the crews on. He wanted no one to lose jobs because of a change in ownership.

Sara had asked Tom to closely watch how well this new company treated the loggers and how well they maintained the land. She knew that she might not be able to hold on to all of the land that Monroe had purchased. If she sold the business and some of the land, she wanted to make sure that it was not going to be raped. This company was working with Samuel and Mary and buying seedlings from them so Sara knew they were replanting.

Caleb had taken over the business and it had grown. He was out talking to other logging companies and they were requesting seedlings in large quantities. Caleb had secured land just outside of town and was building large greenhouses. He had even solicited help from Gus. Caleb caught him at Jack's funeral and asked him to design a watering system for the greenhouse. His job up north wouldn't be finished until spring, so the timing was excellent. Caleb still had to finish putting in the large planter boxes and get the topsoil into them.

Emily was quiet the day of Jack's funeral and had been that way since he died. She had been working long hours during this flu epidemic and she looked tired. She had spent many nights at the hospital, much to Kathleen's dismay. She would encourage her to sleep whenever she could. After the funeral Sara and Emily stood outside of the hotel restaurant and talked.

"Maggie held up pretty well," Kathleen noted. "She'll need our support, though."

"Jack left her in good shape," Tom said. "She won't have to worry about finances for the rest of her life." Sara looked at Emily. It was cold and there was snow on the ground. Emily's face was pale and she was perspiring. She took her arm.

"Emily?" Sara asked. "Are you feeling all right?"

"I'm cold," she said, "and I can't seem to get warm or catch my breath." Kathleen put her hand on her forehead and her fever was high.

"Let's get you to the hospital," Kathleen said. "When did you start the fever?"

"Maybe an hour ago," Emily said.

They got her into a bed and Emily knew better than anyone what she needed to do to get better. She was the only one in the isolation ward and Kathleen had given the nurses strict orders to push the fluids every hour. Most of that first night her fever would rise and fall when Sara told Kathleen about the willow bark that her mother used to boil into a tea.

"We did that when Ivan had Pneumonia," she said. "It seemed to work."

"I think we still have some here," Kathleen said. She disappeared and came back with a tin can. "Let's get some water boiling."

Every 3 hours Emily was given some of the tea, although she complained about the bitter and horrible taste but Sara and Kathleen didn't care. After a couple of doses of the tea, her fever went down, her head stopped spinning, and some of her body aches subsided but her cough still racked her body each time. By the third day she was getting her appetite back and was nagging at Kathleen to let her go home. She finally conceded and let her go home the following morning. Emily was still coughing, but the other cases they saw, this was common and she hoped this would subside over time.

The hospital was empty and the flu epidemic seemed to be over. Kathleen wanted to close the clinic for a week so she and Emily could recover, so with Ben coming in town, he could work any emergencies for them. He arrived just as Emily was leaving the hospital. He looked so young and he was happy to be home. Kathleen looked so proud, and relieved to see him.

Amanda and Annie went back to school after the first of the year. Maggie busied herself with closing up the logging office. She had been alone before in her life, but she always worked. Now she didn't have to work and wanted to. Sara could use some help with her business and asked Maggie if she would take on the bookkeeping duties. Maggie jumped at the chance and could work right out of the bank. Tom had a desk for her and he said he could use her in other capacities also.

Two years later Annie and Amanda returned from college. Amanda had a job teaching at the Indian school. Annie started to work with her mother, Maggie, and Tom to understand the workings of the logging business and the Foundation. She found that this interested her. She even made arrangements to see David Webster and understand the legalities associated with this.

Emily didn't bounce back after she had the flu. She tired easily and never got rid of her cough. She was 60 years old this year and was only working on a part time basis. Ben and another woman, he had gone to school with, were running the clinic. Kathleen had cut her hours also. She consulted with Ben on cases he asked her about, but she let him run his own practice. The woman in town still liked to see his female partner. They were both general practitioners although his first love was internal medicine. They ended up with the cases they wanted and everyone was happy.

Annie really loved what she was doing. She was making all the major decisions for the logging business and the Foundation, and still found time to spend with Amanda. A large timber company had been contacting her about the large tract of land that they owned. She decided to talk with Sara regarding this. It was the same company that bought Jack Regan's business. Sara had watched how they did business and how they treated their workers and the land.

"They're a good company," Sara said. "What are they offering?"

"They want as much as they can get," Anne said. "They'd take the estate and all the land surrounding it, if we wanted."

"No," Sara said. "I will not sell my home. I also want to keep the original 1000 acres that includes the falls. I will not see that touched."

"I agree," Anne said. "I'm going to set up a meeting with these people, you, myself, and David Webster. Is that okay?"

Sara agreed and within a week everyone was sitting at the same table. The timber company owner had no idea that Sara Monroe was an Indian. He sat there a little dumbfounded after David made the introductions.

"Forgive me, Mrs. Monroe," he said. "I didn't realize that you were."

"Indian," she said plainly. "My uncle was Chief Joseph of the Nez Perce nation." She looked him directly in the eye and let this sink in. "Let's get down to business. Our ethnic backgrounds have nothing to do with the subject at hand." He looked at David and back at Sara. "This is what will not be in this sale, should we decide to make this deal. The house," she said as she pulled out a surveyors map, "and this 1000 acres indicated by this shaded area will remain in my possession. The other 107,000 acres will be yours."

"Why this parcel?" he asked.

"This is my home and this is the original land my husband purchased before we married," Sara said. "This area is sacred to me and the local tribes. I will not see a single tree touched here."

As they talked, the timber company owner could see that Sara was no fool and Jack Regan told him years ago that if he ever intended to get his hands on this land, he would have to prove he could take care of it. He found the logging system that Sara and Monroe had developed worked well in all his other operations and with trees were a renewable resource the land would produce forever.

By the meeting's end two hours later a deal had been made that would keep Sara and generations of her grandchildren financially secure, the Foundation would continue to be funded, and the land would be cared for. Sara was a shroud businesswoman, and even Annie marveled at her tenacity.

"Mrs. Monroe," he said as he stood up and extended his hand. "I'm pleased to be doing business with you. I have always been a great admirer of your uncle. He gave the Cavalry a run for its money and I respected him for that. I also admire the fact that you want to preserve part of this land." He looked at David Webster and continued. "Send me the paperwork when it's completed. I'll have my lawyer look it over, but that's a formality. Ma am, Miss, thank you for your time." He tipped his hat and they watched him leave the office.

"What do you two think?" David asked.

"I think we've done well," Annie said.

"I've watched the way this man does business," Sara said. "He bought Jack Regan's business and Tom has kept me informed of any changes to the original deal."

"Have there been any?" David asked.

"None," Sara replied. "The loggers respect him, the mill owners said he keeps to his contracts, and he pays his bills on time."

By 1914 Anne had really taken everything over. World War I had broken out in Europe and the exportation of lumber to build ships had increased dramatically. The stipend that they received was based on 2% of the profits from what was taken from the land. They had paid back the original money that Tom Eichorn had put in plus the extra that was made because the price of the land had increased dramatically. This was turning out to be a healthy sum every three months. Sara made sure that Annie would get cash and it would go directly to the vault. Monroe had started this and the tradition and Sara felt it should be continued, although she was still unclear on the reasons why.

The winter of 1914 was cold and harsh. Everyone in town had come into the clinic with upper respiratory complaints. Emily had contracted Pneumonia for a second time since she'd had the flu in 1908. Each bout seemed to leave her a little weaker. Sara knew that their time together was limited and they both found comfort in just being together. They still shared the same bed after all these years and would have it no other way.

Anne and Amanda bought a house in the city of Renton. The Indian school out at Snoqualmie was in disrepair and there were only a few students. Most of the students were now attending the white school with very little incident. Amanda would be teaching in Renton after this school year was over. They found a house not far from the cemetery they had been too so often. It seemed comforting to both of them to be near this hallowed ground.

When Anne moved out, Sara asked Peter if he wanted to move into the main house. It seemed to need some younger blood. Martin had married a few years earlier so he was alone. He had the greatest respect for Sara and Emily. They would talk for hours in the library. It took a few months but Peter finally admitted opened up and would tell Sara and Emily his innermost thoughts, desires, regrets, and fears.

"We've known that for some time," she whispered. "You're among friends, Peter, and you need to find someone to share your life with."

"It's a little hard to shop for that," Peter laughed. "I think I'll just leave it alone. I like my life. I like it here."

Emily's health was deteriorating quickly. By the spring of 1916 she had trouble walking up the stairs without getting winded. She had seen Ben earlier in the week and there wasn't much he could do.

"It's called congestive heart failure," he said. "That bout of flu you had several years ago damaged your heart and lungs. The Pneumonia you've had over the years just did more damage. It would probably help if you watched your salt intake and get as much exercise as you can."

"Thank you, Ben," Emily said. "You told me what I already

knew." As they left the office they saw Kathleen. She looked wonderful and knew Emily had been ill. She hugged Emily close and grabbed Sara with the other arm.

"How good to see you," she whispered. "I've been meaning to come up to the house to visit, but Ben has had me seeing some patients."

"I'd like that, Kathleen," Emily smiled. "I miss seeing you everyday."

"I miss you too, honey," she smiled. "Plan to see me on Saturday. I'll make Tom bring me up."

"Stay for dinner," Sara said. "I miss our get togethers. We finally got a phone installed. Let me give you our number."

"Anne finally talked you into it, huh?" Kathleen teased.

"Yes," Sara admitted. "She thought it might make it easier if there's a problem but every time it rings, it scares me to death."

Emily lasted through the spring into summer but was getting weaker on a daily basis. The 4th of July party was quickly approaching. She wanted to attend one more. Anne and Amanda had planned a wonderful bash with Peter and Samuel taking charge of the decorations, and Mary was helping the servants prepare some of the dishes. Kathleen and Tom came out the night before and spent the night. Emily felt surprisingly good the last few weeks. After dinner they walked to the falls. This had always been Sara's special place. They stayed and looked at the falls.

"We're going to head back," Tom said. He knew that Sara and Emily needed to spend this time alone. Kathleen kissed Emily and Sara and she and Tom started for the house hand in hand.

"We've had a good life together," Emily said to Sara. "I've loved every day I spent with you." She held Sara's hand and kissed it gently. "Our time together will be ending soon."

"I know this, too, but I can't imagine life without you," Sara said.

"I'll be waiting for you," Emily said. "I'll be standing next to Monroe. My only regret is leaving you alone, but I'll be watching over you."

From the corner of her eye Emily saw the hairy figure. She smiled and nudged Sara and she caught the figure next to the tree. She put her arm around Emily's shoulder and kissed her cheek.

"I hoped to see our friends," Emily whispered. "I was never afraid of them."

"They saved your life," Sara said.

"And then they tore Bobby Palmer apart," Emily responded.

"How did you find out?" Sara asked. "Monroe never wanted anyone to know."

"I had heard how they found him," Emily said. "No bear could have done what was done to him. The bad thing is that I don't feel sorry for what happened to him. He got what he deserved. I'm hoping I don't go to hell for feeling that way."

"There is no hell," Sara said. "It's something the white priests made up to keep all the Christians in line." Emily looked at Sara and laughed.

The next day was wonderful. Emily spent most of the day lounging on the porch and talking with everyone as they came by. She closed her eyes just after the fireworks began and thought of so many things from her childhood, parents, medical school, the train ride to Snoqualmie, and the first time she saw Sara's face. She opened her eyes to look at that face one more time and was greeted with a smile from the lips she loved to kiss. As evening still ended with a grand fireworks display, all the old folks, as Anne said, Samuel, Mary, Sara, Emily, Kathleen, Tom, and Maggie sat on the porch. Emily was lying back in the chaise lounge and holding Sara's hand and when the display was over Sara looked over to see Emily's eyes were closed again. She touched her shoulder and there was no response.

Kathleen saw the look on Sara's face and came over. She checked Emily for a pulse and there was none. She died during the display surrounded by her closest friends and holding on to the woman she loved.

Chapter 28

Kathleen knelt down next to Emily and took her other hand. She bowed her head and started to cry. Within minutes everyone on the porch knew what had happened. The tears fell openly. Emily had wanted to attend one more 4th party and she got her wish. Her first visit was for a 4th party was 40 years earlier. She was young and full of life. She had traveled all the way across the country to find this place and this life.

Sara looked at her beautiful face, which had grown more beautiful with age. She realized that she would never wake and see that face next to hers again. A sob built in her throat and escaped as she put her head on Emily's chest. Her heart was breaking and Kathleen came around and helped her to her feet. She kissed Emily's hand before she released it. She stood upright and swayed slightly as Kathleen put her arm around her waist.

"We'll bury her in our plots in Renton," she said

***

Beth was in tears as they walked through the cemetery. Zack put his arm around her shoulder as he had done to Anne after her mother's funeral. It was on this very path he had first comforted her grandmother and it seemed destined that he did the same for his grand daughter. The time was fast approaching for him to tell her who he really was. As they walked she put her arm around his waist.

Beth was unaware why she felt this was necessary. It seemed natural and comforting. How she wished she could have known these people. She had a rich family history and this same family had shaped the landscape of this area. They were pioneers and visionaries. They were caretakers and risk takers. They planned, gambled, and dreamed of not what was, but what could and should be. They continued to walk and Zack continued with his story. The sun was warm and the headstones stood like sentinels watching for interlopers.

***

The funeral was large. Kathleen looked around and saw many of the babies that she and Emily had delivered. They were adults now, and had children of their own. Patrick Reilly presided over Emily's service. As he spoke words of comfort, Sara's mind was flooded with memories of their life together and everything seemed a hazy blur.

Sara was very specific about what plot to put Emily in. She would be placed to the right of Sara's plot, which would be to the right of Monroe's. Sara and Kathleen placed very special things in Emily's coffin before it was sealed. Sara made a beautiful dream catcher, an art her mother had taught her the art many years ago. Kathleen placed the nameplate from her desk next to her that Charlie Washington had made it for Emily right after she opened her first office. She added her stethoscope around her neck.

Anne watched her mother and looked at Amanda. Would this happen to them in many years? She couldn't think about it. She needed to be supportive and help her mother through this. The train continued toward Snoqualmie. Emily was in the ground. What a cold dark place to leave her. Anne shook her head to get rid of the vision and looked out the window. Kathleen had offered Sara a room for the night. She didn't want her to be alone at the estate. She politely refused, but thanked her for the thought.

"Peter is here to see me home," she smiled. "He'll make sure I'm not alone."

"Is Anne going with you?" Kathleen asked.

"Yes," Sara responded. "She and Amanda will stay for a few days." Kathleen hugged her close.

"If you need anything, you call me," she whispered in her ear.

"And if you need anything, you call me," Sara said. Emily's death was hard on Kathleen also. Sara knew this, but Kathleen put up a good front. She felt she had to be strong for Sara and knew this feeling of loss she had couldn't compare to what Sara felt. She would go out to check on her in the next week just to make sure that she was all right.

A few days after the funeral, Peter showed up at the clinic and would only speak with Kathleen.

"She's not in right now," Ben said to him. "I can give her a message, if you like."

"I really need to see her," Peter pleaded. "Mrs. Monroe is," he stammered.

"Is what?" Ben said in an anxious voice.

"She's not herself," Peter finally said. "I can't get her to eat or sleep and she wanders the house all night long. Doctor Kathleen needs to see her."

"Okay, Peter," he comforted. "I'll send her out right away."

Kathleen accompanied Peter back to the estate. She had taken her medical bag just in case it was more than depression over Emily's death. After Kathleen's arrival, Sara didn't seem to care what she wanted to check out. Her lungs were clear and heart sounded good.

She was gaunt from lack of food, sleep, and slightly dehydrated. She said little as Kathleen finished her exam.

"I can't find anything that a good meal and a night's sleep won't fix," she said to Sara and smiled. There was little response from that comment. Peter was standing in the doorway and Kathleen turned to him. "I want you to bring her some tea, and see if Sally has any soup in the kitchen." He stood there briefly. "She's going to be fine, Peter. Just do as I ask." Sara still wouldn't speak and only answered in one-word responses. He returned with the tray and handed it to Kathleen. She asked Peter to leave the room and to close the door behind him.

"I know the sadness you feel, Sara," she said as she picked up her hand. "I know you feel you have nothing to live for and you are wrong. You have Annie, the Foundation, and so many friends who miss you." Kathleen continued to talk to her about happier times while she got soup and two cups of tea into her. Over the course of the next few hours they talked about all those who had gone before them, their lives, and their dreams until, at long last, Sara started to cry.

It took another hour for Sara to release all of the pain and sadness for those who now lay in that patch of ground so far away. Kathleen held her and cried with her for some time. Finally, at long last, Sara's tears subsided. She sat up and looked at Kathleen with her swollen eyes and tear stained cheeks.

"You look terrible," she said quietly.

"You don't look any better," Kathleen smiled as she dried her eyes.

"I may not look any better, but I feel like a cloud has lifted from my heart," Sara admitted. "I didn't really cry when Monroe or Will died. People thought I didn't love them, but I did. I felt I had to be strong for the children but now…"

"But now, what?" Kathleen asked.

"I don't need to be strong for anyone," she said. "Annie doesn't need me, the Foundation doesn't need me, and Emily is gone. I really don't see the point of going on."

"Don't you dare say that," Kathleen said as she shook her shoulders. "You may be right about Annie, the Foundation, and Emily is gone, but I need you Sara." She looked at Kathleen with surprise. "That's right, I need you. You have no idea how much I admire and respect you. I was always a little envious of Emily and her relationship with you. You are the most remarkable woman I have ever met and you can't just leave me when I've got you all to myself." She paused for a moment and then hugged her close. "I have so much to learn from you before we both leave this world." She looked into her eyes and winked. "I can't lose another friend right now."

The afternoon had passed and Sara was still very week. Kathleen still couldn't be sure that she would continue to eat as she needed so with little resistance from Sara, Kathleen admitted her to the hospital. She found her a private room at the end of a hallway and would spend the next few days making sure that Sara ate, slept, and regained her spirit to live. She would also take this opportunity to spend as much time with her as possible. Kathleen's ulterior motive was to have Sara help her work through her own grief because she didn't know how well she was getting on with life.

Sara went home from the hospital a week later and was a new woman. The time that Kathleen spent with her daily was needed and required for both of them and the bond that developed was wonderful. Through hours of discussions they both grieved in their own way and came through the dark tunnel of loss they were in. They each promised to meet weekly and agreed on a time and day they would spend together, which is really all they needed. They needed to have something to look forward to and someone who remembered the past to recall how things once had been.

Over the next few years, Peter and Sara had become close. He convinced her to start horseback riding again. She had not done that for a few years because of caring for Emily. She had missed it and was pleased with the horses they had in the stable. Peter had foals from her original line that she first brought over from east of the mountains. He had trained them, and cared for them as he would his own children.

She enjoyed her rides and her long conversations with Peter. They would get together with Tom and Kathleen weekly. Anne and Amanda would spend one weekend a month at the estate. Sara didn't seem to be lonely, but Peter knew the nights were hard for her. She remained in the bedroom that she and Monroe, and then Emily had shared. Emily's room remained as it had always been had been. Her antique desk with her medical journals stayed in the corner. The knick-knacks that she had brought with her from Boston remained on the nightstands. The room still had the faintest hint of the cologne she wore.

It was the spring of 1918 when Anne appeared to stay the weekend and Amanda wasn't with her. Sara approached the subject cautiously. Anne said that she was in Seattle looking for an apartment.

"She's taken a job at one of the colleges," Anne said. "The school in Renton isn't challenging enough."

"What are you going to do?" Sara asked.

"I've made plans to move there too," she said. "I can work there with David Webster and still call out here when I need your advice. I'm not going to move until I can sell the house in Renton. It probably won't be until late fall. She's going to find a place for us and move as soon as school is out."

"I couldn't live there," Sara said. "There are too many people for my tastes. The seafood is great, though. I would love to eat that again."

"Maybe you should come to visit me some weekend," Anne suggested.

"I'd like that," she responded.

Amanda did find housing and started at the small college in September. Anne had some nibbles on the house, but no offers she would entertain. She decided if it hadn't sold by the middle of October, she would close it up and move, anyway.

That was exactly how it happened. Anne had closed up the house, packed her clothes and was ready to move into Seattle. She was spending one more weekend with her mother before she left. On Saturday afternoon, Kathleen pulled up in front of the house. Sara was not expecting her. She walked up on the front porch as Sara opened the door. The look on her face wasn't one that came from good news.

"What's wrong?" Sara asked. "Is Tom all right? Ben?"

"They're fine, Sara," she said. "Is Annie here?"

"I'll find her," Sara said. Kathleen came into the house and Sara asked the cook to bring some coffee and called upstairs for her daughter. Annie came down from upstairs and saw Kathleen sitting with her.

"It's so nice to see you," she said as she gave Kathleen a kiss.

"It's nice to see you, too," she said. "Annie I have some news. Sit down here next to me." Annie did as instructed. "I got a visit from Maggie Regan this morning. Honey," she paused with a sigh and a quiver in her voice, "there was a fire in the school where Amanda teaches. Many students and some teachers died. One of them was Amanda." She waited for the information to sink in. "I'm so sorry, honey. Maggie thought it would be best of I gave you this news." She picked up her hand and held it close to her chest.

"Dead? Amanda's dead?" Anne asked quietly.

"Yes," Kathleen said. "She was trying to get the students out of the first floor when the second floor came down on them. I guess the fire started on the second floor." Annie stood up and looked at her mother and went back up the stairs. Sara looked at Kathleen.

"I don't think it's sunk in," Sara said. "I'd better go up and."

"Let her alone for a bit," Kathleen urged. "Let her think about it."

"Can you stay for a while?" Sara asked.

"Tom is in Seattle," she said. "I've brought things to spend the weekend, if you don't mind. I think Annie is going to need all the support she can get." Sara nodded her head and smiled at her dear friend.

Maggie had a memorial service at the cemetery only. She couldn't bear the thought of another funeral. She had attended too many in the recent years. She laid her daughter to rest next to her husband.

"Parents shouldn't outlive their children," Sara said to her after the service as she left the cemetery with Maggie.

"Is Annie doing okay?" Maggie asked. "I don't know what to say to her."

"Just say what's in your heart," Sara said. "That's what she wants to hear." They boarded the train and Maggie sat next to Anne and they talked during the trip back. There were many tears during this conversation, and they seem to come to a better understanding of each other. Kathleen and Sara watched from a few rows back. Sara held Kathleen's hand.

"I think they finally understand one another," she whispered. "They've made their peace."

"They both needed to do that," Kathleen replied. "Closure is so important."

***

Beth and Zack arrived at the gravesites. She saw the markers she had found originally and then read all of the others. She still had tears in her eyes and looked up to stare off into space. Zack didn't interrupt her thoughts. After a moment she spoke.

"All of these markers mean something to me now," she said as her voice quivered. "It seems a sad place to end up after all the wonderful things they accomplished. They all lay here next to each other, but only the physical bodies. Their spirits reside in another place, where they will never be apart."

"There spirits reside in you, Beth," Zack said quietly. "You are a part of this legacy. You're just as much a part as Sara, Anne, Eddy, or Monroe."

"Tell me the rest of Sara's life," Beth said.

***

Sara lived on and she and Anne worked together on the Foundation. Anne remained in her house but would visit on weekends. The last years of Sara's life were happy. In 1927 she started having problems with fatigue and shortness of breath. She contracted Pneumonia but survived that. In the spring of 1928 she had a mild heart attack, which weakened her. Anne was spending more time at the estate than she had in the past.

When she wasn't there, Peter kept a close watch on Sara. On the morning of June 14th, Peter came down the stairs to find Sara was not up yet. This had never happened before. He had a bad feeling about this because she had been so tired the night before. He wasn't going to wait for her to get up. He went to her room and knocked on the door, then opened it. He found her under her covers, and holding two pictures. One was of Monroe, Sara, and the boys taken at Christmas many years ago. The other was of her and Emily. She had passed away sometime in the night.

Peter picked up the phone next to her bed and called Kathleen and Tom. He told them the door was open and come to Sara's room when they arrived. Within 30 minutes he heard their car pull through the gate. They entered the room and saw Sara, who was as beautiful in death as she was in life. Kathleen looked at the pictures she held and smiled at Tom.

"I remember when those were taken," she said quietly. "Look how young and full of life they all were." She sat down on the bed and stroked Sara's cheek. "Did you call Anne?"

"Yes," Peter said quietly. "She should be here within the hour."

"We'll leave Sara right where she is until Anne gets here," Kathleen said. She looked back at Sara. "Have a good journey to the spirit world, my friend. Many are waiting for you." She bent and kissed her forehead. Tom did the same and they waited for Anne's arrival.

***

"That's when I first met your Grandmother, Beth," Zack said. "She bought Sara into the funeral home. I had just arrived from Chicago and when I first saw her, my heart was in my throat. Sara didn't look a day over 50, and was still beautiful." He looked at the grave markers. "You look just like her, Beth. When I first saw you here, I could have sworn you were her."

"You've told me about Sara and Monroe and all the people

344

surrounding their lives," Beth said. "What about Anne? You've not told me anything about her after Sara died. I have questions about my father also. Did you know him?"

"Yes, I did," Zack smiled. "I knew him from the day he was born. Did I tell you that Kathleen Eichorn delivered him? She was 75 years old, and did it as a favor to your grandmother. Anne insisted and Kathleen couldn't refuse her."

"How do you know all these things Zack?" Beth asked although in some way she already knew the answer to her own question. He looked at her and then at the grave markers and back at her.

"Because I'm your Grandfather," he said quietly. "Your father was conceived before your grandmother and I got married." Beth looked at him. She didn't seem surprised.

"I, somehow, knew that," she said. "Don't ask me how, but I knew." She walked over close to him and hugged him close. Zack held her and stroked her hair. "Why didn't you tell me when we first met?"

"I couldn't bring myself to believe that you existed," he said. "I looked for your mother after Russell died, but kept coming to dead-ends. After 5 years, there was no trace of her."

"That's because she died," Beth said. "I went to live with my grandmother until she died a couple of years later. An older couple adopted me. I've had a pretty happy childhood." She paused and looked at Zack. "Why was your name not on my father's birth certificate?"

"That's another story for another time," Zack said as he looked at his watch. "It's 2:30 now. How would you like to take a ride with me?"

"I have no plans," Beth said. Zack motioned to the young caretaker to give them a ride to his house.

They got into Zack's car and headed for Snoqualmie. He thought she should see what she had inherited. On the way he talked about her grandmother and their life together. He also told her about Eddy finally coming home and the last years of his life. She saw the town sign that said "Snoqualmie" and as Zack drove through town he pointed out where the bank, the clinic, the hospital, and Walker's store originally sat. He turned and headed out of town and up a winding road. He did stop at the falls so Beth could look from the same spot, that all of the people she had just learned about, had stood. She had seen the falls from the viewing area below, but this was spectacular. She stood for sometime and gazed at the mist.

"Can you hear the whispers?" she asked timidly

"Those are the whispers that call you home," Zack replied.

They got back into the car and traveled a short distance to the main gate of the estate. Beth had a mental picture of this place in her head, but it didn't compare to what she saw. Zack stopped the car and let her take it all in. He finally got out of the car and she did the same. She walked up the marble steps onto the massive porch. Zack let her take her time with this.

"I've never seen anyplace more beautiful," she said. She turned and looked over the grounds. She could see the stable and the path that lead down to Samuel and Mary's house. Zack went to the door and opened it.

"Come inside," he smiled. As she entered the large foyer she was struck by the large painting of Monroe and Sara. It took her breath away as she slowly walked over to it and touched it. She could see the library, where so many plans, conversations, and tears were seen over the years. She saw the painting of Sara and Emily.

"Oh, my God," she said. "How beautiful they looked. How young and how happy they were." Against the other wall was a portrait of Anne and Zack. She looked closely at it and back at him. She had tears in her eyes. He joined her and looked at the portrait. He saw it differently today for the first time. He didn't know why. He had always looked at this and looked at Anne's beautiful face. Today he saw the couple that they were and saw their happiness.

Beth turned to him and hugged him close. The memories in this house were so thick that you could feel them encase you like a warm sweater.

"Look at you," she said as she looked again at the portrait. "You were a very handsome man, and a beautiful couple," she paused and looked at him, "Grandpa." He looked at her and smiled.

"No one has ever called me that," Zack said. "I like it, how about you?"

"I love the sound of it," Beth said. He took her hand and walked her up the large staircase. None of the rooms had been changed. Sara's room remained as she had left it. It was cleaned every single week since her death. Many of her Indian artifacts were on the walls, and the ivory carvings that Eddy sent her from Alaska still resided in the glass-door cabinet. The pictures that she held when she died were on the bedside table.

Beth picked them up and looked at them with the recent story still in her mind. She ran her hand over the glass as if to caress the figures in the picture. She followed Zack down the hall into Emily's room. The beautiful desk was still in the corner, and the medical journals dating back to 1877 were still neatly standing between bookends. She looked at the fireplace and could picture Sara and Emily making love in front of the fire.

Zack walked down to the new section and showed her the suite that he and Anne had occupied. Most of Eddy's possessions had been moved back to his old room after he died. Anne made sure that his room, her mother's room, and Emily's room were off limits to any guests. This was done out of respect and love for them. She didn't want anyone disturbing these possessions.

They walked down the back stairs to the kitchen. An Indian woman a few years younger than Zack looked at Beth and froze.

"Beth, this is Rosie," Zack said. Beth extended her hand and Rosie shook it timidly. "Rosie is the grand-daughter of Sally One Feather." He waited and then looked at Rosie. "This is Beth Monroe. This is Russell's daughter." The large woman came around the counter and scooped Beth into her arms. She pulled back and looked at her face and hugged her again.

"I thought it was Anne walking into the kitchen," she said. "Russell's daughter?"

"It's a long story, Rosie," Zack smiled. "But you'll have time to hear it from Beth."

They went back out on the porch and sat down. Rosie brought them some fresh coffee as Zack and Beth talked.

"When your grandmother died she left all of this to me," Zack said. "Russell was very clear about not wanting to come back here to live. I'm almost eighty years old and I had no idea what to do with the Foundation, or the land. All of this is yours, child. I know it's a lot to take in right now, but I've had people taking care of these things. All of this is your birthright. I'm sure the lawyers will want to see birth certificates to verify who you are, but that's a formality. All they have to do is to look at you."

"It's a lot to take in," Beth said. "I know that I'm working a job that means nothing to me. I'm living from check to check with no future. I live in an apartment that means nothing to me. Now I sit here and you tell me that this is all mine. Two days ago, I didn't have a family, and now." She stared out at the grounds again. "I feel like Cinderella. I'm happy and scared. I wouldn't know what to do with all of this."

"There are people who are hired to help you," Zack said. "If I can learn all of this, so can you. I don't want to see all of this go to someone other than a Monroe. That wouldn't be right. Your great grandfather wanted this to be handed down to future generations.

That's you, whether you're ready for it or not." Zack stared out over the grounds as Beth had done.

"Grandpa?" she said. "If I move out here, will you move here with me? Sell your little house and we'll both come home." The tears welled up in his eyes.

"I haven't had an offer like that in many years," he said as his voice quivered. "I'd be honored." They toasted their coffee cups. Rosie came out onto the porch. "Rosie, how would you like some company out here?"

"I'd love it, Mr. Zack," she smiled.

"My granddaughter and I will be moving in out here," he smiled. "We're both coming home."

Beth and Zack did move in shortly after that conversation on the porch. Beth had quickly learned the workings of the Foundation with the help of the Webster legal firm. She had met and worked with many of the local residents that knew her grandmother and her father. She also met Andrea, Rosie's granddaughter. Zack saw the electricity as soon as their eyes met. He knew that Beth had found that missing piece of her future.

Andrea moved into the estate two weeks later. She had a degree in business that the Monroe Foundation had helped her to attain. It seemed destined that she come back and work with the Foundation, and find Beth.

Zack had told her the story of her grandmother sitting in front of the fireplace in the library. He was happier than he had been in years. Beth had taken on her role with style and grace. She dearly loved Zack and both she and Andrea enjoyed hearing about his life and the family history. All of the special items he had moved into his house were brought back. Monroe's journals and all the pictures came back and were displayed. Beth had the chance to read the journals and look at the maps.

Andrea had an idea about putting together a small museum in the old cabin that still sat near the house. It was going to need a great deal of work to be restored as it was originally built. She suggested that the interior be redone to the period that it was built, and to have the displays of the items of the family history.

"It will be a historical look at the people behind the Foundation," Andrea explained to Beth and Zack. "We'll show all those involved with the Foundation what great people these were."

As Andrea worked on this project, she and Beth discussed their future with each other. They agreed on one thing. This was something she didn't tell Zack about and wouldn't until she knew if it was possible.

On this day, July 3rd, Beth made a trip to the cemetery. She drove in close to the family plots, to save the walk. She wanted to say the things on her mind and in her heart. She stood there and looked at all the markers.

"I don't know where to begin," she said. "I know you can't hear me, but maybe you can. I want to say thank-you. I wanted to say it to each and every one of you. To Monroe and Sara, my great-grandparents, thank-you for your vision and tenacity your dream will continue to live on and I'll make sure of it. To uncles Will and Eddy, you followed your own path yet never forgot your heritage. To Anne, thank you for keeping everything together and for my father. Kathleen, Tom, and Emily, you were there when my family needed you. You gave them love and support. None of us go through this life alone. It was a long and difficult road to find all of you, but I would gladly travel that road again to find you all." She paused and looked again at each marker. "I can't tell you what's in my heart. I have so much emotion, gratitude, and love for what you have given me. The only way I can repay you is to carry on with what you started and keep this dream alive. Over the last few months I have started to think about future generations and through the miracle of modern medicine, I am carrying that next generation. The Monroe name will go on. I have also found someone to share my life with me. We are kindred spirits, and I love her deeply. We will raise this child together. This child will understand its Native American background, culture, and heritage. The blood of chiefs will run through his veins and he will know the story of how it all began so many years ago in a small Indian village."

Zack was standing behind when she started talking to the grave markers and smiled. He was so happy for them. He remembered a happier time when Anne was pregnant with Russell, which seemed so long ago now. She seemed to glow and so did Beth. She loved taking care of this business. She turned and saw Zack. She smiled at him and touched her abdomen. He smiled and winked at her. There was no need to tell him. He had already heard with the rest of the family. She walked to him and arm in arm they walked to the car.

"Big party tomorrow," he said.

"And many more to come, Grandpa," Beth replied, "so many more to come."

Be sure to visit

www.gjwnovels.com

for other books by G. J. Woosley